Broken COURSE

Aly Martinez

Cover Design by Ashley Baumann at Ashbee Designs **https://www.facebook.com/AshbeeBookCovers**
Edited by Mickey Reed at I'm a Book Shark
http://www.imabookshark.com
Formatting by Stacey Blake at Champagne Formats
http://thewineyreader.com/champagneformats/

ISBN-13:978-1503097568
ISBN-10:1503097560

Also by Aly Martinez

Changing Course (Wrecked and Ruined Book 1)
Stolen Course (Wrecked and Ruined Book 2)

Savor Me: A Novella

Among The Echoes

Dedication

This book is dedicated to the readers. Every. Single. One of you.
Thank you for spending your time with my words. But most of all
thank you for loving my "friends" as much as I do. I never thought
anyone would be willing to read Sarah's story. Thank you for proving
me wrong.

Prologue

"YES," I hiss to myself as the silver metal slices across my wrist. Blood pours onto the bathroom floor as I stare emotionlessly, praying that it takes my life along with it. My breath slips from my chest as my head lightens. The dark-red fluid running down my arm does nothing to quell the loathing that still burns inside me.

That's for Manda.

"I'm sorry. Oh, God. I'm so sorry." But it's not enough just to be sorry anymore.

The tears slide down my cheeks, mingling with the blood on the floor. My life and grief finally meet in the same moment that will enable me to escape both. The numbness overwhelms my body, so I take another swipe across my arm just to remind myself that I'm still here and living—the worst punishment of all. The pain doesn't even register amongst the guilt and hate that devours me.

That's for Emma.

I briefly catch a glance of my blood-streaked face in the mirror. The hollowness I feel on the inside is finally leaking out, filling my soul as it empties from my veins. I can't fight for a life I don't want to live.

I surrender.

My world may be filled with people, but somehow, I still find myself completely alone in the shadows of my mind. It physically hurts to open my eyes every day. As my lids droop, I don't fight the exhaustion any longer. I drag the knife across my forearm, pressing as hard as the pain will allow. My hands are shaking and the pain is agonizing. But I deserve this.

That's for Brett.

"I quit," I announce to the image in the mirror. "I quit," I repeat on a whisper.

I can feel the darkness closing in, freeing everyone who has been tangled in my web since that night. If I'm gone, I can't hurt anyone else. I only wish I could have done this before I'd had the chance to kill the only person who ever loved me unconditionally. I move to my legs and, as quickly as I can, carve the knife across my thigh.

That's for my family.

My only regret is that I can't clean up the mess I made in this life before I leave it. I don't deserve the attention or the love. I deserve to disappear and fade into ashes. I deserve to be nonexistent. While that should scare me, it seems less painful than continuing the façade of living.

I move to my other leg, the only place that remains unscathed. Then I draw the sharp edge diagonally, watching carefully as the blood springs to the surface.

That's for Casey.

"Sarah!" I hear Brett scream as he pounds on the bathroom door.

I just want to forget.

"Sarah, what the fuck are you doing?" he shouts, but I barely lift my shaking arm to slice the tip of the knife across my neck—the final effort that will prevent him from forcing me to fight any longer.

I can't do this anymore.

The cool metal tip forces a cry from my lips, but I'm not strong enough to do much more than superficially wound myself.

That's for myself.

Just as Brett breaks open the door, I glance down at my wrists and legs and let out a relieved breath as I see the irreparable damage.

It's almost over.

I should be frightened. I should be terrified of death. I should be *sorry.* However, as he begins shouting and frantically trying to put pressure on all of my wounds, I feel none of that.

I feel the end—it's euphoric.

"Sarah, don't do this. Damn it! Stay with me." Brett brushes the hair from my face, but I'm too far gone to even open my eyes and take in one last glance of his beautiful face.

Let me go.

"Just hang on, baby. It's all going to be okay."

As I drift off in his arms, I know he couldn't be more wrong.

Chapter ONE

Leo

Seven Years Later...

"HEY, BABE." I answer my phone to hear Erica sobbing on the other end. "What's wrong?" I immediately freeze in the middle of the busy Chicago sidewalk.

"It's a boy!" She laughs across the line. "We're going to name him Adam."

My whole body instantly relaxes and a smile spreads across my face. "Congratulations!" I say, laughing right along with her.

Suddenly, a tall blonde fumbling through her purse and cussing catches my eye. She's gorgeous, but her level of anxiety is what really makes me take notice.

"Are you coming up for the baby shower? Some of the nurses at work are putting together a little something for us in a few months."

"Isn't that for chicks?" I respond, never tearing my eyes off the blonde, who pulls out her cell phone, just to become more agitated.

"No. Slate will be there. You two can hang out while we gasp over baby clothes."

The woman I'm all but gawking at walks away, only to quickly turn back around and head in my direction.

"Erica, can I call you back?"

"Yeah. Yeah. Yeah. You can get off the phone, but you're coming to the shower."

"Okay. Send me the info. I'll be there," I reply just to appease her. "Bye, babe." I hang up and head toward the flustered woman.

The closer I get, the sexier she becomes, and suddenly, I'm approaching her for a totally different reason.

"Excuse me, miss. Do you need some help?" I ask when I get close.

"God, yes! I'm late for an interview and I have no idea where the hell I am. The cab driver dropped me off here, but I think this is the wrong place. Oh, and my phone died, because *really*—that's the kind of day I'm having. You don't happen to know where State Street is, do you?" she rushes out then blows her hair out of her eyes with a huff.

"Yeah. That's, like, two streets back. You're not far. Come on. I'll walk you there."

"Oh, thank you so much." She sighs with relief.

I extend a hand toward her. "Hi. My name's Leo James."

"Nice to meet you. I'm Sarah Erickson."

"Do you need to call and let them know you are running late?" I ask, offering her my phone.

"I wouldn't even know who to ask for. My friend's dad pulled some strings to get me this interview. He didn't even tell me who I'm meeting with." She shrugs, nervously tucking her hair behind her ear.

"I'm sure they'll understand. What kind of work do you do?"

"Uh, I'm not really sure about that either." She smiles uncomfortably and glances at me out of the corner of her eye.

"So, this is, like, a surprise interview?" I laugh, causing her smile to spread across her face. I nearly stumble at the sight.

"Something like that." When she winks, I swear I almost choke on my own tongue.

Fuck, this woman is gorgeous. Her slender figure is covered by a black skirt that hugs the curve of her ass and a white blouse unbuttoned just enough to show a tasteful amount of skin. She's tall in her black heels, but I still have her by an inch or two. Her blond hair hangs down her back and her blue eyes sparkle in the midday sun.

I clear my throat and barely manage to stop my wandering eyes.

"Where are you from? That definitely isn't a Chicago accent I hear."

She looks over and laughs. "No, definitely not. What gave me away? I haven't even said y'all yet."

"No, you haven't. Although I'm sure it will be worth the wait to hear it again." I smile back at her.

She holds my gaze for a minute before biting her bottom lip and looking away. It's not a shy reaction. It appears as though she's just trying to cover her own flirtatious grin.

"I'm from Savannah, Georgia. Born and raised. But I've lived here for years now. How much farther?" she asks, stealing an impatient peek at her watch.

"Just another block or so," I respond as we stop at the crosswalk, waiting for the light to change.

"There is no way I'm going to get this job. I'm, like, fifteen minutes late already."

"So you really have no idea what kind of job you're interviewing for?" I ask when an awkward silence fills the air around us.

"Nah, I do. It's a very glamorous receptionist position at the newspaper, but that's about all I do know. "

"Well, that's bound to be interesting at least."

"Right. Answering phones and filing paperwork all day is my dream job," she says sarcastically before clarifying. "Don't get me wrong though. I'm really excited about having a job again. What do you do?"

"I own a security agency," I answer, and for some reason, it seems to surprise her.

She looks at me with her head tilted. "Like installing security alarms?"

"No, more like personal protection type stuff. Here." I reach into my back pocket and pull one of my business cards out of my wallet.

"Guardian Protection Agency," she reads aloud, continuing her quick steps down the sidewalk. "You're a bodyguard?"

"I don't do much of the actual street work anymore. I run more of the business side of things and train the new guys, but yeah, I guess bodyguard is the easiest explanation."

"Wow. That actually does sound interesting. You're making me feel completely inadequate with my receptionist position now. You know, the one I won't be getting because I'm officially almost twenty minutes late now. Shit." She cusses to herself as I chuckle.

"Well, you're in luck, because we're here." I motion to the large door of the Chicago Tribune. Stepping forward, I open it for her.

"Oh, thank God." She smooths out her skirt and runs a hand through her hair before walking inside.

"Miss Erickson?" an older woman snaps, making it quite clear that my blonde thankfully isn't married.

"Yes, uh, that's me," Sarah responds hesitantly, and I can't blame her for her trepidation. Even with just two words, this woman has made it clear that she's pissed.

"You're late. I'm sorry but the job is no longer—"

I jump to interrupt her before she has a chance to dismiss Sarah completely. "I'm sorry. It's my fault that Miss Erickson is late. Mrs. ...?" I lift an eyebrow, fishing for her name.

"Fernandez," she finishes for me, obviously trying to figure out who the hell I am and why she should care.

"*Ah, hablas español?*" *(Ah, you speak Spanish?)*

"*Sí,*" she answers, still perplexed.

"*De donde eres?*" *(Where are you from?)*

"Puerto Rico."

"*Pasé un verano en la isla. Es hermosa. Me encantaría volver algún día, pero me da miedo que mientras este allí no quisiera volver a casa mas nunca.*" *(I spent a summer on the island. It's beautiful. I'd love to go back someday, but I'm afraid I'd never want to come home again.)* I wink and she narrows her eyes. "My name is Leo James, and I own Guardian Protection Agency." I drag yet another card from my wallet. "You see, I've been trying to recruit Miss Erickson for a position working for me, but she keeps refusing. When I saw her outside today, I had to give it one last shot to persuade her. However, sadly for myself, she politely declined. It seems she is very excited about the prospect of a position here at the Tribune. It's my loss. But please don't penalize her for my persistence. You would be lucky to have her." I finish with a charming smile.

She flicks my card in her fingers. "Guardian, huh? You run security for Slate Andrews, right?" She changes the topic, and it forces the smile to fade from my lips.

"I do," I answer with more attitude than necessary.

"Is it true his new bride is pregnant? Our sports section would have a field day breaking that story."

"I never comment on clients, Mrs. Fernandez. I'm sorry. There will be no breaking story," I almost growl.

She shrugs. "You can't blame me for taking *one last shot*," she says, throwing my words right back at me.

"Of course not." I plaster on a patronizing smile.

"Well, Miss Erickson, seeing as you are in such high demand, even if you did keep me waiting for almost half an hour, I'd love to speak with you more." The bitchy woman drags her gaze away from me to focus on Sarah, who is nervously smoothing her skirt behind me.

"Yes, and I'm sorry again for being late," Sarah stumbles out.

"Follow me." She walks down the long hall.

A wide-eyed Sarah turns to face me and silently mouths, "Thank you."

I smile and wink before pointing to my card she's still holding. "Call me," I mouth back to her while making the universal phone signal with my hand. She quickly nods and heads down the hall.

"I GOT the job!" I hear her scream over the phone as I sit at the computer in my office. It hasn't even been an hour since I left Sarah at her job interview, but I haven't stopped thinking about her yet. "I mean, hey… This is Sarah Erickson from, you know…earlier," she says uncomfortably.

I laugh at her reminder. "Yes, I remember. So I'm assuming the interview with the Wicked Witch went well after I left." I recline back in my chair, pushing my feet out in front of me.

"Well, the first five minutes were questions about how I knew *you*. But after that, she seemed to warm up a little bit. She offered me shit for pay, but hey, whatever. I am gainfully employed."

"Congratulations. I think you should let me take you out to dinner this weekend to celebrate." I smile to myself at the prospect of seeing her again, but the line goes silent. "Sarah?"

"Oh, um…I… Well," she stutters.

"Wow. Don't sound too enthusiastic," I laugh.

"No. I mean. Yeah, okay. Dinner sounds good," she says quietly, but I can still hear the uncertainty in her voice.

I should offer to pick her up, but her hesitance tells me that she would be wary of such a conventional date. "You want to meet me at Shades on Friday night?"

"Yeah. Shades. Seven?" she asks nervously.

"Sounds like a plan."

"Okay, well, I'll let you go, Leo. Thanks again for today."

"Sure. No problem. I'm glad things worked out. I'll see you on Friday."

"See you then. Bye." She hangs up.

And even though it's Wednesday, the weekend just became entirely too far away.

Chapter
TWO

Sarah

"I CAN'T DO it," I say, staring in the mirror and running my fingers through my long, blond hair.

"Sarah, stop. You look amazing," my little sister, Emma, says as she tugs my top down to reveal more cleavage.

"What if he's a serial killer? I've only met him once." I shimmy my top back up to cover my chest.

"He's not a serial killer," she tries to reassure me but pulls my top back down. "You have great boobs. Show a little skin."

I glance down at my chest. She's not wrong. I do have nice boobs, but I'm not sure that is what I want to show off on a first date with a man I barely know. Second date, maybe. Third, definitely. *What the fuck am I thinking?*

"I should just cancel. This is going to be a disaster." I walk over to my phone and grab it off the nightstand. I open my texts and prepare to send Leo a message with some lame excuse of why I can't make it.

A few days ago, I met Mr. Tall, Dark, And Sexy (forget handsome), Leo James, on a busy sidewalk in the middle of Chicago. I was in panic mode and he walked right up and saved the day. Before that, it had been a shit day—one of those that you just wish you could tear from the notebook and start all over with a fresh page. Only, in my book, there are no more fresh pages—I'm writing in the margins these days.

To say my life has been dramatic for the last seven years would be an understatement roughly the size of the Titanic. My life is a mess. I spent the last two years in either a court-mandated rehabilitation center or some form of therapy after trying to kill myself four times. Oh, and let's not forget that I tried to shoot my ex-husband. Yep, I'm every man's dream woman. Yet another reason I can't go on this date with Leo.

"Don't you dare!" Emma shouts, trying to snatch the phone from my hands just as it chirps with an incoming message.

Leo: I've got some bad news. I can't make it tonight. Work emergency. Rain check?

I slowly sit down on the couch and stare at the words on the screen. It's odd—only seconds ago I would have given anything to get out of going on this date. However, now, the disappointment of no longer even having the option is heavy.

"What's it say?" Emma asks, obviously reading my expression.

"He, uh, can't make it." I try to collect my jumble of emotions. Sure, there was a *very* small part somewhere in the back of my head that was excited about getting to know Leo James, but I was more excited—and terrified—about the prospect of an actual date.

It's been fourteen years since I went on my last first date. Although I'm not even sure you can really call that a date. I met Brett Sharp at a bar when I was twenty-one years old. Our first date was the next morning after he'd spent the night at my apartment holding my hair while I puked. He took me to breakfast, and within three hours, we were having sex on the floor in my apartment. Less than a year later, I married him. We spent seven years together before my life was altered forever.

That whole whirlwind, wild-abandon love is not exactly what I am going for this time around, but a real date with someone who has no clue who I am—or, better yet, who I *was*—sounds amazing...and yes, still terrifying.

```
Me: Sure. No Problem.
Leo: Tomorrow?
```

"Why the hell can't he make it?" Emma asks from behind me.

"Work." I continue to stare at the screen on my phone.

"What's he do anyway? Is he loaded?"

"He owns a security company," I answer distractedly, trying to formulate a response.

Do I want to go out with him tomorrow night? I think so. Does the idea of going out with him tomorrow make me want to crawl into a hole and hide? *Completely.* My response must take too long, because my phone chirps again.

```
Leo: Feel free to copy and paste. "Sure,
Leo. I can't wait to see you."
```

"What's he saying?" she asks, settling down on the couch next to me.

"He wants to go out tomorrow night. Em, I can't do this. He's going to realize I'm a basket case and it's going to hurt like hell to swallow that giant pill of rejection. I'm just not ready yet."

"You're full of shit. You should have seen the way your face fell when he said he couldn't make it."

"I can't do it!" I yell more at myself than at Emma.

"What if Caleb and I go with you tomorrow night? We can drop Collin off with his sister and go to a bar. If Leo sucks or if you panic, you'll have us there as a buffer."

I laugh humorlessly. "No fucking way."

My relationship with Emma's husband Caleb is…well, unusual. Up until eighteen months ago, he hated me. I don't mean he just disliked me. I mean he wouldn't have poured water on me if I caught fire. And rightly so—I killed his fiancée. Or at least it had appeared that way at the time.

Emma's husband, Caleb, was engaged to my best friend, Manda Baker. He was the only person in the world who loved that fiery redhead more than I did. Emma is my sister by blood, but as far as I am concerned, Manda was no different. There isn't a single day that passes where I don't wish that she were still here.

Seven years ago, I was involved in a car accident that destroyed all of our lives. I suffered a traumatic brain injury that changed my personality so drastically that it left me lost and confused in a life I recognized but was completely emotionally unattached to. And Manda…well, she paid the greatest price of all. She never took another breath after our car collided with that fated tree. I have no memory of that night whatsoever, and because I was the sole survivor of the accident, no one really knew what had actually transpired. However, jaded and grief stricken, Caleb blamed me. And he wasn't the only one. I blamed myself for Manda's death as well.

Eighteen months ago, our other best friend, Casey Black, shed light on what had really happened that night. No one had any clue that she'd even been there when the accident had taken place—much less that she had been driving the car. Her on-again, off-again fling, Eli Tanner, had helped her leave the scene unnoticed. However, before her shocking confession, I'd lived with that guilt. I knew how it felt to be consumed by it.

The pain of waking up every day knowing what I'd done was crippling. I hated myself, I hated my life, and I hated the very air in my lungs that was absent from Manda's. I didn't even know who I was anymore. I had every memory from my old life but none of the emotions to match them. I didn't get nostalgic when I thought about the past; I felt nothing. The emptiness was agonizing. The only feelings I could remember were attached to the memories of Manda, and she was gone. I couldn't even remember how it felt to be happy, much less how to find it again.

My husband at the time, Brett, fought to save me from myself, but it only made me more anxious and confused. I was supposed to love him. I knew that. But I couldn't figure out why, and I loathed myself so much that I couldn't rationalize why he would want to love *me*. But he did it anyway.

Over those first four years after the accident, I did a lot of things I'm not proud of. I hurt everyone who had ever loved me. As selfish as it sounds, I just needed some way to escape the pain. There was a barrage of people huddled around me, showing me unconditional love, but I felt virtually nothing for them in return. I pushed away my family and friends as I hid from reality. They just couldn't understand the person I'd become overnight. Hell, I couldn't understand it myself. So when it became more than I could bear, I finally decided to end it all.

I survived my every attempt at taking my own life mainly because Brett was absolutely unwilling to let me go. Until, one day, he wasn't. The day Brett Sharp let me go was the same day I hit rock bottom. Coincidentally, it was also the day I was given back my life.

I did a lot of terrible things to the people who loved the old Sarah—especially Brett. He didn't deserve everything I put him through. I was utterly horrible. I'm not too fucked up to be able to recognize that. Even while it was happening, I knew the things I was doing were wrong, but my life had spiraled out of control. Hate and abuse were the only ways I felt I could convey my inner misery.

I don't make excuses for what I did or the people I hurt. Those actions were my own. I chose them—even if it wasn't with a sound mind. That woman fired a gun at the only person to stand by her side—that is what I am capable of. I may not be her anymore, but she still lives inside me. And that alone terrifies me more than anything else.

So, yeah. I'm a real catch. Leo James should count his lucky stars that he got called away for work. He figuratively, and maybe even literally, dodged a bullet tonight.

"So what do you say? Me, you, Caleb, _Leo_—double date?" Emma asks while making kissy faces, snapping me out of my inner pity party.

"Nah. I think I'm going to pass. He wasn't all that good-looking anyway," I answer flippantly.

"Shut up. I believe your exact words were, 'fuck-hot,'" she says, tossing a pair of air quotes in my direction.

"I lied," I snap, rolling my eyes.

Leo: *cricket cricket*

Peeking over my shoulder to read Leo's latest text, Emma says, "Well, he's persistent."

"I don't want go out tomorrow night," I whine.

"Say whatever the hell you want, Sarah, but you were stoked when he asked you out."

"I was just excited. I didn't think it through. Maybe I should talk to one of my counselors before I jump right back into the dating world." I cautiously turn to look at her, knowing she's not going to be happy with that answer.

She curls her lip in disgust. "Seriously?"

"Yeah, seriously," I answer as my phone starts ringing in my lap. "Shit," I mumble to myself.

Emma starts laughing when she sees Leo's name flashing on my screen. I groan but click the little green button.

"Hello?"

Leo

"YOU GONNA answer my text?" I ask as soon as I hear Sarah's sultry voice across the line.

"Yeah. I was just busy. That's all," she responds, but I can hear a woman laughing in the background.

"Look, I'll be out of the loop the rest of the night, so I just wanted to make sure you were good for tomorrow night." I pull into the underground parking garage at my apartment.

I was on my way back from the florist when I got an emergency call from Johnson. Some celebrity client decided to make a stop over in Chicago to hit one of the strip clubs. He wants a full security detail, and with two guys on vacation, I'm understaffed. I love my job, but as I walk upstairs with flowers in hand, I absolutely resent the interruption.

"Sarah?" I question when she doesn't respond.

"I'm here. I'll have to let you know about tomorrow. I just started that new job, and...you know."

"You work on Saturdays?" I ask, knowing that the Tribune doesn't have office hours on the weekend.

"Well, no," she answers nervously, and I hear more laughing in the background.

"Okay, well, I'll pick you up at seven. Text me your address." I walk into my apartment and toss the flowers to Johnson, who's standing in the corner with a grin that's showing off two gold teeth.

"I'll just meet you at the restaurant," she whispers as the laughing fades.

"Why do I feel like you aren't going to show up?" I ask, unbuttoning my charcoal-gray dress shirt while heading into my bedroom to change.

"I'll be there," she assures me, but the slight quiver in her voice reveals her lie.

"Look, if you've changed your mind, you can just tell me. I'm really not used to forcing women to go on dates with me. This whole conversation is not doing good things for my ego right now," I joke, trying to put her at ease. Her anxiety is unexpected based on the woman I met earlier this week.

"No, it's not that. I'm just nervous," she confesses just as Johnson walks into the room, temporarily tearing my attention away from the phone.

"Yo, Leo. We need to move. Sanders arrives at O'Hare in an hour."

"Load up the truck and get the men briefed. I'll be right out," I respond before focusing back on Sarah. "All right. Talk to me. What are you nervous about?"

"No, it's okay. I'll let you go. I'll see you tomorrow night."

"Are you really going to show up? At least tell me how long should I wait before ordering dinner to go?"

"An hour," she says with a sigh.

"Sarah—" I start to let her off the hook, but she interrupts me.

"I mean, given the way we met, we've established that punctuality is not exactly my strong suit. An hour will give me plenty of time in case of a hair emergency, wardrobe malfunction, or cabbie sabotage. I should definitely be able to make it there by eight." Her teasing answer makes me smile.

"Well, you want to plan on eight then? Ya know, just to be safe."

"No way, because then I won't be there until nine. Let's just stick with seven, okay?" I can almost hear the laughter in her voice as she pretends to be annoyed.

"So, I'll see you at seven fifty-nine." I look down, shaking my head. Thank God we are on the phone because I wouldn't be able to contain my shit-eating grin otherwise.

"On the dot," she responds. "Oh, and, Leo, I am looking forward to seeing you. I wouldn't want your clearly sensitive ego to go un-stroked."

I burst into laughter. "Thanks, smartass."

"No problem. Goodnight." She begins laughing before hanging up.

Chapter
THREE

Leo

Seven months earlier...

I SHOULD Feel free. I should feel alive. I should feel like Leo James again. However, even in my own skin, I feel like an imposter. I'm not a man. I'm a coward.

"Leo!" *Erica calls from the balcony of her hotel suite. I tried to duck out before she noticed, but she catches me just before I get to the door.*

"I need to go, babe," *I tell her and the light dims in her eyes.*

"Not yet," *she whispers, taking a step closer, her eyes already filling with tears.*

"We've been dancing around this all day. I need to go."

"I'm not ready," *she says, looping her arms around my waist.*

"Yeah, you are." *I smooth down her hair and gently kiss the top of her head. I glance up to find her brick wall of a man, Slate, watching us while standing in the corner. His arms are crossed over his chest, but his concern is staggering.* "I'll see you next week for the wedding," *I try to reassure her, but the words catch in my throat.*

The truth is that I'm nowhere near ready to leave her. Our relationship is a prime example of codependency at its finest. Her clear, blue eyes are the only things that soothe the self-loathing burning inside me. She's also a reminder of why it burns at all. She's the poison and the antidote wrapped into one tiny, innocent, and foul-mouthed package.

"Come on, beautiful," Slate says, guiding her arms from around my waist.

I clear my throat and give her a weak smile as she silently cries tucked into his side.

Slate extends a hand and I quickly grasp it. We may not have always had the best relationship, but I definitely consider him family now. I'd trust him with my life, and in a sense, by leaving Erica with him, I'm doing exactly that.

"You'll be at the wedding on Saturday?" he confirms, never releasing my hand.

"Wouldn't miss it," I smile, and it might just be the biggest lie I have ever told.

I ARRIVE at Shades just a little before seven. I know Sarah might be late, but I gave myself plenty of time to walk downstairs and across the street. I may have picked this place based on the proximity to my apartment. *Maybe. Probably.*

Shades is a five-star tapas restaurant and martini bar. After nine o'clock, the atmosphere changes into that of a bar, but before then, it's a crisp, clean fine-dining experience.

The hostess guides me to one of the high-tops lining the perimeter of the large, crowded room, and I settle in so I can watch the door for Sarah.

Finally, at only ten minutes past seven, she comes walking in. I can only see the back of her head, but I'd recognize that white-blond hair anywhere. She's wearing a pair of tight jeans that cling to her ass and a black shirt that I can tell is tight as well. I lick my lips and head in her direction, knowing that the front will be even better than the back.

I sneak up behind her and very carefully lean forward to whisper in her ear. "I'm impressed. You actually showed."

She squeaks from surprise and takes a giant step forward. I begin to laugh before, suddenly, a tattooed arm lands hard against my chest, preventing me from following her.

"Back the fuck up," the man growls, and my eyes snap to his. He looks downright pissed, and the minute Sarah turns around, I know exactly why.

"You're not Sarah," I say, lifting my hands in submission and feeling like a total jackass.

"No. But you must be Leo." The woman smiles, and a pair of blue eyes I immediately recognize sparkles in humor. "Hi, I'm Emma Jones. Sarah's sister." She knocks the man's hand off my chest and extends her own.

I give her a confused look but take her hand then turn to the man with her. He still looks pissed, but begrudgingly nods at me.

"Caleb Jones."

"Sorry, man. Leo James. Nice to meet you," I respond, trying to figure out why Sarah's family is here yet she remains nowhere to be seen.

Then something catches my eye from the corner by the door. Sarah is standing in a line at the hostess desk, biting her knuckles to stifle a laugh. She uses the other hand to give me a very slow finger wave.

I shake my head and excuse myself to move in her direction. I weave through the small crowd by the door, stopping directly in front of her.

"Well, that was embarrassing."

"It was really funny though." She bites her lips to prevent the laugh from escaping but fails miserably.

"Hilarious," I say sarcastically.

She laughs for a second longer before collecting herself. "Hey," she says simply, pushing a hand out for a handshake.

First, she brought company, and now, she's trying to give me a fucking handshake? Clearly, she got confused somewhere along the way. Maybe I didn't make it obvious enough that this is a date, not a business meeting.

I lift a questioning eyebrow and stare down at her outstretched hand. *Fuck that.* "You look beautiful." I very purposefully lick my lips while raking my eyes over her body. Given her nerves on the phone yesterday, I know it will make her clam up and look away, but I don't want there to be any misconceptions about what this actually is. I'm interested in her. She should know that right off the bat—even if it makes her uncomfortable for a few minutes.

Only Sarah doesn't seem to be bothered by my overt gesture at all. She tilts her head to the side and does her own head-to-toe assessment of me. I wait for her eyes to travel back up to mine, and when they finally do, she gives me an unimpressed shrug.

I bust out laughing and she quickly follows.

"Come on. I got us a table already," I say, placing a hand on the small of her back and guiding her toward Emma and Caleb.

Sarah

WHEN THE four of us are seated, the waitress stops by to get our drink orders.

She starts with Emma, who asks for some over-the-top specialty martini, and Caleb, who orders a simple scotch neat. Leo motions for me to go next, and I very uncomfortably ask for a water with lemon. Leo doesn't seem to give my beverage of choice too much thought and orders a beer right behind me.

"So, what do you do?" Caleb asks Leo while dropping his hand under the table and into Emma's lap.

Those two are the horniest people I have ever met in my life. I wouldn't put it past Caleb to throw her down on the table in front of us all. Just knowing that his hand is within a twelve-inch radius of Emma's pants makes me question his motives. I roll my eyes, and Emma starts laughing when she catches my reaction. Both guys pause to look at her, but she ignores them and takes a sip of her drink while still smiling at me.

"I own a security company," Leo answers, draping his arm around the back of my chair. He doesn't exactly touch me, but it's still a flirty gesture that makes my eyes go wide, once again sending my loudmouth sister into a fit of laughter.

"Really?" Caleb asks, surprised.

"Yep. Guardian Protection. I opened about seven months ago."

"No. Shit," Caleb says impressed. "It was your men who took down Lucas Wilkes."

Leo swallows hard and his relaxed posture from just seconds ago goes stiff. "I didn't know that was public knowledge," Leo says with a harsh edge to his voice.

"Well, it's not a secret." Caleb winks, and I'm afraid Leo's sudden attitude has flipped Caleb's asshole switch.

"Caleb is a detective with the CPD," I rush out, trying to keep the peace.

"Gotcha," Leo responds and his shoulders relax. "In that case, yes. We took down Wilkes. It's also a topic that hits close to home, so if we could drop it and not discuss work tonight, I'd really appreciate it." Leo grins, but there's something dark behind it.

"Fair enough." Caleb smirks and takes a sip from his scotch.

We sit in uncomfortable silence for a minute before Emma breaks the tension.

"Isn't that Tom Cole over there?" she asks, looking across the restaurant.

"Who?" Caleb follows her gaze.

"It is! We should go say hi," she announces before jumping to her feet.

"Who the hell are you talking about, Emmy?"

"Would you shut up and come on?" she snaps, dragging him toward the bar.

I immediately let out a relieved sigh that makes Leo chuckle beside me.

"I'm sorry. I shouldn't have brought them." I look up to find his chocolate-brown eyes staring down at me.

Leo is a ridiculously good-looking guy. He's not the clean-cut type I usually go for; he's more edgy. His light-brown skin and dark hair make for an exotic look. He has a thin layer of scruff covering his strong jaw, but it's not because he forgot to shave—it's trimmed to perfection. His no doubt designer jeans are purposefully tattered, and the stylish, white button-down stretches across his hard chest. He must catch my eyes drifting, because his already wide smile grows before falling flat.

"Yeah, bringing the family with you on a first date is a little unusual. At least it wasn't the parents though." He moves his arm off the back of my chair and takes a pull off his beer. I can immediately feel the distance he just put between us.

"My parents are dead. This is pretty much the same thing," I blurt out, because clearly, somewhere over the last few years, I've lost all social awareness.

"Wow. This just got even more awkward." He drains the rest of his beer in one long sip.

"Shit. I'm sorry. I warned you this was a bad idea."

Ignoring my apology, he points down at my water. "You don't drink at all or just not tonight?"

"Not at all."

"Good. Let's get out of here." He pulls cash from his wallet and drops it on the table.

"Um, we just got here," I answer, surprised, and glance up to where Emma and Caleb are standing nose to nose at the bar, ignoring everyone around them.

"Right. But this isn't a date with them here. It's an interview. They seem like good people, but the only person I want to get to know tonight is you. There's a little dive Mexican restaurant a few blocks from here. Since you don't drink, there's no point staying at a martini bar."

"They have food here too," I state, trying to figure out his real motives behind leaving.

"And it's really good, but we're starting over. New restaurant, new date. Just me and you. We're doing it right this time. "

"Oh. Um…"

"Say goodnight. I'll meet you outside." He turns and heads out the door without another word spoken.

Well, I guess I'm going on a legit date with Leo after all.

Fuck.

Chapter
FOUR

Leo

"GET YOUR ass up," I hear Slate say as he walks into my room.

I'm sprawled out on my bed, naked, with an empty bottle of Jack on the nightstand.

"Nice. Really fucking nice," he bites out, snatching open the curtains.

"Jesus Christ, Andrews!" I toss an arm over my face to shield my eyes from the unwelcome light.

"What the fuck is wrong with you?"

"Oh, I don't know. I wasn't aware sleeping was a crime," I snark back at him.

I knew he would come eventually. I just hoped I'd be gone by the time he showed up. But I haven't had the balls to leave yet.

"She's called you twenty-seven times. Twenty-seven fucking times she has dialed your number. Twenty-seven!" he roars, rushing the bed, kicking it at the last second. *"We both thought you were fucking dead. I dropped everything and rushed over here two God damn days before my wedding only to find you passed out in bed. Drunk. What the fucking hell is wrong with you?!"* he screams, throwing the empty bottle of Jack across the room.

I have never seen Slate lose it like this before. It's alarming and—

confusing.

"Chill the fuck out." I grab my head, trying to slow the pounding inside.

"Right. Of course." He pulls his phone out of his back pocket and throws it at me. "Call her," he demands.

"Can I have a fucking second to take a piss and maybe put on some clothes?" I snap, dragging myself to my feet only to fall back against the bed when my dizzy head can't catch up.

Slate strides forward, forcing me to take another clumsy step back. He stops only inches from my face. "You fucking call her. She's a wreck. She fought me tooth and nail to come here today, but I was fucking terrified about what she would find. So pick up that phone and call her. Make sure you tell her goodbye because there is a good chance I'm going to fucking kill you when you hang up," he growls, but the only words that register are those when he said that Erica is a wreck.

The last thing in this world I want is for her to hurt anymore, so I drag a blanket off the bed and quickly dial her number. The shattered voice on the other end of the phone knocks me completely on my ass.

"Is he alive?" she cries into the phone.

"Babe," I whisper as the realization of her fear levels me. Tears spring to my eyes, and I turn to the wall to conceal them.

"Are you okay?" she asks, but I know it's not just a surface-level inquiry.

I take a minute to really consider the question. "No," I answer honestly. This is Erica, after all. I owe her the truth at the very least.

"Where are you?"

"At the apartment." I sweep the emasculating tears from my eyes.

"Stay there. Let me talk to Slate," she breathes across the line.

It pains me to hear her concern. I've spent almost four years protecting this woman, but over the course of five days without her, I've forgotten what it feels like be needed.

"Erica—"

"Forget it. I'll call him later. I'm on the way." She hangs up.

I toss his phone on the bed, heading into my closet for a moment alone and to grab some clothes. I pull on a pair of jeans and a white T-shirt while readying myself for the shitstorm I know is approaching.

Slate is staring out the window when I emerge from the closet. He's pissed, but this is Slate. We are going to butt heads no matter what.

"Sit down and start talking," he says in a surprisingly patient tone, which he usually reserves only for Erica.

I decide to start with a lie. After all, I've spent years telling them—it should be easy.

"I'm just making up for lost time. That's all. Went out, got a little drunk. I must not have heard my phone when she called."

"Bullshit," he snaps. "She's been calling you for three days."

"Look, thanks for coming, but I'm not doing this with you."

"You need serious help, Leo. Erica and I have started counseling—"

"I'm glad to see that Erica is getting help, but beyond that, I don't give two fucks how awesome counseling is working out for you!" I shout.

No therapist in the world is going to change the decisions I've made in the past. I'm not dealing with something that happened to me; I'm crippled by the guilt of something I did. There's a big difference— one that can't just be overcome.

"I don't get this sudden change in you. You are probably the most levelheaded person I know. You're finally free to live whatever life you want, but you're spending your days drinking and ignoring the people who love you. You're having some issues, so let's figure it out so we can all move the fuck on."

I'm not sure why his words send fire through my veins. Maybe it's because the very idea of moving on seems impossible and the words of hope are like dangling a steak in front of a starving man.

I just need someone to hate me as much as I hate myself. I know Erica won't do it, so Slate's on deck.

"That night while your beautiful bride was tied to a bed, naked—"

His face morphs and he immediately stops me. "Don't fucking do this. You're not provoking me."

I spit out the venomous words anyway. "You know...when I sent all those men in to rape her."

"Shut your fucking mouth, Leo. Goddamn it, we are not talking about this."

"It must be nice—to be able to just turn it off." I roll my eyes and head to the kitchen.

"I know you're struggling, and it's okay. We're going to get you help," Slate announces, following me from the room.

"I don't need help. I need a goddamn escape."

"Don't spew bullshit like that. What the hell is going through your head right now?" he asks.

The truth explodes from my throat. "Her screams! That's what is always going through my head. The sounds of her screaming while I stood helpless on the other side of that door play in a never-ending loop. All day. All night. No matter what I do. I can't block it out!"

"SARAH! WOW. You look beautiful tonight." I lean in and give her a hug when she walks out of the restaurant. Fuck that stupid handshake shit she tried to pull earlier.

I take a step away, and she watches me blankly, but the smallest smile plays on her lips.

"All right. I've officially ditched the parents. Where are you taking me for my celebratory dinner? It better be good. It's not every day I get a big, fancy receptionist position," she says playfully.

"Come on. I'll show you." I offer her an elbow, and she doesn't hesitate in sliding her arm through mine.

"So tell me about yourself," she inquires as we stroll arm in arm the two blocks to the restaurant.

"Well, hmmm... What do you want to know?" I smile down at the very moment she looks up through her lashes. *Jesus, she is gorgeous.* No one could possibly describe her as anything else, but I know there's more to her than just her angelic looks. There's a depth in her eyes that interests me the most. "Well I'm thirty-three, originally from Nebraska but grew up in El Paso, Texas. However, I've lived all over the place for the last few years."

"Where'd you learn Spanish?" she asks, seeming to be genuinely interested and not just making small talk.

"I worked on my grandparents ranch in Texas as soon as I was old enough to muck the stalls. Most of the other workers were Mexican, so they taught me a good bit in order to communicate. From there, I made some of the best friends I've ever had. Spanish was kind of a necessity."

"Wow. That's really cool that you picked it up all on your own. I figured you were Hispanic, but with a last name like James, I wasn't really sure."

"Nah. The dark complexion fools them every time though," I tease. "You ready for the best authentic Mexican food you've ever tasted?" I ask, reluctantly releasing her arm only long enough to guide her into the restaurant.

But it's the way she arches her back to press against my hand that has my mind spinning in a million different directions—almost all of which end with her naked.

This is just a first date.

First date.

First date.

Fucking hell!

Chapter
~~FIVE~~

Sarah

"I HAVE to admit. That place was delicious. I was looking forward to Shades, but I always give credit where credit is due," I say with an exaggerated bow as we leave the restaurant.

Jesus Christ, Leo James is intriguing. If there were ever a man who knew how to say all the right things at the right times, that would be Leo. There wasn't a single moment of awkwardness at dinner—even at the points where there was supposed to be the normal 'getting to know you' awkwardness. Leo filled every minute with entertaining conversation I couldn't help but feel comfortable with.

I was worried that we would have nothing to talk about. I wanted to stay as far away from my past as possible. A first date is not exactly the best time to air all of your dirty laundry—or, in my case, the entire Laundromat. Though, until tonight, I didn't realize that I don't have a ton of other stuff to talk about.

However, Leo did.

We talked about everything from stupid everyday stuff at work—his difficulty finding trustworthy employees and my switching careers so drastically. I brushed off his questions about why I no longer wanted to be a writer, and I think he actually bought it. But then we got serious. He told me all about his upbringing as an only child and his parents, who sadly passed away about the same time I lost mine. He was a gentleman in every sense of the word. He never pried, but he definitely asked questions as if he were actually interested in *me*. He's distractingly handsome, but his sex appeal is amplified with his every word spoken.

Leo James is smooth. It's not usually a trait I would want in a man, but there's an honesty in his smile that really draws me in.

"How about you let me drive you home? I'm not okay with just calling you a cab," he says suddenly, turning to face me, forcing me to take a step back. "Please."

"I'll be fine," I try to assure him, but he doesn't budge.

"I live in that building." He points up at the tall tower only a block away. "Just let me get my car and I'll take you home. It will be way quicker than hailing a cab from here this time of night." He smiles and it stills my breath. It's the most terrifying sight I have ever seen.

Shit. He's smooth *and* breathtaking. Red flags start flying all over the place. I'm not scared of Leo, but my legs are definitely trembling for a completely different reason.

Fuckity fuck, fuck, fuck.

"IT'S ONLY ten," Leo announces when we walk into his apartment.

His big-ass, expensive, downtown-Chicago apartment. I have a sudden urge to call Emma just to tell her that Leo is apparently, in fact, loaded.

"Wow. This place is gorgeous," I gasp as we walk inside.

"Thanks," he replies, tossing his keys into the bowl next to the door. "You want a drink?" he asks before remembering that I don't *drink.* "Pop, water, juice…anything?" he corrects.

"You know, I've lived here for almost fifteen years, but I can't ever get used to y'all calling it 'pop,'" I laugh.

He groans, turning toward the fridge. "Y'all," is all he says in reply, as if that is clearly the explanation of his groan.

"I've adapted to most things about living in the Chicago. Y'all is not one of those things. I'm taking that one to the grave." I toss him a smile, but it does nothing to match his bright glow.

Damn it. Leo James is officially blinding too.

"So. Drink?" he asks, trying to divert my obvious stare.

"No. I really should get going," I answer while holding his gaze, but my confidence falters when his lips lift in a devilish grin.

"No. You shouldn't," he corrects while peeling off his button-down to reveal an even tighter, white undershirt.

"I…" I stumble. *Hard.*

Who the hell is this guy? I'm a smartass. It's kind of my thing, but he gives me nothing. He doesn't set himself up for my sarcastic comments. He's always one step ahead. And in this moment, taking off his shirt is that step.

He does things to me, but none I'm willing to admit yet.

Until he touches me.

He stops in front of me. His smile is gone, but there's a definite heat in his eyes. Holding a bottle of water in one hand, he reaches forward with the other and brushes the hair off my shoulder, exposing my neck. It's a gentle touch, but no less sensual. His fingers linger on my collarbone, causing chills to prickle my skin. I hold his eyes, fully expecting him to lean in for a kiss, but Leo doesn't move an inch.

"Stay for a little while? I'll take you home in an hour or so." His tries to whisper but it comes out gravelly—and panty-drenchingly sexy.

"Okay," I answer immediately. I never even had a fighting chance to decline.

"Good," he replies with a smirk. He holds my gaze as his hand travels down my arm before moving to my hip. Then he gives me a quick squeeze before releasing me to walk to the couch.

I stare into space, dazed by what just happened. Suddenly, I feel like I'm in way over my head. I should have gone on a test date with a balding accountant to brush up on my skills before stepping into the ring with this man. Leo is going to eat me for dinner and spit me out when he's done, but I can't even bring myself to care right now. He's barely even touched me, yet I swear I have been hypnotized.

Leo is that fucking good.

"Sarah," he calls from the large, leather sofa.

I snap out of my trance and move to sit on the end farthest away from him, but he pointedly clears his throat just before I sit down. His arm is slung over the back of the couch, and his eyes flash from mine to the cushion beside him, making it clear where I'm supposed to be seated. Though I'm not completely sure I want to give him the opportunity to touch me again, I can't even lie to myself. I immediately slide over to underneath his arm, thrilled by the idea of touching *him* again.

Leo flips on the large flat-screen mounted over the fireplace. He doesn't say a word, but his body is relaxed as he drops his arm around my shoulders. It's a far cry from my tense posture, but it's infectious. My nerves calm as he begins drawing circles on my shoulder with his fingertips.

We must sit like that for at least half an hour. He finds some silly reality dating show and we simultaneously start making fun of the contestants. He seems to have the same sarcastic sense of humor I do, and just when I thought he was maxed on out the sexy scale, Leo becomes sexier.

"What the hell is wrong with her? She has known him for, like, ten minutes and she's already sobbing that he didn't pick her. She's cute. Can't she meet guys at a bar where she could get drunk and embarrass herself in private?" I ask while we watch the woman melt down on the TV.

"She might be cute, but she has crazy eyes. Any guy in a fifty-foot radius could tell she is crazy as all hell. The kind that would light your clothes on fire for picking her up five minutes late," he answers, and my body immediately goes stiff.

In other words, me.

He must feel me tense because he gives me a strangely reassuring squeeze and changes the subject. It's confusing, but I'm so appreciative that I don't bother to question it.

"Do you like sports?" He flips the TV to ESPN and I can't help but laugh.

"Um, no." I look up to find him watching me intently. His brown eyes render me unable to look away.

"Good," he responds as his eyes flash to my mouth. "Then I'll leave it on this channel." He whispers his lips across mine. Then he leans away to catch my eyes, seemingly to gauge my reaction to his advance, but I give him nothing. My expression is blank. It's not a façade. I don't know how I feel about it, but his eyes draw me in.

However, a sharp pain in my stomach stops me in my tracks.

"Oh my God! I'm going to puke!" I jump off the couch and sprint to the bathroom.

"Well, that's new." He follows me to the door, which I didn't bother shutting in my race to the porcelain.

I violently expel the contents of my stomach into the toilet, only vaguely aware that Leo is in the room. I would love to be embarrassed, but my stomach is knotting to the point where I'm not sure I will survive. *Leo who?*

"I'm sorry," I manage to say between the heaves. I know he's somewhere in the vicinity. He's not touching me, but I can feel his presence.

"Oh shit," he groans as I hear his footsteps stumble from the bathroom. *Well, okay then.*

For what seems like seven years—maybe longer—I sit, dying on his bathroom floor. I have absolutely no grasp of time, nor can I move. I can't even bring myself to be embarrassed that I'm puking in the lavish bathroom of a man I barely even know. All I know is that I need to start praying. I may not be a religious woman, but if I ever needed the Lord, it would be now.

"Sarah!" I hear Leo's gravelly voice shout from somewhere in the distance. But if he is expecting me to come to him, he might as well be in Antarctica.

"Yeah," I barely squeak out with my head resting on the toilet seat. And just when I thought I couldn't get any more desirable to a man, I'm hugging his toilet.

"Are you okay?" he asks with concern filling his voice, but the sound of him throwing up rings through the air.

"No," I answer honestly.

"Me either," he responds before throwing up again.

I'm assuming he's in another bathroom down the hall, but another pain hits my stomach in epic proportions.

"I think we have food poisoning," he growls.

"I hate you," I say to my stomach, the toilet, and Leo all at exactly the same time, but none of them answer.

Fifteen years later, I fall asleep with sweat covering my face and vomit lingering on my tongue. The cool tile floor is my only comfort.

"SHH," I hear whispered as I'm lifted off the floor.

My head falls back over his strong arm and my legs dangle loosely in his grasp. The devil himself could be carrying me to Hell and I wouldn't care, but thankfully for me, it's Leo's voice in my ear.

"I..." I try to fire off some random thought, but it only rouses me further from sleep, making me wish I could rush back to the bathroom.

"Shh," he repeats, depositing me on a plush bed. "Bucket on the side," are his only real words as he settles beside me.

I reach a hand over to become acquainted with the plastic rim of my new friend, the trash can, then drift off to sleep.

Chapter
SIX

Leo

"EXPLAIN THE note, Leo!" Slate roars.

"Get the fuck out of my apartment!" I shout right back at him while searching through my room for my phone and wallet.

I have to get the fuck out of here.

"Were you just going to leave that shit for her? Let her stumble upon it the day before we got married? Goddamn it, Leo. Fucking talk to me!" He steps up, preventing me from leaving the room. As the former heavyweight champion of the world, Slate isn't exactly someone you can just ignore.

"Jesus Christ, it's not what you think," I lie. "I was just having a bad day and needed to put a few things down on paper."

"Bullshit. You were saying goodbye to her," he snarls, and I feel the rage rolling off him.

I know he would never want anything to happen to me, but that is not where his concern is aimed. He's pissed right now at the idea that I might do something that would hurt Erica. And I respect the hell out of him for that.

"What do you want me to say here?" I pinch the bridge of my nose. "Why the fuck are you going through my shit, anyway?"

"Because when I got here this morning, you had been on a three-

day bender and I was fucking worried." He sucks in a calming breath and cracks his neck. It takes a few seconds for him to push it all down, but he finally looks me in the eye and asks, "Now please explain the note."

I let out a resigned sigh. "I'm drowning."

"Right. I got that," he answers.

"No, you don't understand. When I had Erica, my goal in life was to keep her safe and make her happy. I spent every minute of the day focusing on her. Trying to make some sort of amends for what I did to her. But now she's gone, and I feel like I am dying."

He blinks at me for a few seconds. "Leo, I've never felt the need to ask this before, but right now, I'm really fucking confused. Are you in love with Erica?"

"Oh for fuck's sake." I push past him out of my bedroom and head to the rec room, where I think I left my wallet last night. "See, this is the bullshit I get for trying to talk to someone!" I shout over my shoulder with a sarcastic laugh.

"Well, you're not making any sense."

I pause and spin around to face him. "My life doesn't make sense. No, I'm not in love with Erica. I have never once looked at her like that. Yes, I love her, and in some sick way, she is the only family I have left. But you can rest easy, big man. I'm not in love with your fiancée," I say humorlessly.

"Then what is the big issue with her being gone?"

"She was my distraction!" I shout. "I spent the last four years trying to make her better, but now, she's gone and the choices I've made flash like neon lights around me. I can't focus on anything else. I was wrong. I thought seeing her happy and moving on would release me. It didn't though—it made it worse. I fucking hate myself. I let an innocent woman be raped—repeatedly."

I know my words have made their way under his skin, but he still manages to grit out from between clenched teeth, "You had no choice."

"Bullshit. Everyone has a choice. I should have let them kill me."

"They would have killed her! Get your God damn head straight. I fucking hate you for what you did—or, rather, didn't do—but she made it out alive. You saved her on more than one occasion. Consider your

penance paid!"

"It's not enough. I can't live like this."

"So, what? You're now planning to kill yourself? You think that would help Erica?"

"No, but it would help me!" I scream.

"Leo," I hear Erica squeak from behind me.

Fuck.

"I have to get out of here." I walk past her, not even able to look her in the eye after what I know she just heard.

I pass Johnson, who's standing at the door. He's no doubt the asshole who let Slate up here today. Then I rush down the back stairs until I hit the parking garage only to realize I never found my keys or wallet.

The door swings open behind me and I steel myself for more of Slate and Erica. But it's Johnson who comes leisurely strolling out, immediately lighting a cigarette.

"Come on, boss. I'll take you wherever you want to go." He walks over to an immaculately restored muscle car.

"Shit. Thank you." I climb into the passenger's side, not sure where I'm planning to go. This is the first time I've ever actually wanted to run from Erica.

I HAVE been hit by a car—no, it was definitely a truck. That is the only thing I can imagine to explain why my whole body aches. As my stomach lets out a low rumble, last night comes rushing back to my memory. Food poisoning. Shit...

"Sarah," I groan just as her phone starts ringing.

I glance over at the clock to see that it's well past two p.m., but with most of our night spent throwing up, I'm not even the slightest bit surprised that we slept all day.

Sarah blindly feels around the floor for her phone before finally answering it.

"Hello," she croaks, and I can hear a woman on the other end of the line start laughing. "Emma, hush," she pleads, pulling it away from her ear and looking for the volume button on the side of her pink iPhone.

"So how'd it go with Leo last night after y'all left?" I hear Emma ask just as Sarah puts the phone back to her ear.

"Not good. He tried to kill me," she responds, throwing an arm over her forehead.

"What?" Emma yells.

"I didn't try to kill you," I moan as I try to sit up.

"Oh my God. You're still with him!" Emma shrieks. Even though Sarah turned the volume down, I can still hear her reaction clear as a bell.

"It's not what you think. Apparently, Leo's idea of celebrating is giving me food poisoning."

"Hey, if it had been intentional, I definitely would not have given it to myself too." I stretch my aching muscles before dragging myself to the kitchen.

I fight down the nausea as I open the fridge. Yeah, food is officially off the menu for today. After grabbing a bottle of Gatorade, I pause only to snag two glasses on my way back to the bedroom.

"I'll call you when I'm ready. I honestly don't think I can move right now," Sarah tells Emma as I set a glass down the nightstand. "Okay, bye." She hangs up and curls her lip at the Gatorade as I pour it. "There is no way I'm drinking that."

"Come on. You have to be dehydrated. How are you feeling?" I ask, sitting down on the bed next to her.

"Terrible. My whole body is sore. What did you do to me?"

None of the things I wanted to do. That's for sure.

Luckily, I manage to keep that little tidbit to myself and reply, "Jesus, I'm so sorry."

"This might very well be the worst first date in history." She gives me a weak smile.

"I'm encouraged that you only said 'might' because I can't imagine it going any worse." I lean back as she slides over to make more room. I don't even have enough energy to walk around to the other side.

"I only said 'might' because you carried me to bed and didn't let me sleep on the bathroom floor," she teases with a warm and sleepy smile.

"Well, at least there's that." I smile back. "So, I need to shower. Since I'm relatively sure neither one of us has big plans for the day, why don't you hang out here? I'll get you a toothbrush and some clothes and we can watch movies on the big couch in the rec room. I won't even offer to feed you."

"Oh God, don't even mention food," she groans and covers her mouth.

"No food, I swear. Just you, me, Gatorade, and bad eighties movies." I reach over to grab her hand. It must catch her off guard, because her eyes snap to mine. I squeeze tight, refusing to release it. "I've never had a woman puke to avoid kissing me. You owe me."

"I *owe* you?" she asks amused.

"Yes, you owe me some serious hand-holding for the way you behaved last night."

"Excuse me?" She sits up only to regret the sudden movement.

I chuckle to myself as she clenches her stomach and slowly leans back on the bed. Then I take the opportunity to slide an arm under her and inch over closer.

"Okay, okay. We can cuddle if you insist." I curl her in my arms as she huffs. I can tell she's not really annoyed when she relaxes into my side. "So, what do you say? You want to hang out and commiserate with me?"

"Sorry. I don't like green Gatorade," she responds with a shrug.

"I have red too." I toss her a wink, knowing good and damn well she is making excuses.

"I don't like 'eighties movies," she states, flashing me a smile. Shit. *Her smile.*

"Fine. We can watch whatever you like. But, just so you know, that's a serious issue we are going to have to discuss at a later date."

"Who says there is going to be a later date?" she asks, and her smile grows to full blown. "I don't like you." She bites her lips to contain a laugh, a task I'm learning she is terrible at.

"Oh come on. Now you are just being ridiculous. You like me. You jumped right into my bed on the first date," I tease even though I feel like absolute hell, and the sound of her laughter soothes me as it flitters around us.

"I did not! You carried me to your bed."

"Oh look. We are right back where this conversation started. I carried you to bed, so now you are going to reward my chivalry by spending the day with me." I slowly push up to my feet. My stomach cramps, but I forge ahead to the dresser.

"Here." I pull out a T-shirt and a pair of sweats and toss them onto the bed next to her. They won't fit her, but that is probably for the best. I'm in no condition to even entertain thoughts of sex, but for some reason, I can't stop them from flooding my head.

Even after spending the entire night in the least appealing way possible, Sarah Erickson is fucking sexy as hell. She should've woken up this morning looking like a troll who'd spent the night drowning in the rain. But with her hair pulled back in a ponytail and her eye make-up slightly smeared, she still oozes sex appeal. Yes, she is beautiful. But her lithe body makes her every move sensual. She tries to play coy, as if she is intimidated by her own overwhelming confidence—the same confidence that makes my dick hard every time I even look in her direction.

"You can use my bathroom. I'll use the one in the guest room. Towels are under the sink." I say, swinging my own T-shirt and shorts over my shoulder. "Oh, and call Mama Erickson back and tell her I'll bring you home tonight," I order as I walk from the room.

Sarah doesn't actually agree to stay, but she doesn't argue anymore either. That's more than enough for me.

"I'M NOT watching *Vision Quest*," Sarah declares while lying on the couch.

"Yes, you are. I've had a ridiculously shitty twenty-four hours. Last night, I took a woman on a date and she gave me the stomach flu."

"It's not the stomach flu! It's food poisoning from the restaurant you insisted we go to." She laughs weakly then covers her mouth at the very mention of dinner.

"You say potato, I say—"

"Food poisoning," she cuts me off with another groan.

"Okay, fine. I give up. What do you want to watch?" I ask.

We're lying on opposite ends of the couch; our legs are tangled in the middle. I inch down to get closer. I've given it a seriously less than mediocre effort, but I can't seem to stop touching her. It's just something about the way every connection sends a spark of electricity through... Okay, fine. She makes me hard. Every. Single. Time. I feel like death warmed over, but every time her foot brushes up my leg, even inadvertently, I go stiff.

Sarah Erickson is phenomenal dressed up and flirting over a meal, but surprisingly enough, she's pretty freaking amazing in baggy sweats while laid up on my couch too.

"*Vanilla Sky*," she answers.

I curl my lip in disgust. "Is that a movie or flavor of ice cream?"

"Oh my God. Food. I hate you." She starts kicking me while holding her stomach. "It's a movie."

"I've never even heard of it."

"Really? It has Tom Cruise and Penelope Cruz in it. I'm sure you remember seeing the old clips where Cameron Diaz goes off about swallowing Tom's come."

"What the hell kind of movie is this?" I ask, surprised, and she begins to quietly giggle. "I had no idea Cameron Diaz did porn. I'm seriously out of the loop."

"Oh my God! It's not porn, Leo. It's an amazing, thought-provoking, beautifully filmed emotional rollercoaster." She smiles and it lights her already bright, blue eyes.

"Well, in that case, it definitely sounded more interesting when I thought it was porn. Thought provoking just means I'll spend half the movie confused. And beautifully filmed means I'm going to spend the other half watching sunsets in either slow motion or fast forward."

"Oh, please tell me you are not one of those guys who only watches movies like *Transformers* and *Batman*." She slaps a hand over her eyes.

"Hey! What's wrong with *Batman*?"

"I didn't think it was possible for you to become any less attractive after last night," she says, tangling her legs tighter with mine.

"Liar." I smirk and grab the remote, flipping through the on-demand movies. "Okay, let's see if we can find this *Vanilla Ice Cream* porno you are so eager to watch. But...you have to come over here by me if you want me to watch this crap."

"It's not crap. I love this movie," she responds as I press play.

"Come on. Get up here." I scoot over to the edge, allowing her just enough room to squeeze in next to me. She doesn't move, so I just shrug and hit the menu button on the remote. "Okay, looks like *Vision Quest* will be playing at the James Cinema today after all."

"This is blackmail."

"Just a little," I reply, patting the couch next to me.

She groans before crawling forward and tucking herself into my side. She rests her head on my chest but keeps her arms at her sides. I almost find it comical. However, before Tom Cruise even starts running through Times Square, she drapes her arm across my chest and begins stroking up and down my side.

We spend the rest of the day lounging on the couch. We talk, sleep, and laugh—a lot. We both feel like utter shit, but I'll admit that I'm actually enjoying my time lying around with her. It is a million times better than being miserable alone. She is always touching me. It isn't sexual, but it is definitely flirty. And it doesn't feel forced or awkward either. It feels, well…normal.

Chapter
SEVEN

Sarah

"THANK YOU for calling the Chicago Tribune. How may I direct your call?"

It's an endless cycle.

"Please hold."

All day.

"Thank you for calling the Chicago Tribune. How may I direct your call?"

Fuck my life.

I've worked this job for approximately two point five days and I'm officially ready to quit, but unfortunately, I don't have that luxury.

"Please hold."

"Sarah!" I hear the Wicked Witch call from her office. "Time for lunch," she informs me then quickly begins explaining, for the third day in a row, how to forward the calls to one of the secretary's desks. It's two buttons. Not exactly a difficult task, but she clearly doesn't think I can handle it.

It's only a lunch break, but I walk out of the building eager for all sixty minutes of freedom before I have to reenter that hell. No sooner than my feet hit the sidewalk do I get an eye full of a gorgeous man leaning against a motorcycle, waiting for *me*.

His delicious lips lift in that genuine smile I haven't been able to stop thinking about.

"I didn't take you for the stalking type," I tease, stopping in front of him. "Or a biker."

Fucking hell. Leo leaning against a Harley is a sight to be seen.

"Stalking isn't usually my thing, but I was willing to make an exception for you." He reaches forward, pulling me against him and wrapping me in his arms. This man and his freaking hugs. I would complain if I didn't enjoy every single second of them.

When Leo dropped me off around ten on Sunday night, he gave me a quick kiss on the cheek then promised to call. We made plans to go out again on Wednesday since he would be gone on business in Indianapolis until then. True to his word, Leo called both nights that he was away. He listened to me ramble about the new job on Monday. Then, on Tuesday, I listened to him complain about one of the new guys he'd had to fire for hitting on a client.

Up until now, I was a little concerned about the direction this thing with Leo was headed. During our phone calls, he never once became the flirty man I have grown to know. He called to chat like an old friend. Granted, we don't know each other well. It's not like I was expecting him to whisper sweet nothings or anything. It just felt like the heat in his voice was gone. However, now, as his hand drifts over the small of my back, I know I couldn't have been more wrong.

"Hey," I finally respond, taking a step away, but Leo doesn't release me.

"How long do you have for lunch?" he whispers into my ear, sending chills down my spine.

"Um, an hour." I grab his biceps for balance and, for some strange reason, turn my head to give him access to my neck.

A small moan escapes my throat as his breath teases my skin. Leo and I haven't even kissed yet, but I'm completely okay if he wants start with my neck…in the middle of the street…in front of my office. *Shit*.

I clear my throat and back away, fully expecting to find him smirking at me. Only Leo looks just as affected by our brief moment as I feel. His eyes are hooded and full of absolute *trouble*.

He sucks in a deep breath. "Okay, so I'm going to take you to lunch—sans food poisoning this time. Then we are going to discuss that moan tonight over dinner," he says bluntly.

As much as I would like to be shy and timid in this moment, I can't resist the impulse to deflect his flirty advance. "Oh, we are most definitely not talking about that. Besides, if we are going to talk, we should start with how long you sat outside waiting on me," I respond with a sarcastic laugh.

"You're probably right. Talking would only prevent me from making you moan again. I like the way you think." He winks before grabbing my hand and walking down the street.

I'm left with my jaw hanging open at his forwardness.

He releases my hand and guides me into a very well-known chain restaurant; obviously, Leo isn't any more willing than I am to take another chance on a random food.

"COME ON. I can't afford to be late," I say, dragging Leo from the restaurant.

Lunch went much like everything does with Leo—easy, comfortable, and fun. We didn't talk about anything profound. No deep, dark secrets were revealed. We just ate lunch and enjoyed each other's company. It was by far the best date I've ever been on. All fifty minutes of it. I'd give anything to make it last longer, but knowing that we will be going out again tonight makes it sting a little less when I see the tall tower of the newspaper building only a block ahead of us.

"How long do you have?" he asks.

"Six minutes."

"I only need two." He grins mischievously. I want to be alarmed by the flicker in his eyes, but as he pulls me down the side street, I lose any desire to care. "I need to talk to you for a second."

"Five minutes." I count him down to distract myself from getting lost in his hypnotic ways.

Leo abruptly stops me, pushing me off-balance. I slide my hands over the curved muscles of his shoulders to keep on my feet and... well, just to cop a feel. I close my eyes. As if looking at Leo weren't hard enough, touching him gets me every time.

Fuck. I just moaned again. And Leo verifies it with his smirk when I peek open my eyes.

"Just so you know, I'm going to kiss you."

I stumble back at his honesty. My shoulders meet the cool brick of the building. It's lunchtime on a busy Chicago sidewalk, but I'm with Leo James. Fuck the rest of the details. The sounds of the city whirl around us as I close my eyes in anticipation of finally feeling his lips pressed to mine. Yet they never come. My eyes flash open to find him watching me.

"Not right now," he corrects, and I sigh with a mixture of relief and disappointment, causing his smile to grow. "Sarah, tonight. I'm going to kiss you. Not on a sidewalk, but in my bed."

"You're pretty confident, huh?" I snark, needing some way to disguise my desires. I know there is no way to deny that he turns me on. I won't even try to pretend otherwise.

"Nope, just optimistic." He leans in close, pinning me against the building. His lips taunt me, but it's the look in his eyes that silences my response. "When's the last time someone kissed you, Sarah?" His hands move up my sides as he licks his lips, holding my gaze hostage with his every move.

"Forcibly or by choice?" I ask with my head lost in a fog.

"Excuse me?" he growls as his eyes flash with an odd combination of anger and something else I don't quite recognize.

"No! Nothing like that!" I exclaim.

"Then what's it like, Sarah?" He lifts his eyebrows questioningly.

"It's just… My last kiss wasn't one I wanted. It was from my ex and it was…weird."

"Right. Weird." His reaction leaves me puzzled, but when his shoulders relax, so do mine.

We stare at each other for a few seconds, but the moment is officially gone.

"I need to get back." I push myself off the wall, attempting to regain some sense of composure that doesn't make me look like a starstruck teenager.

Leo catches my arm, stilling me. "I was serious about tonight. I'm just giving you some notice so you could work it out in your head first," he tells me with a surprising amount of understanding.

"We'll see about that." I give him a patronizing smile that only causes the heat to flare back into his eyes.

"Oh, we will, ángel," he says in a Spanish accent that pretty much guarantees that we will, in fact, be kissing tonight. Maybe not in his bed though. I can at least stand my ground on that one, although I'm not really sure why I would want to.

"I'm going to be late," I reply in a dry, bored tone even though, on the inside, I am anything but.

"I'm picking you up tonight."

"I can just—"

"You're going to be late if you stand here and argue with me. I'll see you at seven." He smiles a knowing grin.

I glance down at my watch and realize I have less than a minute to clock back in from lunch. "Shit."

"See ya tonight!" he shouts as I take off speed-walking around the corner and toward the door of the Tribune.

Chapter
EIGHT

Leo

JOHNSON DOESN'T say a word as he drives through town. He silently smokes as I stare out the window feeling utterly lost. After an
hour of driving in circles, he pulls up to a building about ten minutes
from my apartment.

"It's safe to assume I'm going to lose my job for this." He puts the
car in park and gets out.

"What the fuck are you doing?" I ask as I catch sight of the Building Foundations sign above the door.

He rounds the hood and opens my door. "Get the fuck out," he
growls.

"Fuck you," I respond.

"Sorry it's not one of those fancy-ass richy-rich places Slate
would have taken you to, but this is all I know."

"You can't check me into some nuthouse without my permission."
I look at him like he's the one who should be checking in.

"No, but at three p.m. every day, there's a grief therapy group
session. I come on Wednesdays." He shrugs.

I knew Johnson had a dark past, but we've never talked about.

"I'm not going in there. It won't help."

"Well, you won't know until you try." He takes a long drag off his *cigarette.*

"You don't think I've tried!" I yell, jumping out of the car and stepping into his face.

"Well, get your ass in there and try again. It obviously didn't take the first time." He blows smoke into my face. "That bullshit back there about offing yourself is ridiculous. You went through hell and back to save Erica. Now walk your bitch ass in there and take the first step to save yourself."

I open my mouth to tell him to fuck off, but he stops me first.

"Or maybe I'll call Erica and have her meet us up here. You can deal with her face to face. Tell her all about that shit you spewed to Slate back there. Your choice." He smiles, knowing that he's won.

"Goddamn it," I mumble to myself as I head inside.

The meeting is already in progress, and a thin woman is standing on the makeshift stage. I grab the chair closest to the back and try to blend in while planning my escape.

"Hey, y'all. I'm officially done with this place," she says, and the room claps, making me roll my eyes.

This is ridiculous. Just as I ready myself to leave, the frail woman stills me.

"This might be my last day, but you should all know that I'm not healed, fixed, or magically restored to be the person I was before guilt and self-loathing took over my life. I'm still just as broken as the day I walked in here." She sucks in an emotion-filled breath before continuing. "I think it's important for you to know that I sat right where you are sitting for two years. I listened to people tell me how fantastic they felt as they said their goodbyes, but I'm here to inform you that it's all a load of shit."

Her honesty intrigues me and keeps me rooted in my chair. And when she smiles, it's guts me. Even though I've never seen this woman before, I recognize that pain-filled smile. I've seen it almost every time I've looked in the mirror for the last four years. That's my smile.

"This may be shocking to some of you, but even after what seems like a billion hours of therapy, I still hate myself for the things I have done. I physically ache when I think about the people I have hurt. The only difference is that, now, I know how to handle that pain. It doesn't shred me anymore, and that in and of itself is more than I ever could

have asked for when I walked into this room for the very first time. So, today, as my final parting words, I'm not going to fill your head with false hope of ever completely reclaiming your life. I'm going to fill it with the truth about overcoming and starting over. Today, I'm going to tell you my story. It's a long one, so I hope you grabbed some coffee."

She smiles again, and I know I won't be able to budge from the chair even if the building suddenly catches fire. She never even looked at me while she was speaking, but her words hit me harder than any counselors' ever could.

It's as if she were speaking directly to me.

For over an hour, I sit, riveted, listening to her recount her years of struggle— from the attempts to end her life to her seclusion from everyone who ever loved her. She doesn't pull punches or spin it in a way that places her in a positive light. She gives every gory detail. She speaks about her emotional breakdowns, and it's exhausting just to hear her talk about it. I can't imagine how she must feel reliving it. But with every word spoken, I can see an invisible weight lifting from her shoulders.

She's not being broken down—she's being freed.

For a minute, I'm so jealous of this woman's strength and her ability to overcome everything she's been through, that it makes me ill.

"So that's my story." She finishes with a loud sigh. "Just so there is no confusion...I'm still that person. I'm just a better version with better resources and better support. I'm not alone anymore, and neither are you. Every single day, good people do bad things. And I'm no different. The hardest part about life is putting one foot in front of the other to move past that pain. But I swear to you, inch by inch, you will get past it. It doesn't disappear, but it's no longer staring you in the face. You'll see—just like I did."

I watch in awe as a single tear drips down her chin. She nods to the doctor in the corner, who's beaming with pride. He attempts to approach her, but she waves him off. Smiling, she tucks her head low against her chest and walks from the building.

I swallow hard as my eyes frantically race around the room. What the fuck just happened? My mind is left spinning. How did that woman know exactly the words I needed to hear? I only know one thing—just like her, I want to own my regret.

I grab my phone from my pocket.

"Leo." Erica's sob comes across the line.

My voice is shaking, but I finally manage to say the one phrase I hope will release me too, "I need help."

"I NEED you to give me a creepy factor of one to ten."

"Oh God, Leo. This does not sound good," Erica says with suspicious eyes, placing her coffee on the table.

"Remember the woman I saw speak at Foundations?"

"Of course."

"Yeah. Well, her name is Sarah Erickson and I have a date with her tonight," I rush out with an unexpected pang of guilt.

"Excuse me?" Erica says, leaning in close. "I thought she was a severely broken, homely woman."

"Turns out, she is a broken, smoking-hot bombshell with a wicked sense of humor." I shrug and lean back in my chair.

"You are out of your mind. Don't be that dick who takes her out because…well, because you are freaking weirdo," she whisper-yells, very aware of her surroundings—just like I taught her to be. I try to cover my prideful smile, but she snaps at me, "Don't you dare grin at me. What the hell is wrong with you? You can't be with her."

"Slow down. I'm not trying to marry her or anything," I quickly reply.

"Don't say that! That's worse!" she screeches at a decibel that is barely even audible.

"Um…okay?"

"Those are the ones you end up falling in love with. It's karma's way of punking you," she snaps, annoyed with my inability to follow her invisible flow chart. "Jesus, look at me and Slate. I didn't want to be with him either, but now, I'm married and five months pregnant." She rubs her stomach with the smallest tilt of her lips.

I know she's trying to give me a stern lecture on why I shouldn't pursue Sarah, but that brief moment where she reminds herself of her own happiness is overwhelming to me.

"Shit, you're grinning again," she mumbles, recognizing that this is a lost cause.

"I'm going to be grinning for a while. You may want to start getting used to it." I glance down at her rounded stomach and swallow hard to fight the emotion.

"Slate won't let me name him Leo," she whispers.

"Oh, thank Christ for that," I respond on a laugh, but the sentiment cuts me to the quick.

"I would though," she states firmly.

I have to wave her off before this conversation gets too heavy. She can't name that baby Leo—he deserves more than that.

"So. Sarah Erickson? One to ten on the creepy scale?" I change the subject back.

"Twenty-nine," she answers frankly without missing a single beat.

"I guess that's better than thirty."

"It was a one-to-ten scale, jerk. Twenty-nine is terrible," she bites out, but the concern on her face is endearing.

"I went out with her last weekend and gave her food poisoning."

"Food poisoning, huh? The second best gift you can give a date… besides an STD."

"Your jokes are getting worse. Slate isn't helping your sense of humor." I take the last sip of my coffee.

"Leo, I love you." She becomes serious and reaches out to grab my hand. But as usual, her touch makes me retreat. "We have enough shit in our lives without adding broken souls into the mix. You need Suzy Normal who can remind you what something real feels like."

I'm sure she is probably right, but there is a woman I can't stop thinking about who I bet would disagree. Erica knows me better than anyone, and while I'm sure she is just trying to protect my best interests, she has no idea what she is talking about.

"She's not like us. She's honest—bluntly so. It's *inspiring* to watch her rise above all the bullshit," I grit out.

"Holy. Shit. You really like this girl," she announces, obviously surprised.

"I don't know. I guess. It's just… She's different."

"That's lame and cliché, Leo" She calls me on my attempt not to elaborate, making me laugh.

I shrug. "It's also the truth."

"I really don't think this is a smart idea. Is she aware that you know about her past?"

"Not yet," I answer uncomfortably. That is the part I'm most worried about. If someone knew all my shit right off the bat, you can bet that I'd tuck tail and run. I have a sneaking suspicion Sarah might be the same way.

"Well, if you are adamant about seeing this woman, you might want to tell her sooner than later."

"Yeah, I know. Seriously though, Erica. How crazy of an idea is this? I like her despite her past, and in some sick way, I'm hoping that, if I can overlook the things she did, maybe she will be able to do the same with me."

"Leo, that is not a healthy attitude to start a relationship on. I know you respect her for the things she said that day at Foundations, but I don't like this pedestal you have her on."

"I agree with you...to a point. I'm not going out with Sarah because of some misplaced feelings. I ran into her randomly on the street. I didn't even know who she was when I first approached her. But yes, when I did recognize her it, piqued my interest. However, I asked her out for the same reasons I would ask any woman out."

"Because she's hot," Erica laughs.

"No, smartass. Well, yes, but I meant that she's funny and interesting too."

"Okay, fine. I won't say anything else about it, but please be careful. I don't want you to get in over your head until you really get to know her. Just because you know her past doesn't mean you know anything about who she is today."

"Yeah, okay." I let it go. She's right even though I hate to admit it. "Let's get out of here. I'm supposed to pick her up in a few hours and I have to get some work done first. When are you heading back to Indy?"

"As soon as Slate finishes up at the gym. I'm going shopping for a little bit until he's done."

"Take Johnson with you, okay?"

"Yeah, yeah, yeah." She rolls her eyes but nods. "All right. I expect to meet this Sarah chick soon."

"Now look who's rushing into something." I laugh and guide her out of the coffee shop.

Chapter
NINE

Sarah

"UM, WHAT do you mean he said he is going to kiss you in his bed tonight? That's a little cocky, don't you think?" my best friend, Casey, asks while flopping down on my bed, watching me apply my makeup in front of my full-length mirror.

"Nah. You'd have to meet him to really understand. It's absolutely presumptuous, but when he says it, it's not obnoxious."

"I'll have to take your word for it, because he sounds like a douche."

"Stop!" I turn to face her. "Don't say that. I kind of like him. He's easy."

"Yeah, well. It sounds like he thinks you're easy too," she laughs, but I give her an evil eye that makes her hush.

"Oh, shut up. I'm not kidding, Case. It's odd how comfortable I feel around him." I turn back to the mirror to finish up with my mascara.

"You think it's because he's the first man you've allowed to get to know 'new' Sarah." She throws a pair of air quotes in my direction.

"I don't know. Maybe." I let out a resigned sigh. I have no idea why Leo has me letting my guards down—I just know that it feels good. "He doesn't know anything about my past, so it's easy to pretend that I don't have one when I'm with him. There's no pressure. I can be whoever the hell I want instead of who he expects me to be." I catch her sad eyes through the mirror. "Don't give me that look." When I spin around to face her, she immediately looks away.

"I wish you didn't have to feel like that," she says apologetically.

I know where she's headed with this, but it's not a stroll down memory lane I want to take tonight.

"So, is there something wrong with the way I am now?" I ask with a teasing smile.

"No!" She jumps up defensively. She knows this is a trigger for me, but tonight, I'm using it to my advantage just to mess with her. However, I'm apparently transparent because she calls my bluff. "It's just that you don't drink wine or read dirty books anymore. That was, after all, the foundation of our relationship." She grins.

"Yeah, but now, we eat massive chocolaty desserts and watch trashy TV. I think that might trump wine night." I stand up to grab my perfume off the dresser.

"You're right. This arrangement might be better, although my jeans probably disagree."

We both burst out laughing, only to sober when I see the clock.

"Shit! He should be here soon," I announce, nervously smoothing down the long black-and-white maxi dress I picked for tonight. It has spaghetti straps and shows off a fair amount of cleavage. Emma would be proud. I'm not sure where we are going, but I know I want to look presentable…at least on the outside.

"What are you going to do about Mr. Cocky tonight? You getting in *his bed*?" She perks a questioning eyebrow.

"I have no idea," I sigh.

"It's been a while since you were with someone, huh?" she asks jokingly, but for a split second, a flashback hits me so hard that it steals not only my breath, but also my every thought.

Seven Years Earlier…

"GET OUT!" I scream.

"Jesus, calm down!" Brett pleads, dodging the plate I just hurled across the room.

"Why the fuck would you do this?" I yell. The pain in my chest amplifies the anger in my tone.

"Because it's our anniversary. Because I love you. Because I fucking miss you. Take your pick." He swings his arms out to his sides in frustration.

"So, what now? What are you hoping to accomplish with this?" I wave my hand over the beautifully decorated table.

Everything, from the china to the prime rib, is the exact replica of our table the night we got married. He even had a small cake decorated to match the top tier of our wedding cake. I should be laughing and crying at the sentimental gesture. But as I stare at it now, the emptiness I feel in the memory enrages me. I remember picking out the original cake like it was yesterday.

Brett loved peanut butter cake more than anything else, but the brown icing was ugly as all hell. So I had the bakery make a special peanut butter cake just for him but cover it in white icing so it would match my vision for the day. You should have seen my mother's disgust when I told her the flavors I chose. However, that cake was us. I was always the free spirit, while Brett was focused and career-driven. Yet, just like that cake, we fit together despite everyone else's expectations. It just worked.

"I was hoping it would remind you of happier times," he bites out when his overflowing emotions flip to anger from my rejection.

"Jesus Christ, I remember. I just don't care!" I say the words honestly, but I didn't mean for them to be the verbal knife that twists in his gut.

He swallows hard, and it's more than I can take to witness his reaction. He will never understand how much I want to be the person he remembers—the person I remember. Instead, I feel so distant and removed. I'm completely alone, even though there is a beautiful man standing in front of me, begging me to love him.

"So, you remember sobbing your entire way through your vows?" he asks as tears prick his eyes.

I can't do this with him again. I can't watch him melt down—again. I'm not his wife anymore.

"I want a divorce," I say as my own tears begin to fall.

"So, you remember dragging me into the employee lounge at the reception just because you couldn't wait a minute longer to make love to your husband?" he asks roughly, planting his hands on his hips.

"Please don't do this. I don't remember these things the same way you do. Just stop," I beg. My memories don't pain me, but hearing his memories destroys me. I want to be Sarah Sharp again. However, just figuring out the Sarah part is hard enough.

He continues as if his words can force me to feel something. "So, you remember holding me so tight during our first dance that you joked that we were going to meld together?"

Suddenly, my frustration with the whole fucking situation overtakes me. "What do you want from me? Lies? I fucking hate that you do this to me. You can't make me feel it, so I'd rather just forget every single minute of the past with you. Every tear. Every kiss. Every fuck! I want to erase it all. Maybe then you will leave me the hell alone. I am not that woman anymore. No matter how hard you fucking try, no amount of cake or fancy dinners in the world will make me magically come back to you."

My chest is heaving, but if Brett heard me at all, he doesn't show it. He ignores me and takes three giant steps forward, cornering me against the wall. Then he reaches out, grabbing either side of my face and leveling me with his green stare.

"Come back to me," he demands desperately. "Goddamn it, come back to me. I can't do this without you. We can start over—make a new life. Whatever you want. Just… Goddamn it. Please," His frantic tone shreds me.

When his mouth slams over mine, I don't even have the energy to push him away. I stand motionless as he attempts to lure me into a kiss.

"Please, Sarah. Just come back," he whispers against my mouth as he peppers kisses over my lips.

And because I deserve it, I keep my eyes open and watch every heartbreaking emotion as he pleads. Brett Sharp is just one more person I have destroyed.

Finally, he stills and his eyes open. A single tear slides down his cheek, matching the steady stream falling from my own. He begins *shaking his head and drops his hands from my face. Then he roughly shoves them through his hair before letting out a humorless laugh and covering his mouth with a hand.*

"Fuck!" he explodes, spinning around and flipping over the entire dining room table.

The dishes shatter against the floor, and that fucking cake smashes into a million pieces.

Completely ruined—just like us.

"I shouldn't have asked that," Casey says awkwardly, walking into the kitchen, as I stand frozen, desperately trying to escape the memories.

When I turn to tell her it's okay, a knock on the door stops the unspoken words. As nerves flutter in my stomach, I try to calm myself. I run a hand through my hair as I head for the door and pull it open. However, the minute I lay eyes on the gorgeous man holding a red Gatorade with a messy bow and small bouquet of mixed flowers, I immediately relax.

"Hey, babe," Leo says with a warm grin as he steps forward to kiss my cheek.

"Hey," I laugh, taking the Gatorade and flowers from his hands. "You know this does not make me feel positive about going out with you again."

"Well, I figured, with my luck recently, I should at least make sure you're prepared this time." He leans away to catch my eyes, a devilish gleam in his own. "You're beautiful." He gives me a very obvious head-to-toe assessment and pauses on my breasts for a second too long.

"Should I spin in a circle to make it easier for you to check me out?"

"It wouldn't hurt." He smirks but pulls me tight against his body. For a brief minute, I return his embrace, enjoying the simple comfort that is Leo's hugs.

"Eh, hm." I hear Casey clear her throat from the kitchen. Her eyes are glued to mine and her wide grin is unmistakably peaceful.

"Shit. I'm sorry. Casey, this is Leo James. Leo, this is my best friend, Casey Black," I say motioning, between them.

"Hi." Leo extends a hand in her direction, but Casey just glances at it and crosses her arms.

"What are your intentions with Sarah this evening?" she questions with a stern tone that causes Leo's forehead to crinkle in confusion.

"Jesus. Stop screwing with him," I tell her, curling into Leo's side. "He already had the pleasure of meeting Caleb and Emma. He's been interrogated enough."

"Oh God. I bet that was a real treat," Casey mumbles as her face pales. She quickly recovers. "Okay. You guys have fun. Sarah, can I talk to you for a minute?"

"Yeah, of course." I smile up at Leo and walk Casey to the door.

Just as I pull it open, she leans into my ear and says, "I really fucking hope you cleaned the cobwebs out of your panties, because I don't care if he does think you're easy. I want you to run into that man's bed, strip naked, and let him kiss you wherever the hell he wants. You did *not* tell me he was that good-looking."

"Yes, I did!" I whisper-yell back to her while glancing over my shoulder to make sure Leo can't hear us. But, much to my dismay, he's very obviously listening. His confident shit-eating grin is impossibly wide. "Oh fantastic." I push Casey out the door without even so much as a goodbye.

"I like her," Leo says when I turn back around.

"I figured," I laugh and roll my eyes.

"I'm serious. She gives excellent advice."

"I'll be sure to let her know you think so. Let's go." I grab my purse off the table next to the door, but I'm stopped as Leo wraps his arms around my waist from behind and nuzzles into my hair.

"What do you say we skip dinner and you can *run* to my bed? It might not be the most conventional first kiss, but I can definitely think of a few places I'd like to taste. Your mouth only being one of them."

His breath across my sensitive neck combined with his words send chills over my body. I try to lock it down, but as he drags his nose up to my ear, a gasp escapes.

"Mmm, I like the moan better, but the gasp works too," he purrs.

We stand there silently for a minute as Leo holds me tight against his large body. His lean muscles are pressed against my back, and his quickened breath in my ear tells me that he is just as turned on as I am. Though, just to be sure, I reach up and drag the tips of my nails over his neck and into this hair. He lets out a mouth-watering moan that makes me smile.

"We should go," I whisper, unable to trust my voice.

"*Or* we could stay. You have a bed. I could amend my statement to *your* bed instead of *mine*." He brushes my hair off my shoulder and leans down, placing a very wet and promising kiss on the exposed skin.

As very appealing as his idea sounds, I need to clear my head from the fog. Perhaps make a decision about where I want to end the night without Leo's lips muddling with my resolve.

"We should go," I repeat, causing him to growl.

I spin in his arms and look up into his eyes. He has the thickest eyelashes I have ever seen on a man, and they only serve to make his otherwise common brown eyes stunning and unique. But it's the intensity in his gaze that really has me reconsidering his suggestion.

Very slowly, Leo leans down, stopping only a breath away from my mouth. My pulse begins to race as his hands drift from my hips to the small of my back.

"Sarah, go pack a bag. You're staying at my place tonight."

"I am?" I squeak out, completely lost in the moment.

"You are," he confirms then presses his lips against mine for what can only be described as the best-slash-worst first kiss in history. His lips are soft and warm but gone before I can even appreciate them. I want more.

So. Much. More.

"Go," he orders with a smirk as he steps away.

Fuck it. Who needs resolve anyway? Clearly not me, because I find my legs carrying me back to my room to pack a bag.

Chapter
TEN

Leo

"WE DESTROYED them!" Sarah laughs as we leave the sports bar she chose for dinner.

I thought it was an odd choice at first—until she informed me that it was trivia night. I can honestly say that I had an absolutely phenomenal time tonight. Sarah was hilarious and so fucking competitive. Her face would light up as soon as the questions popped on screen. I swear, at one point, she was pressing the button so hard that I thought she was going to break it. The best moment, though, was when she started cussing after someone buzzed in before she did. I haven't heard words like that used since the high school locker room. She immediately looked embarrassed when she saw that I was watching her. But her cheeks really turned red when I informed her how much a love a woman with a dirty mouth. My tone might have made it a sexual innuendo, but she didn't seem to care either way.

She's right. We did destroy them. I've always been a bit of a history buff, so that paired with her brains about pop culture and science made us an unstoppable team.

"I have no idea how the hell you knew some of those answers. I think you might be overqualified for your receptionist position," I tease as we walk arm in arm to my car.

"Yes, but my vast knowledge of Mariah Carey and the latest in celebrity sex tape scandals isn't exactly in high demand these days," she says, stopping me just before we reach my car. "Thanks for tonight." She loops her arms around my waist. "I haven't smiled that much in a *really* long time."

"Funny, I was just thinking the same thing." I tuck a stray hair behind her ear as her smile nervously fades.

When she rakes her teeth over her bottom lip, my attention hones in on her mouth. Slowly, she rises to her tiptoes. While nothing about Sarah was exactly shy tonight, she always seems a bit nervous when it comes to affection. I'm not sure if she's overthinking it or what, but as much as I want to rush her home and into my bed, I'm willing to let her have this move. I stand completely still as she presses her soft and timid lips to mine. The gentle touch ignites me.

God damn, I want this woman, but I'm not doing this in the middle of a parking lot. I quickly shove a hand into her hair, holding her firmly against my closed mouth. I don't allow her to take the kiss any deeper, but that doesn't mean I don't kiss her with everything I have, breathing her in as if I will never feel her again.

When I'm able to drag myself away from her, I rush out like a caveman, "Home. Bed. Now."

"Okay. Yeah," she says shakily while smoothing down her hair.

I walk around the car and open her door, careful not to touch her again. I just need to get her home—and hopefully naked.

IT SEEMS that the kiss in the parking lot was exactly what Sarah needed to loosen up. It wasn't a long ride back to my apartment, but, surprisingly, she held my hand the whole way. In moments when she would use her overly animated hand gestures while talking, she never truly released me. Instead, she very purposefully placed my hand on her thigh. I've never been so turned on by such a simple gesture—or grateful that the darkness cloaked the hard-on I was sporting most of the way.

"You want something to drink?" I ask as soon as we walk in.

"Nah, I'm good," she replies, eyeing me as I walk to the fridge and retrieve a beer for myself. "You've never asked me why I don't drink. Why is that?" she asks curiously.

"I figure you'll tell me when you want to," I say quickly.

But I know exactly why she doesn't drink. There's a lot I know about Sarah. However, those aren't the parts I want to talk about tonight.

"What if I were a recovering alcoholic?" She walks over to the kitchen to stand directly in front of me. "You've never asked about drinking in front of me either."

I can tell by the twitch of her lips that she is just giving me a hard time, but the gleam in her eye exposes her insecurities. Insecurities I plan to put to rest.

"You agreed to meet me at a bar on our first date," I say simply while tipping the beer to my lips. "I'm assuming that, if you were a recovering alcoholic, you wouldn't have chosen a sports bar tonight either."

"Oh, yeah. Probably not." She gives me a weak smile.

I place the beer down on the counter and grab her hips, sliding my hands down to splay across her ass for the very first time. Her eyes go wide, but she doesn't back away. Instead, she casually rests her hands on my chest.

"Just so you know. If you were a recovering alcoholic, it wouldn't bother me in the least." Leaning forward, I place a soft kiss to her lips. Then I slide my hands up her sides and guide each of her arms around my neck. "Because the fact that you no longer drink would mean that you have overcome it. It would mean that you struggled, just like we all do, and that you didn't succumb. You would've had to fight to get where you are today, and that kind of strength should not *ever* be interpreted as a weakness. That kind of strength is a rare thing of beauty."

"Jesus," she whispers as tears sparkle in her eyes.

I watch for a moment as something passes over her. Her shoulders relax and she lets out a sound that can only be described as a whimper of relief. I rub her back as she takes a second to collect herself. Finally, she laughs, dropping her forehead to my chest.

"How the hell did you just make alcoholism sexy?"

"It's a gift." I smile, using a finger under her chin to lift her eyes back to mine. "Now, Sarah, are you a recovering alcoholic?" I ask even though I know the answer.

"No," she breathes.

"Do you mind if I drink in front of you?"

"No." She leans forward, brushing her lips across mine. "But I do mind that you haven't properly kissed me yet." As she drags her hands down my chest, reaching them around to grab my ass, I can't help but smile at her boldness.

"Mmm, we should really take care of that." I cup her face between my hands. My thumbs stroke her flawless skin as her cheeks begin to flush.

"I agree." She sways even closer, pressing her chest against mine.

Very slowly, I move toward her mouth, pausing at the last second to say, "In my bed." I release her and step back against the counter. I casually pick up my beer and take another sip.

"That was mean," she says with a smile.

"I know, but I'm just not sorry." I smirk, using my beer bottle to point toward the hallway. "Lead the way. You remember where my bed is, right?"

"You have lost your damn mind if you think I'm sprinting down the hall and jumping into your bed like some desperate woman just because you told me to." She cocks her head with false attitude. "Don't get me wrong, Leo. You're a good-looking guy and all, but that's not my style." She crosses her arms over her chest, forcing her already large breasts together to the point where they almost pop out of her dress.

"Ah, now you're playing dirty," I groan, staring at her cleavage and praying to God that the thin straps suddenly break. When I drag my gaze back to hers, I find her eyes dancing with laughter. "I see what you're doing here." I release the buttons at my wrists. Then, with one swift movement, I tug my shirt and undershirt over my head.

She bites her lip as I flex my abs just for good measure, and I can tell the minute she sees the tattoo on my side. It's the same look of heat every woman gets until they realize what it says:

Liv

Love

Lie

I'm not sure if it's the name Liv or the word 'lie' that makes women pause, but if history is any indicator, she'll ask about the part that bothers her in three, two, one…

"Nice tattoo."

"Thanks."

She swallows hard, and I once again tip the beer bottle to my lips, preparing my lies for the questions that are sure to follow. But they never come. Instead, she slides the straps of her dress down her arms. My mouth goes dry as she pauses to make sure I am watching. The twinkle of mischief in her eyes is unmistakable.

"See, now I feel like you're challenging me. I've never been able to turn down a challenge." She shrugs then pushes the thin cotton dress down her chest. It falls down over her curved hips and pools on the floor at her feet.

My mouth would have gaped open at her confidence, but that would have required at the very least an involuntary reaction. Currently, every single brain cell I possess is ensnared by the unbelievably sexy woman standing in front of me wearing only a strapless black bra, lace panties, and black heels.

Holy. Fuck.

I suck in a deep breath, loving every second of where this is headed.

"Me either." I toe off my shoes and lean down to remove my socks, never tearing my eyes away from her knowing smile—except maybe to look at her breasts. I stand up and grab my belt, not moving any further. "Your turn."

She lets out a small laugh and slips off her heels. I obviously didn't think that move through very well, because the idea of her long legs and heels wrapped around my waist makes my already hard cock throb.

"You know what? On second thought, you can put those back on."

She giggles and shakes her head. Placing her hands her on her hips, she very pointedly looks down at my pants.

Not one to disappoint, I quickly drag my jeans down my legs and dramatically toss them over my shoulder, making her laugh again. She immediately stops when her eyes make it down to my cock, which is all but tenting my boxer briefs. I tease my thumbs in the elastic waistband and give her a questioning quirk of the eyebrow.

"Jesus, Leo," she breathes and *finally* looks away.

"I vote we call a truce and both go to the bed together," I announce, taking a step toward her.

She nods. "On three?"

"Okay. One, two…" With absolutely zero intentions of ever making it to three, I charge forward, crushing my body into hers and covering her mouth with my own.

I wanted to catch her off guard. Sarah might have just been playing a game with this, but I'd like for her to see how much I *want her.* However, as she frantically shoves a hand into my hair and rolls her tongue in my mouth with a hungry moan, I'm overwhelmed by how much Sarah wants *me.*

Her tongue slides around mine as the tingle of her peppermint gum invades my mouth. I trail my hands over her back and down to her ass. It's only when I meet the smooth, uncovered skin that I realize those sexy lace panties are actually a thong. Suddenly, visions of Sarah's barely covered ass prowling up my bed invade my mind and force a growl from my throat.

It's definitely time to move this to a horizontal platform.

I spin us around and back down the hall, careful to never to break the kiss that has gone wild. Her feet barely move as I begin to drag her toward my room. But *barely* is just not fast enough for me right now. When I lift her up, she thankfully gets the message, wrapping her legs around my hips. Unfortunately, what I didn't prepare for was the moment when her covered core slides against my painfully hard cock. Two scraps of cotton are all that separate us.

"Fuck," I hiss, almost tripping over my own feet.

Sarah lets out her own breathy expletive. It may very well be the only thing that keeps my legs under me and moving toward the bedroom.

Chapter
ELEVEN

Sarah

THERE IS nothing gentle or sensual about the way I'm kissing Leo. It's ravenous. This may make me easy like Casey said, but I don't give a damn what Leo thinks right now. *I want him.* It's an added bonus that he seems to want me just as badly. But honestly, with the way I *feel* right now, I wouldn't even care if he was only mildly interested.

I don't have amnesia. I remember sex. I know it's amazing. I know I used to love it. But what I don't remember is this feeling of passion and urgency. I forgot this physical rush that builds with every stroke of Leo's tongue. I also didn't remember the spark I felt the second I came into contact with his hard-on. It ignited an uncontrollable flame inside me—one that threatens to consume me if I don't get closer to him. But I just can't get close enough to damper it. I absolutely remember sex, but I forgot all of the feelings that made it so spectacular—instead of just a mindless, self-induced orgasm.

Until now.

Leo blindly carries me down the hall. His eyes are closed as he kisses me. He uses one hand to support me, and the other is against the wall to guide his steps—and to occasionally prevent himself from falling. When we get to his room, he crashes us both onto the bed. His body crushes mine and our teeth painfully knock together.

"Shit. I'm sorry," Leo says, leaning away.

"I'm okay." I shove my hands down the back of his boxer briefs, and squeeze his firm ass.

He pushes up on an elbow, resting it next to my head. It lands directly on top of my long hair, which has fanned across the bed.

"Ow, ow, ow. You're on my hair."

He quickly moves his arm away. "Shit. I'm sorry...again."

"I'm okay," I repeat, crawling backwards up the bed, pulling on his shoulders so he'll follow me.

I'm desperate for this to continue. So desperate that I don't pay attention to anything besides trying to regain the full contact we just lost. I'm so focused that I don't realize where my leg is located in relation to Leo's body. I lift my knee to maintain the forward momentum up the bed...

"Fuck," he groans, rolling over on the bed with his hands cupped between his legs.

Oh. My. God. I just kneed him in the balls.

Kill me now.

"Oh my God! Shit. Damn. Fuck. I'm so sorry!" I gasp as my face flushes with embarrassment. "Are you okay?"

Leo doesn't say anything. He just lifts a finger into the air, asking for a minute with his eyes wrenched shut.

Another thing I didn't remember was how much it sucks when that sexual rush is extinguished prematurely. I sit cross-legged on the other side of the bed and patiently wait for him to speak, feeling like a bumbling idiot. I'm out of practice in the bedroom, but for fuck's sake, this is just ridiculous.

"Phew. All right," he says, still recovering. "Come here." He reaches out and grabs my arm, pulling me down onto the bed next to him.

"God, I'm so sorry."

"I'll be fine. You got me good though."

"If I didn't puke the first time we went out, I would consider this the most embarrassing moment of my dating life," I whine, rolling into his side.

"I once spit on a woman's foot on a date." He begins teasing his fingertips up and down my arm.

I tilt my head back to see him better. "What?"

"Yeah. I was walking her to her door and a bug flew into my mouth. I paused to spit it out, but she kept walking forward. My spit landed directly on her sandal-clad foot. Bug and all." He smiles and shrugs.

"No way." I begin to laugh.

"True story. Needless to say, we never went out again."

"She wouldn't go out with you again because you accidently spit on her foot?" I ask incredulously.

"Oh, no. I was just too embarrassed to call her back. *I spit a bug on her.*" He starts laughing, and just like that, whatever awkwardness was still lingering completely melts away.

Easy.

"How do your balls feel?" I ask with a genuine concern.

"Not the way they are supposed to be feeling right now. That really started off well in the kitchen."

I let out a disappointed sigh. "It really did."

"You think, if I try to take this back in that direction, you could keep that ninja knee under control?"

I burst out laughing, but Leo rolls me to my back.

"Is that a yes?" He kisses my lips.

"I can try. Maybe you should start wearing a cup?" I tease then run my fingers through his short, black hair.

"I'll take that into consideration," he responds with a sexy-as-hell grin before leaning in and sealing his mouth over mine.

It doesn't take more than just a few strokes of his warm tongue to transport me right back into a sexual high. His hands travel over my breasts, but it's not nearly enough. I sit up carefully—we don't need any more injuries—and unhook my strapless bra. I toss it off the bed, and before it even hits the floor, Leo sucks my nipple into his mouth.

"Fuck," I breathe, arching off the bed.

I definitely did not remember *this* feeling. Leo is all over me. It's unbelievable. He moves his mouth to my other breast but continues his assault on my nipple, rolling it between his fingers.

After kissing down my stomach, he stops just before my panties. His big, brown eyes flash to mine, and I lift my hips off the bed, giving him silent permission to continue. His fingers loop around the lace and drag it down my legs.

"God, you're beautiful."

I squirm under his gaze, causing him to smirk.

He doesn't touch me like I expected—or hoped. Instead, he prowls back up and takes my mouth in a hard kiss. We become all hands and mouths. He's still wearing his boxers, and it's completely unfair. I begin trying to tear them down.

"Something wrong, ángel?" he asks, amused.

"You're wearing clothes. It's your turn."

He laughs but pushes them down his legs, kicking them off the foot of the bed.

Unlike Leo, I take plenty of time to catch an eyeful of his naked body. He's long, lean, and hard everywhere. Emphasis on the long. While I blatantly stare at his package, he takes the moment and slides a hand between my legs.

"I fucking love that look on your face right now. *That* is how you are supposed to look at a man's cock." He pushes a finger inside me.

"Ahhh," I moan at the surprise.

"Holy fuck, you're tight." He presses his thumb to my clit, and I swear I could probably come right now.

"Yeah, it's been a while," I say breathily.

"A decade?" he teases.

"Not quite. Seven years," I answer as I try to roll my hips against his hand, which has suddenly stopped moving.

"Seriously?" he asks in disbelief.

Yes, it's been seven years since I've been with another man. The vibrator in my nightstand is not a suitable substitution, but it's been good to me for the last few years while I got things straightened out in my head. However, judging by his reaction, he was not expecting that answer.

"Seriously," I confirm.

He stares at me for a few seconds and swallows hard.

"Leo?" I call to catch his attention, which has suddenly drifted— even while his finger remains inside me.

Finally, he shakes his head and gives me a smile that doesn't look even half as genuine as what I have come to expect from him. "Well, then, you are long overdue," he says as he settles on his side next to me and begins moving his finger inside me. His lips glide over my neck and a strangled sound escapes me. "You like my mouth on your neck, don't you? You're always so quick to reward me with one of those moans you know I love so much."

Just out of the goodness of my heart, I reward him with another. It has absolutely nothing to do with the fact that he pushed another finger inside me or his thumb continuously rubbing circles over my clit. Okay, maybe it had a lot to do with that.

"I'd love your mouth just about anywhere, but especially on my neck," I whisper as he rakes his teeth across the already sensitive flesh.

His hand picks up pace, silencing any further conversation. Not even a minute later, an orgasm roars through my body. I cling to Leo's shoulder as I cry out his name.

He places slow kisses over my face as I try to collect my thoughts.

"Seven years," he says against my lips. Obviously, I'm the only one who moved on from our earlier chat.

"Is that a problem?" I ask, feeling very uncomfortable about why he's still stuck on this.

"No, it's great. You're a virgin." He smiles.

"I am not a *virgin*. I was married for seven years!" I exclaim, immediately regretting it when I realize that this is the first time I've ever mentioned Brett to Leo.

But he doesn't even bat an eye. "Sarah, I'm a thirty-three-year-old man. A woman who hasn't had sex in seven years is as close to a virgin as I'm ever going to get."

"Oh Jesus, Leo. You have no idea what you're talking about. I could probably teach you a few things in bed," I huff, and it makes him laugh.

"Maybe. But not tonight." He reaches down and drags the blanket over us.

"What?" I ask, shocked.

Did he just shut me down?

"Don't give me that look. My plan never was to have sex with you tonight. And especially now that I know you're a virgin."

"Stop saying I'm a virgin. And you sure as hell could have fooled me!" I snap, catching a sudden attitude.

This sure stings like a rejection.

"Shhhhh." He wraps me in his arms, pulling me to rest on his chest. "I don't have a condom. I really didn't think things would go this far tonight. Tomorrow, I'll hit the drugstore and we can spend the day in bed. But tonight, I want you to get some sleep."

Well, I guess that's a little better.

"There's other stuff we could do that doesn't require a condom." I place a soft kiss to his mouth.

"There is. But right now, I have the sounds of you coming ringing in my ears. That's more than enough."

"I want to hear the sounds of you coming." I lean forward and lick his lips.

"Go to sleep, ángel. Tomorrow."

Nope. Definitely shut down.

"Why do I feel like I'm missing something here?"

"Because you are. It's called my cock, and tomorrow, I'm going to make you memorize every inch of it so you never have to feel like this again. Sarah, you have no idea how much I want to be inside you right now. Unfortunately, it's not happening tonight."

"Jesus," I breathe at his words.

He kisses me tenderly then says, "Please just go to sleep. And take my word that this is for the best." He drags his nose up to my ear, sucking in a deep breath as he goes. "I could always make you come again if you think that would help you sleep."

Hmm. Well, that's an interesting turn of events. It appears he's not shutting me down completely.

"No, I'm good. I can't let you be two orgasms up on me. I already owe you one."

He squeezes me tightly and chuckles in my ear, sending goose bumps over my skin. "Fair enough." He rolls to his back, dragging me with him. "Goodnight, ángel."

"Night, Leo."

And just like that, Leo James even makes rejection comfortable. He really does have a gift.

Chapter
TWELVE

Leo

THE BUZZ of my phone vibrating on the table has me springing from a sound sleep. I was always a sound sleeper, but over time and out of necessity, I've taught myself to wake from that subtle buzzing.

"Hello," I bark into the phone as my heart pounds in my chest.

"Leo," I hear Erica whisper, and suddenly, I've never been more awake in my life.

"What's wrong, babe?" I ask as I stride from the room. I snag a pair of sweats and a T-shirt and quickly glance back to find Sarah curled into a ball so far onto my side of the bed that I have no idea how I didn't fall off. I quietly pull the door closed behind me but stop just before it clicks.

"There's someone at the gates," she says in a shaky voice.

"Okay. Hey, it's all right," I soothe very calmly even though my chest tightens and panic ricochets through me.

"I don't think it's paparazzi. It's a larger male, and he just tried to climb the gate!" she cries into the phone.

"Where's Slate?" I ask, quickly sliding into the chair in my surveillance room and remotely pulling up the security cameras for her house.

"He's at the gym, hosting a lock-in for the kids."

I know she is trying to hold it together, but for fuck's sake, she's been through enough. No one should be forced to live with this kind of fear. Not even to mention that she's pregnant. This kind of stress can't be good for the baby.

"Okay, I have eyes on this asshole," I answer as the wall full of screens lights up, allowing me to see almost every inch of her house—inside and out. Then I press a single key on the computer and it flips on all the spotlights on her driveway. "Jesus Christ," I breathe out.

"Leo!" she screams, frightened and misreading my reaction. It's a sound that still, to this day, guts me.

"You're fine. It's okay, babe," I quickly clarify. "Your gate's not working. It's just Johnson trying to get in." I flip on her gate intercom with the click of my mouse. "You are scaring her half to death," I tell Johnson, who is once again trying to scale her towering gate.

"Well, it's about fucking time. I've been trying to buzz in for the last five fucking minutes. I got worried!" he shouts back.

"Yeah. I have no idea what's wrong. Your code not working?" I ask.

"Nope. I'm not even getting a connection on the speaker," Johnson answers, notably agitated.

"You know the drill," I say, watching him carefully over the monitor.

Johnson is my most trusted man *and* my best friend, but I still watch for any sign that he has been compromised. I don't give two fucks who he is when it comes to Erica's safety.

"Alpha-Tango-Juliette-one-nine-eight-one," he confirms.

I press the button to open the gate, but it doesn't budge.

"Erica." I turn my attention back to the phone. "You're going to have to go let him in. I can't open it. I'll have someone come out in a few hours to fix it."

"It's three a.m., Leo. You can't find a repair man this time of night," she answers and I can hear her feet against the wooden steps on her porch as she hurries toward the gate.

"You okay, Mrs. Andrews?" Johnson's voice echoes through the room both from the phone and the intercom I still haven't turned off.

"I'm fine, Aiden," she replies.

I lean in close to watch the smile spread across her face. However, Erica flips a middle finger at the camera, forcing me to bark out a laugh.

"Get out now, Leo."

"You sure you're okay?" I ask more for myself than for her.

"I'm sorry I scared you."

"It's okay, babe. I'm glad I could help." My attention is suddenly pulled to one of my own interior cameras. I watch as Sarah tiptoes out of the bedroom with only a sheet pulled around her naked body.

"I love you," Erica says just like she always does just before we hang up.

And I know the exact second her words make their way down the hall when I watch Sarah throw her hands up to cover her face.

"Erica, hang on for a second," I ask then call out the door, "Sarah, get in here!"

Her eyes go wide as she stumbles backwards, tripping over the sheet and trying to drag it back up to cover her body.

"Don't pull it up!" I yell with a smile. She begins looking around the hallway for the obvious camera. "Open door on the left."

I watch on the monitor as she takes a deep breath, seemingly weighing her options. Then she squares her shoulders and glances back at the bedroom only once before heading for the security room door.

"Leo?" Erica's voice rings through the room.

"Shh. Just a second," I hush her. Glancing back down, I see Erica rolling her eyes as she locks her front door with Johnson in tow.

Finally, Sarah's blue eyes peek into the room and I know immediately that she is flat-out *pissed.*

"Hey, ángel," I say with a huge smile, but her glare levels me.

Holy shit. Sarah's not just pissed—she's livid.

"Jesus Christ. What the hell, Leo?" she asks as she tries to contain her… Shit, is that disappointment? "What in the hell is wrong with you? I should have known you are too fucking smooth not to be up to some sort of bullshit. Fuck!" she screams.

"Uhhhh…" Erica says.

I try to stop her from freaking out but only come up with the most trite and incriminating sentence known to man. "It's not what you think, Sarah."

"Oh really? You didn't sneak out of bed with me at three a.m. to chat with another woman? All calling her babe and saying I love you." She says the last part in a ridiculous, deep voice that sounds nothing like mine. Suddenly, her attitude slips, her eyes sparkle with unshed tears, and her shoulders fall in defeat. "Of course this is happening to me. I'm not sure how I didn't see this coming. Clearly, karma has finally caught up to me. I actually meet someone and…damn it!"

I was wrong. She's not pissed—she's hurt.

I know immediately that this is not a time for a joke. "Erica." I call out loud, never taking my eyes off Sarah.

"Shit. Yeah, I'm here," she answers uncomfortably over the speaker.

"Remember when I told you about that girl I was seeing?" I don't pause to give her a single second to reply, fearful of what she might give away about the little secret I haven't yet let Sarah in on. "Well, she spent the night tonight, and judging by the daggers she is shooting at me now, I'm reasonably sure she has gotten the wrong idea about our relationship."

"Shit!" Erica shrieks, looking up into her ceiling-mounted kitchen camera. "I need to see you, Leo."

"Yep. I'm definitely out of here," Sarah says, turning for the door.

"Switching now. Whoa, wait just a second, ángel." I grab Sarah's arm to stop her retreat, all the while trying not to burst into flames under her relentless glare.

Erica forced me to install this two-way camera system as soon as I got back on my feet. She was worried about me back then. I can lie to her on the phone, but if she can see me, I don't even bother trying. She can read my mannerisms like a book. She knew the only way to get honest answers about how I was doing was to be able to video chat with me.

I spin to the large flat-screen in the back of the room above my corner desk. When I click the icon, Erica's living room flashes onto the screen. Not even a second later, she moves into the frame.

"Hi." Erica says, folding her obviously pregnant body onto her couch.

At the sight, Sarah once again throws her hands over her mouth in shock. "Oh, God," she breathes from behind her hands.

Laughing would definitely make me a dick, so I do my best to stifle it. I know she is thinking the absolute worst right now, and that bothers me on some level, but her expressions are priceless.

With her hands preoccupied, the sheet begins to slip from her body. I grasp the top to prevent it from falling to the ground. I should probably correct whatever nefarious ideas she has about me now, but the jealousy in Sarah's eyes has me wishing I could play it off for a few minutes longer. I'm relatively sure, though, that, in a few minutes, she won't still be standing here.

"Sarah, this is my friend, Erica Andrews. Erica, this is my girl-friend, Sarah Erickson." I slip an arm around Sarah's waist.

"Don't touch me," she hisses, quickly stepping away.

"Leo, stop being a dick. You know what she's assuming," Erica growls at me before speaking to Sarah. "Hey, Sarah. Trust me. My relationship with the jackass standing next to you is *not anything* like what you are thinking right now. We're just friends."

"Riiiight," Sarah drawls out sarcastically.

There are no adequate words for how much I am loving this flash of jealousy from her. However, I need to put an end to it, because against my better judgment, I have a strong desire to get between her legs again, and spending time talking to Erica is killing those thoughts.

"Okay. Okay. Seriously, Erica is like a sister to me. She is mar-ried to Slate Andrews...and pregnant with *his* baby, might I add. I had nothing to do with that." I grin as I hear Erica confirm it behind me.

"Wait. Slate Andrews the professional boxer?" Sarah asks, clear-ly confused.

"Well, Slate the ex-professional boxer. I run his security. And they had someone trying to climb their gate tonight." Watching for some sort of reaction, I can almost see her emotions rattling around in her head.

"Really? Well, does her husband know that you call her babe and y'all say 'I love you'?" she snaps at both of us.

"Yes, he does," I say very slowly. "Hey." Stepping forward, I grab her hips. "I swear to you it's not like that. I've called her babe for years. And I do love her, but not in any way that should possibly ever worry you. Erica is the only family I have." I shrug, not having any more of an explanation for her.

I really like Sarah, but this could be a very pivotal moment for us. I need to see her true colors in a stressful moment. I know about her past, but I need to know who she is *now*. This may have started out as entertaining, but now, I'm actually nervous about how this is going to play out. What if she can't handle my relationship with Erica? Where would that leave us?

Come on, Sarah. Prove to me who you really are.

I plead with the universe that she's the woman I think she is and not the person she talked about that day all those months ago. Jealous is one thing; irrational is something totally different.

"I know this looks bad. So I get that you're upset, but you have to believe me. It's not like that." Squeezing her hips tight, I beg for her to be the person I think she is.

Her eyes flash between mine, seemingly searching for the truth. She's warring with her emotions, and there is absolutely nothing I can do to sway the battle.

Finally, her hard expression softens as she asks, "Promise?" Her cheeks heat in embarrassment.

Letting out a relieved breath, I hook an arm around her waist. "I swear."

Her shoulders instantly relax as she drops her head to my chest. "I'm sorry," she whispers. "I must look like even more of a crazy woman getting all upset over a man I've been out with twice. I just assumed…" She shakes her head, rolling her forehead over my chest.

I look up to find Erica leaning toward the screen, closely watching our interaction. Her eyebrow is lifted as she watches our exchange, but the side of her mouth is tipped in a small grin.

Remembering her words from earlier, I say, "Get out, Erica."

"Right. Yeah. Sorry." She grabs the remote and aims it at her TV, but pauses. "I'm sorry to interrupt your night, Sarah. But I have to admit, it was worth it just to see the way he looks at you. I've never seen him do that before."

I cock my head to the screen and give her a what-the-hell-is-wrong-with-you look, but it only makes her laugh.

"Goodnight." She quickly flips off the screen, and I touch the button to fully sever the connection.

"What was that supposed to mean?" Sarah asks, lifting her head off my chest.

"It means Erica has a big fucking mouth." I smile and place a gentle kiss to her lips. "Hey."

"Hey," she responds, never truly meeting my eyes.

"You want to hang out with me for a few minutes while I close things down? I need to make a call and get Erica's gate fixed."

"If you want me to," she says shyly.

"I'm sorry if you got the wrong idea tonight, but you getting all jealous while wrapped in my sheet is probably the sexiest thing I've ever seen. And that's saying a lot, because earlier, I watched you come on my hand."

"I'm in a sheet," she blinks rapidly.

"Yes, but we could remedy that." I start to drag it off when she suddenly steps away.

Her face is shocked as she says, "I just met your only family in a sheet."

"It's just Erica. And don't be too embarrassed. I accidentally tried to cop a feel of your sister the first time I met her. I think that might be worse." I wink and she starts laughing.

Chapter
THIRTEEN

Sarah

"COME ON." Leo leads me to his overstuffed office chair.

When he sits down, he pats his leg for me to join him. I drag up my sheet, but he stops me.

"No more sheet. It's just me and you now."

"You're wearing clothes," I inform him, wondering when he got dressed.

"Really? We're still doing the tit-for-tat?" he asks then sighs before pulling his shirt over his head.

I once again catch a glimpse of the tattoo on his side. I'm dying to ask who Liv is, but tonight is definitely not the time. I've already shown way more than enough crazy for one night.

As I slowly let the sheet sag, exposing my breasts, Leo lets out an appreciative breath through parted lips. I can't help but remember how it felt only hours ago when those lips covered my nipples and his hand teased my clit. My stomach flutters, wanting nothing more than to feel him again. It must read on my face, because his eyes immediately heat.

"I have to make a phone call, but I want you straddling my lap while I do it."

Like I'm going to say no to that. "Okay."

Holding the sheet tight around my waist, I climb onto his lap, settling right on top of his surprisingly hard cock. It's good to know I'm not the only one turned on here.

Leo closes his eyes and sucks in a long breath, which I feel over my entire body. Just this small connection and I don't feel like a wreck anymore. I don't feel embarrassed by my earlier jealousy or even nervous that, one day, he's going to find out about my past. With Leo, I'm safe and sexy, but most of all, I'm just *me*. After too many years of not even knowing myself, I don't feel the struggle when I'm in his arms. I know *Leo*…and that might just be enough. At least for tonight.

For the next few minutes, Leo is on the phone. His hands constantly slide over my breasts. He calls Slate Andrews and informs him that the security gate at his house is broken and Erica was afraid. I can hear Slate cussing at Leo over the line, but it's obvious to even me that he respects Leo and is only worried about his wife. It's an undeniably romantic response, but the real romance comes when Leo makes his move. Just before the two men hang up, Leo roughly pulls my nipple to catch my attention. Then he presses a single button on his cell phone, putting Slate on speakerphone.

"Anyway, *I told her that I loved her*, and last I heard, she was heading to bed," Leo says, and I can't help but bite my lip in embarrassment. His gentle reassurance makes me want to…well straddle his lap, among other things. He rubs a hand up my back and into my hair, using it to tilt my head back to expose my neck. Quickly, he dives in, raking his teeth across my skin.

"Good. She needs to rest," Slate responds while Leo ravages my throat. I'm sure he is leaving marks, and even though my turtleneck collection is not large enough to support his efforts, I still turn my head to allow him more access.

"I'm going to call and get someone out to fix the gate in the next few hours," Leo announces before sealing his mouth over mine, plundering my mouth with a skill that forces a moan.

"Don't bother. I'll take care of it. I'm heading home now. Till just got here to take over. Thanks, man."

Leo pulls away only long enough to rush him off the phone. "No prob. Bye."

"Goodnight, Sarah!" Slate shouts before hanging up.

I give him a questioning look. "Uh…"

"Only further proof that Erica has a really fucking big mouth. Okay, one last call—" he starts, but I silence him.

"Thank you," I say against his lips.

He gives me a gentle nod. "I need you to be comfortable with her. She's like a—"

"A sister," I finish for him. "I've got it. I'm not usually a jealous person. It's just—"

"You thought I was cheating on you. I've got it," he finishes for me, punctuating it by rolling his tongue into my mouth, but he pulls away all too soon.

"We aren't even really together. You can't be cheating on me. I was worried you were cheating on her *with me*."

"Oh, we aren't together?" Leo asks with hint of annoyance in his voice.

I state the obvious. "We've known each other for, like, a week."

"So?" He reaches under the sheet draped around my waist, and with one very gentle stroke, he finds my clit. I was already turned on, but this has me desperate for more. "Ángel, you were mine from the first moment I laid eyes on you. Does this feel like 'not together' to you?" He begins rubbing those amazingly torturous small circles over my clit.

My head goes light as every nerve in my body begins firing—all aimed in one southern direction. "No," I whisper.

"It feels pretty *together,* doesn't it? It feels like we are getting to know each other in every way possible. See, part of the reason tonight didn't bother me is because I'm a jealous guy. And you know what, Sarah? I don't like to think about other people *getting to know you.* Would you be okay with someone else *getting to know me?*"

"No," I respond immediately. The very idea of anyone else being with Leo threatens to send ice through my veins, but his continued rhythm between my legs prevents it. "I don't share well."

"Good. Then we're together. No one else." He leans forward, sucking my nipple into his mouth.

Together. Even if it is temporary.

Leo will be gone when he finds out all the things I've done. The old Sarah will once again ruin things for me. But that person isn't here tonight. She isn't the one straddling a gorgeous man. She isn't the one he wants to be with, so for tonight, I'm ridding her from my mind, wishing I could get rid of her existence altogether.

Of their own accord, my hips start to grind into his hand. Leo pauses his movement and leans back in his chair. Curious about his sudden departure, I still and catch his gaze.

"I want to watch. Keep going." He slides his fingers through my wetness before moving back to my clit.

I push the sheet to the floor and begin rolling over his hand. Sparks surge through my body, and I throw my head back, my long hair cascading down to my lower back. I can feel it teasing right above where Leo's hand is supporting me.

"Why are you so bold in some moments and timid in others?" he growls, suddenly pushing a rough finger inside me.

"Leo," I moan.

"Why?" he asks again, pulling out only to add another finger, stretching me almost painfully. *Almost.*

"Because, in some moments, I'm lost in myself, and others, I'm lost in you," I answer as I begin riding his fingers.

He hooks them forward inside me, finding a spot I completely forgot even existed. An orgasm begins to build inside me, pushing me to an unexplainable high. I can't decide if I want to fall off the edge or remain on this peak for eternity. However, Leo decides for me.

He quickly removes his fingers. "Don't come."

"No!" I cry out from the loss.

"Shhhh. I have an idea, ángel. Let me control this and give you what you want. Let me remind you how it feels to be taken so hard and so wild that you lose all inhibitions in the process." Suddenly, he slides his hand up, grabbing the ends of my hair and pulling hard.

I suck in a surprised breath just as he drags his teeth across the base of my neck. My hips are forced forward from the movement, and for a brief second, I find friction against Leo's straining hard-on. That's all it takes.

"Oh God!" I call out as the orgasm tears through my body.

I barely register him saying, "Fuck," before thrusting up, allowing me to rock against his cock while riding out my release.

"That wasn't the idea," he whispers as I drop my forehead to his shoulder.

"Well, that's a shame, because it was a really good idea," I respond lazily.

"I want to be inside you. No, fuck that. I *need* to be inside you. I *need* to watch my cock disappear inside you, not my fingers. I *need* to feel you pulse around me when you come, and I need to feel this dripping down me, not wasted on my fucking pants." He reaches down, running a finger through my wet folds before bringing it to his mouth for a taste.

I don't care if it makes me easy or if it complicates things. At this moment, he could ruin my whole fucking life and that wouldn't stop me from begging to feel him moving inside me.

"What happened to *not tonight*?" I ask wantonly. I just had the most amazing orgasm of my life, and here I am, desperate for more.

"I changed my mind. Give me your control. Lose yourself in me."

"I'm not sure I'd have any other choice."

"Good answer," he purrs before demanding, "Get up, Sarah. We're going to the bedroom."

I lean back and find that my easygoing man is gone. As if someone flipped a switch, his expression is hard. Instinctually, I climb off his lap. The moment I find his eyes, I know exactly what he's doing. My Leo is still in there, but this is not only the man who is going to make sure I lose myself, but also the man who will ensure that I never want to be found again.

Chapter
FOURTEEN

Sarah

LEO'S LOOKING at me like he wants to ravage me, and it honestly makes me a little nervous. He's a beautiful, strong predator. If he wants to devour me like his prey, I won't stop him. But I won't make it easy for him to catch me either. He stands from his chair and very purposefully pulls his pajama pants to the ground. His length bobs as it's freed.

I lied earlier. I'm willing to lie down right here in the middle of his office and allow Leo to eat me alive. Forget about the chase.

"Go. I'll be there in a minute," he says, reaching down and gently stroking his cock.

Holy fuck. I'm not going anywhere and missing *this* show.

A very knowing smile tilts his lips. "Never mind. Come here, ángel."

My feet move of their own volition. However, my eyes stay glued to his hand that's moving up and down over the dark, angry head of his straining dick. When I stop in front of him, he reaches his entire hand between my legs. Not just a finger like earlier. This time, he rubs his palm across my drenched sex, pulling away with a very strategic tap on my clit. I sway forward at the contact. He then resumes his long strokes over himself, using my release as his own personal lubricant.

I groan loudly at the sight, licking my lips.

"I have to say, Sarah. I like the way you feel on my cock." He sighs and takes my hand. Placing it over his own, he begins moving at a slightly quicker pace. "That's us. *Together*, ángel. You like the way we feel?" he coaxes me since my mouth has dried and I have clearly lost my voice in him as well.

I finally snap out of it and boldly say, "I wonder how we *taste* together." I might have given Leo permission to run the show, but that doesn't mean I no longer get to participate.

"Jesus Christ. Suck my cock, Sarah," he orders.

Knees.

Hit.

The.

Floor.

I suck him into my mouth, swirling my tongue around the head before greedily taking him into the back of my throat. Maybe I was wrong; maybe I'm the predator in this situation.

My release lingers on his shaft, and I very carefully drag my tongue across it—savoring it with every stroke. It's not my taste that sets me on fire. It's the way it mixes with the saltiness of Leo's arousal.

He threads a hand into my hair as I work his erection. I can't remember the last time I did this, but if Leo's breathing and cussing can be considered signs, I haven't lost my touch. I've always loved to give head. There's just something about the thrill it gives me when every stroke can turn even the biggest man into a puddle of ecstasy.

"Fuck, ángel," he cusses, and the way he calls me ángel with a strong, sexy Spanish accent makes me even more impossibly wet. I could listen to Leo speaking Spanish all day.

I slide his cock from my mouth and drag my tongue down to the base. Very gently, I swipe my tongue across the heavy sack between his legs. Then I lift a hand and begin massaging his balls. His entire body tenses, exposing the ridges of his six-pack.

"Definitely not a virgin," he groans.

I try to once again suck him into my mouth, but he stops me.

Tangling his fingers in my hair, he tilts my head so that I'm looking in his eyes. "Go get on the bed. I'll meet you in there in a minute." His voice is deep, gritty, and laced with sex.

I stand up very purposefully, my breasts brushing his chest and my nipples tightening at the contact. He runs his nose from the top of my head down to my cheek and stops near my ear.

"Don't be nervous. I promise I won't bite. I'm saving that for tomorrow night." He winks. When his lips lift into a sexy smirk, I can't help but grin at him. He reaches out and grabs the back of my neck, pulling me the rest of the way to him. "Go lie down on the bed, Sarah. Facedown, ass in the air." Then he kisses me quickly on the lips.

"I, um…" I mumble. I am completely confident in my own skin, but there is never anything truly comfortable about shoving your ass in the air while a man watches. I hesitate, but Leo lets out a growl.

"This is me taking control, Sarah. I'm telling you what I want and I promise you, ángel, I'll make it exactly what you want too." His tongue darts into my mouth, extinguishing my nerves with every roll. "Go," he orders one last time.

Finally, my feet follow his directions. I take one glance over my shoulder on my way out, running my eyes over his strong, lean body, taking him all in. His eyes are hooded and burning with lust. His fingers twitch at his sides, and his hard cock jumps as I turn away.

Just as I get to the door, I hear him call out, "Oh, and put your panties back on. I'm looking forward to peeling those off again."

Suddenly, I'm looking forward to it too.

Chapter
FIFTEEN

Leo

WHAT THE fucking hell am I doing? This so goddamn wrong, but I still can't seem to stop myself. I know a lot about Sarah's past, but I'm suddenly very aware that I know absolutely nothing about her personal life. I had no idea that she hasn't been with anyone in seven years. Seven fucking years. How is that even possible for a woman who looks like she does? Men must be all over her.

When she let me in on her little secret earlier, I felt like the biggest piece of shit to ever walk the Earth—even more so than I already had. I'm terrified to tell her what I know about her. I can't sleep with her and *then* tell her. She's going to lose her fucking mind as it is, but now, I'm about to be a real asshole and fuck her first?

Goddamn it!

I have never wanted a woman more than I do Sarah Erickson. She's a breath of fresh air to me. Maybe it's because I have the upper hand—knowing her secrets and how to dance around them. But she's amazing. It's not all about the broken parts though; somehow, we just mesh.

She gets my jokes and I love hers. She's smart and witty and challenging. I love spending time with her. It's been, like, ten days and I'm already calling her my girlfriend like a fucking twelve-year-old with a crush to anyone who will listen. Yet I hold a secret that could potentially send her running. And I'm only partially talking about the things I know about her.

I have a shady-as-hell past too. I'm going to have to tell her one day how I really know Erica—and, even worse, who I really am. The last thing I need to be doing right now is burying my cock inside her. I shouldn't have even made her come again in the office, but when she thought we weren't together, it pissed me off. Sarah is different. I'm not usually anti-relationships or anything, but my life hasn't been all that stable over the last few years. However, I'm a firm believer that, when you find someone who fits, you claim them. Immediately.

So, now, Sarah and I are together and I'm about to bury myself inside her—completely claiming her. Then, when the truth comes out, she will probably never speak to me again.

I'm on a fucking roll.

I close down my computer, turn off the security screens, and head down the hallway back to the bedroom. I need to lay her down and talk to her—tell her the truth and make sure she understands that I don't care about who she used to be. Maybe I could even share a *little* bit about my past to reassure her. She seems to like it when I do that. It always puts her at ease to know that she isn't alone. I'm sure I can figure a way to spin this to make her stay. We just need to talk before we…

"Fuuuuuck," I breathe as I walk into my bedroom.

True to her word, Sarah is lying facedown, her black-lace-thong-covered ass in the air, and she did me two better. She put on her heels and graciously left the lights on. She's all but showing off.

Okay, so I'll definitely figure out a way to make things work after I come inside her. Hell, maybe I never have to tell her. What's one more lie on my conscience going to hurt?

I clear my throat. "Good girl," I purr, walking over to the bed. Running a hand up her back, I wrap it around the ponytail that wasn't there a few minutes ago and give it a gentle tug. *Perfect.*

I am all about getting a little rough in the bedroom—especially when a woman reacts to it like Sarah does. I don't get down with spankings or unnecessary roughness for my own sexual gratification though. It's just not how I roll. I want my every move to enhance the pleasure for her. Never—ever—should they be painful.

Never.

"Tonight, when you dropped your dress in the kitchen, I didn't immediately realize that this was a thong. However, ever since I found out, I've not been able to think about anything but seeing you like this. So. Fucking. Sexy." Releasing her hair, I trace my hand back down her back and over her rounded ass.

Sarah is thin, but somehow, she ended up with a fair amount of curves—her ass being two of them. I finally make my way down to her covered pussy. Sliding a finger around the lace, I drag it over her sensitive clit before dipping it inside her opening.

"Oh God," she moans a magical sound that speaks directly to my cock.

As much as I love the sight in front of me, I'm not taking her for the first time like this.

Leaning down, I place a wet kiss on the small of her back. "Roll over, ángel."

She quickly flips to her back.

"Legs open," I amend when she closes her knees together.

Without a single second of hesitation, her legs fall to the side.

Gorgeous.

I quickly strip her panties off. Dropping to my knees, I latch my mouth over her pussy.

"Ahhhhh, Leo!" she cries out, running her hands through my hair.

Sarah's already come twice tonight, but I'm not about to make it three without my cock inside her. That doesn't mean I don't want to taste her first.

I lick and suck every inch of her pussy as her body writhes around me. She lifts a leg, draping it over my shoulder. She then gently rakes the sharp heel of her shoe up my back in the most deliciously arousing way imaginable.

Yep, I'm done. My patience is gone.

I stand up, holding her leg over my shoulder. "Other leg," I growl.

She obliges by placing it on my other shoulder. I bend over, supporting my weight with a hand on the bed, next to her head. My face is still covered with her juices, but Sarah still takes my mouth in a rough and desperate kiss.

"You on the pill?" I ask with my dick poised at her entrance.

"No," she answers.

I cuss to myself. Then I move to the nightstand and pull out a condom, making fast work of rolling it on. "Fix that shit this week. Yeah? Otherwise, I have a feeling I'm going to need to buy stock in Trojan," I say roughly, pulling her legs back over my shoulders and kneeling on the edge of the bed.

"I thought you were out of condoms?" she asks, reaching forward to drag her nails over my abs.

"Well, I forgot about the one I save for emergencies. Walking in and finding you like that definitely constitutes a national state of emergency."

When she starts quietly laughing, I can't help but smile. God damn, she's beautiful.

I begin to ease myself inside her and her laughter abruptly stops. Closing her eyes tight, she slaps her hand to the bed, fisting the blanket.

"You okay?" I pause to make sure I'm reading her correctly.

"Yeah," she whispers. "Keep going."

"Kiss me," I demand.

Her eyes pop open for the first time since I pushed inside her. She gives me a sensual smile before replying, "Of course."

She slides a hand over my cheek and into my hair, placing her lips against mine in a reverent kiss. I slide all the way inside, filling her, as I catch her moans in my mouth. Strangely, I don't want to rush this anymore. This was supposed to be fucking. It was supposed to be rough and wild, but with a single touch, Sarah has tamed that urge. I don't want to tell her what to do or take control of it—I just want her. I roll my tongue with the same rhythm as my hips. Slow and steady.

It doesn't take long before I feel her tightening around me. I immediately stop kissing her, wanting to hear the sounds of her coming yet again. That was definitely the truth earlier. I've never heard a more amazing sound in my life.

"Leo. Oh, God." Her body begins to quake as she pulses around my cock. "Leo!" she gasps as I pick up my pace, frantic to join her.

With one final thrust, I plant myself to the hilt and erupt inside her. "Sarah!" I call out as the orgasm courses through my body. Physically, I'm still buried inside her, but mentally, I've never been more lost.

Lost in the moment.

Lost in the sensations.

Lost in *her*.

I remove her legs from my shoulders and begin trailing kisses over her breasts and up to her neck.

"Mmm," she moans when I make it up to her ear, sucking her lobe into my mouth.

"Take a shower with me," I whisper.

"I don't want you to pull out." She clenches her muscles around my softening cock.

"I don't want that either, but I have to get rid of this condom. So how about this? Shower. Then I'm taking you to breakfast. Then we're coming back and trying that again with you on top. Then we are sleeping half the day."

"It's, like, four in the morning. We don't have to get breakfast. We could just go right back to the 'me on top' part," she suggests, turning to capture my mouth.

"As tempting as that sounds, I need to refuel with some serious protein for what I plan to do to you."

"Oh yeah? What's that?" She smiles teasingly.

"Well, now that we've gotten the sprint out of our systems, next up is the marathon." I wink.

She lifts her eyebrows in mock surprise. "I have to be able to walk on Monday for work. Maybe you should ease me into the marathon. It's the least you can do. You know, since you just stole my virtue and all. " She places another kiss on my lips.

"Ah, yes. I deflowered the virgin," I tease back even while a pang of guilt hits me in the gut.

I know she wasn't a virgin. Hell, judging by the way she sucked my dick, I'm pretty sure she hasn't been in a long while, but I still feel like an asshole.

"Come on. Let's get cleaned up. Then we can talk about that marathon you have planned." I slowly pull out, and the immediate loss is staggering.

I absolutely, one hundred percent should not have slept with her. But that's more to salvage my own conscience when this goes up in smoke than anything to do with my honor.

Chapter
SIXTEEN

Sarah

Two weeks later...

Me: So...
Leo: ???
Me: Dinner on Friday?
Leo: Dinner tonight?
Me: Well that too...but especially on Friday.
Leo: Yeah, I'm down. Anything in mind?
Me: Lots of things in mind. All of which involve you naked.
Leo: <drops pants> Your turn.
Me: Lol I miss you.
Leo: I'll be back in town in a few hours. I've got some paperwork to do but I have an insatiable woman to catch up with first.
Me: I like the sound of that.
Leo: But when I'm done with her, I'd be happy to take you to dinner.
Me: You. Are. HILARIOUS. ← Sarcasm.

Leo: I figured.

Leo: So, Friday?

Me: Yeah. It's my birthday and Emma wants to go out to dinner.

Leo: Dinner with the parents!!! Count me in! ← Sarcasm.

Me: I figured.

Leo: I miss you too.

Me: That's not an answer.

Leo: I miss you a lot.

Me: Still not an answer.

Leo: All I can think about is fucking you in the security room with all the cameras aimed at you. Can you imagine all the different views I could get of you coming?

Me: STILL NOT AN ANSWER! (But I really like where you're going with that!)

Leo: Lol. It's your birthday, angel. If you want me there, I wouldn't be anywhere else.

Me: Can we order takeout tonight? You've been out of town for, like, three days. I won't make it through dinner without molesting you.

Leo: Ah yes. Mole-sting. My favorite.

Me: Molesting* Fucking autocorrect.

Leo: Don't lie! If you want to get kinky, just say so. I'm not sure how I feel about moles, but I'm willing to discuss.

Me: I hate you.

Leo: I hate you too. My place at six?

Me: I wouldn't be anywhere else. XOXO

Friday Night...

Leo: What are you wearing tonight?

Me: Just jeans and a top.

Leo: Does it show off your boobs?

Me: Yes.

Leo: Heels?

Me: Yes.

Leo: So...I heard the party was moved to my bedroom. Totally true story.

Me: Your bed isn't big enough for all four of us. I can ask Caleb if he'd like to snuggle with you though.

Leo: Too far.

Me: Yeah, I got a little sick thinking about that one too.

Leo: It's a nice night. I'd like to take the bike, but I wanted to make sure you weren't wearing a dress first.

Me: Yes! That sounds awesome! I've never ridden a motorcycle before. OMG! Does this make me your old lady?

Leo: Well, you are turning 35.

Me: You. Did. NOT. Just. Say. That.

Leo: I bought you a present!!!! Does that help?

Me: Get your ass over here now! I'm going to show you old lady.

Leo: Ohhhh...I like the sound of this. Leaving now.

Two hours later...

"HAPPY BIRTHDAY!" Emma yells as Leo and I walk into the restaurant fifteen minutes late.

My legs are almost shaking from the sheer number of times I came earlier. Leo took birthday sex very seriously. He left the most delicious red burns on the insides of my thighs from the stubble on his beard—a subtle reminder every time I close my legs.

"Thank you!" I yell back, pulling her into a hug. "Y'all remember

Leo, right?"

"What's up, man?" Caleb says, extending a hand.

"Not a whole lot," Leo responds with a warm smile, dropping an arm around my waist.

"Happy birthday," Caleb smirks, giving me a tight squeeze on the shoulder. That's about as good as it's going to get between Caleb and me.

I smile, shaking my head. "Thank you."

"Come on. I have a table reserved," Leo says, pulling me toward the bar and past the long-ass line at the hostess stand.

"They don't take reservations on Fridays," I inform him as he drags me behind him.

"They do if my girl's birthday falls on a Friday," he responds, stopping at the corner of the bar.

The male bartender approaches us. "What can I get you?"

"I spoke with Alexander yesterday about a table for tonight. He told me to come see you when I got here. It's under Leo James."

"Right. Hang on just a second. I'll get a server to seat you."

"You got some connections that I don't know about?" I ask teasingly while pushing up on to my tiptoes to give him an appreciative kiss.

"I have a lot of things you don't know about." He winks and nuzzles his perfectly trimmed scruff against my cheek.

"Score!" Emma exclaims, patting Leo on the back. "I'm sorry, Sarah. I know this is your favorite restaurant, but it's ridiculous that they don't take reservations on the weekends."

"Oh, hush. It's my birthday. And damn it, I want some pulled pork cheese fries. I'd have waited all night."

Leo starts chuckling. "No one's waiting. I brought a client here once and had to get chummy with the owner in order to do a pre-dinner security sweep. I made a call yesterday and got a table. However, pulled pork cheese fries sounds terrible."

"Disgusting," Caleb says at the same time Emma and I gasp.

"They are so good!" we respond in unison.

"Oh my God. You have to try them," I tell Leo, who is barely suppressing a curled lip.

Caleb starts laughing and mouths, "Awful," at Leo.

Emma smacks him on the chest. "You are such a liar. You ate half the plate last time we were here."

"You've lost your mind. That never happened," he replies, pulling her into his side and kissing the top of her head. "Whatcha drinking tonight, man?" Caleb asks, stepping up to the bar.

"Just water. I'm driving. We rode the bike over."

"Really? What kind of bike?" Caleb asks, immediately interested.

And just like that, the two guys start chatting like old friends. Emma catches my eye and tosses me a huge, award-winning grin. We're both casually tucked under their arms, and I can't help but smile as a sense of comfort washes over me. This is how it's supposed to be. There's nothing fancy about tonight. It's low key and simple.

It's absolutely perfect.

"FINE! THEY weren't horrible. I still don't understand how you two love them so much though." Caleb laughs as he polishes off the cheese fries. We had to order a second plate because the guys *hated* them so much.

Despite how awkward it was when they first met, Leo and Caleb really hit it off the second go-round. After they ignored us for the first ten minutes while talking about Leo's Harley, they discussed boxing and football and every other sport imaginable. Leo fits naturally into our little group. It didn't feel like dinner with the parents at all. It felt like dinner with old friends.

We all laughed as he and Caleb told stories about some of the stupid criminals they have come across over the years. Turns out, Leo was a DEA agent before he started his own company. It bothered me that I didn't know this already. We've been dating for a month. I should have known what he used to do. Leo doesn't pry though. He never asks me about my past, and I think I'm just so grateful that I follow suit.

I know the here-and-now about Leo James.

I know he's wearing a two-hundred-dollar pair of jeans, but he still orders whatever beer is on special. (That is when he drinks at all.) I know that he can spend hours at the gym, but he finishes almost every night in bed, wearing nerdy glasses, with his nose stuck in a book. I know he loves to talk to anyone about anything but won't utter a single word during a movie, especially 'eighties films. I know that, when we go out, he makes me feel like the only woman in the room no matter how big the crowd. I know that he always manages to put my insecurities at ease by throwing himself under the bus.

I know that I've never been happier in my life than I have been the last month.

I also know that I'm terrified for when this ends.

"Time for presents!" Emma singsongs, digging in her purse and pulling out two small gifts. "First, this one's from me."

She pushes an envelope in front of me. I grin as I tear open the paper. I may be thirty-five, but I love present time!

"It's a gift certificate for a spa...for both of us. We get to go away for an entire day. Manicures, pedicures, facials, massages. No babies crying or diaper changes. Just you, me, and a hot masseuse named Bruno."

"Oh hell no," Caleb snaps.

And at the exact same time, Leo declares, "You're not going."

Emma and I both bust out laughing as the guys clink glasses in agreement.

"Leo. You're next," Emma informs him.

"Wait. I didn't get her a present," he replies, surprised.

"That's okay, baby. I kind of sprung this on you at the last minute." I pat his leg and look up to find him giving me the look that says he definitely got me something and is insulted that I would believe otherwise. "I, uh, mean...give me my damn present?" I bite my lip.

He reaches into the inside pocket of his motorcycle jacket, which is draped over the back of his chair, and pulls out an envelope of his own. I give him an apologetic smile then snatch it from his hands.

"Hmm." I stare down at a single printed piece of paper.

No pomp or circumstance, just black-and-white paper that was no doubt produced on his office printer. I begin to read the first few lines and my eyes grow wide.

"Is this...a plane ticket? To Puerto Rico? For next weekend?" I turn to find his gorgeous face beaming.

"I confirmed that Erica was pregnant to the Tribune in exchange for the Wicked Witch giving you next Monday and Tuesday off."

"What?" I ask in shock.

"It was bound to leak eventually. You've seen her. She can't hide it forever, and rumors will start circulating soon. So, this way, the truth goes out and you get a four-day weekend for our trip to Puerto Rico."

"I'm sorry. What?" I repeat as Emma gasps from across the table.

"Happy birthday." He smiles and brushes the hair off my shoulder.

"Okay. I'm lost. One, we're seriously going to Puerto Rico?" I ask but don't give him a second to answer. "Two, what the hell happened to not talking about your clients?"

"One, yes. That's your plane ticket." He nods to the paper in my hand.

"And two, Erica and Slate are family and were more than excited to help. I didn't share anything without their permission."

I blink rapidly, trying to allow a minute for my brain to catch up. "Really?"

"Yes."

"Next weekend?"

"Yes," he says slowly as he begins to chuckle.

"That's a really big first birthday present."

"It's a selfish birthday present. I get to go with you."

"I get to spend the whole weekend with you speaking Spanish. I'm pretty sure I win there."

"*Oh, tu no tienes idea quién realmente ganó.*"

"Yes! Just like that." I smile and pull him into a hug. "Thank you so much! I don't even know what to say."

"You don't have to say anything. Happy birthday, ángel." He leans in, placing an all-too-brief kiss on my lips.

When I turn my attention back to Emma and Caleb, they are silently watching us, Emma is chewing on her bottom lip as her eyes sparkle with happiness. Hell, even Caleb looks sentimental from our exchange.

"I want to go to Puerto Rico too," Emma whines, looking up at Caleb.

He shakes his head and looks back at Leo. "Fucking hell. I'm never living this one down."

"Sorry, man." He laughs then takes a sip of his water.

"Okay, Caleb's next," Emma announces pushing a small, un-wrapped box in front of me.

"It's not a present."

My eyes flash to Caleb to find him looking down, uncharacteristically nervous.

"Yes it is," Emma disagrees, cuddling under his arm.

"It's *not* a present," he repeats.

"Shhh. It will be to her," she whispers in a way that almost makes me nervous.

Unable to contain my curiosity, I reach forward and lift the box open.

"Oh my God." I choke on the sob that tears from my throat, and maybe even my soul, as my eyes make contact with the one thing that I never thought I would see again.

Chapter
SEVENTEEN

Leo

"OH MY God." Sarah sobs, and tears immediately flow from her eyes.

I study her carefully, trying to figure out what the hell is going on. But as I glance into the open box sitting in front of her for an answer, I only become more confused when I see a simple gold necklace with a half of a heart that says: *st ends.*

"Shit," I hear Caleb cuss from across the table.

I glance up at Emma to gather some clues. She's watching Sarah with an anxious expression as if she's trying to make heads or tails of her reaction.

Sarah remains motionless, staring at the box with tears streaming down her face.

All I can do is try to comfort her. I move over an inch, teetering on the edge of my own chair. But she remains stiff at my side.

"You okay?" I ask, kissing her temple.

"Where… How… I thought this was gone," she cries.

She reaches out with shaky hands to touch the necklace but pauses just inches away and brings her hands back to her mouth. I stroke up and down her back, unsure of what else to do.

"Caleb found it in a box last week along with some of her other things," Emma tentatively fills in the blanks.

Caleb clears his throat and finally speaks up. "I should have given it to you a long time ago. I forgot that I even still had it. I'm sorry," he tells Sarah, but she never drags her eyes off the necklace. "You're welcome to come over and look through the box it if you want. See if maybe you want any of the rest of it."

"I want all of it," Sarah answers quickly as her eyes fly to Caleb's. "I mean, if you don't want it." She looks away sheepishly.

"I picked out a few things already. You can have everything else." He smiles warmly, fighting back his own emotions by kissing Emma on the head.

Sarah remains silent for another minute before jumping to her feet. "I need some air." Her tears are still consistently falling even as she tries to dry her eyes and compose herself.

"I'll go with you." I begin to stand, but she stops me.

"I just need a few minutes alone. Please. I won't go far." She offers me a fake smile.

I reach out and squeeze her hand. "Yeah. Of course."

"Girl time," Emma announces, standing from her chair.

"No. *Alone*," Sarah repeats and walks away only to pause just a few steps from our table. She backs up and quickly grabs the box, taking it with her.

"See! That went well," Emma tells Caleb, who is shaking his head at her.

"She's outside crying, Emmy."

"She took it with her though. She'll be okay. I promise."

I clear my throat. "Can one of you enlighten me on what the hell just happened?" I growl, becoming increasingly frustrated by being left in the dark. I have a pretty good idea what this is about, although the necklace confuses me.

"She told you about the wreck, right?" Emma asks.

"No," I answer, and it's not a lie. I know about it, but Sarah has never uttered a single word.

"Not at all?"

"Nope."

"Oh my God. What the hell have y'all been doing for the last month? Clearly, it's not talking."

"Excuse me?" I reply, surprised by her sudden frustration.

"Okay, calm down. This is not his fault," Caleb tells Emma before turning his attention back to me. "Look, Leo. I'll be honest with you here. Sarah has a shit past. That necklace belonged to her best friend, Manda, who passed away about seven years. That's all I'm giving you, but I highly suggest you start asking her some questions."

"What kind of questions exactly?" I play dumb because there is something about his words that pisses me off.

"The kind that enables you to decide if you can overlook her past…or *not*."

What the fuck is happening right now? I just blink at him, not sure I can honestly trust my own ears.

Is her own family actually warning me off her? I begin to choose my words very carefully while trying to keep my anger at bay. *Her past*. This is her family. God damn. He might not have said anything wrong *yet*. But I sure as hell don't want to give Caleb a chance to get there. Luckily, Emma chimes in before I have a chance to act on my impulse to become a real dick.

"She likes you. A lot. Probably more than you even know. I know y'all haven't been seeing each other long, but she's smitten." She laughs. "I love it! She's always so happy, and I've really missed that. I've missed seeing her just genuinely happy in life as a whole." Tears well in her eyes. "You just have to understand. You would be lucky to have her. Sarah is an amazing person. But it terrifies me that she isn't talking to you. I'm only telling you this because, if you can't handle all that is Sarah Kate Erickson, I need you to leave…like, yesterday." Emma implores.

"I'm not going anywhere," I respond firmly

"It's easy to say that now. But you don't have enough information to make that decision. I love my sister, but—"

"You are not listening," I start as my temper begins to slip. Sarah's outside bawling her eyes out and I'm stuck inside listening to them spew warnings. "I'm not going *anywhere*."

"Then ask her about the necklace. Don't let her brush it off as nothing. Everyone in Sarah's life has known her for years. I think someone finally needs to hear her side of the story without the clouds of the past fracturing her truths. Someone needs to finally know that woman standing in the parking lot right now."

"See, right there. That's a big part of the problem I'm having right now. That woman standing in the parking lot shouldn't be out there at all. She should be sitting in here, laughing and eating chocolate cake. I think your heart is in the right place, but this shit is seriously fucked up. It's her birthday. Why would you even give her that necklace tonight?"

"What? Are you kidding me?" Emma asks in awe.

"Hell no, I'm not kidding," I snap.

"All right. That's enough. You need to calm the hell down and watch how you talk to my wife."

"Right. Of course. Well, I'm going to extend you the same courtesy. Watch how you talk about *my woman*. It doesn't sit well with me that we are even having this conversation tonight. You should have talked to Sarah about what she feels comfortable telling me. I shouldn't be privy to anything about her until *she's* ready to tell me. Now I'm suspicious. Where does that leave the two of us? What's if she's not ready to talk yet, but I can't stop asking questions?"

Hypocrite. Fucking. Hypocrite. But Christ, this is too much.

I didn't seek out information about Sarah. And I feel guilty as shit that I know about her past—but not guilty enough to tell her.

"Just so you know, I'm smitten with her too. I'm not blind. I know she's keeping some things to herself, and I appreciate you looking out for her, but I think it's up to her when she wants to open up."

"She won't ever tell you! She has you so high up on a pedestal, Mr. Perfect."

"I'm not perfect." I quickly correct.

"Maybe not, but she sees you that way. You don't understand. You weren't here when things went down."

"No, but I'm here now." I push to my feet and dig some money from my wallet. "Dinner's on me. I'm sorry if I've come off as an asshole tonight, but I'm not going to just sit around while Sarah gets bashed."

"Who the fuck was bashing her?" Emma defensively jumps to her feet and shakes off Caleb's arm as he tries to restrain her. She's not yelling, but her reaction is definitely drawing attention.

"No one as long as I have anything to say about it," I answer matter-of-factly.

"I all but kicked her out the door for y'all's first date." Emma steps around the table with Caleb sliding out behind her. "She's my sister and she hasn't exactly had the easiest road the last few years. And when she showed even the tiniest bit of interest in you, I pounced. I fully expected her to hate you—come home with some terrible story about what a cocky douche you were... And after this little outburst, I can't say I was wrong in that assumption. However, Sarah is enamored by you. And if you left because of her past, I'm not sure how that would affect her. Jesus, all I'm saying is if you break up with her, do it because she's a bore or lazy in bed—not because of her past. If you care about her at all, you will recognize that I'm only looking out for her."

"I don't need you to remind me that none of us are perfect. Not Sarah. Not you. And certainly not *me*. Emma, I do recognize that you're trying to help. But what you aren't taking into account is that I'm doing the same damn thing. I just have a very different opinion on what help looks like. She's your sister, but I care about her too."

"That's really good to hear." She crosses her arms over her chest.

"I'm going to get Sarah," I announce over my shoulder as I walk away, dismissing any further conversation.

When I push open the door, I suck in deep, filling my lungs with the cool, crisp air I hope will calm me down. I glance around, searching for Sarah, but don't see her anywhere. Once I walk to the side closest to the parking lot, I find her sitting on a bench. She's leaning over and her hair is curtaining her face. Damn it, I hate seeing her this upset. Why the fuck did they give her that necklace tonight? It ruined everything.

"Sarah," I say quietly so as not to scare her.

Her head snaps up, and I swear, for a minute, every planet orbits around her. I have never in my life seen a smile so breathtakingly genuine. It doesn't show just on her gorgeous mouth; it radiates through her entire body. Damn it if Emma wasn't right. She's so fucking happy. I fully expected her to be a wreck, but she's anything but right now.

"Hey." She slides over an inch and pats the bench next to her.

"You're beautiful," I tell her, knowing it's not nearly enough.

"Yeah, I'm sure I look amazing right now. Is my eye makeup running?" She sweeps a thumb under her eyes, holding the open box tight in her other hand.

"Nah, you're good." I drape my arm around her shoulders and pull her into my side.

She cuddles in close and lets out a content hum. "I think this is the best birthday I've ever had."

"Really?"

"You have no idea how much this means to me." She uses a finger to toy with the heart charm.

"You want to tell me about it?" I look down questioningly.

"Yeah. I think I do." She smiles then kisses me softly on the lips. "You want to take a stroll with me?"

"Sure. Where we going?"

"Memory lane." She stands up, dragging me up with her. "Will you put this on me?" She lifts the necklace from the box and very carefully hands it to me.

I fasten it around her neck, finishing with a wet kiss on her shoulder.

"Let's go back in. I need to ask Caleb something."

"I may have screwed up and showed my ass," I tell her awkwardly.

"What?"

"I got pissed that they gave you that tonight. I thought it upset you on your birthday." I decide to leave out the rest of the argument. "It appears this is one of those very rare occasions in which I'm wrong."

"Very rare, huh?" She begins laughing—and not because she heard something funny. She's straight up laughing *at* me.

"Extremely."

"Aw, did you get upset because someone made me cry?" she questions in a mocking baby voice.

"I'm serious, Sarah. I was pissed."

She wraps her arms around my waist and starts laughing again. "Oh God. What did you say?"

"I don't even remember exactly. But I'm pretty sure I called you my woman and pissed on someone's leg."

"Damn. I would have loved to see you go head-to-head with Caleb. I'm actually really sorry I missed that." She folds over in hysterics.

"Sarah, stop," I say seriously then burst out laughing right alongside her. "Caleb didn't even have a chance to say anything. Emma had it all covered."

"Oh, well, she probably deserved it then. She's always trying to get up in my shit. I think she forgets that she's my baby sister sometimes."

"She called me a cocky douche." I feign injury and Sarah laughs even louder.

"Damn it. Why do I always miss the good stuff?"

"I'm glad you find this entertaining."

"I absolutely do. Now, come on, tough guy. Time for round two."

I let out a groan as she pulls me toward the restaurant door.

Chapter
EIGHTEEN

Sarah

"THANK YOU so much." I throw my arms around Caleb's neck the second we get back to the table. I can tell that he doesn't know how to react, but he finally gives me an awkward hug.

"You're welcome. I'm really sorry I didn't give it to you sooner."

"No, really, today was the perfect time." I look down to see Emma's prideful grin. I'm one hundred percent positive that giving me this tonight was not Caleb's idea. I reach up, clench the necklace in my palm, and mouth, "Thank you," to Emma.

She replies with a wink.

"I think I may have overreacted," Leo says, extending a hand to Caleb.

He smirks and shakes his hand. "I've done worse."

Leo turns to Emma, but before he can even open his mouth, she smacks him on the arm.

"You are really lucky that I like overprotective assholes."

Leo nods and Emma and I both bust out laughing.

"Hey, any chance we can swing by tonight and get that box?" I ask as we start gathering our stuff to leave.

Emma's eyes go wide and flash to Leo. "Yes!" she exclaims loudly.

I give her a suspicious look, but she shrugs and rushes out of the restaurant.

AFTER A brief stop by Leo's apartment to drop off the bike and pick up his car, we headed over to Emma and Caleb's house. Much to my dismay, their little boy, Collin, was sound asleep when we got there. I did, however, sneak in and give him a kiss even though Emma threatened me with my life if I woke him up. Thankfully, the little guy didn't move a muscle.

There didn't seem to be any lingering awkwardness between Leo, Caleb, and Emma. But I could definitely feel them exchanging quite a few knowing glances as we left. The box of Manda's belongings was a lot bigger than I'd expected. I had no idea that Caleb still had this much of her stuff. I feel like a kid in a candy shop tonight.

There was a day not too long ago where I couldn't have imagined smiling while reminiscing about Manda. Back then, I was struggling with handling all the guilt. Her death still hurts, and I don't think you can ever really let go of someone you loved when they die so suddenly and way too soon. However, I'm in a good place right now, so this is a treat, not a punishment like it would have been a few years ago. The truth is that, if Caleb had given me Manda's necklace at any other time, it would have killed me. But as I ride back to Leo's apartment with his hand wrapped tight around mine, the gold around my neck doesn't burn.

"Come on. I'll carry it up," Leo says, taking the box from my hands.

"Thanks," I respond as he drags a keycard over the sensor to unlock his private entrance to the stairs.

"Here. Put this in your purse. Now I won't have to let you up every time you come over." He hands me the card.

"Are we exchanging house keys?" I squeal sarcastically.

"Uh, no," he responds with a lopsided grin. "It's a keycard so you can park down here when you come visit. It's safer than parking on the street."

"Is that why you always pick me up instead of just letting me drive over here?"

"Yep. And now, you can park and make it all the way up to my door. I'm not giving you an apartment key until I'm absolutely certain you won't randomly sneak into my bed naked at night. Wait, change of plans. I'll get you a key made tomorrow." He waggles his eyebrows suggestively.

"No, don't do that. I'm not sure I want you to have one of my keys. What if you come over on a nonscheduled night and catch me with my other boyfriend?"

He narrows his eyes at me. "A nonscheduled night, huh?" He nods. "All right. Looks like I'm going to be dropping by your place unannounced randomly this week."

"Oh, the torture! How will I ever manage knowing you could just show up at any time?"

"I find out you got another man, Sarah, and I'm going to end up in jail for killing him. You aren't the only one who doesn't share well," he says as we ride the elevator up to his apartment. It's a short trip since he only lives on the third floor.

"Oh, shut up. You know I was kidding."

"I know, ángel." His arms are preoccupied with holding the box, but that doesn't stop him from leaning down and smacking his lips, asking for a kiss—one I'm more than willing to give.

"So we're really going to Puerto Rico next weekend?" I ask as we walk to his door.

"Absolutely. I got a room right on the beach in San Juan. It's going to be amazing. I haven't been on vacation in at least five years. I should be thanking you for having a birthday and giving me an excuse to take my girl somewhere relaxing."

"Thank you, Leo. Tonight…" I trail off when words fail me.

The truth is that I don't actually have the words at all. This night was more than I could have ever even hoped for. However, I know, the moment we walk through that door, it's time to come clean. I need to tell Leo about the wreck. I need to tell him about Manda, Casey, and even Brett. One *baby* step at a time though.

I'm not going into details about after the accident tonight. I'm just not there yet. I should absolutely tell him, without question, but that would mean risking him. I can't take that chance. I can't gamble with Leo. Waiting will make it worse—I'm well aware of this. But I'm just not ready to let him go. Then again, I have a feeling I'll never be ready for that.

"Where do you want me to put this?" he asks when we walk inside.

"Do you have carpet anywhere?" Leo's floors are all beautiful hardwood, but right now, I want to take my shoes off, put on some pajamas, sit on the floor, and introduce Leo James to Manda Baker.

"The rec room is carpeted," he answers with a confused tilt of his head.

"In there then." I smile as butterflies take up occupancy in my stomach.

The nerves sneak up on me from out of nowhere. It must show, because Leo puts the box down on the couch and folds me into a hug. It's a good one too. I swear his hugs could be the solution to world peace.

"You don't have to do this tonight," he whispers.

"No. I want to," I respond, nuzzling up against his scruff. "I want to get comfortable. Can I wear one of your T-shirts? I like the way they smell."

Suddenly, he releases me and steps away. He pulls the fitted, black T-shirt off his back and hands it to me. I begin laughing and he smiles.

"Well, that wasn't exactly what I meant. But it'll work."

"Get comfortable, ángel. I'll put this in the rec room." He loops an arm around my lower back and pulls me in for a hard kiss. It's not passionate or heated—it's reassuring and exactly what I needed to soothe my nerves.

A few minutes later, I walk into Leo's rec room wearing his black T-shirt and a pair of pink pajama shorts I stashed in his drawer at some point over the last few weeks. He's reclining on the large leather sofa with a book in his hand and a beer at his side. He's gotten comfortable too. He's wearing a pair of gray workout pants and a white tank top. I've come to know this outfit as Leo's pre-sleep attire. Because the minute he climbs into bed, he strips completely naked.

I flop down on the couch at his feet and suck in a deep breath.

"You're strange."

He looks up from the book with a humor-filled expression. "If, by strange, you mean insanely sexy, then yes, I would have to agree with you." He smirks.

I roll my eyes. "I love how humble you are."

"Why am I strange?" He sits up and places his book on the table next to him.

"Because you don't pry. I broke down sobbing tonight and you haven't asked a single question about the necklace or the box."

"Caleb told me it belonged to your best friend who passed away. I don't need to know the rest. You'll tell me when your ready."

This man.

I swallow hard, but not because I'm nervous to talk about the wreck. I'm touched by how simple Leo makes everything. Nothing is messy or scary. It almost makes me want to tell him everything. *Almost.*

"Well, I think I'm ready."

"I'm listening, ángel." He reaches out and grabs my hand, intertwining our fingers before kissing my knuckles.

Here we go.

Leo

SARAH TAKES a deep breath and squeezes my hand tight. I'm desperate to hear this story. This could be the moment where she tells me everything, where she lays it all out, and the secrets I've been keeping about knowing her past become null and void. This could be the beginning of something real. She'll still probably be pissed that I didn't tell her the truth earlier, but I doubt she'll flip. How can she be pissed if she's willing to tell me herself?

"Seven years ago, I was in a car accident. My best friend and Caleb's fiancée was killed. Her name was Manda Baker. She was my other half. We met in college and just clicked from day one. We were inseparable. I'm not exaggerating when I say we talked probably twenty times a day. Casey made our duo a trio about six months later when she moved in across the hall from us. The three of us did everything together. But while I love Casey, there was just always something special about the bond Manda and I shared.

"When she died, it ruined me. I was dealing with some other issues in my life at the time. Caleb was in a bad spot too, and his anger got the best of him. He blamed me for some of the circumstances that led up to Manda's death. He went so far as to say I was driving drunk. Which I wasn't!" she quickly corrects.

I nod and brush the hair away from her face, purposely dragging my fingers across her neck in the way that I've found calms her. She leans in toward my hand and tears begin to sparkle in her eyes.

"The necklace?" I ask to encourage her.

"Manda and I got it one drunken night while we were in Vegas on a girls' trip. It was just something silly. They were cheap and nothing fancy, but we pooled our slot winnings because we just had to have them. They started out as a joke, but neither one of us was willing to take them off. She used to play with it when she worried about stuff." The tears finally begin to slide down her cheeks. "Anyway, after Manda passed away, Caleb and I had a bit of a run-in over that necklace. It ended with him throwing it in his front yard. I searched for hours but never found it. I thought it was gone forever. I had no idea he ever recovered it."

"What a dick," I mumble.

Sarah barks out a strangled laugh. "He really is, but he's a good guy. He was struggling just like I was. He missed her a lot. Caleb was a mess for years until he met Emma." She waves off the comment. "But that's a different story. So yeah. That box is what's left of her stuff. I'd really like it if you'd hang out with me while I go through it."

"Of course," I quickly answer.

"Thank you." She leans forward and places a brief kiss to my mouth before moving to the floor.

Damn it. That was certainly the abridged version of her story. No brain injury. No husband. No suicide attempts. No Casey revelation. No court-mandated therapy. *No Sarah.* She actually didn't tell me about herself at all—she gave me Manda's story and nothing more. And just like that, any hope I had of the truth coming out tonight vanishes. I guess it's a step in the right direction, but damn. I had high hopes for this conversation. Selfish hopes, but high nonetheless.

She pulls the box over in front of her and begins fidgeting with the lid. I grab my beer off the table and head to join her, but just before I sit down, she stops me.

"Wait. Do you have any wine?" she asks with a small smile.

My eyebrows pop up in surprise. "I think I have a bottle of something white."

"Can I have a glass? Manda and I used to sit and drink wine for hours, and well, this might be the last time I ever get to have wine with her. It just seems fitting."

"Yeah, absolutely. Let me go grab it."

She nods and goes back to staring at the closed box.

A few minutes later, I come back into the room with the bottle of wine in an ice bucket. It wasn't cold and I figured she might want more than just one glass.

"Sorry. It's warm," I say, setting the bucket down on the table next to her then handing her the glass I poured.

"That's okay." She reaches into the bucket, scoops out a few pieces of ice, and drops them into her wine. She smiles at the glass for a second before lifting it up with a trembling hand and weakly saying, "Cheers."

"Cheers." I clink her glass with my beer and watch as she takes a sip of the fruity wine.

No sooner than the liquid passes her lips, her chin begins to quiver and tears pool in her eyes. I immediately sit down on the floor behind her and pull her between my legs. Wrapping my arms around her shoulders, I hold her tight, wishing I could magically piece her back together.

"I lost someone once," I whisper into her ear. "It almost destroyed me, and every time I think back on those days, it shreds me. It still hurts, no matter how much time passes. You know what though? When I focus on the good times, it makes all the pain melt away. Tell me about the good times with Manda, ángel."

She reaches up with one hand and rubs my arms, which are crossed over her chest. Her whole body relaxes as she leans back against me. She lifts the wine to her lips once more before setting it down and opening the box. As soon as the lid clears the box, she lets out a loud laugh. When I peek over her shoulder, she's holding a bottle of wine with a yellow sticky note stuck to the front.

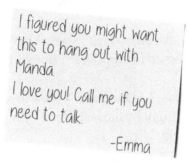

I figured you might want
this to hang out with
Manda.
I love you! Call me if you
need to talk.

-Emma

For the next two hours, Sarah pulls the contents one by one from the box. It seems to have a little of everything packed inside—a few pictures, some earrings, random knickknacks, and even some clothes. She tells me random stories about the stuff she recognizes, and some things make her laugh before she puts it aside. Finally, she packs it all back inside and closes it.

Her second glass of wine is almost empty by the time she turns around to face me. "I'm done." She sighs. "Thanks for, you know, listening to all that."

"Thanks for telling me. I like knowing who you used to be," I say pointedly, but she doesn't react. I give her what I expected to be a gentle kiss, but her tongue snakes into my mouth unexpectedly. I moan loudly when she boldly reaches down between us and into my pants.

"Take me to bed, Leo James. I'm ready for my birthday sex." She giggles. Clearly, the wine has gone to her head. It's cute, but it concerns me how quickly she switched as soon as that box closed.

"Why don't we just go to sleep? I'll give you birthday sex all weekend." I wink.

"No way. I'm happy. Like, really happy, and I want to be with my man now. So please. Take. Me. To. Bed." She kisses me after every word, and it makes me feel a little better about her current mindset.

She's happy.

It's funny. When I'm with Sarah, I'm happy too.

"Yes, ma'am." I salute her and quickly rise to my feet, dragging her up with me.

"You know about birthday spankings, right?" I tease.

"You remember my ninja knee, right?" she responds, and I bark out a laugh at the memory.

Yeah, really fucking happy.

Chapter
NINETEEN

Leo

One week later...

"WHAT TIME is it?" I ask as Sarah's cell phone alarm starts beeping from the nightstand.

"Seven," she answers.

Seven's not early at all unless you spent the entire night before buried to the hilt inside Sarah Erickson. Then, in that case, seven is damn near the crack of dawn.

"I'm going to go start the coffee. I might even have a cup with you." She yawns then pushes to her feet. "What time does our flight leave?"

"Eleven," I mumble burying my face in the pillow.

"Get up, baby. It's time to take your girlfriend to Puerto Rico."

"Cancela los boletos. Déjame dormir unas horas más y yo reservaré un vuelo privado donde podemos unirnos al mile high club.» (*Cancel the tickets. Just let me sleep a few more hours and I'll book us a private flight where we can join the mile high club.*)

"I have no idea what you just said, but I understood 'mile high club,' so I penciled us in an extra twenty minutes in the shower so we don't get arrested on the way." She drags her hand over my ass.

"Coffee," I moan, sweeping an arm out and pulling her back into bed.

"I can't get coffee if you are holding me in bed against my will." She laughs, but there have never been words to ruin the mood more quickly. I immediately release her as my pulse spikes. She rolls to the side and eyes me warily. "Leo?"

"Coffee," I repeat, but she can read my discomfort.

Rubbing my eyes, I smile sleepily while trying to play it off. But Sarah doesn't buy it for a single second. She bites her lip and rolls her eyes when I don't attempt to explain. I know she wants to ask; I also know she won't. Yet another reason Sarah has me buzzing like a broken streetlamp. Aren't we just two of a kind? I don't ask questions because I don't want her to have to face her demons by answering. And I think she wants to avoid asking questions to keep me from reciprocating with my own inquiries. But then again, that might just be my reason too.

"Woman, get me some caffeine stat." I rake my teeth over her shoulder and push her from the bed.

She smirks and pulls on one of my T-shirts before heading to the kitchen.

I scrub my hands over my face, wishing I could scrub my memories too. Well, everything except Sarah.

"Oh God!" she screams from the other room. Her voice isn't jovial or teasing—it's filled with fear and sends me flying to my feet. With a whoosh, my heart dips in my chest and I dash from the bed.

"No, no, no, it's okay." I hear a man's voice as I round the corner into my dining room.

The sun is peeking through the windows, but with the curtains drawn, it's still dim inside. Sarah is quickly backing up and we crush against each other as I rush forward. With one quick swoop, I force her behind me.

"Who the fuck—"

"Alpha-Tango-Juliette-eleven-nineteen," he says before he finishes with, "And you're naked."

Fucking Johnson.

"Jesus Christ. What the hell are you doing here?" I bark, turning to hold Sarah.

"Covering for you while you take your girl on vacation," he responds.

"Yeah, but you don't come in until nine."

"I'm covering for you—and you start at seven."

"How about you call next time you decide to come in early? I do live here, ya know," I snap before turning to Sarah, who's peering over my shoulder with a confused look on her face. "You okay?" I ask, but she doesn't respond to me.

"Aiden?" she questions.

Still as naked as the day I was born, I turn back to find the same confusion on Johnson's face.

"Oh shit! Sarah Erickson?" He laughs.

"Oh my God. Hi!" she squeals and rushes toward him, throwing her arms around his neck. "How the hell have you been? You scared the shit out of me."

"Sarah, go get dressed," I growl as her shirt lifts, exposing her panties.

"I could say the same to you," she replies, not even bothering to look back at me. "God, how long has it been since…" She stops and her shoulders tense.

"Dressed. Now," I bite out, desperate to get her out of the room.

I had no fucking idea she knew Johnson. Sure, they went to the same place for therapy, but what are the fucking odds that they were friends? It's suddenly very clear to me that my worlds have officially crossed. Johnson knows everything about me while Sarah knows absolutely nothing. If I can't get Johnson alone and tell him to keep his mouth shut, this could become a really fucking bad game of Six Degrees of Separation.

"Sarah," I warn.

"Oh good Lord," she complains but walks out of the room, heading toward the bedroom.

"We need to talk," I say the minute she turns the corner.

Johnson crosses his arms over his chest and nods. "It seems we do."

"Let me put on some clothes. I'll meet you in the office in five."

I head down the hall, trying to figure out how I'm going to play this. When I walk in the room, I find Sarah pulling her jeans over her hips.

"How do you know Aiden?" she asks.

"He works for me."

She nods and mildly relaxes.

"And he's a close friend."

She closes her eyes and drops her head cussing.

"What's wrong? How do you know Johnson?" I ask just to make her nervous and stop her from asking any more questions until I can formulate a plan. But as I watch her face pale, I immediately feel like an asshole for putting her on the spot. "Hey. I'm going to go brief him on some work stuff. You should really get packed. We need to leave for the airport around nine."

"Leo, we need to talk." She sighs, sitting down on the edge of the bed.

"We have a five-hour flight ahead of us. We can talk later." I pull on a shirt and shorts and squat down in front of her.

She's a mess of nerves and I hate it. I'm assuming she's worried that Johnson's going to spill it all about her past and it cuts me to the quick.

"How long have we been together?" I ask, brushing her hair off her neck and kissing just below the ear.

"Like six weeks." She tilts her head to the side to allow me more access.

"That's it?" I lean away, framing her face with my hands. "Sarah Erickson, I'm crazy about you. So crazy that, even after only six weeks together, the very idea of spending four days uninterrupted with you on a beach is about to push me over the edge of insanity. I can't wait to get out of here and spend the weekend getting lost in *you*." I press a kiss to her lips, holding her tight against my mouth as I siphon off every bit of her anxiety.

She sighs as I release her. "How do you do that?"

"Do what?" I ask, standing up and pulling her to her feet.

"Always say the exact thing I need to hear." She drops her forehead to my chest.

"I've told you. It's a gift. Now, go get naked. I'm going to brief Johnson. Then I'll meet you in the shower. I plan to take full advantage of those extra twenty minutes you penciled in this morning." I squeeze her ass before walking away.

When I push open the door to my office, I find Johnson's sitting at the computer, no doubt checking the business e-mails like he does first thing every morning. His eyes immediately flash up to mine.

"How did you end up meeting her?" he asks, rising to his feet.

"It was random." I walk around him to sit behind my desk.

He crosses his thick, tattooed arms over his chest. "Bullshit."

"It's the truth. I ran into her on the street." I shake my head and begin absently staring at the computer screen.

"Okay, well, let me rephrase. How long did it take you to recognize her before you were taking her to bed?" he growls, and I continue to act unaffected.

If there were ever a person to call me on my bullshit, Aiden Johnson would be that man. He has a no-nonsense personality and feels zero need to pull punches. I've never heard him even partially lie. He's honest to a fault. He might have a sketchy past, but without question, he's one of the best men I have ever met. I have no secrets from Johnson. He knows me better than anyone else, including Erica.

"I swear. I approached her because she was gorgeous. She was all flustered and I was just going to help her out. It wasn't until she started talking that I recognized her."

"Does she know that she changed your life?"

"No," I answer after a few seconds.

"Son of a bitch. This is fucked up, Leo."

"So people keep telling me," I snark.

"Is she the girl you've been seeing for the last few weeks, or is she just something new on the side?" He sits down on the couch, running a hand over his shaved head.

"Jesus Christ, I'm not that big of a dick. Of course she's the one I've been seeing."

"She know about your past?"

"For fuck's sake, can you stop with the twenty-question bit? I'm not a sullen teenager you need to reprimand."

"Oh good. Then being an adult who is not a prick, you'll understand that I'm about to fill her in on all your fucking shit just so you can be on an even playing field."

I jump to my feet. "The hell you are!"

"Why not, asshole? That seems fair to me." He shrugs.

I walk around the desk and step into his space. Johnson is a big dude, and between the tattoos, piercings, and gauges in his ears, he's scary as fuck. Hence why I hired him. But if he thinks he's going to screw things up for me with Sarah, he has another thing coming.

"I swear to God, you fuck with my relationship, I will fire your ass so fast."

"You can't afford to fire me." He lifts his eyebrows knowingly.

"Keep. Your. Fucking mouth. Shut."

"No problem—as long you open your fucking mouth and at least tell her that you know her. I'm not saying you need to bare your soul, but I think it's a really dick move not to at least give her all the information. Sarah's a nice girl. She's made some mistakes, but last I heard, she was really putting her life back together. She doesn't deserve to be blindsided by something like this."

"Don't act like you know her like I do. I'll admit that this isn't the ideal situation, but it is what it is. If you think my informing her that I know about her rap sheet is going to endear her to me, you've lost your damn mind. She'd be gone before I even got the words out of my mouth. What I know changes nothing."

"You're full of shit. It changes everything and you know it. So what is this with her, some weird obsession?"

"Fuck no. I genuinely like her."

"Right. And if you didn't know every detail of her sordid past to make you feel better about your own, how would you feel about her?"

"That's not fair."

"Oh, but it's somehow fair to Sarah?" He throws his hands out to the side before running them over his dress pants.

I put my hands on my hips and start shaking my head. "I don't know. Things have been going really well recently…and she's going to flip."

"Probably." He shrugs. "But, hopefully, she'll get over it. If you're serious about her, you need to say something soon."

I laugh humorlessly. "That's what Erica said."

"I knew I liked her for a reason. She's a smart lady."

"Yeah. Whatever." I run a frustrated hand through my hair. He's right. They're both right, but damn. Telling her is going to suck.

"Oh, hey. Speaking of Erica, who do you want me to send down to Indy since I'll be stuck here running things this weekend?"

"Not one of the new guys. See if Long would be willing to go. His wife is pregnant, but it's just a weekend and I don't think she's due for a while. Check Slate's schedule first though. He may not want anyone if they don't have any plans."

"So what are you going to do about Sarah?" he asks as I walk toward the door.

"I'm going to take her on a trip. This is her birthday present. I fully intend to make good on it. When we get back, I'll sit her down and talk to her. I have no fucking idea what I'll say, but I'll figure it out I guess." I breathe a defeated sigh.

"Just tell her the truth. She's gonna be pissed, but she'll get over it. Leo, when I was going through my shit, she was there. She reached out to me, and we became friends over coffee and drama. I have zero desire to talk about any of it with you, but I'll tell you she's good people. Crazy as hell, but I mean that in the best possible way. Her mind is always spinning. She overthinks and tries to rationalize everything—even the irrational shit. She looks for a greater meaning and symbolism in everything. The truth is she looks so hard sometimes that she misses the obvious shit right in front of her."

I blink at him, waiting for his words to sink in, but it never comes. "I have no fucking idea what the hell you just said."

He laughs a deep, throaty sound that you rarely hear from such a stoic man. "You'll get it eventually."

"No, I'm serious. I think you were speaking in hieroglyphics. I wasn't expecting it. You didn't put 'bilingual' on your job application," I joke, and he flashes me a smile and some shiny gold on his teeth.

"How about this? I know you can understand this. *Cállate la boca, cabrón.*" (*Shut the fuck up, asshole.*)

"*Sí, eso lo escuche alto y claro, puta.*" (*Yeah, I got that one loud and clear, bitch.*)

We both begin laughing, and I reach a hand out. He slaps it before pulling me in for a chest bump.

"I'm gonna jump in the shower. You think you can drive us to the airport around nine?"

"Yep. Oh, and if she asks, tell her I told you we know each other from yoga."

"You do yoga?"

"Nah, and I haven't seen her since she left Foundations, but she'll think it's funny." He winks.

"Hey, Johnson," I call just before I leave the room. "You might want to start saving up. Because if you ever hug Sarah while she's half naked again, you're gonna need to invest in some new gold teeth." I don't even wait long enough for him to respond, but I hear him chuckle as I close the door behind myself.

Chapter
TWENTY

Sarah

"FUCK, LEO!" I moan against the shower wall as he drills inside me.

"Don't you fucking come. I swear to God, ángel, if you come before I do, we're starting all fucking over. I don't give a fuck if we do miss our flight."

Those twenty minutes I penciled in for a joint shower are almost up and Leo is showing no signs of slowing. When he prowled into the bathroom after his talk with Aiden, I was a nervous wreck. I had no idea what he might tell Leo about me. Things that happened at Foundations are supposed to be confidential, but when you find out your best friend is dating a basket case, those lines might get blurred. My hands were trembling at the very thought of coming clean with Leo. I might have taken the first step by telling him about the wreck, but I knew the accident wasn't what would send him running. Who I became after the wreck would take care of that.

However, the moment he stopped behind me, I knew nothing had been said. His eyes weren't full of disgust or betrayal—they were blazing with desire. He didn't say a word as he pushed me forward against the sink. He snatched my panties down my legs and thrust a finger inside me from behind. It was so fucking hot that I almost came on the spot. And now, I wish I had.

Leo's left me teetering for the full twenty minutes. Like some sort of sexual terrorist, every time I get close, he stops and changes things up.

What started at the sink quickly moved to the shower, where he pinned me against the wall and pushed inside me so fast that I almost lost my footing.

It's rough, deep, and *hard*.

"Please," I beg, moving my hand down to my clit, desperate to find the release he has been denying me.

"Don't. Come." He pulls my arm back up, holding both of my wrists in one hand above my head. "You've never come with me. I want to feel that tight pussy milking me while I empty inside you."

"Then fucking come, because I was ready the minute you gave me your cock," I snap as the need becomes too much.

"Mmmm," he purrs. "I like when you catch attitude while I'm fucking you." He slams inside me, forcing a cry from my throat.

Oh, fuck this.

I push back, grinding against him. If he wants to come with me, I can speed up this process.

"Damn it," he groans as I tighten my muscles around his dick, all the while matching his every stroke. "Oh, fuck," he moans, and I feel him swell inside me. His hand drops between my legs. "Come, Sarah," he rasps on a breath.

His words do nothing to force the orgasm, but those circles over my clit that Leo has perfected set me off like a bolt of lightning. My knees go weak as he pulsates inside me.

My head is light as I come down. "I need a nap," I say as he slowly continues to slide in and out of me.

"You can sleep on the plane."

"That was amazing," I sigh, and he lets out a soft chuckle.

"We need to get going. We're going to be late." He slowly pulls out, but before I can even groan from the loss, he snakes a hand down and pushes a finger inside me.

"Mmm."

"Like, really soon. We need to go." A second finger joins his first.

"Okay," I answer wantonly, pushing back against his hand.

He glides his other hand up to my breast and squeezes gently. "Do you have one more to give me, ángel?"

"I'll give you as many as you want." I drop my head back against his shoulder as his hand speeds inside me.

"I want to claim every one of these. You want to come, you do it with *me*."

"There's no one else," I whisper.

He reaches up and grabs my hand, pulling it down to join his own, which is playing between my legs. "That's not what I mean. Not even these fingers get what's mine," he growls, raking his teeth over my shoulder.

I let out a breathy laugh, but his fingers suddenly twist, silencing me.

"You want to come, you do it with me," he repeats.

"You go out of town a lot," I manage to squeak out just to be a smartass as another orgasm builds inside me.

"That's what Skype is for, ángel. Now tell me you got it and come on my hand."

I reach between us, grabbing his softening dick and giving it a gentle stroke. "Then these belong to me."

"Not a problem." His fingers begin a deliciously frantic rhythm.

Seconds later, I give Leo exactly what he asked for. As pleasure tears through my body harder than even the first time, I have absolutely zero problems giving Leo James every orgasm I ever experience while we are together.

Hell, maybe even forever.

AFTER OUR flight was delayed, Leo and I arrived in San Juan at around seven p.m. We were both exhausted, but I insisted we at the very least grab a drink and hit the beach. I haven't had any wine or alcohol since my birthday, and I'm not exactly sure how I feel about drinking at all anymore. After the accident, it seemed logical to give up alcohol. However, now, I don't particularly have any strong feelings about it. Although I'm not too fond of the idea of getting drunk off one drink and making a fool of myself in front of Leo.

"I want a virgin Sangria," I announce as we approach the bar.

"So you want fruit punch?"

"With fruit floating in it," I finish with an excited grin, and he shakes his head at me.

He turns to the bartender and orders our drinks in Spanish. I'm pretty sure he makes fun of me too because he and the bartender both start laughing and eyeing me. But it's hard to be annoyed by something like that when Leo is rolling his Rs with his hand possessively resting on my ass. When I look up, he gives me a sexy smirk before leaning down and placing his warm lips to mine in a sensual kiss.

"Here. Let me pay for the drinks," I say, digging into my purse to pull out my credit card.

Leo lets out a loud laugh that makes me jump.

"What?" I ask.

"Sarah, you have lost your damn mind if you think you are paying for anything this weekend. This was my birthday present to you."

"Um. No. Your birthday present was flying me down here, putting me up in a gorgeous hotel, sleeping naked next to me, and sexing me up every time I so much as get wet."

His eyes go wide and he quickly looks around the almost empty bar to see if anyone overheard me. "Jesus Christ, woman. Not so loud."

"Your birthday present did not include buying our every drink or meal. So please let me pay for some stuff while we're here."

"No," he responds shortly before pulling me in front of him and wrapping an arm around my waist. He brushes the hair off my shoulder and whispers in my ear, "This is my birthday present. You don't get to define the limitations. You want to do tit for tat while we're here? Fine, but you're going to do it in a different way than paying for things. You feel the need to take a turn, you take my dick in your mouth while I'm sleeping naked next to you." He finishes by rolling his hips into my ass, revealing a hard-on that definitely wasn't there a few moments earlier. He then pulls out his wallet and tosses some money around me on the bar. I don't argue.

"You know, the beach will still be there in the morning. Maybe we don't need to go out there tonight. I suddenly feel the need to take a turn. You did, after all, buy me a drink," I say and he busts out laughing.

"There's plenty of time for that, ángel. First, we are going to need to stand here for a few minutes while I recite the periodic table. Then how about we go out to the beach for a little while before you take your turn?" He winks.

"Okay," I respond, pressing my ass back against him.

He lets out a cuss and quietly starts mumbling, "Hydrogen, Helium, Lithium…"

"I HAD no idea you did yoga," Leo says as I sit between his legs, staring out at the waves crashing on the beach.

"What?" I look at him over my shoulder.

"Johnson told me y'all know each other from yoga."

I quickly turn back around and bite my lip. Of course he did. He obviously remembers when I got pissed and told the staff at Foundations that I thought that the yoga class they were trying to force me to take was the beginnings of a religious cult. He laughed his ass off, which in turn made me laugh my ass off. The staff, however, didn't find me even remotely humorous and made me take the class anyway.

"Yeah, I don't go much anymore," I answer, trying to stifle my laugh.

"Yeah, you didn't strike me as a yoga girl."

When I spin around, he's grinning down at me. I drape my legs over his and wrap my arms around his neck.

"What kind of girl do I strike you as?" I ask curiously.

"I don't know. Down to earth. Someone who doesn't follow all the hottest trends, but rather forges their own path." He kisses the tip of my nose.

"I like that you see me like that."

"How do you see me?"

"Easy," I answer without hesitation.

He gives me a put-off look. "Hmm. I'm not sure how to take that."

"Oh hush. I can be a little anxious and high strung sometimes, and you have this natural ease about you that doesn't allow my mind to spiral. Just something as simple as the way you touch me or the stories you tell me—it keeps me grounded."

"I like that you see me like that," he says, repeating my words back to me, and this time, he kisses my mouth.

"Hey. Can I ask you a question?" I lean away but only long enough to tangle my legs around his waist.

"Sure. Then I'm taking you up to bed." He slides his tongue into my mouth, kissing me with such passion that I have no choice but to join him. His hands drift down over my breasts but pause when we hear voices down the beach. He lets out a growl then drops his forehead to mine. "Ask."

"What's your tattoo mean?"

"And time!" he exclaims, looking down at his watch. "Five weeks, six days, eight hours. This might be a new record."

"What?" I ask, thoroughly confused.

"Most women ask me about it the moment they see it. I'm actually impressed, Sarah."

"Thanks?" I respond.

He laughs, pulling his shirt up to his shoulders so I can see the tattoo on his side.

I trace my fingers over the top line of the ink and ask, "Who's Liv?"

"What? Holy shit, they forget to put the 'e' on the end?" he teases.

"Hilarious," I deadpan.

"I had a serious girlfriend in college. I fell for her hard." He slides my hand down to the word 'love' for a second before moving it on to 'lie.' "Then she started sleeping with my best friend. They kept it a secret for months until he finally told me the truth the night before I was about to propose."

"Oh damn," I whisper, and he nods his head in agreement.

"So, yeah, it's actually three separate tattoos." His shoulders tense and a flash of pain flickers in his gorgeous eyes.

For a second, I stare. It's so unlike the Leo I know that it almost hurts me to see it. I need to wipe away that look as quickly as possible, so I reach up and cup his face.

"I should probably send her a 'Thanks for being a whore' Hallmark card. It's the least I can do for the woman who handed me the most amazing man I've ever met."

"I'd hardly say all that," he responds, brushing his lips across my mouth.

"I would. I might even go so far as to send her a fruit basket." I crawl closer to close the invisible gap between us.

Leo smiles. "She hates apples."

"An all-apple fruit basket then," I whisper, kissing the underside of his jaw.

He groans and pulls me impossibly closer. "Christ, ángel."

"And look at the bright side. At least her name wasn't something ridiculously long like Seraphina-Jo-Lynn." I try to kiss him again, but Leo leans back to catch my eyes. I have no idea what that look means, but a very slow smile lifts the corners of his lips.

Suddenly, I'm flying through the air as he flips me to my back. I let out a startled scream, but Leo's mouth absorbs the sound as he crushes it over mine. Holy hell. What the fuck just happened? His hands are in my hair and his kiss is rabid. I try to keep up, but it's worthless—Leo's gone savage.

"Goddamn it, Sarah." He trails kisses down my neck.

"What did I do?" I ask breathily.

"*Tu lo haces muy fácil.*"

"English," I moan as his hand sneaks under my skirt and into my panties. "Fuck, Leo."

"Mmm, ángel, You're wet. I believe that's my cue." He jumps up and pulls me to my feet after him.

My head is spinning from how quickly this started. However, he's right. I am wet and I *crave* him. So as he takes my hand and heads back toward our hotel, I follow behind him without hesitation or any other conversation.

Chapter
TWENTY-ONE

Leo

Two weeks later...

"BABY, YOU ready yet? We're going to be late," Sarah coos as she walks into my bedroom.

"We're always late. I don't think we should mess with our perfect record now." Tugging a tight, gray T-shirt over my head, I give her a kiss.

"You're probably right."

"Sarah, I'm always right." I give her the best stern expression I can fake.

"Oh please. You're so full of yourself."

"Well, if we stand here any longer, you're about to be full of me too." I wink and allow my hand to drift down to her ass. "How was work, ángel?"

"It was horrible. I hate that damn job so much. I need to go back to school, because if I have to work as a receptionist for the rest of my life, I think I'll lose my mind. What about you? How was your day?" Sarah asks, rubbing her hands over my chest.

"It was pretty good actually. I got a new client. It's a politician who wants two men full time. So it looks like I'll be hiring some new guys pretty soon."

"Oh, that's fantastic! Full time? Any chance he wants a female bodyguard? And when I say bodyguard, I mean personal shopper, secretary, or dog walker?"

"Dog walker? Guardian hasn't dabbled in those services yet. I'm pretty sure you're completely overqualified if I do though. I know you went to college. What'd you major in?"

"English," she answers with a shrug.

"Well, that's a worthless major," I tease.

"Hey!" she exclaims, sliding a hand under my shirt and raking her nails up my side.

"Okay. Okay. I give up. It's an extremely useful major."

"No, it's not." She rolls her eyes and gives me a knowing smirk.

I release her and head to my closet. "We need to get out of here," I say, pulling on the baby-blue button-down I know she loves. It's funny, because ever since she mentioned it the last time I wore it, I've loved it too. I'm not particularly attached to the shirt. I'm utterly addicted to the way her eyes heat when she sees me wearing it.

"Are you sure this is a good idea?" she calls from outside my closet.

"It's fine. Erica is dying to get out of the house. She's also been harassing me for weeks to meet you."

"Yeah, but aren't you worried someone will bother them if we go out. Slate's pretty famous."

"He is, but I'm bringing three men, and if for some reason things get out of hand, we can just leave. Besides, we're going to that hole-in-the-wall place that Caleb suggested." I emerge from the closet.

"What if—"

"Ángel, let me worry about the what-ifs. This is what I do for a living, remember? It will be fine. I promise. Now, are you worried about meeting Erica or Slate being asked for an autograph?"

"I love this shirt." She leans up on her tiptoes and whispers her lips across mine.

I ignore her compliment, unwilling to let her change the subject. "It's okay if you're nervous. Although you have absolutely no reason to be. Emma and Caleb are still coming, right?"

"They are. And thank you for inviting them. Caleb has been giddy all freaking week about meeting Slate. He's a huge boxing fan."

"Yeah, I know. I was a dick last time we all went out. Maybe this will smooth things over."

"Oh, I'm pretty sure this will more than just smooth it over."

"Good. Then let's get out of here." I kiss her nose and step away.

I was preoccupied when she walked in, but as we prepare to leave, I finally take the time to slide my eyes over her tight-fitting black pants and heels. She's wearing what, on any other woman, would be described as a conservative white top, but somehow, Sarah's sensual body turns it into something sexy as hell.

"You look gorgeous by the way."

"Is it okay? I wanted to go casual but still look nice."

"Well, I'm not sure 'nice' is how I would describe that outfit. Sex kitten may be more fitting, but either way, you definitely look amazing. Now, lets go before I'm tempted to undress you."

CALEB WASN'T lying. From the outside, the restaurant is a fucking hole in the wall. However, when we get inside, I'm happy to find that it's actually a semi-nice place. Very quaint. All the furnishings are new and the smell of fresh garlic made my stomach growl the second we stepped through the door.

"Get a room," Sarah teases when we find Caleb and Emma are already sitting at the small bar, having a drink. Emma's sitting on a barstool with Caleb standing close between her legs, whispering something in her ear.

"Hey! You're only a few minutes late tonight," Emma laughs, standing up to pull Sarah into a hug.

"Yeah, well, we didn't want to be too late. I know how you love to take off your bra and put on yoga pants as soon as the sun goes down," Sarah smarts back.

"Your sarcasm would hurt if it weren't the truth."

"What's up?" Caleb extends toward me.

"Not much. What have you guys been up to?" I ask as Emma gives me a friendly hug.

"Well, I'll tell you one thing. We haven't been gallivanting around Puerto Rico," she says sarcastically, giving Caleb an unimpressed smirk.

"Oh for fuck's sake," he responds, pulling a sip off his beer.

We all start laughing and fall into a casual conversation.

"What you drinking, ángel?" I ask Sarah, who is involved in a very animated discussion about her boss with Emma.

"Um. I don't know." She toys with her bottom lip and glances up to Caleb.

He stands there for a moment before quirking an eyebrow. "What?" he asks, clearly confused.

"I was thinking about maybe having a glass of wine," she replies nervously, causing Emma to let out an excited squeak through tight lips.

"Jesus, Sarah. Yeah, of course. Come on. Let me buy it for you." Caleb turns to the bar.

"No, you don't have to do that. I just... I don't know..." she trails off, wrapping her arm tight around my waist.

"It's fine. I swear. Come on. My treat."

"Yeah, okay." She smiles weakly and looks up at me.

My only answer is to give her a wink and squeeze her tight into my side. But that's all it takes with Sarah. She lets out a sigh and her tense posture disappears from the simple gesture.

The bartender places a round in front of Caleb, who passes them out. Lastly, he hands a wine glass to Sarah and smiles pridefully.

"Pinot Grigio, if I recall correctly."

"Chardonnay, actually. But this will work," she laughs, taking the glass from his hands.

Emma and Sarah do a ridiculous toast, and Caleb and I clink beer bottles while simultaneously rolling our eyes at them.

A few minutes later, I hear a familiar voice from the door. "This place is cute!"

I spin to find Erica walking in, dragging Slate behind her.

"Hi," she says, waddling her way over to us.

I haven't seen her in weeks, and her stomach has definitely grown quite a bit over that time. Erica is a very small woman, so maybe getting pregnant with Slate's sure-to-be huge son wasn't her smartest decision. The smile on her face says otherwise though.

"Hey, babe." I pull her into a one-armed hug, never releasing Sarah. Then I turn my attention to Slate and give him a quick nod. "What's up, man?"

"Sorry we're late. We had to make a quick stop to look at a crib. However, that turned into looking at baby bedding, which turned into looking at car seats, which turned into buying half the baby store. Which is currently about to turn into me chugging half a gallon of beer."

"Oh shut up! You loved it," Erica laughs.

"Wow. I am terribly happy I missed that," I say sarcastically.

"You shut it, too," she mumbles, looking over at Slate, who is silently laughing.

"Hi," I hear Sarah greet Erica.

"Oh, sorry. Mom, Dad, this is my girlfriend, Sarah Erickson, and her parents, Emma and Caleb Jones."

"Stop." Sarah slaps my chest.

"Why? This is exactly that awkward step in every relationship where your parents meet the future in-laws," I joke before I really think it through.

Sarah's big, blue eye bounce to mine, and she looks almost embarrassed for a second as her cheeks heat to pink. She swallows before glancing over at Emma, who might as well be glowing.

I didn't mean to insinuate marriage, love, or even a future to Sarah. Although I'm not sorry I said it. I mean, who the hell knows if this will end up working out, but I've dared to dream that it will.

I've had many conversations in my head where I tell Sarah that I know about her past. Some days, in my alternate universe, she's relieved that I know, and others, she gets pissed—but only slightly. She's always rational and talks everything through then cuddles up next to me and listens to me explain my past as well. She's more than just accepting—she's unfazed. Then we get to be together without the secrets shrouding us and guilty consciences weighing us down.

So maybe I've done more than just dare to dream. Maybe I've plotted it out completely and, in a sense, set myself up for nothing but heartbreak. It's hard not to, though, when I'm this happy. I've figured out over the years that, for me, happiness isn't centered on another person. It's molded and shaped around moments and experiences that leave you breathless. However, suddenly and without warning, my happiness begins and ends with Sarah. It's exhilarating and distressing all at the same time.

I stand casually at the bar of the small restaurant with Sarah tucked under my arm and everything feels right—even all the way down to a very fundamental level. I know it's not perfect, but for the first time in over four years, I can actually hope that it will be eventually. Erica, Sarah, and Emma are huddled together, chatting about pregnancy and babies, and Caleb and Slate are lost in conversation about boxing and some of the up-and-comers from the gym in Indianapolis. I pull a sip off my beer and revel in the peace and quiet inside my own head.

"You okay?" Sarah looks up at me with a warm smile.

"I'm perfect, *mi cielo.*"

"*Mi cielo?* That's new." Her smile grows.

"Heaven," I answer on a whisper, tucking a stray hair behind her ear. "*Cuando la verdad salga, no se donde esto nos dejara. Pero aqui contigo es como yo imagino deber ser el cielo.*" (*I don't know where this is going to leave us when the truth comes out. But here with you will always be what I envision heaven to be.*)

"I have no idea what you just said."

"I said you are beautiful and I'm starving."

"Well, that's not as romantic as it sounded, but I'll take it." She laughs, giving me a soft kiss that goes straight to my head.

I look up to find Erica and Emma staring at us with their mouths all but hanging open. Slate and Caleb are awkwardly toying with the labels on their beers.

I clear my throat. "Well, okay. Now that we're all here, I'm going to grab us a table."

"I'm going to the restroom," Sarah announces with Emma and Erica both agreeing to join her.

I watch as the three woman walk away laughing. Then I make a quick trip to the hostess stand before heading back to the guys.

"I'm telling you. I have this kid who is about to break out. I've never seen such raw talent before. He's a good kid too." Slate drains his beer and sets it down on the bar.

"No shit?" Caleb asks while signaling for another round.

"Yep. Till Page, and I swear, within the year, he's going to explode onto the scene."

"I'll have to keep an eye out for him." Caleb tilts back his beer.

"Come on. Our table's ready. I'll wait for the…" My words are frozen as I see Caleb's eyes grow impossibly wide and he barely manages to keep from spitting out his beer.

"You asshole. I thought you two were staying in tonight?" I turn to find a tall man smiling and walking over from the front door. A tiny brunette is holding his hand with a kind grin.

"Yeah…" Caleb responds slowly and takes a few quick steps toward them.

His behavior immediately puts me on alert, and I glance around for Johnson, who seems to have also read Caleb's body language and has already started heading our direction.

"What's wrong with you?" the tall guy asks before recognizing Slate. "Oh shit." His eyes flash to me with a huge grin.

This guy doesn't look even the slightest bit menacing, so Caleb's reaction has me puzzled. I have a horrible feeling in my gut, but I can't for the life of me figure out why. Unwilling to be left in the dark any longer, I take a step forward.

"Hey, how's it going? I'm Leo James" I extend a hand and Caleb groans as the tall guy quickly takes it in a friendly shake.

"Nice to meet you. Brett Sharp."

Fucking hell. The pieces snap into place. The ex-husband.

"You need to leave." Caleb tells Brett before focusing on the brunette.

He says something else, but my attention is drawn away when I hear Sarah laugh as she returns from the bathroom. I stride away from Brett and Caleb and head toward her. I need to warn her at the very least. But as she rounds the corner, her laughter is abruptly silenced. I can actually see the color seep from her face as she stumbles backward.

Chapter
TWENTY-TWO

Sarah

"SON OF a bitch," I hear Brett cuss as he pushes Jesse behind him.

I can't blame him for having that reaction, but when I see it first-hand, the pain still consumes me.

"Brett, stop," Jesse responds, offering me an uncomfortable smile.

With a flash of understanding and two quick steps, Leo closes the distance between us and wraps me in his arms.

Time suddenly freezes and the world tilts on its axis. With just one glance of Brett's green eyes, I'm transported to a different time.

A different life.

A different *Sarah*.

Two years earlier….

I PULL up to Brett's apartment knowing he's at work by now. Years ago, he gave me this key with some ridiculous hope that I would one day use it. I held on to it despite my desire to throw it in the garbage. There's nothing in this apartment that I want. Including him.

He sold our old house within months of my moving into my new apartment, and it left a searing pain in my already shattered heart. If I'd thought there was any way I could have convinced him to leave, I would have stayed there for all eternity. I had memories in that house. Memories with Manda. I could care less about the rest of them.

Manda and I did everything together. She used to bring her clothes over and get ready at my house almost every weekend. It worked out for everyone. Brett would go over to Caleb's and they'd watch sports for a few hours while we talked and got ready for whatever we had planned for that evening. There were physical reminders in that house too—like the black spot on our bedroom carpet. If I close my eyes tight, I can still hear Manda's laughter when she spilled that nail polish. If she were here, she would say that I slapped it out of her hand in mid-stroke. She also would be right. Friends don't let friends paint their nails black in August. She tried to make me clean it up so Brett wouldn't get mad, but we were both laughing so hard that it had almost dried by the time I pulled myself up off the floor.

God, I miss her so much.

But today's not about Manda. Today is about Brett.

I hate him. On the outside, he's a really nice guy. I can see how I once fell in love with him. But I'm not the only one who changed after the wreck. Brett's basically unrecognizable these days. He's always so needy and harassing me about something.

"Sarah, did you pay your electric bill?"

"Sarah, did you take your medicine?"

"Sarah, did you eat yesterday?"

What the actual fuck is wrong with him? I'm thirty-three years old. I don't need a babysitter. The whole fucking world treats me like a child and it's so damn frustrating. He's just another prick who always talks down to me and refuses to let me live my own God damn life.

But I have to hold on to him.

Brett's all I have left, and that speaks volumes to how screwed up my life truly is. He's finally trying to move on with this Jesse chick. I just can't in good conscience allow that to happen. I don't love Brett, not even a tiny bit, but I need him to love me. I spend all day every day wanting nothing more than to be alone, but when the sun goes down, the solitude becomes terrifying. My mind races and images of Manda lying dead on the highway invade my every thought. I never actually saw that visual, but that doesn't mean it's not branded into the backs of my eyelids. My overactive imagination is a cruel bitch. I have even conjured up a whole scene from the night of the wreck where I get trashed and laugh as I drive directly toward the tree.

Yet, every Thursday night, Brett shows up at my house and the world inside my mind goes quiet for a few hours. I focus on slinging all of my pent-up pain at him. It releases some of the constantly build-ing pressure that threatens to overtake me. I know my words kill him, but it's better him than me. Each time he visits, he always leaves just like I want him to. Hell, I spend hours trying to force him to leave. But he always comes back. It's Brett's biggest flaw and greatest attribute.

I don't know why I picked today to come over to Brett's apart-ment. But I woke up this morning feeling even more on edge than usu-al. I've been hiding out in my room since the seven-layer-dip fiasco a few weeks ago. The sound of his words still rings in my ears.

"There will never be another Brett and Sarah Sharp."

The best part was the look on his face when he said it. I honestly had to fight back a laugh. It was as if that were the very first time he ever admitted it to himself. We haven't been together in four years, and he is just now catching on to this? And they say I'm the one who suffered a brain injury.

I laugh to myself as I swing open Brett's front door, quickly lock-ing it behind me. If I'm going to be successful in my plan to break him and Jesse up, I'm going to have to give her doubts that Brett can't talk himself out of. I'd known that the appearance at the coffee shop prob-ably wouldn't be enough, but it was just too damn easy. His sisters still have my old e-mail address on their family e-mail distro. They send what feels like a million pictures a day. It was all too easy to print out that picture of Brett's niece. She looks just freaking like him. It's defi-nitely not a stretch to believe she could be his child. When I slammed it down on the table that day at Nell's coffee shop, I thought Jesse's eyes were going to bulge out of her head.

However, Brett clearly managed to weasel his way out of that one. Now, it's time to step this up a bit. I reach into my purse, pull out one of my earrings, and toss it under the pillow on the couch. Just so there is no doubt about who it belongs to, I picked the same ones I wore the first time I met Jesse.

Damn it. I really liked that pair too.

I then move to the bathroom and search through the drawers. Just as I hoped, I find a few women's toiletries. I pull a handwritten note from my purse and begin to search for somewhere to hide it. Just for good measure, I grab the pink toothbrush before shoving them both in the drawer.

Brett,
I'm so glad we have decided to give our marriage another try. Thursday was amazing and exactly what I needed. I'd almost forgotten how amazing it felt to make love to you.
Love always,
Sarah

I pull the red panties from my purse and make my way to his bedroom. The minute my eyes lock with the wooden picture frame on his nightstand, the breath is stolen from my lungs. My arms fall limply at my sides and I stagger forward. With every step closer, a knife is twisted in my gut. I immediately recognize the picture of Brett holding Jesse, but it's the frame that causes a sob to rip from my throat.

It's one of Manda's frames. Caleb made them for her all the time. His house used to be littered in them before she passed away. She loved to take pictures and he, well...loved to display them. As far as I know, he has never once made a picture frame for anyone else. It was something special he did only for her. Yet here on Brett's nightstand sits an image of Jesse Addison inside one of them. The pain starts to subside as my blood begins to boil.

Jesse...in Manda's fucking frame.

Did Brett ask Caleb to make this for him?

No. No! There is no way he would have made this for Brett. This is Manda's!

My pulse begins to race and I fight to breathe. Anger rages through my veins, struggling to find it's way out.

That fucking home-wrecking whore is inside my Manda's frame.

I snatch it off the nightstand and sling it as hard as I can to the floor. It shatters the glass, but the sturdy frame remains intact. I roughly pull the picture out, purposely ripping it in half as I go.

Why in God's name would Brett put her picture in Manda's frame?

"Manda." I gasp her name out loud when just the thought of her isn't tangible enough. "Fuck!" I scream.

Suddenly, a thought explodes into consciousness. Jesse must have stolen this from Caleb. Oh my God! She isn't just replacing me—she's trying to replace Manda as well.

The roaring in my ears becomes almost deafening as the very thought renders my mind unable to process anything else. My vision tunnels, blocking out everything around me except the severed picture in my hands. I purposely rip it again—this time dividing it directly across her face. She can fuck with me, but I will never allow her to make people forget about Manda. I fucking hate that manipulative bitch for even trying.

Then again, if I hadn't murdered Manda, no one would even have the chance to forget her. Oh God, this is my fault.

"No!" I croak as I begin to hyperventilate. I might be the reason Manda is gone, but I am not going to let the world just move forward without her.

How is it so fucking easy for Brett and Caleb to move on without her?

Why am I the only one stuck?

Why? Fuck! Why?

Time is frozen as I stare at the jagged glass still attached to the inside of the frame. Right about now, it would feel fucking amazing slicing across my skin. And fitting. So. Fucking. Fitting. The silence it would give my mind is so attractive that it makes my mouth water. But I'm sick of playing games. If I'm going to end this once and for all, I'm taking her down with me. She has no right to try to fill Manda's shoes. She can try to take Brett from me, but...she has no right to fill that frame!

I rush to Brett's closet, praying that the combination on his safe is still set to my birthday. My hands are shaky, but I somehow manage to type in all the correct numbers. With a click, the door swings open, revealing three guns. I tuck one into my purse and head to the front door.

I'm over it. I'm over Brett.

I'm over trying to ruin his life.

I'm over my life as well.

Today, this ends for me...and Jesse too.

I suddenly snap back to the present. It's been years since I've seen Brett Sharp. I saw him briefly the day Emma had the baby, but before that, the last time I laid eyes on him was while holding a gun after firing it at him. My stomach twists, and the guilt in my memories is more than enough to send me on a wild spiral downward. Tears fill my eyes and my legs become unsteady. I brace myself on Leo as the shame spreads like wildfire through my veins.

"I've got you, ángel. You're my Sarah. Nobody else," Leo begins to eerily repeat in my ear. His innate ability to say all the right things has never been more unsettling—or appreciated.

I scour for the truth in his words. I search within myself as the broken bits crumble and I mentally try to piece them together.

"What the fuck?" I hear Brett growl, but Leo's breath against my ear reels me back in from the approaching breakdown.

I focus on his warm arms, which make me feel safe and cared for—and, if I'm being honest with myself, *loved*. In some ways, Leo *only* knows the real Sarah. Then again, maybe it's Brett who knows me—the terrible woman who put him through absolute hell. If I can't distinguish the difference, how can I expect anyone else to? My hands begin to tremble and my mind races in circles between my past with Brett and my present with Leo. Seeing Brett isn't the problem at all. But remembering who I was is searing.

"You're not that person anymore," Leo whispers.

As much as I want to question how the fuck he is reading my mind, I allow his words to infiltrate my thoughts. I'm not that person anymore. At least I don't feel like I am, and Leo's words confirm it. I take a few deep breaths and finally get my emotions under control.

When I lift my head and swipe the tears from under my eyes, I give Leo a weak smile.

"Let's get out of here." He brushes my hair off my neck, dragging his finger over my skin like he always does. And just like that, Leo does far more than just center me. He anchors me to his soul in a way that solidifies that I'll never be the same without him.

"I'm okay," I mumble, pretending to be strong, all the while wishing I could crawl into a hole and sleep for a hundred years. I turn to face the rest of the group with Leo securely at my side. "Hi," I say softly, trying to keep my voice from shaking.

Brett's eyes bounce between me and Leo, curiosity and confusion covering his face.

"Hey, Sarah," Jesse responds with a sweet smile.

"We're out of here," Brett bites out, giving Caleb a nod but not bothering to acknowledge anyone else.

"Brett, wait. I can leave. You don't have to," I call out, feeling horrible that, once again, even inadvertently, I'm ruining something for him.

"Don't do me any favors, " he replies roughly.

"Hey," Leo interrupts, but I quickly silence him with a shake of the head.

"Right. Okay, then. I'm sorry, Jesse," I tell her around the lump in my throat.

For reasons known only to her, Brett's new wife has always been kind to me. I don't know her well, and she has more than enough reason to hate me. But even with all the hell I put her through, she spoke on my behalf at my sentencing and has reached out to me several times over the last few years, all of which has been behind Brett's back.

"Don't worry about it. Goodnight," she calls over her shoulder with a smile. Her eyes flash to Leo as Brett marches her out of the restaurant.

"Come on, ángel. I'll take you home." Leo strokes a hand over my back.

"No. I'm okay. Really," I answer with an Oscar-winning smile. On the inside, I'm freaking the fuck out. "I'm just going to go fix my makeup. Come on. Let's eat."

"You sure?" He eyes me warily.

"Of course," I say sweetly, securing my Golden Globe win as well.

"I already have to pee again anyway," Erica announces, bracing her swollen stomach.

"All right. Girls' trip to the bathroom two point oh," Emma says, linking her arm through mine.

Not even a half second after the bathroom door closes behind us, I sprint to the big stall and dry heave into the toilet.

"You need to ignore Brett," Emma calls out. "He can be a real asshole sometimes."

"He's not the asshole," I grumble from behind the closed door.

"No, but it's more fun to talk shit about him than it is to listen to you puke," Emma states with a laugh.

My hands are sweating, and I lean against the wall as Erica decides to join the conversation.

"I dated this guy in college who used to whisper sweet nothings in my ear like, 'You'd be really hot if you got a boob job.' Unfortunately for my apparently small breasts, it didn't work out. A few months ago, when news broke that I was with Slate, he tracked me down and asked to borrow ten thousand dollars. We all have an asshole ex."

"Brett's not a bad guy. I'm his version of the guy who asked for money." I walk out of the stall and start washing my hands.

"We still all have them. Everyone gets a turn in life at being the asshole. We're no exception," she replies, and I stare at her curiously. "Regrets will only hold you down. Own the wrongs and move on." She shrugs. "Come on. Let's get back out there. If I know Slate and Leo, they are probably arguing about something by now. You going to be okay?"

"Yeah. I think I am. Sorry you had to witness that."

"Sarah, you never have to explain yourself to me. Just keep doing what you're doing to make Leo happy and I'd be willing to forgive anything." She smiles kindly.

"Thank you," I say, returning her smile. Then I clean my face, apply lip gloss, and head back to Leo—needing to feel his touch more than ever.

"Hey, ángel." He stands from his chair as soon as I walk up.

I fold my arms around his waist and fill my lungs with as much of Leo as I can possibly hold. "I'm sorry about all that. That was—"

"The ex-husband. No biggie. Caleb filled me in."

My eyes immediately flash to Caleb, who gives his head the tiniest shake, letting me know that my secrets are still safe.

"Okay then." I slide into the booth with Leo right behind me.

The rest of the evening is spent laughing. I am quiet at first, but the atmosphere at the table is infectious. Caleb and Slate get along like old friends, and Erica is great too. It's clear why she and Leo are such good friends. She's really funny. A brief argument ensues at the table as all the guys fight over the check. Finally, it's Erica who wins. She sneaks out to go to the bathroom and pays for it behind everyone's backs.

Chapter
TWENTY-THREE

Sarah

Wednesday at five p.m.

> Leo: I can't make it tonight.
> Me: Well, you suck. ;) Want to do lunch tomorrow?
> Leo: I'll let you know.

Thursday at ten a.m.

> Me: Lunch?

Nine p.m.

> Me: Hey, where you been today? I've missed you!

Eleven p.m.

> Me: Okay, I'm starting to worry. Did you fall off the face of the Earth? This isn't

```
like you to not respond.
```

Friday at eight a.m.

```
Me: So, are you speaking to me today?
```

Friday at noon.

```
Me: I'm not really sure what to do here.
I can't decide if something is wrong or
if you're trying to brush me off. Care to
enlighten me?
```

Friday at six p.m.

```
Me: Are you kidding me with this? Together,
huh? Now, you're just going to disappear?
What a load of shit.
```

Friday at eight p.m.

IT'S BEEN three days since I last heard from Leo, and for seventy-two hours, I've been a bungee cord of emotions. Finally, tonight, I decide to just get pissed and confront him.

"Where's Leo?" I snap at Aiden as if he has any control over Leo's being a dick.

"Shit," he cusses under his breath, stepping out from the guard's desk. "He's upstairs. But you shouldn't go up there," he answers and my heart sinks.

"Is he with someone?" I whisper, my hands beginning to tremble at my sides.

"Oh God no!"

"Then why the hell can't I go up there?"

"He's…" he starts but doesn't finish.

"He's what?"

"He's just busy. That's all," he lies unconvincingly.

"Bullshit," I bite out, pulling my security card from my purse.

"Sarah, don't. He's not in good shape right now." He grabs my arm to stop me.

I pointedly look down at his hand, which he promptly releases. "What the fuck is that supposed to mean?"

"Just… Go home and I'll get him to call you."

"Aiden, don't screw around with me here. What the hell is going on?"

He shakes his head and toys with one of the gauges in his ear. "Sarah, I don't talk about his shit any more than I would talk about yours. Just know that this happens occasionally. Just give him a day or two. He'll snap out of it. He always does."

"While I appreciate your discretion, I'm going up there regardless of whether you tell me or not. So I'm going to highly encourage you to do both Leo and me favor and give me a heads-up about what the hell I'm going to find up there."

He stares at me for a minute before finally answering. "Damn it, Sarah. He's dark right now. It happens. I've tried to get him to see someone about it, but he won't listen. He doesn't do anything but mope around for a few days, so I just try to keep the business going and let him do his thing."

"Dark? Like depressed?" I ask in shock. "Leo?" I question, because we are clearly talking about two different people.

"It's not as bad as you're thinking," he answers, and I can't do anything but tilt my head in confusion.

What weird alternate universe am I in? I suffer from depression and take a little pill every single day to keep it at bay, but Leo? He might be the happiest person I have ever met. He's always smiling, and even when his jokes are bad, he never stops making them. I am fully aware that depression can affect even the loudest laugh in the room, but I never would have suspected that it was hiding behind those chocolate-brown eyes.

Without another word, I scan my card and head up the stairs. I'm not even willing to wait for the elevator. No one should be completely alone during a dark spell. Using my key, I let myself in. Quietly, I head down the hall, searching for any sign of Leo. When I reach his bedroom, I slowly swing open the door. His blackout curtains are more than doing their job. Not even the moon breaks into the room. But the hall light behind me reveals him sleeping facedown on his bed with a pillow covering his head. I take a deep breath at the sight. I've really missed him.

I toe off my shoes and crawl fully dressed into the bed next to him. He doesn't budge at first, but as I drag the pillow off his head, he lets out a low growl.

"I was worried about you," I whisper, kissing his naked shoulder.

"Sarah?" His voice is jagged and filled with sleep.

"Yeah, it's me." I lean in and kiss the lips I have been starved for. It may not bring him any comfort, but just that brief second of contact is like a drug to me. It tingles on my mouth and glides through my body, soothing me in its wake.

"I just want to be alone for a while. Can I call you tomorrow?"

"Yeah. Of course, baby. Go back to sleep," I whisper against his cheek while inhaling his scent. Then I simply roll over and pull the blanket over my body.

"Uhhh…" he says questioningly. "Alone?"

"Oh, I'm not leaving," I respond frankly. "You do whatever you need to do. I won't bother you. But if you decide you want to talk, I'll be right here."

"Sarah, I can't argue with you right now. I really need some space."

"Then roll over. It's a king-sized bed."

"Please," he begs, but the word catches in his throat.

"I know you think being alone is the solution. And I'm not saying it's not. I'll leave if you want. But you should know I'm going to be sleeping on the floor just outside the bedroom door. I've been where you are. I know it gets easier. I also know easier is an impossible notion for you to even entertain right now. I'm well aware you think wallowing by yourself is the only answer. However, tomorrow morning, I'm making you breakfast. You don't have to eat it, but I'm making it all the same. I can't fix the way you feel, not even with my famous bacon, egg, and cheese sandwich, but I can be here while you suffer. You may *want* me to leave, Leo. But as long as I'm breathing, you will never truly be alone." I almost choke on the words. They might just be the closest thing I have to tell him that could ever adequately portray my feelings. Love wouldn't even be enough right now.

"Sarah," he starts but never finishes.

"Together. You told me that a while back. So let's do this."

With a simple nod, he scoots over to the far side of the bed and rolls away from me. It may seem like a dismissal, but it's a victory in my book.

Leo

Saturday...

"HEY, CAN I buy something on your Kindle?" Sarah asks from the other side of the couch.

"Have at it," I answer, uninterested.

"It might be construed as porn."

My eyes snap to hers and I blink twice. Her only response is a shrug.

"Sure," I respond then go back to staring at the ceiling.

"AS YOUR woman, can I ask Johnson to run errands for me?" Sarah asks randomly.

I lift my head from the dining room table and give her a questioning look.

"Just a small one, and it's not like 'go fetch me lunch' or something."

"Then, by all means, go for it," I answer dryly.

Sarah smiles wide and I look away.

"YOU WANT something to eat?" Sarah asks.

"No," I answer shortly.

Sunday...

"I SENT Johnson to buy it for us." Sarah smiles proudly, popping in a DVD. *Breakin' 2: Electric Boogaloo.*

"What in the fucking hell is that?" I ask with a curled lip.

"Ohhhh, Leo. You are seriously missing out. From the self-proclaimed master of terrible eighties movies, I'm actually disappointed in you right now. This might possibly be the worst eighties movie ever to be made," she laughs.

I stretch a leg down the couch to tangle with hers.

Monday...

"I'M STARVING," I inform Sarah.

"You want me to cook you something?" She puts the Kindle down on the nightstand and rolls to face me.

"Chinese?" I suggest.

"I'll order delivery. Sesame chicken?"

"That works," I answer absently.

"YOU DIDN'T eat much," Sarah whispers from across the bed. "You want me to get you something else?"

"Nah. That new place wasn't very good."

"That's the same place we always order from." She offers me a small smile.

I reach out and grab her hand, entwining our fingers. "Really? It tasted different."

Tuesday...

"YOU'RE OUT of man shampoo," Sarah says, pouring some of the shampoo she keeps at my house into her hand.

"I've been too busy to shop," I respond as she reaches up with both hands, scrubbing my hair into a lather.

"It's okay. Mine smells better anyway."

"WHEN I first met you, I remember thinking how gorgeous your eyelashes were. They are seriously wasted on a man. I'd kill to have them," Sarah says while lying in bed, tracing a finger across my eyebrows.

I don't even bother responding. I simply snake out an arm and pull her against my chest.

I WAKE up with my cock throbbing and my hips moving of their own volition against Sarah's ass. I'm desperate to get inside her. She's still sound asleep, spooned in front of me. Her hair is in a ponytail, but the ends tickle my nose as I greedily breathe her in. Sarah's beautiful, and that's not a superficial observation. On every level, both inside and out, she's...well, *it*.

Sarah hasn't left my side in...fuck. I have no idea how long it's been. The numbers on the calendar have most definitely changed, but if it's been a week or a day, I couldn't even venture a guess. All I know is that Sarah was there. Every minute of the day, and especially in the minutes when I needed her the most, which coincidentally were also the minutes when I've never wanted her less.

She begins to stir, so I know I must have woken her. She pushes her panty-covered ass back against my erection and we both moan. Desperate to feel her, I roll her to her stomach and drag her panties down her legs. She pulls her shirt over her head as I rise to my knees behind her, looping an arm under her stomach to tilt her ass into the air.

"Still just as beautiful as the first night you did this for me." I push a finger inside her tight pussy only to find her not nearly wet enough to slam inside her the way I'd like to. I guess I haven't exactly been the sexiest company the last few days. "You know what else I wanted to do that night?" I slide a hand up her back, giving her ponytail a slight tug.

"What?" she gasps.

"Back up." I step off the bed and lead her down until her feet are on the edge. I drop to my knees and roughly seal my mouth over her pussy.

"Ahhh, fuck, Leo," she cusses, pushing harder against my mouth.

I dart my tongue inside her while gripping both her ass cheeks in my palms. I begin the circles I've learned Sarah loves so much over her clit, and within seconds, an orgasm quakes through her body. I press a finger inside to find her more than primed for me now. She's barely coming down as I drag my tongue up and over the puckered flesh of her ass.

"Oh God!" she cries out as I smile to myself. Chills spread over her body as she pulses around my finger, which is still moving inside her.

I position myself behind her and trail kisses up her spine. "We'll talk about that 'oh God' later."

I suddenly stand all the way up and bury myself inside her with one quick thrust. She lets out a blessed curse, but nothing escapes my throat. It's not surprising. I'm not sure anything could pass the huge lump of emotions I'm desperately trying to keep under wraps. I've barely even begun pumping inside her when I reach a hand down between her legs. The moment I touch her clit, she comes hard on my cock. I begin a chaotic rhythm, wanting nothing more than to join her, but with every thrust, something else escapes me.

"You didn't leave." I slam inside her.

"Never," she moans.

"I just wanted to be alone." I fold over her, finding her breast and rolling a nipple between my fingers.

"I just wanted to be with you." She presses her hips against me.

"Promise me you'll always stay. No matter what," I plead as I speed up my pace inside her.

"There's nowhere else I'd rather be."

With her words lingering on my heart and conscience, an orgasm builds to an all-time high before tearing through my body.

"Fuck, that was a lot faster than I planned," I pant while trying to catch my breath. "But thankfully, you were faster."

"It's been a week, and I'm not allowed to get myself off, remember?" She reaches back and scratches the back of my head.

I silently pull out and collapse onto the bed. She follows suit and crashes on top of me, snuggling in tight.

"Mmm. Morning sex is quickly becoming my favorite," she mumbles.

"So I think we should talk about that 'oh God' now."

She laughs before nuzzling her face against my beard. "You need to trim that. It's getting soft. I miss the stubble."

When I chuckle, she stills in my arms. She peeks up with a small smile.

"Welcome back."

They are two simple words, but they hit me harder than thirty-three years of vowels and consonants combined. I have absolutely no way to stop the words before they tumble from my mouth.

I gently cup her face in my hands and bring my lips to hers. "I love you."

Her eyes go wide, but she doesn't immediately respond. "Stop," she whispers as the tears pool in her eyes. "You don't owe me that."

"No, I do owe you something, but that's not it. I'm telling you because it physically aches to try to keep it in any longer. I love you, Sarah."

"Leo, please don't. You don't know all of me, and I want to be able to say it back, but I need to tell you some things first." She nervously sits up and pats around the bed until she finds her T-shirt.

"See, this is the other part that physically hurts to contain." I run a hand though my hair and let out a loud sigh. "I know about your past."

"What?" she questions, clearly confused.

"I know about the wreck, your head injury, Brett, your suicide attempts, and the reason for your stay at Building Foundations," I rush out as she throws a hand up to cover her mouth. "I know about it all, but I don't care. I love you anyway," I finish, and she stumbles.

I snag a pair of shorts off the floor and pull them on. She backs away as I round the bed, but I don't stop advancing. Cornering her against the closet door, I gently brush the hair off her neck and whisper in her ear.

"I don't care, ángel. You aren't that woman anymore. So please believe me when I say I am absolutely and unquestionably in love with *you*."

When her shoulders relax, hope springs to my chest.

Until she explodes.

"Oh my God!" She pushes me, catching me off guard and causing me to rock back a step. "Oh my God. That's how you do it. You… You…" she stutters and begins snatching up her clothes off the floor. "You don't say the right things to calm me. Fuck, you manipulate my past to make them the right things! It's all lies!"

"Sarah. I'm not lying about anything."

"I have to get out of here."

"You're overreacting. Listen to me. I'm not perfect either," I call after her as she rushes from the room.

She begins shoving her clothes in her oversized purse. "How long have you known? Did you already know on my birthday when I went through Manda's box?"

I nod and she chokes out a sob.

"Of course you did. You know you could have told me then. If there had ever been a fucking moment to tell me that you knew my life story, that would have been it. Before I shared one of the most special moments of my life with a fucking liar."

"I was worried you were going to react like…well, like this. I wasn't ready to lose you." I toss my arms out to my sides in frustration.

"And what about now? You ready now?" she asks, snatching her keys off the table.

I step in front of the door to prevent from her leaving. "No! I'm not ready. And truth be told, I don't think you're ready either."

"Fuck you, Leo. You can stop pretending you know what I need."

"So what exactly are you mad about? The fact that I knew or the fact that I didn't tell you."

"All of the above!" she shrieks, stopping in front of me.

"Please just talk to me. You aren't being rational here."

"Bullshit. This might just be the most rational I've been since I fell under your spell." She pushes past me and storms down the stairs.

"Can I please have a goddamn minute to explain?"

"Sure. Build a time machine, because I've given you all the minutes you're ever going to get from me."

She swings open the garage door and Johnson steps out of the guard station.

"Everything okay?" he asks.

Sarah starts to breeze past him but freezes just a few steps away. With a humorless laugh, she spins to face him and levels him with a glare.

"You son of a bitch. That was confidential! You had no right to tell him!" she yells.

Johnson shakes his head and turns to me. "I'm not getting involved in this. I highly suggest you start fucking explaining things to her."

"He didn't—" I start, but I'm immediately interrupted.

"You know what? I'm done. Fuck you both. Aiden, you're an asshole. I never would have told him you were gay. Oops. I guess it just slipped." She spins on a heel and walks to her car.

She doesn't spare another word for me. I watch helplessly as she drives from the garage. I want to chase her down the street, force her to listen to me, but I have a feeling none of that would help my case. I can't fight with her until she cools off and is ready to listen. I'll give her some time. I don't believe for one second that Sarah's really done, but more than that, *I'm* not done. She just needs to organize her thoughts. It's going to hurt like a motherfucker to sit back and let her figure this out. She doesn't even have all the facts. But if it ultimately ends with her in my arms, I'm more than willing to endure.

"Well, that went well," I say to Johnson, who is suddenly enthralled with the cracks on the concrete.

"Yeah. Awesome," he growls.

"Hey. You want me to go back to pretending I don't know or you want to bring Chris out to dinner when I iron this shit out with Sarah?" I ask and his head snaps to mine. "You might want to be more discreet on the work cell." I smirk uncomfortably and his eyes grow wide. "Oh, don't give me that look. I learned a long time ago not to look at the pictures you guys exchange."

He closes his eyes, but a tiny smile tilts his lips. He doesn't utter a word as he walks back into the guard station.

I head back up to my apartment and snatch my phone off the nightstand. When I turn it on for the first time in a week, messages from Sarah, Erica, and some clients flood my screen. I clear them all and type out a text.

Me: You don't have to believe me, but that doesn't change the way I feel. I love you. Take all the time you need. I'm ready to explain whenever you're ready to listen.

Chapter
TWENTY-FOUR

Sarah

Two days later...

"UM, WHY the hell are you not at work?" Emma questions when she walks into my apartment.

"I took the day off," I respond mindlessly while flipping through the TV channels.

"She got fired," Casey pipes up from beside me.

"You what?" Emma shouts.

"She called in sick on Monday and Tuesday, then no-showed on Wednesday. I stopped by today to see if she wanted to go to lunch only to be informed that Sarah Erickson was no longer employed by the Tribune." Casey smiles and I flip her off.

"You done tattling?" I ask before resuming my hunt for a nonexistent TV show.

"Why didn't you call me? What's going on? You not feeling well?" Emma rushes out a barrage of questions that makes me roll my eyes.

"Because I didn't want to deal with this." I motion between the two of them.

"Leo out of town?" Emma asks, sitting down in the chair next to the couch.

"Don't know. Don't care," I drone emotionlessly as my stomach knots and my chest aches.

"Ah. So you're that kind of sick. Y'all have a fight?"

"No. We broke up," I answer shortly, hoping to close the conversation just as quickly as it opened.

"All right. Spill it," Emma says, propping her feet on the table.

"Yeah, not happening." I stand and head to my small kitchen, which overlooks the living room.

"I thought things were going really well," Casey tells my back.

"They were. Now they're not."

They have to stop talking about Leo before the anxiety creeping up has a chance to turn into a full-blown panic attack. It won't be the first one I've had since I left Leo. I barely even made it a block from his apartment before I had to pull over and catch my breath.

Losing Leo hurts far more than I thought possible. I miss him so much. This is such a sucky situation because I want nothing more than to turn to Leo right now. I know he'd be able to make me relax. It was also a false sense of comfort, but I'd give anything to feel again.

"All right. I'm headed to Leo's to get some answers." Emma jumps to her feet and walks to the door.

"No, you are fucking not." I rush after her. Just as she grabs the handle of the door, I snag her arm. "Don't. It's not a big deal. We just broke up. It was nothing scandalous or dramatic," I lie. "It just didn't work out."

"So if it's that simple, why are you calling in sick and getting fired from your job? That doesn't sound like 'no big deal' to me." She slings a pair of air quotes my way. "It sounds like you're hurting."

I try to give her a bitchy smile, but my chin begins to quiver, giving away my impending breakdown. "I, um…" I stutter as my hands start to shake and tears spill from my eyes. I don't even know why I'm crying except that she's right. I'm hurting so fucking bad.

"Okay. Casey, go get sushi. Spare no expense. Stop and grab an overnight bag too. It's a girls' night," Emma announces, wrapping me into a hug that does nothing to calm me down. "You want wine or chocolate tonight?" She leans away, catching my eye.

"Chocolate," I answer, trying to fight a losing battle with my emotions.

"I'll be right back." Casey gives my shoulder a squeeze and darts out the door.

"Go get in some ugly-ass pajamas. And lend me some sexy ones." She walks to the kitchen and calls over her shoulder, "I'm not even kidding. I don't care if you did just get broken up with. I'm not hanging out with you tonight if you wear one of those tank tops that makes your boobs look better than mine."

I let out a strangled laugh, and just like that, the floodgates open. "I think I love him," I admit out loud for the first time.

"Jesus, Sarah. What happened?"

"He's a liar, and I hate him, because even though I know that, I can't stop thinking about him or stop wishing he were here."

"Did you open up about your past?" she guesses, grabbing the ice cream from the freezer and two spoons from the drawer.

"I didn't have to. He knows everything. His best friend was at Foundations with me. He filled Leo in on all my bullshit. The wreck, my suicide attempts, trying to shoot Brett. Everything."

"Fuck," Emma breathes. "I'm assuming that didn't go over well?"

"He told me he loves me anyway," I barely even whisper, unable to trust my voice with the ludicrous words—yet another one of Leo's lies.

"Wait. What?" she asks, putting the ice cream down on the counter. "So he knows everything and he told you he loves you anyway? Please tell me I'm missing a part of this equation."

"He's known for a while. At least since my birthday. He's lied to me so many times that I can't even begin to recount them all."

"Lied how?"

"He does this thing where he always knows exactly what to say when I get nervous or stressed out. I thought that's just who he was, but come to find out, he just knew enough about me to know what I *needed*. The man I was falling in love with wasn't Leo at all. I don't have a clue who he really is." I wipe the tears from my eyes and take a quick breath to get myself back in check.

"Okay…let me try to get this straight one last time. You have somewhat of a troubled past, you meet a hot man, and you *do not* disclose aforementioned past. Then you fall in love with said hot man because he makes you feel safe and comfortable, only to find out that he already knows the shit—that you never told him but should have—and he used it to his advantage to make you feel…well, safe and comfortable all the while falling in love with you. And now that you know this information, you have decided that he's a liar for not being a dick and heading for the hills?"

"That is not at all what I said, so stop twisting it," I snap, crossing my arms over my chest.

"Maybe I'm not the one twisting it, Sarah."

"I feel like everyone knew the full story except for me. Leo didn't get to know *me*. He heard stories about who I used to be and used it to his advantage. It's embarrassing, Emma. I should've been the one to tell him those things about myself."

"Okay, now *that* I understand. Embarrassed is one thing. Breaking up with a man you are obviously in love with is something altogether different."

"You don't get it, Emma. What if Leo had never done all of those things that made me fall in love with him? How would I feel about him? Hell, what if he just told me he loved me because he thought I needed to hear it. I don't know this new guy at all any more than he knows new Sarah. And it hurts because, even if we get back together, I'm not sure that I'll ever feel for this new guy like I did my old Leo."

"Jesus, listen to yourself. New Sarah. Old Sarah. New Leo. Old Leo. I honestly can't keep up. I'm sorry, sis, but you've worn out that phrase. You are still the same Sarah from before the accident and Leo is still the same man you came home raving about after your first date. People change and evolve every single day. It's not exactly a novel concept that people act differently when they first start dating than they do later in relationships.

"So he knew some stuff about you. It sucks. And yes, he should have told you. But I don't think that makes him a liar any more than your not telling him makes *you* a liar."

"I guess we will just have to agree to disagree," I huff and head toward the bedroom.

I can't just let this go. I get what Emma's saying and I hear her rational words. It's just that I've spent so much of the last few years feeling like an outsider even in my own skin. I can't go back to that. I need some sort of control in my life. Maybe I handed Leo too much of that control over me. That could be why this hurts so much. Leo didn't just betray me; I betrayed myself.

I walk into the bedroom, and instead of digging through my drawers to find pajamas, I crawl into bed. I don't want to think about Leo anymore. But when I close my eyes, all I can think about is the deep hum of his chuckle before everything fell apart. If Leo ever does manage to build that time machine, the first thing I'm doing is stealing it and going back to those two seconds in time when everything *felt* perfect. I'd happily relive that moment for all of eternity.

An hour or so later, Emma wakes me up by throwing a T-shirt at my head. Ultimately, she ended up in tight yoga pants and one of my low-cut tank tops, which does, in fact, make her boobs look fantastic. And because I appreciate her leaving Collin and Caleb at home just to spend the night with me, I don't even argue when I pull on the stained sweats she laid out for me.

"Casey, where's Eli tonight?" I ask while grabbing the last piece of sushi.

"Hell if I know. We haven't spoken in a few weeks."

"Oh dear Lord." I roll my eyes and she lets out a small giggle. "You better be amazing in bed because you give that man hell and he always comes back."

"He's a dick, but yes, I am amazing in bed."

We all laugh.

"Oh, hey. I read those Fifty Shades books y'all were talking about the other day. I thought I was fucked up. Christian is crazy." I laugh but neither of them utters a word. I turn to look at Emma and she's blinking rapidly at me. "What?" I ask, looking at Casey, who looks equally as shocked.

"You read?" Emma asks.

"All three books?" Casey clarifies behind her.

"Yes," I answer suspiciously.

"I thought that was, like, against your religion or something?" Emma says seriously, but a smile grows on her face.

"Oh, shut up. I used to read all the time."

"Used to." Casey emphasizes. "You haven't read anything since the wreck."

"Oh stop. It's no big deal. Leo wasn't feeling well over the weekend, so we just laid around. I didn't want the TV to bother him and his Kindle was on the nightstand, so I decided to read instead of dying of boredom."

"I'm not sure which part of that sentence is weirdest. The fact that you willingly chose to read an actual book or that Leo has a Kindle." Emma laughs.

"He's a big nerd, actually. I tried to read one of his books, and dear God, they were boring. They were all classic literature or, like, books on great wars in history."

"Oh jeez. That sounds torturous. So how'd you like Fifty?"

"It was good. Although I'd punch a man in the face if he ever tried to spank me. But it was hot reading about it," I respond and they both bust out laughing.

The rest of the night is spent on the couch with Emma and Casey. Thankfully, no one brings up Leo again. No questions, no arguments. Nothing. Just sushi, chocolate, and terrible reality TV.

Chapter
TWENTY-FIVE

Leo

SPACE.

I told myself I'd give Sarah time to clear her head and think things through without emotions dictating her reaction. But for fuck's sake, it's been three days now. I really thought she'd come over the next morning after she'd had a chance to cool off. But she hasn't so much as even sent me a text.

I've tried to throw myself into work, but no matter how many hours I spend approving timecards, nothing seems to take my mind off Sarah. I have no fucking idea how to make this right. In a few days, she'll come around.

She has to.

The intercom on my desk buzzes, snapping me out of my thoughts. "What's up?" I call through the speaker.

"Yo. Leo, you got a visitor," Johnson responds from downstairs.

Thankfully, he's been here a lot the last few days, because I've been worthless since Sarah left. Due to her parting words about his sexuality, things were awkward at first. But not another word has been spoken about it, and things have *basically* gone back to normal between us.

"Shit," I cuss. Flipping through my calendar, I try to figure out what appointment I've forgotten about only to find today blank. "I'm not expecting anyone. Who is it?"

"Brett Sharp," he announces.

What the fucking hell is Brett Sharp doing here?

I quickly run through a few scenarios until my pulse suddenly begins to race. Oh God. What if something happened to Sarah? Could she have possibly tried to kill herself again? He's a cop. Did he draw the short straw and is here to notify me that something happened?

"Let him up!" I call out and rush to open the front door.

As I wait for the elevator to arrive on my floor, I try to calm myself by taking a rational step back. There is no way Brett would have been the one chosen to inform me. Emma or Caleb would have called. Shit. Do they even have my number? I should really call Emma and have her check up on Sarah. When Brett walks off the elevator, I'm still lost in my worries.

"Is she okay?" I bite out, praying that he doesn't have an answer.

"Who? Sarah?" he asks, notably confused and my shoulders fall in relief.

"Hey, can you give me Caleb's number real fast. I need to ask him something."

He narrows his eyes but rattles off a few numbers.

"You got Emma's too?" I ask while adding the contact to my cell phone.

"What's going on? Something happen?" he asks curiously before sliding a Magnolia Photography card from his wallet with Emma's number on it.

"Just give me a minute," I say, typing out a text to Caleb.

Me: Hey, it's Leo. Has Emma seen Sarah the last few days?

I begin to type out a message to Emma when my phone pings back.

Caleb: She's okay. Emma spent the night at her place last night. You want to grab a beer tonight and talk about this shit?

Me: Probably not, but I'll let you know. Thanks.

I rush out a relieved breath. What the fuck is wrong with me? Why is this the first time I bothered to think about how Sarah is doing? I've been so lost in all the ways I could think of to try to fix this and get her back that didn't even think about how this was affecting *her.* Maybe she's better off without me. I'm such a fucking mess. I can't even—

"Everything okay?" Brett asks, reminding me that he's in the room.

"Yeah. Fine. Thanks for the numbers."

"No problem," he responds, awkwardly shoving his hands in his pockets.

"So what can I do for you?"

"Look, I'm sorry about just stopping by tonight. I've spent over a week talking myself out of coming over here, but I truly feel like this is something I have to do."

"Oh yeah? What's that?" I question with a little more attitude than I originally intended.

"Sarah. She's not…right," he says, which causes me to bark out a laugh.

"Really?" I ask in a tone dripping with sarcasm.

"You don't know who she is, and I don't know what she's told you, but I feel like I need to maybe fill in the gaps."

"Get out," I growl while walking past him toward the door.

"Just hear me out. There's some shit you need to know."

"I don't need to know any of your shit. Because that is exactly what it would be—shit."

"How long have you two been seeing each other?" he asks, turning to face me but not budging even after I open the door.

"I'm not even remotely interested in listening to anything you have to say about Sarah. Especially when you start a conversation about the woman I love with bullshit about her not being 'right.'"

"Fuck," he breathes and runs a hand through his hair. "I didn't mean it like that."

"She's your ex-wife. There's a reason for that," I remind him just to be a dick.

"No, she's not. I was never married to the woman you're in love with."

"Even better. Then this conversation really is moot. I have work to do, so I'm going to need you to leave now."

"Did Sarah tell you what happened that night at Jesse's apartment?"

"Oh for fuck's sake. What is it with you people needing to warn me about shit? Yes. I know all about Sarah's past. I don't give a shit. She's not perfect. Yeah, yeah. I get it." My frustration is palpable. I slam the door closed because Brett obviously isn't planning to leave until he says his piece.

"Well, there are some facts you should know."

"Well, there's a fact you should know as well. I don't give a fuck about your facts!" I roar, but it doesn't seem to faze him.

"Her favorite color is blue. Not just any old generic blue. She's very specific," he rushes out oddly.

"Baby blue," I finish for him.

"For Sarah's twenty-fifth birthday, I ordered her a custom Walther P22 with a baby-blue grip. It was ridiculous and I paid a fortune for it. She was never big on guns, so she was pissed when I bought her one. She didn't speak to me for a week. But I was a rookie back then and worked a lot of nights while trying to work my way up to detective. I saw all the crime that happened while on patrol, and it killed me that she was always alone. I just wanted to know she was safe. So I ordered this gun, started taking her to the range, and taught her how to shoot. She was hesitant at first, until I made it a competition on who could hit the most targets. You know Sarah—she's so fucking competitive." He pauses to quietly laugh.

I nod in agreement. That is one thing I definitely know about Sarah, and even though Brett is standing right in front of me, I can't help but smile as my mind drifts back to that first night when she dropped her dress in my kitchen.

"Anyway, she got good—like, really good. We spent at least one night a week at the range for years." He smiles and it annoys me.

As ridiculous as it sounds, I'm fucking jealous of his time spent with Sarah. I should have been the one to spend seven years with her. Not fucking months. But I guess Brett should understand how I'm feeling. He somehow survived losing her. Maybe I could learn a thing or two from him.

Or I could continue to be a jealous dick.
"Is this going somewhere?"

"I'm getting there. So, that night, at Jesse's apartment… Sarah pulled the trigger only inches away from me, yet she somehow managed to miss. Sure, she may have been a bit rusty after four years, but a toddler could have hit me at that range."

"Wait. You don't think she tried to shoot you?"

"Nope. Now listen, the only reason I'm telling you this is because I want you to understand I don't hate Sarah. I just personally can't deal with her. Every time I see her or think about her, I turn into a brand of asshole that would give Caleb a run for his money. I remember the way it felt when I thought she had hurt Jesse. I'll never be able to get over that. But I'm not here to fill your head with a bunch of bullshit about what a terrible person she is. Sarah's just broken."

"Was," I quickly correct him. "She *was* broken. She's not anymore."

"Right. Well, then, what was all that shit when I first got here then? You planning a party and just happened to need Emma's and Caleb's number?"

"No. I fucked up. Not Sarah," I snap. "But that's—"

"None of my business." He waves me off. "Look, I saw Sarah with you last week at the restaurant. The way you kept her together… I have no idea what the hell you said to her, but it was the most amazing thing I've ever seen. After the wreck, I wasn't able to do that for her. I've never seen anyone affect Sarah like that, actually."

"The truth. I told her the truth. Sarah doesn't believe it herself, but up until a few days ago, she believed me." I drop my head and pinch the bridge of my nose.

"You cheat on her?" he asks.

My eyes fly up to his. Not that it's any of his fucking business, but I feel compelled to answer anyway.

"Jesus Christ, no."

"Meh. Nothing that can't be fixed then." He shrugs.

"Yeah? How'd that work out for you and Sarah? You didn't cheat, right?" I smart back.

He crosses his arms over his chest. "I was never supposed to be with Sarah after that accident. I tried really fucking hard though, and that was ultimately my own demise. I may not know Sarah now, but I sure as hell know how to alienate her."

I laugh humorlessly. "I think I've got that covered. Thanks for stopping by."

"I'm here because I wanted to reach out and tell you all the ways I fucked up so you don't make the same mistakes. It's been seven years since that wreck, and we've all gotten better. Well, everyone but Sarah. She's been stuck in this holding pattern, yet it appears you made her better...even for just a minute.

"You have to understand, Sarah was always high strung. She was wild—always the first to be dancing on the bar or fluttering around socially. It was hard for me when she changed. I tried so hard to make her the woman I remembered. And you know what it did? It drove her away."

"Gosh, as enlightening as this has been, I didn't know Sarah before any of this, so I'm not trying to make her anyone she isn't."

"No, you're missing what I'm saying. *I tried.* There was nothing natural about it. Whatever the hell you did in that restaurant wasn't forced and *she responded to it.*"

"Yeah, well, things have changed since then." I grab the back of my neck and let out a loud exhale.

"Well, fix it," he says simply. "Leo, there's an invisible chain that has bound the six of us together since the wreck. When I met Jesse, it severed a link. Emma snapped one and then Eli's betrayal shattered another. However, there's one left. And I need *you* to break it. Sarah deserves a happy ending too, and I'm going to need *you* to give that to her."

"No pressure, right?" I laugh then swallow hard. *Fuck, I want to give that to her too.*

"No one's been able to touch Sarah in seven years. Don't fuck this up. I spent a third of my life with Sarah Erickson, and when she loves, she loves harder than anything you have ever experienced. However, your problem is going to be making her remember that."

"Damn it, I'm trying!" I yell, causing Brett to shake his head.

He walks to the door and pauses just before he passes me. "Then stop. I'm assuming you weren't trying before. Don't fucking start now." And without another glance, he walks out my door, ending the weirdest virtually one-sided conversation I have ever experienced in my life.

Just as the door clicks, I snatch up my phone and call Johnson. He's only downstairs, but I need to talk to someone—preferably someone who hasn't slept with Sarah.

"Yo."

"Would you leave her alone?"

"Erica?"

"No, asshole. Sarah. Tell me I'm wrong for giving her space."

"Would you be doubting it if Sharp hadn't just been up there?"

"Probably," I answer honestly.

"Then yeah, you're probably doing the wrong thing."

I let out a long string of expletives and snatch my keys off the table next to the door. "Does Slate need you this week?"

"Nope. They are laying low until Erica has the baby."

"I'll be gone for a few days. I just finished payroll, so things should be smooth."

"I won't let it explode, I swear." He laughs and I can hear it as I step off the elevator. He meets me as I walk to the car.

"Will you close down the house? I'm sure I left every light on."

"No problem. Hey, can I say something without you being a prick?"

"Right now? Probably not," I snark.

"Oh well. I guess I'll take that chance. Leo, I can almost guarantee she's overthinking all of this. All her gears are probably spinning, but none in the right direction. If you want any type of future with Sarah, this is the time to lay it all out there."

"I know," I answer curtly.

"No. I mean *all of it*," he reiterates.

Chapter
TWENTY-SIX

Leo

"OH MY God!" I hear Sarah scream, causing me to jump to my feet.

"Jesus Christ. Shhh."

"What the fuck are you doing here? You scared me to death."

"Change of plans. You parked your ass at my apartment for days while I worked through my shit. I'm here to do the same."

"Leo, it's two a.m. Go home," she says calmly.

"Nah. I'm good, thanks. We don't spend nearly enough time here. Your couch is actually really comfortable." I recline back down, propping my feet on the coffee table.

"You have lost your fucking mind. Get out," she demands with attitude creeping into her voice.

"You got anything to eat?" I ask, and for a brief second, I think her eyes might pop out of her head.

"Are you kidding me here? What the hell is wrong with you? Get. Out," she snaps right alongside her temper.

She's beautiful when she's pissed. And also a tad bit scary. I decide to stick with being a smartass. She'll have to laugh eventually. *Hopefully.*

"Jesus, calm down. I didn't eat dinner. It's not the end of the world."

"I'm not doing this with you. Get the fuck out of my apartment or I swear to God…" Her chest begins to heave.

"I'm not going home. I miss you."

"Well, I don't miss you. Now, leave," she bites out.

Even though I'm relatively sure she's lying, it still feels like a punch to the stomach. But I refuse to back down. I have my mind set on making this right, and I can be stubborn as hell when I need to be.

"Look who's lying now." I smirk and can almost see her fuse disappear.

"Get the fuck out of my house." She races forward, grabs my keys and phone off the coffee table, and heads for the door.

"Hey, what are you doing?"

"Goddamn it, Leo. Leave me alone."

"I'm not here to bother you, ángel," I reply with a sweet smile.

The vein on her neck begins to show, and I have a sudden and irrational urge to lick it. However, I have a stronger desire to keep my nuts intact.

"Get out!" she shrieks, throwing my keys and phone into the breezeway.

"Hey! That was a new phone." I rush out the door after it.

She slams the door behind me and I hear the deadbolt click as I pick up my belongings. I count to thirty before using my key to let myself back in.

I walk in and find Sarah leaning over her kitchen sink, crying. It all but breaks me. But I'm not willing to show her that.

"We need to get you a chain or something for this door."

She stares at me for a minute and I swear I see something flash through her eyes. Humor, maybe?

"You're hurting me," she cries. *Nope, definitely not humor.* "Just you being here physically hurts."

"I'm not trying to hurt you, Sarah. But you should know it's excruciating for me to stay away."

Her shoulders fall and she drops her chin to her chest as tears once again begin to flow from her eyes. "I hate you so much," she chokes out.

"Well, I love you enough to supersede that," I respond more honestly than I have ever been in my life.

"No, you don't. If you loved me, you wouldn't have played me for the last two months. Lying and filling my head with bullshit at every turn."

"I omitted. I never lied to you, ángel. Well, maybe once. I hated *Vanilla Sky*." I grin. It's lost even on me why I'm making jokes right now, but I can't seem to stop. If I can just lighten the mood, maybe she will come around. And I desperately need her to come around right now.

"Is this a fucking joke to you? Are you getting off on watching me fall apart? You enjoying the show, Leo?" She grabs the plate on the counter and hurls it across the room, shattering it against the wall. "There! Is that better for you? Is this what you wanted all along—a front-row seat to see Crazy Sarah Erickson firsthand? Well, here she is!" She moves to the cabinet and pulls out another plate, which quickly joins its mate broken on the floor.

"You're not crazy, Sarah. You're mad. I get it. I really fucking do. I'm sorry I wasn't more up-front with you. But—"

"But what? Waiting for me to lose it was more entertaining?" She throws another plate at the wall and finally...*fucking finally*, I lose it too.

"You want crazy, Sarah?" I walk to the kitchen to join her, grabbing a mug from the open cabinets. "I've found coffee cups to be more gratifying." I throw it as hard as I can against the wall. "You are not the only person in the fucking world who has issues. If you want to talk crazy, let me tell you a little fucking story."

I grab another coffee cup and send it flying. "I know Erica because, while I was working undercover for the DEA, I stood outside her door and allowed over eight men to rape her."

Sarah stumbles back a step, her look of horror matching the way I feel inside. I snatch up another cup and throw it.

"I was so riddled with guilt that I couldn't breathe at night. I became obsessed with making it up to her, even despite the fact that it was in her best interest to remove myself from the situation. She was scared of *everything* back then, and in some sick way, I loved it because it gave me a purpose and silenced her screams that were constantly ringing in my ears."

Sarah throws her hand to cover her mouth.

"Yeah. Crazy, right?"

The last two coffee cups go flying across the room.

"Oh, but wait. I'm just getting to the good part. When she and Slate got married, I was devastated. I was never in love with Erica, but I *needed* her. We spent three years in the Witness Protection Program together. And the moment she moved in with Slate, all the shit I had done came storming back into my head. It was too much. I decided to kill myself—the day before her wedding."

Sarah's eyebrows pop up.

"One hell of a way to say sorry, huh? But I was too fucked up to even realize it."

Tears stream down her face. My heart is racing, but the dam has been opened. I can't stop now. I move to her bowls, slinging one over my shoulder into the pile of broken dishes on the floor.

"Slate found me before I had the opportunity to follow through with my plan. Johnson drove me straight to Building Foundations and forced me inside. It just so happens that it was the day you gave your goodbye speech. You remember that one, right? When you bared your soul to a room full of strangers just to give them hope. You don't know this, but there's a reason why I call you ángel. Sarah, your words saved my life."

"Oh my God," she breathes.

"That's it. That's all I've got." I shrug and throw one last plate at the wall. "Oh, wait. And I love you. I love you despite it all, and now, I'm standing here, begging you to love me despite it all too." I run my hands through my hair and wait for her to respond.

However, she doesn't move a muscle. Her eyes stay glued to me, but I'm not completely sure she's even breathing. It becomes unnerving.

"Please say something," I whisper.

Her silence wounds me deeper than her words ever could.

Chapter
TWENTY-SEVEN

Sarah

"I SHOULDN'T have come here," Leo mumbles as he turns to walk away.

How the hell am I supposed to respond to something like that? So much of what he said doesn't even make sense. He allowed men to rape Erica? No way. He and Erica are close. There has to be more to that story, and as much as I want to run to avoid any further discussion, I need the answers more.

"Leo, wait. Just give me a minute. That was a lot for me to process. I'm going to need you to explain a little more about the part where you allowed Erica to be raped," I call out, and he blows out a relieved breath.

"Anything." He takes step toward me, but I immediately back away. I can't let Leo touch me—not until I get some answers.

"So start talking," I urge.

"Yeah, so, about five years ago, I was hand-chosen for an undercover position in the DEA. The dark complexion and Spanish really came in handy. For ten months, I worked as the right-hand man to one of the biggest drug dealers in Miami. One night, everything got shot to shit. Literally. My boss flipped on his family and merged with another crime family—one that did not trust me. I didn't know Erica before that night. She was just an innocent witness in all of it. They kidnapped her and I was tasked to kill her."

"Holy shit," I cuss. Leo is either telling the truth or he's a hard-core pathological liar. This isn't your everyday type of drama. However, the anguish on his face makes it easy to believe him.

"I never would have let that happen to her," he rushes out to clarify. "Under new leadership, my weapon was taken from me. I knew if I didn't play along, they would kill me—and ultimately Erica too if I wasn't there to protect her. When it was my turn"—he pauses and nods, not willing to say the words—"I convinced them that she might fight back, so they momentarily returned my gun. I ended up killing three men and wounding another to get the two of us out of there."

"Oh my God!" I throw my hands over my face as my heart dips in my chest.

"Sarah, listen to me. I don't feel a single ounce of remorse for killing them. They were bad fucking men. They deserved far worse than just death. There are a lot of things I have done wrong, but that is *not* one of them."

I take in a deep breath and try to picture Leo as a cop, defending an innocent woman. And as a vision of him swooping in and saving the day flashes behind my eyes, I begin to relax. It's easy to imagine Leo doing that. Truth be told, Leo always makes things right.

"Leo, that's a far cry from 'allowing Erica to be raped.'"

"I was there. I could have stopped it. End of story."

I nod knowing there is no talking him out of feeling that way. It would be wrong of me to even try. Telling people that they shouldn't feel guilty about something is useless. It's showing them that they aren't defined by those actions that usually gets them to come around. At least that's the way it worked for me.

"So you heard me speak that day. It triggered something for you. Then what?"

"Erica and Slate dragged me to a doctor. They tried to put me on anti-depressants, but I refused and agreed to start seeing someone several times a week and going to group therapy with Johnson."

"Were you seeking me out after that?"

"Absolutely not. It was pure coincidence when we ran into each other. I didn't recognize you until you started talking and I heard your accent. You looked a lot different a few months back."

"So once you did recognize me…is that why you asked me out?"

"I want to say no. I've told everyone else no, but if you want total honesty, I'm not sure." He lets out a loud sigh and runs a hand through his hair.

"Great. I never thought my mental history would be an alluring quality for a man, so you'll have to forgive me for trying to figure out how the hell this isn't just another sick obsession for you." I quickly clarify with, "Your words. Not mine."

"Please, God, tell me you don't believe that. Have I ever once made you feel that way? This is not an obsession. Well, maybe it is, but really isn't that all love ever is?" He takes a step forward, and I once again retreat.

"Leo, we shouldn't be together," I rush out even though my mind is screaming otherwise.

"Why the hell not? We were fucking perfect together. Nothing has changed."

Suddenly, my pulse begins to quicken and I have an overwhelming urge to spew everything I've wanted to tell him since day one. However, I do it selfishly because I know deep down he'll make it all right. Leo makes everything right—even something as fucked up as me.

"Because I'm shit for a person!" I scream manically then start pacing. "I'm the worst fucking kind, because I actually think I'm reformed. I hurt people, Leo. I ruined lives."

"Who, Sarah? Whose life did you ruin? Because from where I'm standing, everyone made it out of that tragedy okay. I get that you didn't make it out unscathed. You have issues besides loss and guilt, but damn it, Sarah, you're not crazy! You struggled and then you *overcame*. Focus on the right fucking part of this scenario. You didn't kill anyone—and that includes yourself." He pauses. "God damn it. You saved me!" he roars.

"I tried to shoot my husband." I quickly inform him because he obviously doesn't have all the facts. "Is that the kind of woman you want to be with? Is that the person you fell in love with?"

"No, you didn't try to shoot him. Don't pull that bullshit. But yes, the woman who struggled and got better is absolutely the woman I fell in love with."

"I did. I pulled the trigger."

"Oh for fuck's sake. Sarah, the only person who believes that you were trying to kill Brett is you."

"Leo, you deserve better than me."

"I'm sorry. Did you hear what I just said about myself?" he asks, popping an eyebrow.

"I don't care about your past," I whisper.

"Then why do I have to care about yours?"

"I don't know," I respond, defeated, as his words begin to sink in. "I know it's been years, but I still just feel like a mental case in a sea of sane people."

"Sarah, we're both crazy. That's the best fucking part about this relationship. Together, we're just normal."

"We can't do this, Leo. It's a recipe for disaster." I begin to pace again.

"I need you to shut down for a minute."

"What?" I ask.

"Close your eyes. Take a deep breath. Hell, maybe even let me hold you. But stop spinning this into something it's not." He once again steps forward.

This time, I stay still. "I don't know how," I whimper.

"Then let me show you." He takes two giant steps forward, pulling me into his arms. "We're going to be okay. I refuse to accept it any other way," he tells my hair before kissing the top of my head.

I try to step away, needing the space to clear my head—or, in actuality, to clutter it back up with the shit Leo just cleared—only he squeezes me tighter.

"Nope. I'm still hugging," he says and I hide my smile in his chest.

Leo stands in the middle of my apartment, surrounded by my entire collection of dishes broken on the floor, and simply holds me. This time, he doesn't whisper encouraging words in my ear like he has in the past, but I don't need to hear them. I just need to feel *him*. Finally, after a few minutes, he scrubs his stubble across my cheek, and I sigh and give him a soft laugh.

He leans away to look down at me, uttering the familiar words that started this all. "Welcome back."

Taking a play from Leo's flashback playbook, I cup both sides of his face and brush my lips across his. "I love you, too."

He smiles and presses another kiss to my mouth. "I know we have a lot to talk about, and I'll answer any question you want to ask, but can we at least just agree to do it together? No more running."

"Okay."

"I'm keeping you, and I hate to say it, but you're stuck with me. So don't make me chase you again, or next time, I'm going to take you over my knee." He kisses me again and my eyes grow wide.

"No, the fuck you won't," I snap, and his smile grows to epic proportions.

"Oh, yeah. I read that shit you bought on my Kindle."

"Oh my God. You did not read that." I begin to laugh.

"Only a small part. But I got a few ideas." He winks and all of the drama fades into the background.

Even the hard stuff.

So. Fucking. Easy.

Chapter
TWENTY-EIGHT

Leo

"YOU SHOULD call in sick to work tomorrow." I try to persuade as I lead her down the hall and into her bedroom.

"Ah, well. Funny you should mention that. I got fired," she replies sheepishly.

"Why? What did the Wicked Witch do?" I release her only long enough to undress down to my boxers and crawl into her bed.

She follows behind me and settles into my side. "I wouldn't know. I haven't been to work in a week."

"What?" I ask, surprised.

"Yeah. I called out on Monday and Tuesday. Then…"

"Shit," I cuss when I remember that she was parked next to me those days. "I'm sorry."

"Don't be. Even if we weren't here together right now, I'd still be happy that I was there for you."

"Sarah, I don't deserve you," I say, kissing her mouth.

She replies with a laugh. "Not many people do."

"I'm serious." I kiss her again, a little more deeply.

"I didn't get fired for calling out. I got fired because, after everything went down with us, I crawled into bed and shut down the world. I didn't go in or even let them know that I wouldn't be there on Wednesday and Thursday either. So yeah, now I'm back to being unemployed."

"Come work for me," I rush out.

"Um, no," she says simply.

"Come on. I've taken on some new clients and I don't have enough men for the positions. I'm going to have to fill in until I can hire some. I'm barely keeping my head above water in the office as it is, and now that I'll be in the field all the time…well, it's going to be a mess. I need some help."

"Maybe it will be easier to understand if I say it in Spanish. No." She begins laughing.

"You can start on Monday." I ignore her joke, causing her to laugh louder.

"Leo, there is no way I'm working for you. We'd kill each other. We just got back together not even ten minutes ago. You think we could work—"

"Whoa!" I interrupt her. "We did not just get back together. We never even broke up."

"See. Right there. I'm not working for a delusional man." She rolls over on top of me, straddling my hips. Bending down, she begins kissing up my neck.

I tease her nipple through her tank top. "Get naked. We can talk while I'm inside you."

"I don't want to talk anymore," she whispers, and I drop my hand.

"Sarah. We *need* to talk. I don't want to just brush the last week under the rug."

"I know. I don't either, but I have a feeling this isn't going to be a quick conversation. I'm exhausted. Maybe we can set aside some time to talk each week as things come up. I know I have some questions for you now, but I swear, by tomorrow, I'll have a ton more. I just want to make love then go to sleep—for like a week."

"Promise me. We set a specific day and time to figure this shit out."

"I promise," she assures me, sealing it with a kiss.

"Okay. But I just feel like going to sleep. I have a grueling day ahead of me tomorrow. I have to try to find someone to help me out in the office. That is unless you happen to know someone who's looking for a job?"

"I'm not working for you." She pulls her shirt off and I fold my arms behind my head to get a better view.

"Then sorry, ángel. It's a work night." I smirk.

"That's too bad." She slides a hand down into her tiny sleep shorts, holding my gaze the entire time.

"You get yourself off, I'm gonna be really upset," I growl as I stiffen between us.

"Then stop trying to blackmail me into working for you." She pulls one of my arms out from under my head and places it on her breast. Just to prove my point, I let it fall back down to the bed. She groans. "Okay, you want to play it that way…fine."

When I see the sparkle of a challenge in her eyes, I know I've lost, but I have a feeling I'm never going to enjoy losing more.

She rises from the bed and drags down her shorts and panties before tugging my boxers down my legs. Immediately resuming her position on top of me, she begins kissing up my neck. She alternates between playing with herself and grinding her wet pussy against my painfully hard cock.

"Fuck," I cuss as she slides over me, never pushing it inside. "Just take the damn job, Sarah."

"No," she moans, rolling her nipple between her fingers. "You know, technically, Leo, if I keep this up, I'm going to be coming on your cock. So you can't be upset. I'll be a little disappointed that I won't be able to feel you inside me though. You're so long. I always come so much harder when you fuck me deep."

I bite my lip and fist the back of my hair to keep my hand from joining her. Sarah's always been a beast in the bedroom, but she's not usually a talker. It's killing me because I want to hear that voice screaming my name.

"Take the job," I growl again.

"No," she whispers with a sexy grin.

It hits me that I'm handling this all wrong. I quickly sit up and push her to the bed beside me. Covering her breast with my mouth, I suck hard. As I settle between her legs, she lets out a giggle, thinking she's won. I reach between us and grab my cock so it strokes across her clit as I roll my hips against her.

She throws her head back. "Shit, Leo. Please."

"Take the job," I repeat.

Her eyes pop open and just as quickly narrow. "I hate you," she murmurs.

"I love you, too. Now come work for me. I need the help. This isn't charity. It's just a job."

"No," she whines in frustration.

I continue to rub the head of my cock over her opening and she arches off the bed at the contact.

"Damn it. Fine. I'll work for you temporarily while I look for a new job. Then I'll help you find someone else before I leave. Okay?"

"Okay, ángel."

"Now, please just fuck me."

"My pleasure." I slam inside her and we both cry out. "Just so you know I pay shit, but the position does come with daily sexual harassment."

She lets out a soft laugh that quickly becomes a moan as I begin to move inside her.

"MONDAYS," SARAH announces just I begin to doze off behind her.

"Huh?" I mumble.

"Let's talk on Mondays. That way we can enjoy the entire weekend before dealing with all the shit that I'm sure will come from our chats."

"Sarah, why the hell are we only talking once a week? Shouldn't we be talking every day?"

"I don't work like that, Leo. If you lay too much on me at once or expect me to put my stuff out, I'll get lost in the words. It's not that I can't deal with the stress. I'm just not the most optimistic person these days. You present me with a problem and I immediately jump to the impossible before even trying to rationalize it out."

"Your gears begin to spin in all the wrong directions."

"Yes!" she exclaims, rolling to face me.

"Johnson told me that as I was leaving to come over here."

At the mere mention of his name, her face goes pale. "Oh my

God." Her chin begins to quiver. "Fuck, fuck, fuck. I outed him. I thought—"

"I've known for a while, Sarah. You didn't out him."

"Oh Jesus. I'm going to throw up," she announces, bolting from the bed.

"Stop." I pull her back down, but as she threatens to make good on her promise to puke, I decide maybe helping her to the bathroom is a safer option.

"I can't believe I said that!" she shouts at her reflection in the mirror.

"Why are you puking all the time?" I tease, sitting down on the side of her bathtub.

"Oh God, why did I tell you that? I am such a fucking bitch."

"You really are," I say with a laugh, and she glares at me in the mirror. "I'm kidding! You were pissed. We all say stupid shit when we're mad. Just apologize. He's a big boy. He'll get over it."

"Leo, you don't understand. That is not a line you cross. Even if you're pissed."

"Well, it happened. Now, all you can do is try to right the wrong."

"That sounds like some seriously hypocritical advice." She crosses her arms over her naked chest.

Reaching up, I snag her elbow and pull her down to sit on my lap, teetering her off balance so she has no choice but to hold my shoulder to stay upright.

"See, now that was a bitchy comment."

Her shoulders fall. "I'm sorry. I just—"

"Feel guilty. I got that. But stop being defensive. I'm not here to judge you and I sure as hell don't expect you to judge me either."

"I'm really sorry." Tears begin to well in her eyes.

"It's okay, ángel. It's been an emotional night. But don't let it happen again. Next time, I won't be so forgiving." I sit her back upright and she curls into my chest.

"We're a mess, Leo."

"I can handle a mess," I say matter-of-factly, rising to my feet with Sarah securely in my arms.

"Are you sure? Because I wouldn't blame you if you wanted to go now."

I set her down on the bed. "I just spent the entire night fighting to get you back. I'm not going anywhere. We might be a mess, but you're my mess, Sarah."

"I don't think you really understand what you're getting into."

"I don't think *you* really understand that I'm not getting into anything. I'm already in so deep there isn't a chance in hell that I could ever turn back." I relax on the bed and sling out an arm, nodding for her to crawl into my side. She quickly obeys. "Besides, I've known from the beginning what I was getting into. It's you who just got all of this sprung on you tonight." I look down to find her staring up at me.

"I meant it earlier when I said I don't care about your past, Leo. I have questions, but none of them are whether I should be with you. I just want to learn more about who you are so I can better understand what goes on in your head."

"So the only thing you question is why I should be with *you*?"

"Um, pretty much." She gives me a tentative smile.

"Well, how about this? I'll make all the decisions for Leo, and you make all the decisions for... Hmm, just let me make the decisions," I tease.

She slaps my chest. "I love you," she breathes on a content sigh.

"I love you too. But I want Thursdays."

"Huh?"

"I want to talk on Thursdays, so in case things get rough, we can spend the weekend together making it smooth again."

"Of course he would pick Thursdays," she mumbles to herself.

"What'd you say?" I ask.

"Nothing. Yeah. Thursdays will work."

"Good. Now go to sleep. I have a few days off, so we're going somewhere tomorrow. I don't know where yet. But we need a vacation."

"We just got back from Puerto Rico," she laughs.

"Sleep," I repeat.

She doesn't say another word. Moments later, her arm grows heavy across my chest and her breathing evens out.

I close my eyes and drift off to sleep, knowing this won't be the last time I have to fight for Sarah.

I didn't tell her nearly enough.

Chapter
TWENTY-NINE

Sarah

THE MORNING after Leo and I got back together, we slept until noon then got up and headed for the airport. Leo had no bag or clothes with him, and he convinced me to do the same thing. So, armed with only my purse and the toothbrush I snuck inside, we left for an impromptu vacation.

When we arrived at the airport, Leo walked to the desk and asked for the cheapest flight they had going anywhere. We were given two choices: Detroit or Boston. Two hours later, we were in the air and on the way to Massachusetts.

We didn't do a lot while we were there. We stopped at a local mall and picked up a few necessities then found a hotel downtown. We were only there for two nights, but Leo was right—it was a much-needed vacation. We didn't get deep or talk about the issues that were looming over our heads. But that doesn't mean I didn't ask him some questions. The fact that he already knew most of my drama made me brave enough to ask. He didn't bat an eye as he told me about the ten months he'd been working undercover before meeting Erica, but I always stopped him before he got to that night when everything went wrong.

Leo had a few questions as well. He didn't understand why I hadn't dated anyone in seven years—or, more importantly, why I was willing to break the pattern and go out with him. I didn't have an answer. I don't know why either. I told him that it had to be some cosmic pull that forced me to immediately recognize that he was *the one*. I only made it about halfway through the sentence before I doubled over in laughter. He replied with a shrug and told me that he just assumed I was horny after all that time. I can't say that he was wrong, but I secretly think I might have been partially right too.

The minute we got back to Chicago, I started mission 'Apologize To Aiden.' I decided to cook him dinner. Men love food—at least that's always been my experience. So I made him my famous chicken and dumplings. I was worried that he wouldn't like it, but he raved when he brought the Tupperware back the next day. For two weeks, I cooked him food to take home for dinner. Finally, he asked me to stop. He used some excuse about all the butter forcing him to stay at the gym longer. Then he gave me a hug and told me not to worry about it anymore. But I still felt bad, so I started making him protein smoothies for breakfast every morning. It made me feel a little better at least.

It's been four weeks since we got back from our little getaway, and I have to say that, even despite how dramatic things got before we left, it's been smooth sailing since we returned. True to his word, Leo sits down with me every Thursday night to talk. We started out just talking about generic parts of our relationship and how to navigate them.

On the first night, I asked him to start taking anti-depressants. He told me no. I didn't push. I'm also not letting it go. I'll let him say no for now, but not for forever.

For such a dramatic couple, Leo and I sure handle these chats like professionals. It's obvious that we have both spent many of hours in therapy. We can fight like cats and dogs over what movie we are going to watch on Friday or who is doing the dishes after dinner, but we dive into deep stuff with level heads.

Tonight is our fourth conversation, and while Leo usually sits back and lets me take the lead, tonight, he jumped right into a tough topic.

"How are you still friends with Casey and Eli after what they did to you? They let you bear their cross for all those years. You should hate them!" he shouts.

Hmm… Okay, maybe we were *doing a great job at keeping level heads. Clearly, we're not anymore.*

"Why are you yelling?" I ask, propping my feet up on the couch between us.

"Because, when I think back on all the things you've told me about your past, ninety percent of it all stems from guilt—guilt they could have relieved you of by not sitting on the truth for five fucking years." His chest heaves, but something just doesn't sit right.

"No. I don't believe you," I say calmly.

"Don't believe what?" he snaps.

"I don't believe that the way you're acting is because of your feelings toward Casey and Eli. What else is going on with you?"

"Nothing. I get pissed every time I think about it. Sarah, I'll be really fucking honest—I don't like you hanging out with them. It's not good for you," he declares sternly.

"Well, I'm sorry you feel that way. But it's not going to change anything." I cross my legs at my ankles and point my toes so they brush his leg.

"Well, don't expect me to hang out with them." He scoots away an inch so my feet can no longer reach him.

"Okay," I respond simply, not wanting to match his intensity. It's a rare day when I'm the levelheaded side of our relationship, but it makes me smile to myself.

"You know what. I don't feel like doing this right now."

"It's Thursday, Leo," I gently remind him.

"We aren't bound to Thursdays, *Sarah.* I don't think the world will end if we move it to Friday for one week. I'm in a shitty mood, and if we try to do this, I'm just going to find shit to be an asshole about."

"I can see this, but what I'm trying to figure out is why you are in a shitty mood."

"Please just let me take you to dinner or something. I can't do the talking thing tonight. I just can't."

"All right. Let's go." I stand up, sliding on my heels then heading for the door.

"Thank God," Leo breathes as he follows me.

DINNER DID little to improve Leo's mood. He sulked for most of the evening, barely even talking to me. He even moved away once when I tried to take his arm. It's completely unlike the man I've come to know, and quite honestly, it worries me.

"You spending the night?" Leo asks as we get to his car in the restaurant parking lot.

"I guess that depends if you want me to or not. I'm feeling a bit like a burden on you tonight."

"You're not a burden, ángel. I'm in a terrible mood. That's all. I think I'm just going to work out then head to bed."

"Since when do you work out at night?" I ask curiously.

"Since I have some shit to work through tonight, and taking it out on the weight bench seems like a better plan than being a dick to you," he answers, and I have to agree with his assessment.

"And just to be clear, there is nothing you want to talk about?" I ask, hoping to draw something out of him.

"No." He tosses me an insincere smile and reaches down to squeeze my thigh.

"Okay. Well, my car's at your place, but when we get back, I'll go home and give you some space." I intertwine our fingers and kiss his knuckle.

He squeezes my hand in response before pulling it to his own lips. "Thank you," he tells the windshield.

WHEN WE arrive at his apartment, I walk upstairs to get my keys but decide not to linger.

"I'll see you in the morning. Okay?" I say, heading right back out the door.

"Yeah. Sounds good." He gives me a gentle kiss and pulls the front door open.

"I love you," I call over my shoulder, but the door closes without another word spoken.

As I walk into the parking garage, my mind whips around, trying to figure out what's really going on with Leo. I might have agreed to let him have some space, but that doesn't mean I don't want to know what the hell is going on inside his head. I play back as much as I can remember about the last forty-eight hours, but nothing stands out. Nothing except for our odd conversation about Casey and Eli—the very same conversation we never finished.

He's never even met Eli, and he's only seen Casey a few times in passing. I can't imagine that he has just suddenly developed these strong feelings. Yet, out of the blue tonight, he got pissed off about them still being my friends. It's not like I have issues with his relationship with Erica—

Shit.

Finally, it hits me.

I rush back into his apartment, using my key to let myself in. I find him sitting on the couch with his elbows to his knees and his hands fisting his hair.

"I never answered your question about Casey and Eli," I announce.

He lets out a groan when he realizes I've returned. "We can talk tomorrow," he replies, not even turning to look at me.

"No. It's Thursday and I want to tell you now."

"Sarah, for fuck's sake. Please!" he shouts as his frustration gets the better of him.

Ignoring his outburst, I begin to talk. "For five years, I carried the weight of that night on my shoulders. The guilt ate away at me until, eventually, the hate and anger seeped out onto everyone I came in contact with. Brett caught most of it because he was always there. He just wouldn't leave me alone."

"Boy, do I know that feeling," he comments while leaning back against the couch.

"No, you can't compare me to the way he handled things. Brett tried to force me to talk with hopes of me returning to our happy little life together. You don't need to say a single word. I just want you to hear *me.* Then I'll leave."

He rolls his eyes but motions for me to continue.

"I was absolutely vile to Brett. In some ways, I enjoyed the fact that he suffered right alongside me. I hated seeing people happy back then. I guess you could say I was jealous. I had no idea how the hell to get there, and it enraged me to see people moving forward with their lives when I was frozen in the past. I was horrible, Leo. I physically assaulted Brett on numerous occasions. I would just fucking lose it. I threw things at him and slapped him more often than not. Hell, I even punched him once."

"Shit," he mumbles.

"You remember his wife from the bar? The tiny woman with the kind smile? Yeah, I hit her once too."

His eyes pop in surprise, and I walk over and crawl into his lap, straddling his legs. He may want to get rid of me, but for the next part of this, I need his full attention. If I'm right about why he's on edge tonight, he needs to hear this more than anything else.

"It was the only way I could express the feelings that were constantly multiplying inside me. But I had an outlet. It may have been the wrong way of expelling the anguish, but it was something. Now I want you to imagine how excruciating it would have been if I had kept all of that shit bottled up. That's what Casey went through. She had to live alone with the secrets and the knowledge of what she did."

"She didn't have to, Sarah," he bites out.

"No talking, remember? I won't get into Casey's story or the whys. You should know there are a few factors from that night that may not excuse their actions but will definitely shed a new light on the choices that were made. One day, I'll let her tell you her side, but tonight, I'm telling you *mine*." I loop my arms around his neck. "If I could go back to that night I broke into Jesse's apartment, I would. Actually, I would change something about almost every day of my life, but that's not possible. Casey is no different. She took off and left town, unable to face any of us. And Eli took a slightly different approach. He tried to make things right."

Leo's shoulders stiffen, confirming my suspicions from earlier.

"Eli decided to become Brett's and Caleb's best friend. Did you know he once bought twenty chairs from Caleb when he found out that woodworking took Caleb's mind off life? He dumped a huge amount of his savings on chairs that he just ended up giving away because he had no where to keep them.

"And if Brett needed something, Eli was always there. For the first few months after the wreck, I ran off every sitter Brett could hire. He didn't want to leave my side, but he had to get back to work. He started working nights so I'd be asleep while he was gone. He still worried though, especially after the first time I tried to kill myself." I pause as the emotions creep into my throat. "Eli volunteered to start sleeping on our couch. They didn't think I noticed since I never really came out of my room. But about ten minutes after Brett walked out of the house that first night, I heard Eli break down. I didn't understand it back then, but the sound of this otherwise strong man sobbing lulled me to sleep. I'll never forget it as long as I live.

"So, yes, Eli fucked up. He did a terrible, horrible thing, but if a terrible, horrible person like myself can't forgive him, who will?"

"And I love that you feel that way, ángel. But it doesn't change the fact that he ruined your life. He should have done the right thing to begin with. He should have been a fucking man and not left you for dead." He brushes the hair off my shoulder, trying to offer me his magical comfort, but I'm not the one who needs it tonight.

"You're not Eli, Leo," I whisper.

"I didn't say I was," he quickly answers.

"No, but you were thinking it. That's why you got so pissy earlier, isn't it?"

"No," he responds, but even though it's only a single word, I can tell it's a lie.

"Let me tell you why—" I start, and Leo suddenly lifts me off his lap and shifts me to the couch next to him as he jumps to his feet.

"No! I don't want you to tell me why. For fuck's sake, I feel like I'm dating a shrink. I want you to let this shit rip me to shreds because that is what I deserve. Don't make me feel better. Tell me I'm a fucking piece of shit!"

"Then tell me I'm a piece of shit. Because if you are, I am too!" I shout back at him.

He stares at me for a minute before beginning to pace the room and speaking Spanish so fast that I can't even pick out a single word.

"Stop speaking in Spanish. If you're going to talk shit about yourself, at least use words I can understand."

He stills and looks over at me blankly.

"Well, since you don't seem to be able to adequately express yourself in English, I'm going to be forced to repeat: You. Are. Not. Eli."

"Fuck," he growls, stomping past me into the kitchen.

I flop down on the couch and begin picking at my nails, waiting for him to settle down. It's not a quick process, so I start scrolling through my phone as I listen to him pace.

"Here," Leo says, walking back into the room, placing a beer and glass of wine down on the table in front of us.

"You know, if I drink that, I'm not leaving."

"Well, it doesn't appear that you're leaving anyway," he snarks but then gives me a quick kiss. He grabs his beer off the table before letting out a resigned sigh. "Four years ago, I sat next to Erica as our identities were stripped from us upon entry into the Witness Protection Program. I spent over two hours arguing with them because they tried to separate us. They *should* have separated us," he quickly clarifies before leaning forward and passing me the wine. "We had formed this completely unhealthy bond—her fears and my need to keep her safe. The whole team was convinced we were romantically involved, because back then, I would sleep on the floor of her hotel room every night. I want to sit here and tell you she needed me. She didn't. *I needed her.*"

He takes another sip of his beer and I follow suit with my wine.

"She freaked out, screaming and crying, when they told her they couldn't allow us to be together. I knew they were right. She would have been better off without me, but I was so fucking selfish. I knew *I* wouldn't be better without *her*. So I fought them. I argued them in circles and finally told them we wouldn't testify if they tried to split us. I didn't know what the fuck I was going to do. Half of the drug dealers in the country wanted my head for all the incriminating evidence I had against them. But I grabbed her hand and marched out of the office. We got all the way to the street before they thankfully stopped us. We both would have been dead by the end of the night if they hadn't. I was just so desperate back then..." he trails off, covering his face with his free hand.

I try to scratch his back, but he shrinks away from my touch. "Leo, that sounds like you were in a really bad situation, but I don't necessarily think anything you did was wrong. You wanted to protect

Erica after everything that happened to her. Can't you see that it was a somewhat noble thing to do?"

"I had lunch with Caleb today," he announces, suddenly changing the topic.

"I thought you had a business meeting at lunch?"

"I did. It was with Caleb," he answers frankly.

"Um, okay."

"I wanted to ask him about Eli. He applied for one of my open positions. I recognized his name from hearing you talk about him and Casey. I never really got the full picture there though. I knew it was Casey who was driving the car that night, but I didn't really understand Eli's role in the accident until today."

"Wait. Why the hell didn't you just ask me?"

"Because I know you, Sarah. You can forgive everyone in the world except for yourself. I wanted the truth, not your rose-colored version of it."

"That's not fair. The truth is the truth no matter which way you spin it. He's not a bad guy because he was trying to protect Casey."

"He left two woman for dead on the side of the road—one of them being *my* woman."

I let out an exasperated sigh, knowing that this conversation is going nowhere. When he puts it like that, I can't honestly blame Leo for being pissed.

"Okay, fine. So you don't like him. Don't hire him. There are other jobs he can get."

"Sarah, you don't get it. Yes, Caleb told me all about the chairs and how he really stepped up for Brett. The reason people hate him is not necessarily because of what he did. It's how he handled it afterward. He befriended the people he'd wronged. Can you just for a second take a step back and look at this whole situation objectively?"

"Fine, yes. It was messed up," I begrudgingly answer.

"Ding, ding, ding," Leo chimes before draining his beer and standing to get another one. "Which is exactly why I wanted to be alone tonight. Eli and I have entirely too much in common. The person I wronged is now my best friend." He walks to the kitchen.

"You're not Eli!" I call out, jumping to my feet to follow him.

"I don't think I am Eli. I just think he's a selfish son of a bitch in a 'Hello, kettle. You're black' kind of way."

"Why the fuck are you even concerned with Eli? You want me to stop hanging out with him? Fine. Whatever it takes for you to stop acting like a brooding child. Casey is my friend though. I won't accept you dictating my relationship with her."

"A brooding child? Jesus, aren't you one to talk!" He laughs manically.

"So, we're doing it like this, huh? You want to take some stabs at me to make yourself feel better? Go for it!" I swing my arms out to my sides. "But when this shit is over, you're going to feel worse."

"God damn!" he screams so loud that it echoes off the walls, but I stand my ground.

"There you go. Get pissed. We haven't broken your dishes yet. Have a go at them."

He shakes his head and begins to crack his knuckles. "I hate you sometimes," he fumes, but his voice cracks at the end.

"I hate you too. But only because I love you so fucking much and you always talk shit about my boyfriend." I cross my arms and give him a pointed look. "I'm not going to sit here and try to fill your head with all the ways that what you did wasn't wrong—even though it wasn't. All that matters is how you feel about yourself. You know what I love about our relationship? We can forgive each other anything, but looking at ourselves in the mirror is damn near impossible. So how about this? I'll love you and you love me. And maybe that will be enough."

"That sounds like a terrible plan," Leo responds, grabbing the back of my neck and pulling me into his chest. "How do you always make things so bearable?" he asks, kissing the top of my head.

"The same way you do it for me. When my vision tunnels, you always find a way to remove the blinders. You also have to remember I've been dealing with my shit a lot longer than you have. You should see the hours I've logged in therapy. It was my full-time job for almost two years."

He sighs, and I can feel his pulse gradually slowing in his chest.

"Any chance I can convince you to start seeing someone again?" He laughs.

"Maybe start taking some anti-depressants?" I continue. "I think they would help you a lot."

"Seeing someone, yes. Drugs, no." He releases me but only long enough to grab my hand and guide me back over to the couch.

"Can you at least agree to explain to me why?"

When he lets out an exasperated sigh, I quickly amend my statement.

"Not tonight. Maybe next week. We've done enough talking for one Thursday night. Hell, maybe even an entire month of Thursdays."

"Yeah. Next week," he mumbles then places a gentle kiss on my lips.

I have a sneaking suspicion that it's not going to be that easy to get him to explain this one though.

Chapter
THIRTY

Sarah

Emma: So apparently Kara and Hunter are back together. Are you going to freak if she comes to Collin's birthday party with him?
Me: Jesse's best friend, Kara?
Emma: Yes
Me: The one who lived with Jesse when I broke into her apartment?
Emma: Yes
Me: Yes, I'm going to freak if she comes!

My phone begins ringing in my hand and I see Emma's name flashing onto the screen

"Stop," she orders immediately.

"No way. I'm not coming if she's there," I answer, putting the tape and scissors down.

"You've seen Jesse since that night and she married your ex-husband. I figured that would be way more reason to freak than Kara."

"Saying hi to Jesse is a far cry from hanging out with Kara at a twelve-person birthday party. Aren't y'all doing a party with Brett and Jesse anyway? Invite them to that one."

"Yes, but Hunter and Alex are only in town this weekend. In my defense, I originally invited them to come up this weekend because Hunter was trying to avoid Kara. But apparently she found out he was in town and they got back together last night. I've spent the morning listening to him replay their sexual escapades. That girl's a freak. I really think you'd like her." She laughs, but I find nothing humorous about this situation.

"How the hell, in a city the size of Chicago, does this group seem to be getting smaller and smaller?"

"The cool people have to stick together."

"Maybe Leo and I can just meet you guys at one of those kids' places next week and do a mini party with just the four of us then."

"Sarah, come on. She's nice. Plus, I asked her first and she said she would love to get to know you."

"You have no idea how awkward this is going to be for me."

"Oh stop and just promise you'll come."

"Leo's already on his way over here. I love the way you spring this on me fifteen minutes before we are supposed to be there."

"Well, I know you. I didn't want to give you enough time to think of an excuse. Now, tell me you're still coming. Collin would be so disappointed if you—"

"Fine! I'll come," I resign and Emma actually squeals.

"Okay! Love you! Bye." She quickly hangs up before I can change my mind.

I toss the phone on the counter, and just as Emma predicted, I begin trying to think of excuses why I don't have to go.

"Hey, ángel," Leo says as he walks into my apartment.

"Do you think we could make a quick stop at that little Mexican restaurant we went to on our first date?"

"The one that gave us food poisoning? Have you lost your mind?"

"No, it's just that food poisoning would be the perfect excuse to get out of Collin's party."

"I thought you were looking forward to this? You made me wait for an hour the other night because you couldn't find the perfect wrapping paper."

"Hey, if my boy wants trucks, then trucks he shall have!"

He chuckles before leaning in to kiss me. "What's going on? Why the sudden change?"

"Jesse's best friend is going to be at the party. She's dating Emma's best friend, who's up from Savannah just for the party."

"Jesus, you people really keep it all in the family."

"Right? That's what I said."

"You nervous about seeing her?" Leo walks behind me and begins massaging my shoulders.

"I guess. I'm not sure why though. Maybe I'm more embarrassed than anything else."

"When I was in middle school, I had to give this speech in front of the whole class. I got so nervous that, as soon as I opened my mouth, I puked all over my shoes. I know it's not quite the same thing, but I know you're a puker, so I just wanted to tell you to at least aim for the carpet instead of my favorite heels."

I bust out laughing. "I think you might be the strangest man I have ever met."

"But it worked, didn't it?" He kisses my neck and folds his arms around my waist.

"A little bit. Thank you."

"No. Thank *you*. I plan on fucking you with those heels on tonight. I'm going to need them to stay vomit-free," he responds making me laugh again.

WHEN WE pull up to Emma's house, the butterflies begin again. Leo doesn't tell me any more stories, but as we walk to the door, he grabs my hand and gives it a reassuring squeeze.

"Just breathe, ángel. I won't leave your side. I promise."

I tentatively nod and knock on the door.

"Sawah!" Collin screams as soon as Caleb opens the door.

"He's been waiting for you." He passes Collin over to me and extends a hand to Leo.

"Happy birthday, buddy!" I begin tickling Collin and blowing raspberries on his cheeks.

"Oh God, don't hype him up any more than he already is. Caleb let him have a cupcake for breakfast," Emma says.

"It was a muffin with a candle," Caleb calls out in defense.

"Oh hush. It had icing. That makes it cupcake," she responds as Collin launches himself into her arms.

"Mommy! Sawah!" he says, pointing over at me.

"I see her. Come on. Let's go put her present on the table." Emma grabs the skillfully wrapped gift from my hand and walks into the other room.

I glance up at Leo to find the oddest expression on his face. I give him a questioning look, but he just shakes his head.

"Hey hey!" I hear Alex greet as he walks into the room.

"Hi." Releasing Leo's hand, I throw my arms around Alex's neck. I grew up with him, but when I moved to Chicago for college, we lost touch. He's a quiet guy, but once you get to know him, he is chatty as all get-out. Now that Emma lives here too, Alex and Hunter come to visit quite a bit. I make it a point to see him every time he comes.

"How are you, hon?" he asks warmly.

"Good. *Really* good," I answer honestly. "Alex, this is my boyfriend, Leo. Leo, this is my old friend, Alex."

"You need a job?" Leo asks randomly, and I can't help but give him a crazy glance. "You're a big dude. Seriously. You need work?" He digs in his back pocket and pulls out a card.

"I live in Savannah. That'd be one hell of a commute." Alex grins but tucks the card in his wallet.

"Well, if you change your mind, you give me a call. But yeah, nice to meet you."

I laugh and Leo looks down at me.

"Hey, I need more men. Size is half the requirement in my business."

"Of course." I smile patronizingly.

"Oh. My. God." I hear a woman's voice I don't recognize and my stomach drops. *Kara.* Judging by the tone of her voice, I fully expected to look up and find a disgusted look on her face. However, when my eyes meet hers, she's not looking at me at all. She's staring at Leo.

"All right. Girl time!" she announces, walking forward and grabbing my arm.

"Um...I'm good." I tug my arm away and lean into Leo.

He steps between us and very obviously pulls me into his side farthest away from her. "Hi. I'm Leo."

"That was hot," she whispers. "Hi. I'm Kara Reed. Can I borrow your girlfriend for a minute?"

"Kara! Leave her alone!" Emma yells from the kitchen.

"I can't do that and you know it! I need some answers!" she calls back to Emma.

My pulse begins to race as I nervously slide impossibly closer to Leo.

"Jesus Christ, Kara. They just got here." Emma walks over and hands me cup of punch. "You're freaking her out."

Kara clears her throat and pointedly tilts her head to Leo.

"Seriously?" Emma laughs.

Kara shrugs unapologetically.

"It's not what you think," Emma tells me. "She's not mad or anything."

"Oh God no!" Kara exclaims from behind her. "Shit, I'm sorry. I didn't even think…" Her face heats to pink and I begin to feel bad about my reaction.

"It's okay." I smile weakly while trying to get my heart to slow.

"Come on. We can chat in my room. I need to change anyway. I'm covered in shrimp dip. The mixer just went haywire."

I glance down to Emma's shirt to find it covered in an orange mess. "You made shrimp dip?" I ask in shock and immediate excitement. It's my favorite, but you can't find the mix in Chicago. It's only sold at one of the touristy shops in Savannah.

"Yep. Alex brought some up just for you."

"You still love that stuff, right?" Alex asks, shoving his hands in his pockets.

"Um, abso-fucking-lutely," I quickly respond before Emma scolds me for cussing.

"All right, gentlemen. Food's in the kitchen. Go eat. Come on, Sarah." Emma turns and walks away with Kara giggling hot on her heels.

"You going to be okay?" Leo whispers in my ear.

"I think so." I stand on my tiptoes to give him a kiss. "However, while I'm gone, I need you to put on a professional face. Go in there, find that bowl of shrimp dip, and guard it with your life. No one touches it until I get back. You got it?" I pat his chest, causing him to grin.

"Yes, ma'am," he answers before whispering into my ear, "Since this is a professional job, I will expect payment in the form of your mouth on my cock later."

"Leo," I chastise.

"Sorry, ángel. That's the price you pay for professional bodyguard services these days."

"I'm going to check your bills on Monday. I better not find you charging anyone else like that."

He laughs and gives me another kiss before walking away unfazed. Unfortunately, I can't say the same.

When I walk into the bedroom room, I find Kara rummaging through Emma's closet.

"Wear this one. It gives you great cleavage."

"Um, I'm not wearing a backless cocktail dress to my child's second birthday party," Emma responds, pulling an orange T-shirt from her drawer.

"Can I wear it then?" Kara asks.

"Sure, but it would be a floor-length, ass-less dress on you. Hunter would lose his crazy shit."

"Damn it. Why do I have to be so short?" she complains, flopping down on the bed.

"You're not short. We're just giants," I say, walking up to her. "Hi. I'm Sarah."

"I'm really happy to meet you again."

"We've met before?" I ask, confused.

"Well, kinda. You waved a gun in my face," she says bluntly.

My eyes go wide as I stumble back a step.

"Kara!" Emma scolds.

"Oh my God. I totally did that," I breathe, beginning to feel sick when I catch a flash of her coming home early that day I broke into her apartment.

"No. It's okay. I swear. Don't get upset. I was just really worried about you for a while."

"I'm so sorry." I attempt to apologize, but the words lodge in my throat.

"No, stop. I'm just glad to see you doing so well."

"You have to understand. I was a mess back then. I'm not..." I

205

trail off before claiming not to be that woman anymore. I honestly don't know if I am or not.

"I know you're not that person anymore," she finishes for me. "It's been my experience that fuck-hot men like that one don't do crazy."

My anxiety immediately begins to subside as she mentions Leo. "Leo's really good at crazy actually." I grin awkwardly.

"Jesse's been keeping me filled in on your progress over the years."

"Jesse should really learn how to hate me," I respond matter-of-factly.

"Nah. She has this huge heart. She really wants to see you happy. However, if you need her to hate you, just hit on Brett. She'd go nutso on someone over him." She lifts her hands like cat claws and hisses. "She told me you had a new stud. And I have to say she was really freaking right."

"Jesse did not say *stud*," Emma interjects, causing Kara to laugh.

It's infectious. I glance down at my feet to try to hide my smile.

"Nah. She said something completely appropriate like 'attractive.' I translated it to what she really meant though. I'm a good friend like that. Now, Sarah, tell me where you met that fine piece of meat out there. If Hunter doesn't get his shit straight, I might be in the market soon. Is there an auction where you can go purchase men like that? Because I have to say I wasn't sure you'd be able to top Brett, but damn, woman. I think you might have pulled it off," she rushes out and ends with a huge grin.

"Leo is pretty amazing," I answer dreamily.

"Soooo…" Kara drags out exaggeratedly.

"Oh God. Here we go." Emma laughs, sitting down on the bed cross-legged next to Kara.

I look at her warily before glancing back to Kara, who is beaming with excitement.

"I need the vegetable report," she announces shamelessly. "I know we just met and all, but I can already tell we're going to be good friends. So spill it."

"I can honestly say I have no idea what you are talking about, and judging by your excitement, I'm slightly frightened to know what it is."

"You should be. But I'm with Kara. I'd like to know what Leo's hiding behind those designer jeans too." Emma laughs and Kara gives her a high five.

"Wait. Are we talking about his dick?" I ask as it dawns on me.

"No. We are talking vegetables. But yes, I want you to compare his junk to what vegetable it resembles."

"Are we middle schoolers?" I ask, glancing between the two of them. Their eyes are wide with anticipation.

"No, and please tell me he isn't hung like one either. That would be such a waste," Kara says seriously.

I have to admit that this is a funny conversation—ridiculous, but still humorous. However, I'm not quite sure I want to be sharing this with a woman I barely even know. Emma and Casey, sure. Women talk; that's not exactly a secret. But to just come right out and ask the first time you meet someone is freaking weird.

"What's Hunter?" I turn the tables on her.

"Well, Emma originally told me eggplant. But upon further inspection for the last few years, I'd have to go with one of those huge parsnips."

My jaw drops open at her honesty and also just a little because Hunter's hot. It's not right for him to be packing something that big.

"And Caleb's a—"

"No!" I shout, throwing my hands over my ears. "I've known that man for way too long to want to hear what he's using to give the business to my sister every night."

We all bust out laughing.

"Okay, fine. Let me think." I tap my chin while mentally inventorying the produce department. "I guess I'd have to say one of those long plantains. It's not exactly a vegetable, but it's very fitting since Leo speaks Spanish. "

"No way," Kara breathes.

"Really?" Emma asks, standing up on the bed.

"Wait, is it like the really skinny ones at least?" Kara asks for clarification.

"Nope." I laugh.

"*Damn*," Kara groans.

Emma waggles her eyebrows in my direction. "Impressive."

I shrug and smile. They don't have to tell me.

"Okay, are we done now, Kara? Did you get all the information required for your report?" Emma asks, but Kara just stares into space with a glazed-over look in her eyes. "Kara!" Emma snaps her fingers in front of her.

"Oh, yeah. Let's go eat. You got a veggie tray, right?" She makes a show of licking her lips, causing us all to howl with laughter.

We exit the room, still laughing. Caleb and Hunter flash us knowing smiles when we meet up with the guys in the kitchen. Leo gives me a puzzled look when I stop in front of him.

"Everything okay?" he asks, draping an arm around my waist.

"Yeah, it's great. Oh, but stay away from Kara. She makes us look like the definition of sanity."

"Um. Okay?" he says as more of a question than an answer.

Hunter walks over and pats Leo on the back. "Welcome to the group, my man."

Chapter
THIRTY-ONE

Sarah

"SARAH! WHERE is my new client notebook?" Leo asks, walking into the security room-slash-office.

"The same place it always is. Top drawer on the left," I respond from behind the company laptop.

I've been working for Leo for the last six weeks. And when I say "working for," I mean trying to get him organized. How the hell this man has been running a successful business is beyond me. The day I started, Johnson walked in with a yellow sticky note covered in numbers. When I asked him what the hell it was, he told me that was how he turned in his time to Leo.

Head. Exploded.

I thought I was laid back about proper business practices, but a Post-it note time card? Really? Leo has thousands of dollars' worth of high-tech security equipment, but his client list was handwritten in a spiral notebook. It was almost comical.

"No," he drawls. "That's the old notebook. I've asked you to add at least twenty people since it was last updated. None of them are in there. Fuck, please tell me you added them. Those were some big-name clients, and now I have no way to reach them."

"Oh! The *new* one. It's in your phone. I added them all to a spreadsheet then merged it with the contacts on your phone."

"Seriously?" he asks, surprised.

"Yes, seriously. I can't believe you had a freaking notebook to begin with. Aren't you Mr. Technology?" I ask, leaning back in the chair, propping my feet on the desk.

He gives me a slow, sexy smirk. "Yes, but I'm not Mr. Time. I've been doing this alone for a year now." He walks around the desk and sits on the corner. "What else have you been up to?" he asks, running a hand up my thigh.

"Well, the guys now have time cards. They're still handwritten though. You need to figure out a way to allow them to clock in and out remotely. There has to be an app or something for that. Because I'm really sick of importing all that shit every week. You have too many guys now. It takes me forever."

"Okay, ángel. No need to get feisty. I'll figure something out." He leans in and kisses me.

This might be the only perk of the job. Leo wasn't lying. He really does pay for shit, but it's still more than I was making at the newspaper.

"Mmm. You want to do lunch in bed today?" I stand up and wrap my arms around his neck. Yeah. Lunchtime quickies are definitely a perk.

"I am pretty hungry." He sucks my bottom lip into his mouth before raking his teeth across it.

"I have something you can eat." I'm guiding his hand under my dress just as the phone begins to ring. I let out a groan and he chuckles against my lips. "Guardian Protection Agency," I say when I pick up the phone, but I'm greeted by the sound of a dial tone.

"It's the TV, Sarah." He clicks a button on the computer to answer the incoming call.

Erica flashes onto the screen, but her face is twisted in pain. "I can't find Slate. My water just broke," she moans, and Leo jumps to his feet.

"Shit. Hang on, babe. Where's Johnson?" he asks, but Erica doesn't answer.

Supporting herself on the arm of the couch, she shakes her head.

He moves to the screen of monitors and brings up the inside of

Erica's house. One by one, he goes through each room, looking for any sign of Slate or Johnson. For the last few weeks, Johnson has been staying in Indianapolis so he can be there when Slate goes to train the kids at On The Ropes. They never leave Erica alone. *Someone has to be there.*

Not a second later, Leo locates both Slate and Johnson laughing in the basement gym.

"Andrews!" he calls over the intercom and Slate's head snaps up. "Get your ass upstairs. Your wife's having a baby."

"What?" Slate responds, but he takes off at a dead sprint with Johnson right behind him.

Leo tracks Slate through the house until he reaches Erica. Slate immediately scoops her off her feet and hauls ass toward the front door. Erica screams out just as he gets to the door, and I swear you can see the pain move through Slate's face as well. It might be twisted, but it makes me smile.

"He really loves her," I say to Leo as he watches them peel out of the driveway.

"Yeah. He does. You want to go to Indy with me or stay here?" His voice is void of emotion as he begins shutting down all the monitors.

"I'll go. Let me grab some stuff. You want me to pack you some clothes too?" I ask just as Leo turns to face me. His eyes are nervously flashing around the room and his chest is heaving. "Jesus, are you okay?"

"Um, yeah," he confirms, but he looks anything but okay.

"Leo, she's not dying. You know that, right? She's just having a baby."

"Yeah, I know. It's just…hearing her scream. I…um… Fuck, it just brings back some shit. That's all." He shoves a rough hand in his hair and strides out of the room. As he heads for the hall bathroom, I decide to give him a few minutes to collect himself.

I quickly pack an overnight bag for both of us before going to the kitchen to make a few sandwiches for the road.

"How long does that labor shit last?" he nervously questions, suddenly appearing behind me.

"It all depends. If we leave now, I bet we can make it before she has the baby."

"No. I don't want to be there for that. I can't listen to her scream. I'll lose it. I, um…" His voice cracks and it cuts me deep. He reaches up and grabs the back of his neck. "I can't be there, Sarah. I…I just can't." His chin quivers, exposing exactly how much this is affecting him.

"Leo," I breathe, dropping the mayo-covered knife and rushing in his direction. I throw my arms around his waist and desperately try to offer him the same comfort he always provides me.

"I know this isn't rational. But my whole body is thrumming because she might be scared right now and I'm not there to fix it. Shit…" His hands begin to tremble and he nervously cracks his neck. "I also know that, if I were there, I'd be tearing the hospital apart trying to get to her."

"She has Slate. She's not alone," I try to reassure him.

"I get that. But that doesn't make the instinct to protect her any less consuming."

"Okay, so what do you want to do? Go or wait? I've never actually had a baby, but I don't think it's as dramatic as they make it out to be in the movies. We could always just drive to Indy and check into a hotel until she has him. That way we are close by but you won't end up brawling with a doctor."

"Yeah. That sounds like a plan."

A few minutes later, Leo walks silently to my car after I inform him that I'm driving. He doesn't argue, nor does he eat any of the food I packed. About an hour into the trip, he reaches over and grabs my hand, giving it a tight squeeze.

"I'm sorry. I get a little wigged out about her sometimes," he apologizes, bringing my hand to his mouth.

"This probably isn't the best time to ask this, but you know me… so I'm going to ask it anyway. Have any of your therapists ever mentioned that you might have some form of PTSD from the events of that day?"

"Yeah. They have," he responds quietly, but he doesn't elaborate. He goes back to silently staring out the window.

Another hour later, Leo's phone chirps in his lap. He picks it up and lets out a loud relieved laugh. He turns the phone to me, revealing a picture of Erica smiling while holding a tiny baby with thick, brown hair. You can't really see the baby, but God bless Slate for knowing exactly which face Leo really *needed* to see.

As we continue our trip, Leo glances down at the picture several times. His mood significantly lightens as well. Holding my hand tight against his thigh, he even leans over to give me a few kisses. About ten minutes from the hospital, he asks me a question of his own.

"Do you want kids?"

My head snaps to his. "Um, I don't know. I mean, I always planned to have a family. It's just things haven't exactly worked out that way. Plus, I'm getting older, so I'm just not sure it's in the cards for me anymore."

"Sarah, you're thirty-five. You're not too old to have kids."

"Well, 'I don't know' is still my answer. What about you?"

"I just don't see how I could ever have anything to offer a kid. I just freaked the fuck out over Erica giving birth. Can you imagine what a whack job I would be as a dad?"

"I think you'd be a great dad. That's kind of how I think you treat Erica already. It's weird in some ways but really freaking sweet in others. My dad was this big, tall, quiet guy. He loved me and Emma more than anything in life, but he was never that over-the-top, don't-touch-my-daughter-or-I-kill-you type of dad. However, I can see you being that way. Cleaning guns in the living room when her fifth-grade boyfriend comes over to play." I laugh, but Leo just turns to stare back out the window. "I'm okay with no kids, Leo. In case you were worried about that."

He nods and squeezes my hand but doesn't say anything else.

"YOU WANT to hold him?" Erica asks.

"No, babe. I'm good," Leo declines while staring down at Adam Slate Andrews wrapped up in a blanket sleeping in his bassinet.

"Can I?" I ask when I'm not able to resist any longer.

"Of course," Erica answers warmly.

Stepping around Leo, I lift all eight pounds of baby Adam into my arms and cradle him tight against my chest. "He's gorgeous," I say, lifting his tiny hand from under the blanket.

As shameful as it may be, jealously immediately creeps into my heart. I was supposed to have this. I'm thirty-five years old. I shouldn't be starting over from scratch. I should have a baby with my blue eyes…or maybe even chocolate-brown. I glance up to find Leo watching me intently. I try to give him a forced smile, but it only makes the tears spill from my eyes.

Leo walks behind me, wraps his arms around my waist, and drops his chin to my shoulder. "You okay?"

"He's just really cute," I half lie, wiping the tears from my eyes.

"I love you," he whispers into my ear, making the world right again.

The fact is that, if I had a school of kids running around my feet right now, I wouldn't have Leo. No matter how fucked up it may be, in this moment, I'm thankful for the broken course that led me to here. All of the wrongs somehow feel right. And if Leo James is all I ever get, I can honestly still say that this life would be an absolute win.

"I love you, too." I turn my head and find his lips for a brief but no less meaningful kiss.

"He looks like you," Leo tells Slate.

"He does. Poor kid." Slate settles on the tiny hospital bed next to Erica.

"All right, Mr. Andrews. I've told you twelve times. That bed has a weight limit," a nurse says, walking in the room.

"I'll buy you a new one," Slate responds, not budging an inch.

"Okay, everyone. I need to check on our new mom now, so I'll need you all to step out into the hall for just a minute. Out you go."

"I'm not going anywhere," Slate growls.

"Oh lord, I don't mean you, Dad." She tosses him a sugary-sweet grin only to roll her eyes when she turns to face us.

"We'll be outside." Leo reaches, forward squeezing Erica's foot, while Slate takes Adam from my arms.

"So, gift shop?" I ask as soon as we exit the room.

But Leo's hands are suddenly in my hair. His mouth slams over mine as he pushes me up against the wall, stroking his tongue against mine. Screw the fact that we are standing in public—I meet his every thrust.

"Cásate conmigo," he says against my lips. *"No quiero ninguna parte de esta vida sin ti. Fuistes, mi* ángel. *Despues mi cielo y ahora necesito que seas mi todo."*

"Are you talking dirty?" I whisper, laughing.

"It might just be the dirtiest thing I've ever said." He leans away and tosses me an insecure smile. "Thank you for coming with me, ángel."

"You're welcome. I'm glad to be here." I give him a tight hug.

We stand in the middle of the hospital hallway holding each other. It's nothing overly sexy like it was a few minutes ago. It's just comfortable. *It's Leo.*

When the door swings open, Slate comes walking out with the nurse.

"I'm going to get some coffee. Can you sit with her for a minute?" he asks Leo.

"Oh, coffee sounds great. I'll go with you." I smile and pat Leo's arm. He needs a few minutes alone with Erica, and it doesn't appear that Slate is going to leave her side often.

"Grab me some too." He kisses my forehead before going back into Erica's room.

"So, how bad did he flip the fuck out earlier?" Slate asks as soon as the door clicks.

"Um, well…it wasn't terrible. But seeing her in pain really affected him," I respond evasively. I feel bad talking about Leo behind his back, but I don't exactly want to hide his struggles from the people who love him either.

"Right." He nods, not bothering to look at me. "Did Leo ever tell you that I used to have a real issue with their relationship?"

"No," I answer shortly. I'm unsure, yet very concerned, about where this conversation might be headed.

"Well, I had a big problem with it at first. I've heard Leo told you about their past." He glances over at me questioningly.

"He did." I once again give nothing away.

"Come on, Sarah. You have to admit it's a weird friendship they have." He stops walking and turns to face me. His expression is kind, but his words are starting to annoy me.

"No. I don't think it is. Sometimes, your only choice is to stick to the people who truly understand. It's easier than opening up to those who don't." I lift an eyebrow with a little attitude, causing Slate to grin.

"Is that why you and Leo are together?" he asks bluntly.

My eyes snap to his. I guess it's not surprising that Slate and Erica know about my past as well. To hear Leo tell it, I had a big impact on his life back then. But his question still catches me off guard.

"I…uh…" I stutter, not exactly sure how to answer. I like to think that our pasts aren't the only reason we are together. However, it might be the reason I truly fell in love with him. He gets me and accepts me for who I am. *God, I love him for that.*

"Leo needs you."

"No, he doesn't, but I'm more than happy to stay anyway," I inform him.

Slate's smile widens a fraction of an inch, and I decide to close the conversation.

"Erica and Leo's relationship is unconventional, but it's real. I think, fifty years from now, they will still be close. And it's not because they have some twisted dependency on each other. I don't disagree with you that it might be how it started, but every day, I think it evolves. In my eyes, they are just two people who bonded over a shared experience, but isn't that how all friendships start? Just because it was something ugly that brought them together doesn't make the bond any less pure." I begin to walk away.

I didn't exactly intend to be a bitch with my parting words, but I have a feeling that's exactly how it came off. Slate struck a nerve with this conversation though. I'm well aware of how Erica and Leo feel because my relationship with Casey has been scrutinized by everyone who knows our story. This all just hits a little too close to home for me.

I hear Slate bark out a laugh from behind me as I march away. With one giant step forward, he catches up and grabs my arm to stop me.

"Sarah, I agree with you *now*. So stop getting upset. This isn't what I was trying to say at all. You have no idea how fucking happy it makes me to hear you say all this. The truth can be a little overwhelming with those two, and I wanted to make sure that it doesn't intimidate you. I like you with Leo. I think you are really good for him. I just wanted to make sure your head was in the right place and you don't view Erica as some sort of competition."

"No, not at all. I mean, maybe I did that first night I heard them on the phone together," I say sheepishly.

"I can't blame you there, but you have no idea what a relief it is for me to hear all this from you. See, if you give Leo hell about spending time with Erica, she's going to, in turn, give me hell about…well everything." He scratches the back of his head.

"I promise. I'm okay with all of it. You don't need to worry about me." I smile reassuringly and it seems to sink in.

"Okay, coffee. Come on. My treat." He holds the hospital cafeteria door open and motions for me to enter.

Chapter
THIRTY-TWO

Leo

Two weeks later....

"WHAT DO you think about moving in with me?" I ask Sarah over the computer during our Thursday night chat. Broaching this topic over a video chat while I'm in LA is probably not my most romantic move, but I couldn't wait any longer.

I've been thinking about it for weeks now. We stay together most nights, but a few times a week, she goes home to clean her apartment or get more clothes. Slowly, the contents of her closet have been trickling their way over to my place. First, it was just some shampoo and pajamas. But it gradually became more. Now that she's working for me, it's not too hard to convince her to spend the night at my place.

"Seriously?" she asks, surprised.

"Yeah, seriously," I laugh. "Don't look at me like that."

"Leo, we haven't been seeing other each that long."

"You planning on breaking up with me anytime soon?" I ask, leaning back against the bed, suddenly wishing I hadn't blurted this out tonight. I'll be home tomorrow. I should have done it then when I could have coerced her with my body. *Mmm, her body.*

"I don't know. I like to keep my options open," she responds sarcastically.

"You know what I like for you to keep open? Your legs. Jesus, I can't wait to get home."

"Focus, Leo. Moving in together," she scolds.

"Right. Break your lease. I'll pay the fees."

"I'm less worried about the fees and more worried about how it's going to affect us."

"Ángel, we already basically live together. This will just make it permanent. And I'm not sure if you have missed this somehow, but *we* are absolutely permanent."

"I know we are. It's just… It seems like a huge step. We still have so much talking to do and stuff," she says quietly.

"What else exactly do we have to talk about? You might not have noticed, but we don't actually do much talking on Thursdays anymore. We mainly talk about our days and then have sex. Thursdays are officially my favorite day of the week." I smile and she lets out a soft laugh. "I think we've covered all the hard stuff and we're both still here."

"Yes. We are getting along so well. Clearly, it's time to move in together and start fighting about who should pay the electric bill and who left the cap off the toothpaste."

"I like those kind of fights," I tell her honestly. "Because I know they always end with me apologizing, even if I don't mean it, and then you get naked."

"Leo James! I'm going to pretend I didn't hear that part about you not meaning it!" she shouts, making me laugh.

"Come on. Move in with me," I exaggeratedly beg. "Besides, I don't like the idea of hiring a maid, so really this would be a win for me."

"And they say romance is dead," she deadpans.

"I love you, Sarah. You know I was joking…kinda." I wink. "But I'm serious about you moving in with me. I want you there all the time. I want to come home to you every night and know that you're safely tucked into my bed when I'm away. I want a life with you, ángel."

"I'm wet," she replies out of the blue.

I sit blinking at the screen for a minute. My neck should ache from whiplash after that sudden change of topic. I'm reasonably sure she's just trying to distract me, but I can't say that I really care.

"Show me," I answer, leaning in close to the computer, but she doesn't move a muscle.

"Last night, I woke up about an hour after I fell asleep. I was so turned on. I was having a dream that you snuck into the bedroom and pinned me on my stomach as you slide in from behind. I swear I could feel you inside me, Leo."

"I like this dream." I lick my lips as I immediately go hard.

"When I woke up, my hand was between my legs. It was a sad substitute for you, but it was working."

"Fuck, ángel." I begin to rub my growing cock.

"It was amazing until I completely woke up and remembered I told you I wouldn't come without you. Then it fucking sucked." She crosses her arms over her chest in an adorable show of attitude.

"Well, I'm here now." I tug down my pants, revealing my erection.

Her eyes glance down the screen for a second before she lets out a groan. "It was all hot and sexy at first when you claimed my every orgasm, but I'm not playing games anymore. I shouldn't have to ask for permission to get myself off. Especially on nights like last night when you were gone."

"Take off your pants. Show me what you would have done."

"I'm just letting you know that the deal is officially off."

"No. Every time you come is for me and me only. I'm sorry I was gone, because had I been there, I would have rolled you over and made good on your dream. You should have called me. I would have told you all about what I would have done then listened to you moan my name as you came."

"You were working," she says, pulling her shirt over her head, exposing her fucking perfect tits.

I begin stroking my cock as I watch her fingers roll her nipples. "Take. Off. Your. Pants. I want to see that wet pussy," I growl.

"See, I figured you would get all caveman. 'Grunt. Your orgasms belong to me.' So I will repeat. I'm not asking here. I am, however, willing to make a compromise."

"Oh yeah? What's that?" I continue to stroke myself as she reaches down to the button on her jeans.

"What if I agree to only make myself come while I'm in your bed? Well, I guess it would be our bed at that point." She smiles and my hand stills.

"You moving in with me?" I ask as a huge smile creeps across my face.

"I don't know. Are you going to throw a macho shit fit about me rubbing my clit while imagining your long cock buried inside me?"

Holy. Fucking. Hell. I can't decide if I'm happy or so turned on that I need to push the computer back a few inches to keep it from forever glowing under a black light.

"Yeah, I'm going to throw a fit." I pause, and I can tell by her face that she's about to get annoyed and shut me down. "But only because I like the idea of you coming in my shower too."

She smiles and temporarily disappears offscreen only to reappear a second later completely nude. "Our shower," she corrects, reclining on the bed and dropping her legs wide open.

"Fuck," I whisper as she pushes a single finger inside her heat. God, I'd give anything to feel her. I know exactly how tight that pussy is and how good it feels milking my cock.

I quicken the pace over my shaft as I watch her add another finger.

"Talk to me," she says, using her other hand to glide over her breasts.

"You are fucking beautiful. Christ. I'd give anything to fuck your tits right now."

"Mmm. My tits, huh?" She sits up, pushing her breasts into the camera.

"Yep. I'm going to come on them as soon as I get back. I want to see you covered in me." I switch hands so I can tilt the camera down to give her a better view.

"Fuck, baby," she breathes, lying back down with her eyes glued to the screen.

"Circle your clit. I want you to come for me now, ángel."

She quickly follows my direction and licks the finger on her other hand before dropping it between her legs. I move my hand over my cock with the same rhythm of her fingers.

"Come on your stomach. I want to watch," she demands between moans.

My pace quickens as I feel the orgasm traveling up from my balls. I'm close, and I fight to keep my eyes open. I want to see her face.

"Oh fuck. God, Sarah." My release lands right where directed and she lets out an approving moan.

Not a second later, I watch as she loses herself in her own high. She doesn't utter my name. Instead, she whispers a string of unrecognizable expletives as an orgasm courses through her body.

She silently relaxes against the bed, and I head to the bathroom, snagging a washcloth to clean myself off. As soon as I settle back in the picture, Sarah lets out a laugh.

"Fine. You can come on my tits. That was hot."

"Oh, I was coming on your tits whether you agreed or not." I laugh and roll to my side, taking the computer with me.

"Why do you have to travel so much? I miss you," she whines.

"Well, it won't be as bad next month. Things should plateau off pretty soon. I have enough men now, I think. They can travel for jobs and I'll be able to stay at home more."

"Good."

"Hey, next week, I have to be down in Florida for a meeting. You want to come with me? We can shut down the office and just have a couple of days to ourselves," I ask.

She smiles excitedly. "You love to take me places, don't you?"

"I just like being with you," I respond honestly.

"Well, I can't deprive you of that then."

"Okay, good. I'll have my secretary buy your ticket tomorrow." I wink.

"Hilarious. If you expect me to do it, I'm buying myself first class," she answers before changing the topic to something random.

We spend the next hour lying in bed naked, talking about how quickly we can get Sarah moved into my apartment. She tries to convince me to wait the two months until her lease is up, but I refuse. I'm more than willing to buy it out. If I had my way, I'd hire movers first thing in the morning, but she refuses, stating that we need to work out the details a little better. I promptly decide to hold her hostage at my place until then.

Chapter
THIRTY-THREE

Sarah

One week later…

"EVERYTHING OKAY?" I ask as Leo drops his keys on the dresser of a lavish hotel in Florida.

"Yeah, why? What's wrong?" He eyes me suspiciously.

"Nothing. I was just worried. I thought your meeting was over, like, an hour ago."

"It was, but I had to make some stops. No big deal. Just work shit." He removes his suit jacket and walks to the bed to kiss me. "You look gorgeous," he says, raking his eyes over my chest.

Upon Leo's insistence, I went shopping today and bought a new dress for tonight. It didn't take much convincing. Now that we are moving in together, the old purse strings have loosened up a bit. He tried to give me his credit card, but I enjoyed paying for the short, emerald-green cocktail dress myself, even if it is Leo's hand writing my paycheck.

"Thanks. You look pretty nice too." I pull his baby-blue tie, dragging him down for another kiss.

"*Cásate conmigo*," he whispers as he releases my mouth.

"Will you teach me some Spanish?" I ask. "I hate not understanding you when you say stuff like that. And I know you lie to me when I ask."

He laughs and nods. "Of course. Although I'm not sure what's Spanish for 'y'all,'" he teases before stepping away. "We're going to be late. I made early reservations so we could go out and hit some of the nightlife later."

"Oh, that sounds great. Let's go." I stand up in my four-inch heels, meeting Leo almost eye to eye. In these shoes, he's only an inch or so taller than I am. He doesn't back away, even when I try to take a step around him.

"New shoes too?" he asks, brushing the hair off my shoulder.

"I *needed* them," I explain. "Which reminds me. I *need* a raise too." I turn my head, and he trails wet kisses up my neck, sending chills over my body.

"*Cásate conmigo*," he repeats into my ear.

"What does that mean?" I grab his biceps to balance.

He leans away with a full-blown megawatt smile and answers, "I'll tell you later. Let's go eat." Grabbing my hand, he pulls me from the room.

"WOW. THIS place is gorgeous," I say as we walk into a stunning restaurant that overlooks the beach.

"See, aren't you glad I talked you into getting a new dress?" He smiles, resting a hand on my lower back, guiding me toward the maître d'. "Leo James. We have reservations," he tells the older gentleman, who leads us to a table right by the large bay windows.

"I feel like we're eating on the beach," I tell Leo as he pulls out my chair.

"I think that's the idea, ángel."

The menus are placed in front of us and I begin studying the entrées as Leo orders a bottle of wine.

Growing up in Savannah, I was exposed to every possible seafood you can imagine. I loved it all. Fresh shrimp and fish are some things I've missed while living in Chicago. As my eyes race over the menu, my stomach lets out an audible growl.

"You hungry?" he jokes.

"Well, I didn't think I was, but the sight of this seafood section has changed my mind." I glance up to find his menu closed and resting on the table in front of him. His smoldering eyes are locked on me. "You already know what you're getting?" I ask curiously, wondering how the hell he could have possibly decided that fast.

"How about you just order two meals and we can share? I think you are frothing at the mouth." He laughs.

"It all just looks really good." I go back to reading the menu and moan when my eyes find shrimp with truffled grits.

"I can tell." He laughs again, reaching out to hold my hand.

"Okay, it's decided. You are getting the salmon and scallops because they are calling my name. And I'm getting the shrimp and grits because what kind of Southern girl would I be if I didn't?" I look up to find him watching me intently once again.

"Whatever you want, ángel." He interlocks our fingers and rests them on the table.

The waiter shows up with the wine, but Leo never releases my hand. We fall into comfortable conversation with his thumb lazily stroking mine.

When dinner arrives, I have to fight my hand out of his grasp. Just as I suspected, the food is amazing. It isn't until I am halfway done with the grits that Leo informs me that he doesn't like salmon or scallops. I want to be annoyed with him for not having told me before I ordered, but he just shrugs and pushes his plate toward me. I, on the other hand, do love salmon and scallops, so I gladly switch with him.

As he polishes off my grits, I may fall in love with him all over again. He tells me how his grandmother used to cook grits when he was a kid. Finding a man in Chicago who loves grits may very well be as rare as hitting the lottery, but somehow, I did it. Maybe karma doesn't hate me after all.

"As an employee of Guardian Protection Agency, I am officially volunteering to accompany you on all further business excursions to Florida. That was delicious." I place my napkin on the table and take the last sip of my wine while Leo pays the bill.

"Well, as the owner of Guardian Protection Agency, you are welcome to join me on all further business excursions to…well, everywhere." He pauses before lifting my hand and kissing my palm. "*Cásate conmigo,* ángel."

"Please tell me what that means? That's, like, the third time you've said it tonight."

He ignores my question and stands up, using my hand to pull me to my feet beside him. "You want to go down to the beach?"

"Only if you promise to speak in English."

"No promises." He winks and leads me from the restaurant.

We walk down the long boardwalk toward the beach. It's the middle of the week, so there are only a few people milling around. We both remove our shoes, and Leo stashes them under the boardwalk before heading into the sand.

"God, look how big the moon is," I sigh just as my toes touch the water.

"It's a beautiful night." Leo wraps his arms around me from behind and drags his nose up my neck. I suck in a deep breath, reveling in the mixture of his scent and the salt in the air. "*Cásate conmigo,*" I feel him say against my skin.

"Okay. You are really starting to freak me out with that. Please just tell me what that means. I feel like you're calling me fat or something." I turn to face him, and Leo bursts out laughing.

"I'm definitely not calling you fat, ángel."

"You know what? Fine. I'm going to Google it." I look down and realize that I didn't bring a purse. "Give me your phone," I demand, snapping my fingers at him, making him laugh again.

When he hands over his phone, I quickly bring up the search engine.

"Okay, now can you spell it?" I ask when my first attempt at phonetics doesn't return any results.

Leo shoves his hands in his pockets, and I swear I can see the ripples of his muscles thought his shirt. It's almost distracting as he begins to rattle off consonants and vowels, but I forge ahead. I click enter and stumble back a step as the translation flashes on the screen.

Marry me.

My pulse spikes as my eyes fly to Leo, who's watching me with a nervous grin.

"I…um…think Google is broken," I rush out then quickly hand him his phone and speed-walk down the beach.

Oh my fucking God. Is he proposing? Surely, 'marry me' must mean something else in Spanish. Fuck, his first language is English! Maybe his Spanish isn't as good as I thought. Maybe he thinks it's some sort of term of endearment like ángel or *mi cielo*. Maybe he—

"Sarah." He interrupts my inner panic attack by grabbing my arm from behind. "Stop overthinking this. Let me explain."

I let out a relieved breath. "Oh thank God. I thought you were about to propose." I laugh and wipe away the tears that started to form in my eyes.

"No, I *am* proposing. I'm just not okay with letting Google do it for me."

"Oh my God," I squeak, throwing my hands up to cover my mouth. "Leo, I, um…" I begin to stutter.

"Shh. It's my turn to talk." He grabs my hand, and my vision begins to swim. Dropping to a knee, he pulls out a ring I can barely make out among the unshed tears.

Apparently, marry me does mean the same thing in Spanish.

"I'm going to be sick," I say from behind my hands.

Leo lets out a chuckle but stands back up and pulls me into his chest. "No puking," he breathes against my ear while rubbing his scruff against my cheek. "Here. Just let me hold you. Maybe that will be easier." He silently holds me for a few minutes as I try to compress the emotions into something more manageable but fail miserably. "You okay?" he whispers, and I shake my head. "Well I'm going to start talking. You let me know if you need to puke so I can at least get out of the way."

I can feel the smile on his lips as he kisses my neck.

"Sarah, I love you. I know I told you once that you saved my life, but oddly enough, that isn't even the most spectacular thing you've ever done for me. I've lived a lot of years, and none of them have been as fulfilling as the last few months with you. You've given me back a life that I had long since given up on."

My hands begin to tremble between us. Leo only acknowledges it by squeezing me tighter before continuing to talk quietly into my ear.

"We have a long road ahead of us because of our pasts. We both

227

still struggle on a daily basis, and I can't swear to you that will ever stop. But it doesn't feel impossible when I'm with you. You make me smile and laugh. You make things right even when the world feels completely wrong. Sarah, it's easy to remember why I should open my eyes every morning when the first thing they see is you."

I hiccup a breath and lift a hand to cover my mouth again.

"You need to throw up or can I keep going?" he asks in the most romantic way one can ask such a question.

"Keep going," I whimper.

"I love that I'm able to be your rock even though, sometimes, I feel like I can barely support my own weight. But more than that, I love knowing that, even on my weakest days, you understand enough about how I'm feeling to be my rock also. We can do this, Sarah. I know you're going to worry about jumping into a marriage, but you have to know I have never been more confident about something in my life. Individually, we've been through hell and lived to tell about it. Together, there isn't a force in the world that could bring us down."

"Leo, I…" I start, but I'm afraid to even finish the sentence.

Leo

I DECIDED weeks ago that I was going to propose to Sarah. It never included a beach or her getting sick, but I knew I was going to do it. I've proposed in Spanish no less than twenty times since I made the decision. I proposed over breakfast when the light from the window twinkled in her ocean-blue eyes. I proposed on a random night after dinner when she got frustrated and began cussing because she couldn't find the words to make me understand how we might benefit from time spent apart. I proposed in the middle of a heated game of Trivial Pursuit right before she cheated so I couldn't get my final pie piece. I even once proposed in the middle of sex as I emptied myself inside her. But up until now, I've never had the balls to say it in English.

"Sarah Kate Erickson, will you marry me?"

She sucks in a deep breath but remains silent in my arms.

Asking a woman to marry you is terrifying, but I didn't exactly go into this with visions of her screaming yes from the mountaintops. I knew this was going to be a hard sell. I also knew that I wouldn't take no for an answer. We might be taking up residence on this square foot of the beach because I'm not budging until she agrees to be my wife.

"We're right together. You know it just as much as I do," I say, hoping to convince her, but she only continues to cry. "Ángel, say something."

"I don't know what to say," she tells my chest.

"Start with what part of this has you all worked up. Are you excited, nervous, scared?" I prompt as she begins to wiggle out of my arms

"What if I break you like I did Brett? What if that's, like, my curse—I ruin men."

"And you think not marrying me will make me any less ruined? Sarah, if something happened to us, I would never be the same again, ring or not."

"This is a big commitment," she says, looking down at her feet.

"No. This is just us showing our friends and family how committed we already are. Tell me you can imagine a day where you don't love me. If you can envision that, then I'll let this go. Otherwise, I'm not leaving this beach without a yes."

Her eyes bounce around the night sky. I know she's trying to work this out in her head, but Sarah doesn't exactly have the best track record in that department. She's going to make this into something dramatic and work herself into an over-the-top frenzy.

"Just listen to me—" I start to talk her down, but before I get all the words out, she renders them useless.

"Yes," she rushes out.

"Yes?" I question because I was definitely not expecting it to be that easy.

"I'm really scared, but you're right. We're better at this life thing together." She tosses me a tentative smile.

"Yes?" I repeat one more time just to make sure I'm not hearing things.

"*Sí.*" She shrugs and starts laughing around the tears still flowing from her eyes.

I instantly take her mouth in a hard kiss. "Give me your hand." I reluctantly pull away long enough to retrieve the ring from my pocket. I swiftly slide the oversized ring onto her finger as if it could prevent her from changing her mind.

"Leo!" She gasps, running her fingers over the large, round diamond and down over the blue topaz stones I had embedded in the band itself. It was the closest thing to baby blue I could find. "It's gorgeous."

"Just like you," I respond, only vaguely aware of how cliché it sounds.

"Are you sure about this? I mean, like, really, really sure?" she asks, looking up at me nervously, causing me to begin laughing all over again.

"I was ready to set up camp on this beach like Tom Hanks in *Cast Away* until you said yes. So I can say with absolute certainty that I'm ready for this."

"Shit. That would've made me Wilson." She sniffles.

"You have better hair." I smile wide, unable to wipe it from my face.

"I'm not going to lie, Leo. I'm glad that you are so optimistic about this because I'm really fucking worried." She pauses and begins inspecting her ring. "But I'm really fucking happy too."

"We're going to be amazing, Sarah. I can feel it. Now, come on. Let's go upstairs. Suddenly, I feel ready for something else too."

"No, wait. I have to call Emma and Casey. They are going to flip. Give me your phone. Let's text them a picture of the ring." She begins wiping the mascara from under her eyes. I watch as she tries to capture the perfect picture of her ring using only the flash on my phone as light.

A half hour later, Sarah and I consummate our engagement in the hotel shower. My phone vibrates its way off the counter with incoming messages from not only Emma and Casey, but also Erica. However, as I bury myself in the woman who will forever be my wife, they all go unanswered.

Chapter
THIRTY-FOUR

Sarah

THE MORNING after Leo proposed, we immediately started talking about getting married. He wasn't keen on the idea of a long engagement. And while I may have been hesitant at first, once that ring was on my finger, I couldn't wait to become Mrs. James. For the first time since the accident, everything actually *felt* right—including the imperfections in our relationship.

Leo and I decided to have a small ceremony in a few weeks. Just something intimate with our closest friends in attendance. Originally, he just wanted to rush to the courthouse as soon as we got back. That was until I reminded him that Erica would probably murder him in his sleep if she didn't get to come to his wedding. He quickly agreed, and we sat down to set a date around his schedule.

We went over our finances on the plane ride home. It was really important to me to help contribute to our new life together. When Leo broke down his monthly bills for me, it became blindingly obvious that he made a hell of a lot more money than I did. I would have been lucky if I could even cover our electric and cell phone bills every month. I still had some money from the wreck, but it was dwindling quickly, and with overhead like Leo's, it wasn't going to get us far. I got panicky at the idea of depending on him for everything, but he squashed those fears by telling me that, by accepting his proposal, I had just signed on for a twenty-four-seven job at Guardian. I began to relax as I worked out the math of my new paycheck in my head while Leo laughed beside me.

The day we got back from Florida, Leo hired movers. I thought his head was going to explode when they told him it would be a few days before they could add us to their schedule. I giggled as he marched to my bedroom and dumped all my underwear into a box, mumbling something about how "home is where the panties reside." He also confiscated my keys so that I had to stay at his apartment until the move was final. He could have just asked. It's not like I would have argued, but it was more entertaining watching him try to force me to stay with him.

When the movers finally came, it didn't take long to empty my apartment since I didn't have much to take with me. Leo has a house full of furniture, so we donated most of mine to the Building Foundations's yard sale. They were more than appreciative.

"Leo, where did they put the stuff from my bathroom?" I ask, walking into *our* room just as the last mover leaves.

"I'm going to go out on a limb here and guess the bathroom? But come here. I have something for you."

"Mmm. Is it something new or something hard?" I ask seductively, swaying my hips as I walk toward him.

"Well, first, it's something new. *Then* it's something hard." He pulls me against his chest and presses his hips into mine. Walking backwards, he scoops up a bag next to the bed then leads me into the bathroom.

"So, now that we are living together—"

"And getting married," I add with a huge smile.

"And getting married," he confirms, "there are a few things you should know that I'm not willing to share." He pulls out a rectangular box from the bag. "This is your very own Kindle. No more borrowing mine. I swear, Sarah, I opened it the other day and there was a naked man on the cover of nearly every book in my library."

I let out a quiet laugh. He's not wrong. I've been reading a lot more recently, and every single day, Casey sends me a new recommendation. It's not my fault they all have half-dressed men on the covers. Okay, fine, I might buy them exactly for that reason.

"Well, you didn't have to do that. But thank you. I'll put it to good use." I give him a quick kiss and throw in an ass grope, well… just because I can.

"Secondly,"—he opens the bathroom closet, revealing a shelf full of my body wash—"you stink. Take a shower."

"Excuse me?" I cross my arms over my chest.

"I know you ran out of body wash while we were in Florida, but you are not allowed to use mine anymore. You smell like me…and I hate it." He gives me a serious look but returns the ass grope.

"I like the way you smell." I make a show of sniffing his shirt, but he ignores me.

"And lastly, here are the forms from the bank I need you to fill out in order to add you to my checking account."

"Wait. Already? Shouldn't we wait until we actually get married?"

"Nope. Because I'm not paying you anymore. And I'm assuming you'll need money for groceries and shit." He releases me and digs back through the bag.

"I have money, Leo. But the hell you aren't paying me anymore."

"Joint account, Sarah. It's *our* money now. It seems like a waste of time to write you a check just to deposit it right back into our account."

"I don't know, Leo."

"Just fill them out," he orders before revealing a stack of bridal magazines from the bag. "Here. I dog-eared the pages I liked."

"Um…why are you reading bridal magazines?" I ask confused.

He cocks his head. "Um…because we're getting married."

I have to bite my lip to force back the laugh that is dangerously close to escaping. "Well, okay, then." I continue to chew on my lip.

"I made a few notes too. According to the quiz, you're a rustic bride, so I took that into consideration with my preferences."

When he winks, I completely lose it.

I burst into a fit of laughter, keeping myself from toppling over by grabbing his arm. Leo watches me curiously while I try to collect myself. He doesn't say anything, but it's obvious that he's trying to suppress his own smile. I wrap my arms around his neck and kiss his nose.

"You are an amazing man, Leo James. I had no idea wedding planning was part of your repertoire."

"If it gets you down that aisle with the bare minimum amount of panic attacks, wedding planning can be my main priority," he answers, rubbing his scruff against my cheek.

"I love you," I whisper.

"I love you too, ángel." He sucks in a deep, content breath. "Now, get in the shower." He reaches out, snagging one of the new bottles of my body wash and all but shoves me into the shower fully dressed.

"WHERE'S LEO?" I ask while wringing out my freshly washed hair with a towel.

"One of the new guys had an issue with a client, so he went to talk to him," Johnson responds from behind the desk in the security room.

"Hey, thanks for helping the movers out earlier. I was just about to make a late lunch. You hungry?" I drape the towel over my shoulder.

"I could go for some food." He smiles. "Hey, I need to make a few phone calls. You think you can listen out for the buzzer? Leo has a potential client coming up in a little while. I told him I'd meet with her if he wasn't back yet."

"Yeah, no problem. Chicken salad work for you?"

He gives me a thumbs-up as he lifts the phone to his ear.

A few minutes later, I'm sobbing my way through chopping an onion when the buzzer for the door goes off. I take a quick peek at the security monitor to find a woman in a business suit carrying a small leather briefcase. I press the button allowing her entrance to the building. Then I wash my hands and drag my still-damp hair up into a ponytail. Just as I swipe my fingers under my eyes, I hear her knock at the door.

"Hi. I'm looking for Leo James," she says professionally as soon as I open the door.

"Come on in. Leo's not here right now, but Aiden Johnson is expecting you." I start to lead her back to the office.

"I'm sorry. You must have me confused with someone else. My

name is Judy Price and I'm with the Department of Child Services. I didn't have an appointment with Mr. James today." She pulls a card from the side of her briefcase.

"Can I ask what this is about?" I request curiously.

"I'm sorry…?" she prompts for my name.

"Sarah."

"I'm sorry, Sarah. This is a personal matter. Can you please see that Mr. James calls me as soon as possible? I have a very urgent matter to discuss with him."

"Personal? So this isn't related to Guardian Protection?"

"I'm sorry. I can't discuss this with you."

I stare down at her card, trying to piece together what the Department of Child Services could possibly want with Leo.

"I'll see myself out," she says when I don't immediately respond.

"No, wait. Can you please just tell me what this is in reference to? I'm Leo's…wife," I lie, knowing that I'll need to be family in order to get any type of answers.

"I'm sorry, but I'll still need to speak with Leo." She offers me an apologetic smile then lets out a huff. "But you can tell him my visit is in regard to his daughter, Liv."

"I'm sorry, what? His daughter?" I ask, incredulous.

"Right. Okay, then. I can see this is news to you. Please relay that I was here to your husband. Have a nice day, Mrs. James." She turns and lets herself out the door.

I stand immobile as the bite from her announcement ricochets through my body, shredding my hopes and dreams at every turn.

There has to be a mistake. Maybe another Leo James?

His daughter?

It's just not possible. He would have told me.

His. Daughter.

Liv.

Suddenly, the memory of Leo's tattoo flashes into my mind, igniting a spark that roars into a wildfire in a matter of seconds.

"Son of a bitch!" I scream, rushing to the office, knowing one man who will have the answers.

Just as I enter the door, Johnson's eyes jump to mine. The phone is to his ear, but he immediately stands as if he is able to sense my anxiety. He tilts his head and uses a hand to cover the mouthpiece.

"You okay?" he questions.

"He. Has. A. *Daughter*?" I deliver very slowly.

He physically dodges the word 'daughter' as I spit it at him. "I'll have to call you back," he says into the phone then quickly hangs up. "Sarah, calm down." He begins to move around the desk, but I put a hand up to stop him.

"I need some fucking answers. Like, yesterday." I take a few deep breaths in an attempt to reel in my rapidly growing anger. Though it does nothing to extinguish the betrayal that is surging through my veins.

"You need to talk to Leo. He should be back in a few—"

"Goddamn it!" I scream. "Tell me the fucking truth. It's plain to see Leo won't do it." My chest heaves and my stomach threatens to revolt.

"It's not my truth to tell," he responds with a shrug that enrages me.

"You know what? Fuck you." I rush forward and decide to get the answers from the only other person in the world who might be willing to give them to me.

I use the remote to flip on the TV and find the call button on the computer like I've seen Leo do numerous times in the past. Then I listen to the drone of a phone ringing as my hands nervously knot in front of me.

"Sarah, please don't bring Erica into this," Johnson begs from behind me.

Fuck that. Someone is telling me what the hell is going on.

I don't respond, and after only a few seconds, Erica flashes onto the screen with a baby held tight against her shoulder.

"Sarah? Is everything okay?" she asks, concerned.

"Tell me about his daughter," I demand as Johnson begins to cuss behind me.

"Whose daughter?" She shakes her head in confusion.

"Leo's!" I try to scream, but it catches on a sob.

"He doesn't have any kids," she answers with certainty.

"Fuck!" Johnson bites out, rubbing his hand over his shaved head. His outburst catches Erica's attention.

"Aiden, what's going on?" She disappears offscreen only long enough to put the baby down.

"Shit," he mumbles before looking back at Erica. "Yeah. Fuck. Fine. He has a daughter. He's never met her. He sends money every month, and extra during the holidays. This is not my place to be telling you, so I'm begging both of you to calm the hell down and just talk to Leo about this."

"Excuse me?" Erica shrieks, apparently hearing this information for the very first time.

"Her name is Liv, like his tattoo," I fill in and both their heads snap to mine.

"How the fuck do you know that?" Johnson asks, perplexed.

"A social worker was just here looking for him," I reply, dropping my head into my hands. "I can't believe he would lie to me...again."

"Oh my God," I hear Erica whisper in disbelief. "He got that tattoo our first year together in the program. Oh God." She begins to cry. "How old is she, Aiden?"

"Please. Wait and talk to him," he answers.

"Aiden," she pleads.

"Don't go there, Erica. I know what you're thinking and he did not abandon her to take care of you," he responds.

Erica begins to sob loudly. I try to figure out why she's so upset, but my attention is stolen away when I hear the front door open.

Chapter
THIRTY-FIVE

Leo

AS I pull into the parking garage at my apartment, the strangest feeling of excitement washes over me. After dealing with an idiot client who expected chef services from fucking security, I should, by all accounts, be in a shitty mood. However, I have a fiancée waiting for me upstairs and that idea has me darting from the car and jogging up the stairs. Just as I push through the stairwell door, I see a woman exiting my apartment.

Even better. I didn't completely miss my appointment today.

"Mrs. Brown?" I say as I approach her.

"Mr. James?" she asks in return.

"That's me." I smile and extend a hand. "Leo James. Nice to meet you. Sorry I—" I start but am quickly cut off.

"I'm glad I ran into you, Leo. My name is Judy Price. I'm with the Department of Child Services." She pulls a business card from the side of her briefcase. "I'm here to talk to you about your daughter, Liv."

The sound of her name sends a pang of guilt through my system. That one syllable spikes my pulse and knots my stomach.

"What about her?" I ask roughly, glancing around to make sure no one else is within hearing range.

"Is there somewhere we can talk?" She glances to my front door.

No fucking way I'm taking her back inside when I know Sarah's in there. "This is fine," I respond, crossing my arms over my chest.

"Well, okay, then." She pulls a manila file folder out of her briefcase and hands it to me. "Your daughter is currently in the care of Social Services in the state of Texas. I was asked to come here to inform you of this fact. To gain custody of your child, you must return to Texas and fill out the appropriate paperwork. It's quite simple, actually."

"What? Where's Amy?"

"I'm very sorry to inform you, but Amy Avila passed away last week, Mr. James."

"Wait. Amy's gone? What the fuck happened?" I choke out around the lump in my throat.

"Heroin," she answers with the shake of her head.

Bile creeps up into my throat. "Amy?" I ask again for clarification, because this can't be happening.

She silently nods a confirmation.

"No, there must be some confusion. She wasn't into drugs. I was a fucking DEA agent. I'm sorry, Mrs. Price, but something's not right here. She would *never* have touched that shit. She knew better." I start to become irate when nothing adds up the way it should.

"Things change, Mr. James. *People* change," she answers, but it does nothing to remove the five hundred pounds that have taken up residence on my chest.

"Oh. Fuck." I feel sick and have to throw an arm against the wall to remain on my feet. "Jesus Christ."

"I'm sure this is shocking, but I'm going to urge you to stay focused on Liv. We attempted to place her with Amy's parents in the interim, but they only agreed to take her on a very temporary basis, ending tomorrow. They gave us your name and asked that we reach out to you, as her father, for a more permanent situation for Liv. It seems they haven't had much contact with her, nor are they in any position to care for a young child."

Foggy memories of the many altercations I had with the Avilas flash into my thoughts. At the forefront of my mind is the verbal abuse they passed out like lollipops when Amy was growing up.

"She shouldn't be with them. The Avilas are fucked-up people," I manage to grit out through clenched teeth.

"While I haven't met them personally, judging by the urgency in which Texas sent me to find you, I assume they would agree with that assessment."

"Wait, where's Max?"

"According to the paperwork, Max Young hasn't seen Liv since he was removed from the birth certificate four years ago—the very same time you were added."

"Fuck," I mumble as my racing mind tries to sort out all of the details. "What am I supposed to do?" I plead for guidance. I know there is only one option, but I can't seem to wrap my mind around it.

"You need to go to Texas as soon as possible. The Avilas will be turning Liv over to Social Services tomorrow. You should be there or she will be placed into foster care."

"How am I supposed to do this?" My hands begin to nervously twitch at the very idea of taking on something this big.

"She's lost her mother and has been left in the care of virtual strangers. She could use a parent right now."

"I'm a stranger!" I yell at the entire fucking cruel world. "I've never even seen her," I choke out.

"Well, there has never been a better time than the present to change that."

"No!" I yell. "You don't understand. She deserves better than me. She deserves parents who can offer her a stable life. I can't give her that. I have nothing to offer her."

"Mr. James. I'm going to be very candid with you here. I don't know much about this case except what was faxed over to me this morning. So let me just state the facts. Her mother was addicted to heroin and ended up dying because of it. She has two grandparents who acted like it was a burden on them to even keep her for a week. She is on her way to foster care, which, in some cases, works out well and in others, not so much. I have no idea what her life has been like, but I'm relatively sure you and your wife can give her better."

My wife? Oh my God. Sarah. I haven't even stopped to think about how this is going to affect her.

"I'm not saying you have to take her, but you need to contact Texas regardless. The numbers are in that folder. Please don't hesitate to contact me if you have any further questions." She gives me a tight smile and heads toward the elevator.

I lean against the wall for a moment longer, unable to trust my shaking legs.

Amy's gone. My *child* is with her borderline-abusive parents. Either I have to claim custody or she will be placed in a foster home.

What the fucking hell is going on right now?

This can't be my life.

Yet, somehow, it is.

I make my way to my front door, desperate to find something—or, preferably, someone—who can make sense of the questions overwhelming my mind.

I barely even make it through the door before the chaos continues.

"So, when exactly were you going to tell me?" Sarah asks the minute she rounds the hall corner.

I stumble for a minute when I realize she has obviously already heard. But I can't deal with it right now. My thoughts are still firing in a million different directions.

"Not now, Sarah," I say over my shoulder as I stride to my office.

"No. Fuck you, Leo. It's right fucking now or never," she demands in the bitchiest tone I have ever heard from her, but when I glance up, her eyes are filled with tears.

"What do you want me to say here?" I ask in a surprisingly calm voice even to my own ears.

"The truth, Leo. How about, for once in our entire fucking relationship, you give me the entire goddamn truth." She throws her arms out to the sides in frustration.

Maybe she's right. What the hell can it hurt at this point? This might actually be the perfect time to unload it all. I'm just numb enough to not care how much it's going to hurt when she leaves.

"I've got a kid. She's five and her mother just died from a drug overdose."

Sarah's mouth drops open. So maybe she didn't know all of it.

"Tomorrow morning, I have to fly to Texas to keep her from entering foster care. I'm all she has left, yet my mind is screaming at deafening levels that she's better off without me. Sure, I can put a roof over her head and food in her stomach, but that is fucking *it*. I have nothing else to offer a kid. Every fucking day, I struggle to keep my own head straight. Now, I'm supposed to drag an innocent child along in that journey? I can't do it, but I'm not sure I have any other choice." My words become increasingly louder as the absolute truth flies from my mouth.

"What the fuck?" she breathes from behind her hands.

"Exactly!" I laugh humorlessly. "My thoughts exactly!" I breeze past her and head for the security room. I want nothing more than to hold Sarah as the tears flow from her eyes, but I don't have even an ounce of myself left to give another human being right now.

I round the corner into the office only to find Erica crying on the TV screen. Her red-rimmed eyes flash to mine, and it's painfully obviously that she heard the great revelation as well.

Fuck.

"I don't have time for a lecture, babe." I move to the computer to sever the connection, but Johnson swats my hand away before I have the chance.

"Don't you fucking dare. Clear the goddamn air once and for all," he growls just as Sarah appears in the doorway. Her tears have dried, but I can tell she's even more livid than before.

I lock my fingers and rest them on my head while feeling the mounting pressure from the three sets of eyes I would easily classify as those of my family. Only tonight, they are all shooting daggers at me. If my life weren't crumbling under my feet, I might pause to laugh.

"For fuck's sake. Can you people give me just a fucking second to form a coherent thought?"

"No. I can't. You've had months to figure out how to tell me this story. I'm done waiting," Sarah says from the doorway. "Start talking or I'm gone."

I pinch the bridge of my nose and look up to see Slate standing behind Erica, holding baby Adam. I guess it's now or never.

"I met Amy my senior year in college. We spent five years together, and I had these grand plans of proposing. I was already part of the DEA and progressing quickly. Everything was perfect until she popped up pregnant."

I take in a deep breath, finally turning to face Sarah. I don't owe this story to anyone but her.

"Initially, I was ecstatic about the idea of starting a family with her. There wasn't a baby in the world that would have been more welcome. That is until I found out that Amy had been cheating on me with my best friend, Max. They had apparently been seeing each other for close to a year. It happened mostly while I was away training, but sometimes right under my nose. I showed Max the engagement ring I had bought and he spilled it all. Everything right down to the fact that the baby she was carrying was his. To say I was devastated would be the understatement of the century. I lost the woman I loved, my best friend, and what I thought was my future child all in the same day.

"Amy tried to stop by and talk to me, but the only thing that came out of it was her confirming that the baby was Max's. I called her a whore, and Max and I ended the day brawling on my front lawn. It was a really fucking bad time for me. That was the first time in my life I ever struggled with depression. I called out of work and went dark for a few days. The pain was agonizing.

"When I was able to go back to work, my boss called me into his office and offered me a long-term undercover job. Desperate for something new, and with nothing to leave behind, I immediately accepted. A week later, I was on my way to Florida."

I turn to Erica, who silently nods in understanding, before facing Sarah once again. "We were already in the Witness Protection Program by the time I was sent word that Max had a DNA test performed and it ruled him out of being Liv's father." I shake my head and take a step toward Sarah only to have her back away. "I called in a favor and had them add me to her birth certificate as soon as Max petitioned to have his name removed. At least, that way, she would be entitled to my benefits if something happened to me. Back then, I didn't think I'd ever live long enough to meet her. It's not like I could come out of hiding to see her on the weekends or anything. If I had shown her any interest, she would have become a target as well. It was safest for me to stay as far away from her as I could get."

"You've been out of the program for over a year now, Leo," Sarah snaps.

I can tell my explanation is doing nothing to help our current situation. "All right. I'm done here. There's your story. Now, everyone out but Sarah," I say roughly.

"You haven't told me shit!" Erica yells.

"No. But we can talk about it later. Right now, I need to talk to Sarah. Alone." I quickly click the button on the mouse to end the call. "Out," I tell Johnson, who slaps me on the back before exiting the room. Then I settle down in the chair and motion for her to join me. "Come here, ángel."

"No. Talk," she demands from across the room. "I heard what you said. I understand your situation, but I can't for the fucking life of me figure out how you thought it would be okay to never mention that you have a kid? We're getting married, Leo. You don't think you should have been a little more upfront about something this big?" She pauses. "Just so you know, I wouldn't have cared. It wouldn't even have fazed me, but you making yet another lie of omission is damn near killing me. God damn it, Leo! I can't spend the rest of my life wondering what else you are keeping from me."

"I didn't tell you because I didn't want to admit it to myself!" I explode out of the chair. "Sarah, if I told you I had a daughter I've never met, what would you have done? No, wait. I can tell you what you what you would have done. You would have given me some grand pep talk and forced me to go find her. You wouldn't have stopped until she was calling me Daddy and I was walking her to school. That's what you do. You try to fix me. But this is *not* something I was ready to face yet."

"You're damn right I would have tried to fix this."

"And it would have ruined us!" I yell at her. "I would have fought you, and it wouldn't have been pretty. Fuck, Sarah, I should have the right to deal with my own shit on my own time without you forcing it down my throat."

"Forcing it down your throat, huh? So let me get this straight. You don't mention that you have a kid, and somehow I'm in the wrong for some assumed transgression that never even happened? Don't worry, Leo. I won't try to fix anything for you anymore." She reaches down, rips off her engagement ring, and throws it at me. It bounces off my chest then clinks against the floor, but I don't take my eyes off her. "You can do it all on your own from now on."

"Sarah, stop. That's not what I meant." I rush after her, grabbing her arm before she can make it to the front door.

"I don't give a fuck what you *meant*." She snatches her arm from my hand. "Your words and actions have said more than enough."

"What do you want me to say? I know I should have mentioned it to you, but saying it out loud feels a whole lot like accepting it."

"She's a person, Leo. It's a fact. It's not some idea you have to accept."

"God damn it. You're already doing it. Stop."

"That is not me trying to fix you. That's me telling you the fucking truth. Although now I understand why you might not recognize what that sounds like," she seethes.

"That's not fair and you know it. Damn it, Sarah. I'm sorry. It's just... I'm not the same person I was a few years ago. I know you wouldn't have listened to that though. You would have pushed me to make contact. But what exactly am I supposed to say to her? 'Hi, Liv. I'm your dad. I've allowed women to be raped, planned to kill myself, and spend a week every few months depressed and hiding in my bedroom. I hate myself most days and suffer from paralyzing PTSD when it comes to your Auntie Erica, who coincidentally is the same woman who I allowed to be assaulted. Come to Papa'?" I say sarcastically.

"Jesus Christ, Leo." She shakes her head.

"Too much?" I ask roughly. "You wanted the truth right? Well, there it is." I suck in a breath and try to calm down. She doesn't deserve this. I push my hands in my hair as the entire day becomes just too much for me to take. "I love you. I'm just so overwhelmed right now. Yes, I hate that you try to fix everything for me, but I'm not sure I could do it without you."

"Maybe you should have thought about that before you decided to keep all of this from me." She heads for the door and my eyes go wide.

"Stop. Just wait. Please. *Stop!*" I shout as loud as my jagged voice will allow. "I can't do this now. I can't keep up. I have to figure out everything with Liv right now, and I can't process all of this at once. I'm sorry. Just...please." I panic.

"I'm sorry, too." She snatches her purse off the table and walks out the door.

I silently stare at the door for a few minutes, completely lost on how to even begin processing the last hour. Sarah's gone, Amy's dead, and Liv is alone. *Oh God.*

I end up on my couch, though how I got here will forever remain a mystery. It's still light outside, so I know it hasn't been hours, but the Earth might as well have done a full rotation for the way I feel. I'm lost. My life barely even resembles what it was when I woke up this morning, but lying here won't change anything. I need Sarah in order to breathe, but right now, I can't be selfish enough to worry about the ache in my lungs. There's a little girl who's never even seen my face and needs me most of all right now.

I stand on shaky legs and head for the office. When I push open the door, I find Johnson sitting behind the desk.

"You back so soon?" He cocks an eyebrow.

"I need to make some phone calls, but most of all, I need a flight to Texas."

Chapter
THIRTY-SIX

Sarah

FOR THE first three hours after leaving Leo, I drove around aimlessly. I was in no hurry and had no real direction to follow. My phone buzzed on the seat beside me numerous times. First, it lit up with Leo's name, then Emma's, then Casey's. I ended them all. Instead of talking, I drove to see the one person who I knew wouldn't ask me any questions.

"I have no idea what the fuck I'm doing." I admit into the cold night air. "Fuck!" I yell, dropping my knees into the grass. "You're laughing, aren't you?" I ask the granite that expectedly remains silent. "Damn it, I miss you Regina Phalange." I trace my fingers over the indentations of Manda's name on her headstone, tucking my knees to my chest under my jacket.

"That can't be comfortable," Caleb says, walking up and scaring the shit out of me.

"Fuck!" I scream, toppling over when my legs get stuck.

"Chill. It's just me." He puts his hands up in surrender.

"Shit, you scared me. Jesus. Don't sneak up on people in a cemetery in the middle of the night."

"Perhaps you shouldn't come to a cemetery in the middle of the night, then. It's not safe."

"Yeah, well. I didn't have anywhere else to go."

"So I heard. Leo called," he informs me, sitting down on the cold ground next to me.

I scoot over to add a little more space between us. "Did you draw the short straw?"

"Collin's sick. Emma was worried about leaving him."

I immediately become worried. "Is he okay?"

"He's fine. The doctor said it's an ear infection, but he's running a nice little fever."

"Poor guy," I respond before turning back to face Manda's headstone.

"Come back to our place for the night. Emma's way better at this talking shit than I am." He tosses me apologetic smile.

"No, I think I'm just going to a hotel or something. I can't deal with her tonight. She'll just lay it all out and make it rational. Maybe I'll call that Kara chick. She seems like she'd be good guy-bashing company." I laugh without humor.

"I can't let you go to hotel. Your sister will hang me by my balls."

"Well, apologize to your balls for me, because there is no way I'm talking with Emma tonight."

"Okay, fine. Talk to me, then." He lies down on his back and crosses his legs at the ankle.

I laugh at the idea of having a heart-to-heart with Caleb Jones, but he's probably going to do the least amount of preaching of anyone else.

"Come on. I can't go home and leave you here, so start talking and let's see what bullshit we can figure out."

I sigh. "What'd Leo tell you?"

"Just that you took off and he was worried."

"He has a kid," I say bluntly, and it burns coming off my tongue.

"Okay? I'm assuming you are just finding out about this?"

"Yeah. She's five. He's never seen her. But her mom just passed away and Leo's on deck." I shrug at how simplistic yet sad my explanation sounds.

"Shit," he breathes.

"Pretty much," I say, chewing the inside of my lip.

"So you guys going to take her?"

"There's no *you guys* anymore. I basically told him to go to hell."

"Jesus, Sarah. Since when do you have something against kids?"

"Since my fiancé has one with another woman," I answer matter-of-factly.

"Ah, so you're jealous." He points out the obvious, and I can't say that he's wrong.

"Maybe a little. I'm also just pissed that he never bothered to mention this to me. We were supposed to be getting married in a few weeks, Caleb. Now, he's going down to Texas tomorrow morning to pick up his daughter. Where does that leave me?"

"You?" he questions loudly and it echoes through the night.

"Yes. Me," I confirm.

"Sarah, I'm going to be really honest here. I think you sound like a bitch who has her head stuck up her ass."

I swing my head to face him, shocked that he would be such a dick. Well, that is until I remember who I'm talking to.

"Excuse me." I jump to my feet, dusting the dirt off my jeans. "You have no right to talk to me like that. You don't know the whole story."

"I don't need to. You told me the only thing that matters. Leo has a kid who just lost her mother. Honestly, it infuriates me that you two aren't on a plane tonight. If something happened to Collin, I'd hitchhike across America to get to him if I had to."

"Caleb, it's not that easy. He never told me about her."

"Well, given the fact that he's never seen the child, I'm going to assume something else was going on. There's not a cop in town who doesn't know Leo spent years in the Witness Protection Program, so I'm going to put two and two together and guess his difficulty in opening up has something to do with that."

I look at the ground and wish I had just gone to Emma. She at least would have sugarcoated the lecture.

"So, tell me this. Did Leo lie to you or did he just decide not to deal with his own shit?" He quirks an eyebrow as my chin begins to quiver.

"He was paying child support," I answer as some sort of proof, but it only supports Caleb's theory.

"Well, good. That makes me respect him at least."

"He could have told me. How am I supposed to marry a man who just leaves out details this big?"

"As I recall, it took you months to tell him your bullshit. If he didn't know all about it, you think you would have just dumped it all on him over coffee one day?"

"No, but I sure as shit wouldn't have proposed to him without telling him everything," I bite out.

Caleb releases a loud sigh. "What's your gut say? You think he's some big asshole who purposely duped you or do you think he fucked up big time but really fucking needs you right about now?"

I drop my chin to my chest and fight back the waterworks. "What if there's more? I feel like I'm in the dark. I hate surprises, and Leo James had been nothing but." I sniffle.

"That's life, Sarah," he announces. "You're going to have to learn to roll with the punches or that bitch will beat you down in no time."

"Well aren't you poetic," I say sarcastically.

"You remember that day Collin was born. You gave me this whole speech about our lives coming full circle. Could this be the point that closes your own circle? You found a man who accepts you for exactly who you are. Now you just have to be willing to do the same."

"Jesus Christ, where the fuck did you come from? Does Emma know you get all deep like this?"

"Nope. And I'd appreciate it if you didn't mention it." He smirks.

"I don't know if I can do this."

"Just listen to yourself. You're more concerned that Leo was dealing with his own issues instead of telling you all about it. I'm not saying he's right, but I *am* saying your spat can be dealt with after he gets that little girl somewhere safe. If you are going to commit to being part of Leo's life, she's going to need you too."

"Oh my God." I panic when that little realization hits me. "I can't be someone's stepmom."

"Good, because now that her real mom is gone, she's probably going to need more than that."

"Stop!" I shout as my heart begins to race. Surely, Manda of all people would understand if I puked on her grave.

"Okay, okay. How about you just start with supporting Leo and worry about your relationship with the kid later."

I take a few deep breaths. "Yeah, that makes more sense."

"So, should I start cleaning out the guest room for you to move in?" He tosses me his signature smirk.

Chapter
THIRTY-SEVEN

Leo

ONE PHONE call, two plane tickets, and three hours later, I'm half-way to having a daughter. Although I guess in reality I've had a daughter for a while now. From what the Department of Child Services in Texas told me, when I arrive tomorrow, it should be an easy process. As her legal father, there isn't a ton of paperwork to be done or a long, drawn-out custody battle to be won. Basically, I show up and they give me a pink bundle of joy. Or, in my case, knowing her mother, a sassy-mouthed five-year-old.

As soon as Sarah left, I called Emma and let her know that she was gone...again. She didn't ask any questions and I didn't provide any answers. I just needed to know that Sarah was safe. She can hate me all she wants, but I love her. That will never change. Deep down, I don't believe for a single second that things are over for me and Sarah, but that doesn't make the hole she left behind any less unbearable.

I'm terrified of how I'm going to manage to be a full-time father. I don't know the first thing about kids. Much less how to deal with one after something as traumatic as losing her mother. I can't imagine what she has been through for the last week, and that alone has managed to snap me out of my usual doom-and-gloom spiral. For once since my life changed, I feel like I'm actually doing the right thing. No matter how much it scares me.

After packing a small bag, I try to call Sarah one last time. She's been gone for just over five hours and I ache for her already. I didn't lie to her when I proposed. We're better together. Alone, the what-ifs become overwhelming and tomorrows seem impossible, but with one embrace, she makes even the most difficult parts of life seem manageable. While I don't want her to fix this for me, I'd give anything to just have her at my side while I navigate the winding path to right the wrong.

I head for the shower with only the visions of blue eyes and blond hair preventing me from breaking down completely. As I stand in front of the mirror, I take a hard look at the same man I saw this morning, but for some reason, I now no longer recognize him. Let's just hope that's a good thing.

Tomorrow's a big day, and I'm completely exhausted. I wrap a towel around my waist and head into my room with big plans for a date with the backs of my eyelids. I don't make it two steps into the room before I'm suddenly very awake.

Sitting in the dark on the edge of my bed is the most beautiful sight I have ever seen. Her cheeks are tear stained, but her shoulders are squared and confident.

"Ángel," I breathe.

"You let me down, Leo. You took the trust that I gave you and made me regret it once again."

"I know. I—" I start, but she quickly interrupts me.

"Shut up. Let me talk."

I take a step closer, desperate to feel the comfort only Sarah can give me, but I stop when she lifts a hand.

"And don't even think about touching me."

"Okay." I grab the back of my neck to still my hands, which obviously did not understand her words.

"I'm pissed. And hurt—so fucking hurt. I hate that you didn't trust me enough to open up to me about something as big as a child. But I get it. You're right. I would have tried to make you reach out to her. So, for that, I'm sorry."

"Sarah, please don't—"

"Shut. Up." She silences me again. "It's who I am and I know it's overbearing and probably annoying as hell. That's me and I'm sorry to say it, Leo, but I'm probably always going to be like that."

"I don't want you to be anyone else," I whisper, taking another step forward.

She stands up and backs away to maintain the distance between us. "After the accident, I used to cry myself to sleep, wishing someone could fix me. I actually used to dream about this hero rushing in to save me and magically making all the static in my mind silent." She laughs to herself. "But no matter how much everyone around me tried, that person never came. Finally, I was forced to fix myself, and it fucking sucked. It was grueling, and it took so much goddamn blood, sweat, and tears to get me where I am today. So when I see you struggle, it breaks me all over again. It transports me back to how hopeless I used to feel. I have this ingrained need to make things easier for you because, in turn, it heals me as well.

"You have told me a million times that I saved you, but I disagree. With one simple, 'Hi. I'm Leo James,' you rescued *me*. You shattered my force field and magically began repairing parts of me I didn't even know were broken."

"Please let me touch you," I beg as her words pierce through me.

"Not yet," she answers simply.

It's only the fact that she said *yet* that keeps me rooted in place.

"Leo, you showed me that crazy is the new normal and that it shouldn't hurt to breathe. With one stroke of your fingers across my neck, you make the entire crazy world disappear. That savior I dreamed about may not have looked like you, but I have absolutely no doubt that it was *always* you. And I think the part I still can't get over is that I never in a million years could have imagined being able to help you too."

Tears begin to slide down her cheeks, and every drop of moisture is like a knife to my gut.

"So, back to my point. I'm pissed. Like, fucking pissed, but I have a sneaking suspicion that, if the tables were turned, you wouldn't have batted an eye at my omission. You would have brushed it off, pulled me into your chest, and figured out a way to take on the whole goddamn world if that's what I needed. So here I am."

"Sarah," I breathe as emotions spring to my eyes.

"I have some terms though."

I nod in understanding.

"One, I want you to start anti-depressants. Like, tonight. We've never talked about what your hangups are with medication, but I'm not budging. You can't be going dark with a child in the house. And if a pill helps you manage things a little better, then, Goddamn it, I'm going to start lacing your lunch if I have to."

"Okay," I quickly agree. I may not like it, but she's right.

"Tonight, Leo. Erica's a doctor, right? Get her to call you in something. Then, when we get back, you can go see someone for a full regimen. I know the next few days are going to be rough, and I can't have you withdrawing into your head."

"Okay," I repeat as my heart begins to swell at the possibilities.

"Two, I need you to accept my apology for flipping out earlier. I wasn't focusing on the right part of the issue. But you have to stop surprising me with shit. I do a really bad job at processing it."

"Okay," I agree once again as a smile starts to creep across my lips.

"And three, I want my ring back."

And that's it. There is nothing in the world that can keep me from touching her for even a second longer. With three giant steps, I rush across the room and crush her into my arms.

I hold her tighter than I ever thought was possible. I'm wishing I never had to leave this moment where everything is right. However, knowing that Sarah will be at my side for the next twenty-four hours doesn't seem so hard.

It actually seems easy.

"We need to buy plane tickets," she whispers.

"I already did." I lean away to catch her eye.

"For both of us?"

"Yep. I wasn't sure when to make the return flight, so for now, they are just one way."

"Wow. I'm that transparent, huh?" She leans her neck to the side, silently asking for a kiss.

"No, I just had big plans of kidnapping you. I bought the chloroform, zip ties, and everything," I say, trailing wet kisses up her neck as she rewards me with the most amazing laugh, which I swear I can feel all the way down to the marrow in my bones.

"No chloroform necessary, but hang on to those zip ties. We can probably think of a use for them later." She smiles.

Yeah. I can do this.

Chapter
THIRTY-EIGHT

Sarah

"YOU READY?" I ask for the ninth time since we arrived at the Department of Child Services in Texas.

Leo quickly shakes his head and begins pacing again. He's squeezing my hand, dragging me along with him. I'm sure we look ridiculous, but I can't bring myself to care.

We arrived in El Paso bright and early this morning and drove straight here. Leo received a voicemail while we were in the air that let him know that the Avilas had already dropped Liv off and left. This led to a loud rant in the middle of baggage claim about what assholes they are. Since every other word was a curse, I tried to quietly remind him that we were in public. The only way I knew he had even heard me is that he switched to Spanish. We were in a Texas airport just minutes from the Mexico border, so I'm not sure how much good it did, but at least I tried.

Most of the morning, Leo's mood was all over the place. He was convinced that she was better off without him, and I tried to reassure him that he was wrong. Then he got emotional thinking about all the time he missed only to swing to anger at Amy for having turned to drugs. I could barely keep up. I've been so preoccupied with worrying about Leo that I haven't even had a chance to stress myself out about becoming a kinda-sorta parent as well. She might be Leo's child, but Caleb was right. I'm going to have to step up and be more than just an every-other-weekend type of stepmom. *Oh. Shit.*

"Um. I think I'm going to puke," I say with a quiver in my voice.

Leo stops and turns to look at me. I must have a serious case of crazy eyes, because he immediately switches gears and pulls me into a hug.

"Jesus Christ. Aren't we a fucking pair?" Leo whispers into my ear, rubbing his stubble against my cheek. "She's a little girl, not a T-Rex. Let's go in there. I'm just going to keep working myself up into a frenzy out here, and now I'm starting to take you down with me. Only one of us is allowed to have an anxiety attack at a time." He kisses the top of my head and I melt into his arms.

Sucking in a deep breath, I look up into his eyes. "I love you. I know this is scary, but we can do this." I try to be encouraging for both of us.

"Yeah. We can." He smiles sincerely.

"But you have to stop cussing," I scold.

He starts laughing, pulling me even tighter against his chest. With one brief kiss, he releases me and takes my hand before guiding me to the front door.

"Hi. I'm Leo James. I'm here to pick up my daughter," he says, and I have a feeling he says it more for himself than the receptionist.

"Mr. James." A thin woman with long, black hair and a warm smile makes her way from around the desk. "I'm Suzanne Moore. We spoke on the phone earlier. It's nice to meet you."

"Nice to meet you as well. This is my fiancée, Sarah Erickson," he introduces us while curling me tight against his side.

"Well, you two can come on back. I have a couple of forms for you to sign. Then I'll take you to meet Liv."

"Can I see her first?" Leo asks, surprising me. "Yeah, I'd really just like to meet her now. Please," he rushes out.

"Um. Sure. Right this way."

Leo takes in a deep breath and pauses for only a second before grabbing my hand and following her down the long hallway. When we reach the door to a conference room, Suzanne gives us one last glance before swinging the door open and walking in ahead of us.

"Hey, Liv," she greets a gorgeous little girl with dark-brown hair and chocolate-brown eyes I would recognize anywhere.

"Hi," she responds quietly as her eyes flip to Leo then to me.

I feel Leo's entire body tense at my side as he squeezes my hand painfully hard. I try to nudge him to get him to say something, but when I look up, I know not a single word is going to come from his mouth. It's all he can do to fight back the tears that are sparkling in his eyes.

"Hi, Liv. My name's Sarah, and this is your dad, Leo." I yank on his hand and he finally manages a smile and wave.

She nods as her eyes flash back and forth between Leo and the social worker, rarely landing on me.

"So. Mr. James. How about that paperwork now?" Suzanne interrupts when Leo fails to utter a single syllable.

"Yeah," he says quickly, offering Liv a tight smile before exiting from the room.

"I'll be right back," I tell the obviously uncomfortable little girl before following Leo out the door. I find him leaning against the wall with his head in his hands. "You okay?" I ask, rubbing a hand up his back.

"I always thought she would look like Amy. I know it's stupid. I'm her dad, but it never really occurred to me how much she would look like my family. This is just so fucking surreal." He scrubs his hands over his face.

"Okay. I need you to put on your big-boy pants for just a minute," I say teasingly, and he gives me an unamused glare. "She's scared, Leo. She's about to leave with two people she doesn't know from Adam. I know this is emotional for you, and we can hash all of that out later tonight. For now, I need you to pack it down."

"Shit. You're right. I know. I'll do better." He sighs, running a rough hand through his hair.

"I have no doubt that you will." I pat his chest. "Oh, and stop cussing." I stand on my tiptoes and give him a brief kiss before heading back into the conference room.

I move around the table and sit down in the chair next to the frightened girl. Jesus, Leo isn't wrong. She looks just like him.

"So how old are you, Liv?" I ask, propping my purse on the table between us.

"Five," she answers, looking down at her lap.

"Wow. I thought you were at least twenty," I say seriously, and her eyes pop to mine—a small smile twitching at the corner of her mouth.

"Are you his wife?" she asks quietly.

"Not yet. We're engaged though. So I'll be his wife soon."

"Oh. Okay." She looks back down at her lap.

"What's your middle name, Liv?" I try to keep her talking.

"Kaitlin," she responds but gives me nothing else.

"Really? Mine's Kate. That's kinda close."

She once again looks up at me, but her expression is timid.

"Let's see what else we have in common. What's your favorite color?"

"Purple."

"Mine's baby blue," I respond, and I can see her trying to hide a smile.

"That's a boy color." A full-blown smile creeps across her face and it renders me speechless. Definitely Leo's child. Unexpected emotions begin to manifest in my chest as tears leak from my eyes.

"No, it's not," I laugh and begin digging through my purse to keep her from seeing my eyes.

"Yes, it is." She lets out a small giggle before going quiet again.

"Hey, you like makeup?" I ask when I run across my compact at the bottom of my purse. I look up to catch her nodding quickly. It's so freaking cute that it makes me laugh. "Okay, then. How about I give you a little makeover? Don't tell your dad I'm letting you wear makeup though. Just a little secret between us girls, okay?"

"Okay," she whispers, and it seems whatever headway I made with the makeup has been quickly erased at the mere mention of Leo.

For the next few minutes, she sits while I apply a very thin layer of makeup. Most of the time, I just use the brush without any color on it, but she doesn't need to know that. Finally, I let her pick between my three lip glosses, and of course she choses the bright red that is sure to earn us a few looks as we walk out of here. As a show of solidarity, I apply some too even thought it completely clashes with my pink top.

Just as we are finishing up, Leo comes walking back in carrying a plastic bag. I give him a questioning look and he only shrugs before aiming his attention back on Liv.

"Wow. Um. You look beautiful," he tells her, barely containing his laugh.

She quickly looks away, embarrassed by his compliment.

"So, you ladies will never believe where I've been. Did you know that there is a machine filled with candy here?" he says exaggeratedly, and my heart melts as her head snaps up to his. "You have to use quarters, but luckily, I met a nice lady who made change for me." He tosses me a wink.

I let out a relived breath. Yeah, he packed it down all right.

"Well, I decided I should bring you some candy to try to get us off on the right foot. I mean. Everyone loves candy, right?"

Liv excitedly nods.

"Then it occurred to me that I don't know you so well. I had no idea which kind of candy would be your favorite." He leans over the table, puts his hand up, blocking his mouth from my view, and whispers, "So I got them all." Then he flips the bag over, dumping at least twenty candy bars onto the table.

I let out a loud laugh as her eyes go wide at the sugar coma waiting to happen before her.

"Liv, I'm sorry I was so weird earlier. I was just a little nervous. My name is Leo James and I'm your dad. I know I haven't been around much, but I'm here from now on. Forever. Okay?" He leans forward to catch her eye.

"Okay." She answers, reaching for the candy.

"Oh, and there are some crackers in there too just in case you don't have a sweet tooth." He reaches out and snags his own chocolate bar off the table.

"All right, you two. How about, before we dig into this mountain of candy, we grab some lunch. Everything settled?" I ask Leo.

"Yep." He barely tears his gaze away from Liv long enough to answer me.

As I gather my purse and makeup, from the corner of my eye, I see Leo sneakily slide a candy bar across to her before packing the rest back in the bag. She even giggles as she tucks it inside the backpack that's beside her on the floor.

Just as we get to the door, Liv quickly moves to my side farthest from Leo and grabs my hand. She gives me a wary glance that makes my heart drop. I squeeze her hand reassuringly and her small body seems to relax. Leo watches our interaction and kisses my temple with gratitude. Although I'm not sure why he's thanking me. I'm loving every second of this.

Chapter
THIRTY-NINE

Leo

"THEY'RE ALL dirty," Sarah whispers as we get back to the hotel.

"What do you mean dirty?" I ask for clarification as my head starts to pound.

"Calm down." She pushes me into the bathroom and eases the door behind us.

Lunch was fantastic and entirely too short. I guess Liv hasn't been sleeping very much recently. I have no idea if five-year-olds still take naps, but it was clear that she was in need of one as her eyelids drooped while we sat at the kid-friendly restaurant Sarah had picked out. As soon as we got back to the hotel, Sarah put on some cartoons, and within minutes, Liv was out.

Sarah started going through the two small bags that consisted of all of Liv's belongings. The social worker had warned me that the Avilas sent very little with Liv when they'd dropped her off. I hadn't exactly expected to need a moving van for a five-year-old or anything, but with the exception of one doll and two books, there wasn't even a toy in sight. Her entire life didn't even amount to a full suitcase.

Among those belongings wasn't a single picture of her mother. I have a few pictures of Amy from years ago tucked away somewhere, I'm sure, but I'd be hard-pressed to find them. Thankfully, after an uncomfortable phone call to Max, he agreed to e-mail me everything he still had. He didn't say much during our brief conversation, but before he hung up, he left his parting words.

"Things had gotten really bad, Leo. I'm just glad she's with you now."

And as Sarah stands in front of me telling me how half of her clothes won't fit and the other half are tattered or stained, I can't help but agree with him.

"What the fuck!" I boom and it echoes in the small bathroom.

"Hush," she urges. "You're going to wake her up."

"Do you have any idea how much fucking money I've been sending Amy?"

She shakes her head.

"I've sent her at least four thousand dollars a month in child support for the last year. The minute I got my first big contract after starting Guardian, I sent her a lump some of twenty grand to make up for everything I didn't send while I was in the program. For fuck's sake, I didn't even pay Johnson that first month because I sent it all to *her*."

"Jesus," she mumbles.

"And now my child doesn't even have clothes that fit? I'll admit that I'm a piece of shit for not visiting her, but I at least went out of my way to make sure she would never be without the way Amy and I were growing up. Goddamn it!" I roar. "She couldn't even buy her clothes? Where the fuck did all that money go?" I run a rough hand through my hair.

"I'm going to guess drugs," Sarah whispers, wrapping her arms around my waist.

"Awesome. Now I get to live with the guilt that I killed her."

"I've listened to you spout a lot of crap, Leo. But please tell me that you don't believe that."

"No. I don't. But Christ, it pisses me off." I blow out a breath and look down at Sarah. "So what do we do?" I ask, managing to get myself back under control.

"We go shopping and buy her a few outfits to travel in. She'll love it. Then, when we get home, we start from scratch." She tosses me an encouraging smile.

I have no idea how the hell I would have handled any of this without her.

"I love you. So fucking much." I kiss her deeply, trying to return to her even an ounce of the way she makes me feel. But the most amazing thing happens—Sarah's lips somehow give me more.

"Come on. Let's go take a nap too. I'm exhausted." She opens the bathroom door and the sound of Liv crying meets our ears at the exact same moment.

We rush around the corner to find her sitting up on the bed with her knees pulled to her chest. Tears are rolling down her face.

"Liv?" Sarah says gently, walking over to the bed and sitting beside her.

Liv quickly scrambles onto her lap. I have no idea what to do, so I stand at the foot of the bed and watch Sarah comfort her.

"You okay?" She smooths down the back of her hair as Liv begins to calm in her arms.

"I thought maybe you left," Liv finally squeaks out.

It rips the remaining shards of my heart in half.

"No, we're not going anywhere, baby," Sarah reassures her as I let out a Spanish curse in frustration that this child would even have to worry about that.

Liv's eyes immediately snap to mine.

"Sorry," I respond for my outburst and offer her a smile.

"That's a bad word," she informs me while wiping the tears from her eyes and moving off Sarah's lap.

"*Hablas español?*" (*You speak Spanish?*) I ask in shock, although I'm not sure why. It should have been more surprising that she speaks English. Amy's parents were from Mexico and she spoke almost exclusively Spanish at home.

"*Sí,*" she answers, giving me a small smile I can't help but return.

"*Bien. Ahora ella no entendera cuando nosotros le hacemos una broma.*" (*Good. Now she won't be able to understand us when we play tricks on her.*) I tilt my head to Sarah and Liv begins to giggle.

"*No le hagas bromas feas, pues ella es muy buena.*" (*Not mean tricks. She's nice.*)

"*Sí, ella lo es.*" (*Yeah, she is.*) I respond with a wink.

"Oh no. I think I'm in trouble now," Sarah exaggerates, making Liv laugh even louder. "Looks like I'm going to have to learn Spanish pretty soon."

"I can teach you," Liv volunteers.

"Really? That would be great. But let's stick to English until I get the hang of it." She reaches out and brushes the hair off Liv's neck in the most familiar way. "Hey, so I was thinking maybe we could go shopping. Have a little fun before our plane ride home tomorrow. Maybe I can pick out an outfit for you, and you can pick out one for me. What do you think?"

"Is Leo coming?" she asks.

"Of course. Oh, let's pick out an outfit for him too!" Sarah responds excitedly.

I let out a playful groan, causing them both to laugh. I swear it's the sweetest harmony I've ever heard in my entire existence.

"I CAN'T afford to keep her," I mumble to Sarah as we walk back into the hotel.

What started out as a quick trip to grab the essentials quickly turned into a full-fledged shopping spree. I had to stop and buy more luggage just to be able to get it all home. My credit card is not just smoking. It's on fire from the amount of times it was swiped today.

"Well, you could have said no," Sarah responds with laughter in her eyes.

"Jesus. And I thought I had my hands full telling you no. Together, as a team, there will be no way to stop you. I'm going to need a second job."

We walk into the bedroom and find Liv trying to open the box on her new iPad.

"Hey, how are you doing?" Sarah asks quietly as we watch her.

"I think I'm okay. I know it will be different when we get home, but I really think it's going to be good. For all of us." I finish by kissing her on the forehead.

"Leo," Liv calls. "Can you help me?"

"Absolutely." I smile and head her direction.

Chapter
FORTY

Sarah

NOT EVEN forty-eight hours after we landed in Texas, we leave as a family of three. Liv has definitely warmed up to me, and several times, I've caught her watching Leo out of the corner of her eye too. She's a little more hesitant with him though. As far as Leo and I can figure, she hasn't had a strong male presence in her life. We aren't exactly sure what kind of a life she has had at all, but at first glance, she doesn't seem to be overly affected by her mother's drug use.

As soon as her iPad was out of the box, Leo spent even more money on games. When he handed it to her, we were both shocked to see that she could already read. She informed us that she spent a lot of time with the elderly woman who lived next door when her mom would go out at night or sleep too long the next day. This time, Leo at least had the good sense to go out into the hallway before exploding into profanities. Although the door didn't muffle his voice nearly enough.

While waiting for our flight, Emma's name flashes on the screen of my phone as it begins to ring.

"Hello," I answer.

"Y'all on your way home yet?"

"We're at the airport." I stand to walk out of hearing range, but

Liv jumps to her feet to follow me.

"How is she?"

"Amazing…and adjusting." I reach down and run my fingers through her hair. I glance up to find Leo watching us intently from his chair.

"So, I was thinking. You know Jesse is a grief counselor, right? Well, I happen to know for a fact that she's done a good bit of work with kids over the last year. I was thinking about maybe seeing if she'd be willing to come out and talk to Liv and help you guys get her settled in."

"Emma, no. That's weird. I appreciate it, but I don't want to bother them."

"It's no bother. I can't confirm this, but she *might* have reached out to me when she heard about Liv and your situation. She also *might* have begged me not to tell you she really wants to help."

"Wow. Remind me never to tell you something in confidence again," I deadpan.

I glance down at Liv, who has completely abandoned her iPad and is clinging to my leg. Emma's not wrong. We could really use the help. Last night, Liv woke up crying no fewer than five times. Each time, she'd settle back into my arms and drift off muttering words in Spanish.

"Let me talk to Leo," I answer before hanging up and moving back to my chair, Liv tight at my side.

"Who was that?" Leo asks from behind his book.

"Emma." I reach out and pull Liv into my lap when I realize she has zero intention of sitting anywhere else. "Listen, she had an idea. Jesse Sharp is a grief counselor and she has offered to come over and help us all get settled in." I silently tilt my head to Liv.

"Oh, that would be fantastic." Leo blows out a loud breath. Apparently, he's a little more nervous than I thought.

"You don't think it will be awkward?" I move Liv to the chair beside me and pass her one of the new books Leo bought her at the airport gift shop.

"Sarah, I don't give a damn… I mean, I don't care if it's awkward. It's Friday, so it's not like we're going to be able to find anyone else until next week. Last night killed me. I can't go through that again. I'd love to get some advice from a professional about how to handle stuff like that." He grabs my hand and brings it to his lips. "Now, is it going to upset you to see Jesse?" he asks as concern fills his eyes.

"I love you. So even if it did upset me, I can deal with it if it will help both of you feel better." I bring his hand to my mouth to return his kiss.

He sucks in a breath and closes his eyes reverently.

"We're going to be okay, Leo. We can do this together," I whisper.

Liv interrupts our tiny moment in the middle of a busy airport. "Sarah, I need to go to the bathroom."

"Well, then lead the way." I give Leo a quick kiss and wrap her small hand in mine.

"THIS IS your house?" Liv asks as we ride the elevator up to our apartment.

"No. This is our house," Leo answers her with a smile that makes her shyly look away.

"Can we ride the elevator as much as we want?" She tugs on my hand as the doors open.

"Of course." Leo answers. "I'll have to take you to the roof later. You can see half the city from up there." He reaches down and strokes her hair.

"Really?"

"Yep. Now, come on. Let's put these bags down in your room before they break my back." She begins to giggle as he squats low to the ground, exaggerating how heavy her small backpack is.

As we walk into the apartment, Johnson greets us at the door.

"How was your trip?" he asks.

Liv only takes one eyeful of the whole scary package that is Aiden Johnson before hiding behind me.

"Liv, this is my best friend, Johnson," Leo says, introducing her. "He's just ugly, but don't let him scare you. He's a nice guy."

"Hey, Liv," Johnson replies, peeking around behind me to catch a glimpse.

"Hi," she shyly tells my back.

Johnson lets out a chuckle. "Okay, well, I'll let you guys get settled in. I'll be in the office if you need anything. I took the liberty of tidying up the guest room for her. I put a few of Sarah's boxes in the storage closet downstairs."

"Thanks, man," Leo answers, giving him a quick handshake before addressing Liv. "You want to see your room?"

She peeks up at him and nods quickly.

"Okay, well, it's not much right now, but you and Sarah can decorate it however you would like."

When Leo pushes the door open, the three of us let out a gasp in unison.

"Oh my God," I exhale as I take in the sight in front of me.

Gone is the simple, conservatively decorated guest room, and in its place is every little girl's fantasy palace. The walls have all been painted a pale purple with butterflies stenciled randomly across them. A collection of feather boas hangs in the corner and a large, white, antique dresser supports a jewelry box and colorful butterfly lamp. The bed has been covered with a princess comforter and matching sheets, complete with a toy tiara resting on the pillow.

Liv squeals and rushes over to the bed. I look to Leo for answers, but I can tell that he's just as surprised as I am. Suddenly, Johnson appears in the doorway behind us with a huge shit-eating grin.

"You did this?" Leo asks, blinking back his emotions.

"Well, no. Chris did this. I just used the company credit card to pay for it."

Leo shakes his head and gives him a handshake, which is immediately pulled in for a man hug. "Thank you," Leo chokes out. Then he steps away, allowing me enough room to squeeze in to give Johnson my own embrace.

"No problem. I figured you'd want her to have something nice."

"Jesus. Tell Chris thank you for me."

"Tell him yourself. He wants to meet her as soon as she gets settled in. Maybe dinner one night?" He smiles, and it's not lost on me that this is the first time he has ever spoken about his boyfriend openly to Leo.

"Absolutely." Leo gives his shoulder a pat before turning back to Liv, who is currently examining the small shelf filled with books.

Definitely her father's child.

A buzz from the front door sounds and my stomach flutters nervously when I realize who's behind it.

"I'll get that," I announce.

Leo tosses me an encouraging smile before heading over to join Liv on the floor.

I nervously smooth down my shirt. It's just Jesse. She's always been so sweet to me. I have nothing to be nervous about. However, the minute I open the door, I'm given a six-foot-five, green-eyed reason to be nervous.

"Hi," I say to Brett before my eyes drift down to Jesse, who's standing in front of him.

"I'm sorry," she immediately apologizes.

"For what?" I try to pretend that I'm not about to puke up my dinner on their shoes.

"Because I wouldn't let her come alone," Brett answers for her.

She gives me a tight smile followed by an eye roll.

"No. It's fine," I lie. "I just appreciate you coming, Jesse. Y'all come on in."

Jesse walks in and begins looking around the apartment. "Where is she?"

"She's in the bedroom with Leo." I nervously eye Brett.

"Oh, well, I was thinking I could meet her and just get to know her a little then talk to you and Leo about a few things you could expect and the best way to handle the million questions she is sure to have. I probably won't be very beneficial to her tonight, but hopefully I can supply you two with some tools."

"That would be great," I sigh.

"Sarah!" Liv screams, rushing from the bedroom. She runs at a full sprint before slamming into my legs and starting to cry.

"Liv!" Leo calls, jogging behind her, slowing only when his eyes find Brett.

"I thought you left," she whimpers, holding me tight.

"No, baby. I'm not going anywhere. I just had to answer the door." I squat down in front of her as she throws her arms around my neck.

I look up to Jesse pointedly and she gives me an understanding nod.

"Hi, Liv. My name is Jesse."

Liv turns to face her, realizing for the first time that someone else is in the room.

"I'm a friend of Sarah's," she tells her, and I can't help the small laugh that erupts from my throat. "Look. I brought you some coloring books and Play Doh, but judging by the size of that suitcase in the corner, you probably don't need them." She laughs at her own joke, and Liv smiles.

"Oh, you have no idea. You should see her room. I'm a little jealous." I brush the hair off Liv's shoulder and stand back up.

"Really? What's it look like?" Jesse asks excitedly.

"You want to see?" Liv perks up, all signs of her anxiety gone.

"I'd love to!" Jesse replies.

"Come on." She pulls on my hand, but I stop her.

"Hey, how about I make us a snack? I have some cookie dough in the fridge. Why don't you go show Jesse your room and I'll be right here in the kitchen."

"You won't leave?" she asks, and it pains me.

"I swear." I make a show of crossing my heart. "Hey, why don't you take Leo with you? I bet he would look fantastic in one of those feather boas." I wink.

She rewards my effort with a laugh. "Okay. Come on, Leo." She grabs Jesse's hand and motions for Leo to follow her.

He gives me a knowing glance, flashing it to Brett. I nod and shoo him away.

"Good to see you again, man." He lifts his chin to Brett.

"Yeah. You too," Brett replies stoically.

"Now, if you'll excuse me. Apparently, I have a drag show to give."

I laugh as he heads back down the hall. Leaving me completely alone with Brett. *Yep. Puke time.*

"Can I get you a beer or something?" I inquire, remembering my manners.

"I could use a bottle of whisky right about now, but yeah, a beer sounds great."

"Look. I'm sorry. I know this is weird. Leo just really wanted to talk to Jesse. This has been overwhelming for us. I'm sorry to bother y'all. I'm sure this was definitely not how you wanted to spend your Friday night. You didn't have to come," I rush out uncomfortably.

"It's fine. Happy to help," he says shortly.

"It's just… She's only a little girl, and she's just lost her mom. I really want to make this a smooth transition, and…quite honestly, we have no idea what the hell we are doing," I ramble, completely unsure why I'm still talking. Brett must feel the same way because he quirks his eyebrow. "Anyway, yeah. Beer."

"I figured you'd have this on lockdown," Brett speaks up. "I mean, you've been in her shoes. You know firsthand how it feels to lose someone. Let's just hope she handles it a hell of a lot better than you did." He throws the verbal blow and it lands hard in my gut.

"I'm sorry," I choke out as tears spring to my eyes.

"Shit. I'm sorry," he mumbles. "I shouldn't have said that." He runs a hand through his hair in frustration.

"No. I deserved it." I walk into the kitchen to retrieve his beer. As I pull open the fridge door, I burst into tears.

Brett suddenly appears behind me. "I know I shouldn't have come here tonight, but I didn't like the idea of her being around you without me."

"I get it. I really do. I can't blame you one bit." I wipe my eyes and grab a beer before turning to face him.

"I didn't mean to upset you. It was a low blow."

"Really, it's fine." I pull the cookie dough out to keep my hands busy so he hopefully won't notice that they're trembling.

"She pregnant," he blurts out before picking up the beer I placed on the counter.

My head snaps up. "Really? That's great," I respond sincerely. Brett always wanted kids. It actually surprises me that they don't already have a litter.

"God, if you thought I was a overprotective before… I've taken it to a whole new level since we found out. We fought for two full hours before coming over here. She even cursed." He laughs at the memory.

"I'm sorry," I once again apologize, regretting having asked Jesse to come in the first place.

"It's not your fault. She was thrilled to be able to help tonight. That's who she is. It makes me insane, but as you can tell, I have zero ability to change her mind once she sets it on something."

"She's a great person."

"Yeah. I won't argue with you there." He shoves a hand in his pocket and looks down at his shoes. "Listen, I'm gonna go wait outside. I shouldn't have come. I'm sure this is a tough time for you guys right now. I'm just making it harder." He turns to walk away.

"You don't have to do that. Brett, wait," I call out as he heads for the door.

"Just tell her I'm in the car. No rush." He pulls open the door but pauses, not even turning to face me. "For what it's worth, I'm really happy to see you doing so well."

As he leaves, he closes the door behind himself, but surprisingly enough, it's not the only closure I feel.

I take a deep breath and look around the room. I've been here for hours, but suddenly, the air seems lighter. I walk to Liv's bedroom but stop just before entering. She's sitting on the floor, reading a book to Jesse with Leo, complete with a boa around his neck, sitting beside her. I lean on the doorjamb and just watch, reveling in the life I never thought I would have. Leo's eyes immediately jump to mine as if he can sense my presence.

He gives me a suspicious look as tears fill my eyes. Immediately standing, he heads over to pull me into a warm Leo James hug.

"Are you okay?" he whispers.

"Yeah. I really think I am," I choke out, and never have words been truer.

Chapter
FORTY-ONE

Leo

Three months later...

"I DO," Sarah says through a mixture of laughter and tears.

"I now pronounce you husband and wife. You may kiss your bride," the minister announces.

I quickly follow his direction, pulling Sarah in for a kiss. She keeps her mouth closed and denies my tongue entry, laughing as I try to force it on her.

She leans away, wiping her mouth on the back of her hand, and asks the minister, "Is it too late to return him?"

"I'm afraid so," he replies.

"You hear that? You are *stuck*." I laugh, dragging her in for another quick kiss.

Liv giggles from beside her.

"Oh you think that's funny?" I say to Liv, who is all but glowing in a pale-purple dress that's tied at the waist with a bow. I scoop her up into my arms and blow a raspberry on her cheek. "Now *that's* funny." I begin to tickle her.

"Daddy, stop!" she calls out.

Even though she's been calling me Daddy for several weeks now, it still gets me every time.

"Okay. Okay." I put her back on her feet.

"Come on, Sarah. There's cake inside!" She grabs her hand and drags her down the small makeshift aisle.

Sarah and I got married in the patio garden of a downtown restaurant. One night while walking home from dinner, Liv spotted the small fountain and wanted to go in and check it out. I dug a few pennies out of my pocket and she tossed them in. It was then that she turned to Sarah and told her that she wished for us to get married. Until that point, I hadn't realized that she even knew we weren't. And honestly, our lives had been so busy becoming a family of three that I'm not even sure Sarah and I realized that we weren't either. We felt like a family. No paper was going to change that. But in that moment, nothing had ever been more important. I dropped to my knee and asked Sarah to marry me all over again, this time with Liv laughing and clapping beside me. Of course she said yes, and less than a month later, here we are, in that same little garden, only now the three of us share a last name.

"Oh my God. I can't believe she actually married you," Erica says, pulling me in for a long hug.

"Babe, are you crying?" I tease.

"Shut up," she mumbles, releasing me.

I glance up to Slate, who is standing behind her holding baby Adam. Sarah is standing just a few feet away with Emma and Caleb, watching Liv try to pick up Collin like a baby and laughing when he wants absolutely no part of it. Liv bonded quickly with Emma. She loves Collin, and surprisingly enough, she actually warmed up to Caleb pretty quickly too. Last week, she spent an hour sitting on the couch beside him, adding more designs to the tattoos on his arms with a Sharpie. I tried to stop her, but Caleb just laughed and continued to point out empty spots for her to fill in. They were kind enough to invite Liv for a sleepover tonight to give Sarah and me some time alone. *God, do I have plans for those twenty-four hours.*

Having a child has been an interesting transition for us, but we are all doing the best we can. Jesse comes over once a week to hang out and talk with Liv. I can't imagine what we would have done without her. She is absolutely amazing. I pay her every week, but it's not nearly enough. No check in the world could adequately show my appreciation for how far she has helped Liv come in such a short period of time.

Thankfully, Brett never came back after that first night. He's not a bad guy, and I have nothing against him. But hanging out with the ex-husband is pretty fucking low on my list of ways I'd want to spend an evening.

We still have our Thursday nights. Sarah thought it was important to keep those, and I can't say I disagreed with her. However, now, with Liv in the mix, it has turned into more of a family night. We talk about our week while the girls cook. Then we end the night playing board games, which Sarah almost always wins. I think even Liv has learned to not bother trying to beat her. Sarah is not above cheating at Candy Land.

I snake a hand out to the side and tug Sarah into my side. "Hey, ángel." I lean forward, kissing her exposed neck. She picked out a simple, white, strapless dress to wear today. But like always, her svelte body transformed it into something that could have come straight off the catwalk at Fashion Week. There isn't a word in English *or* Spanish that would ever do justice to how beautiful she looks today—or, really, any day.

"I'm hungry," she murmurs, turning her head to the side to allow me access to her neck.

"Well, dinner's next, then cake, then we have to drop Liv off, but *then* I'll be happy to give you something to put in your mouth." I graze my teeth across her neck.

"Leo," she moans.

I swear to God, if there were not children present, I would take her right here in the middle of a restaurant. Or at the very least make her come on my hand under the table.

"All right. Save something for the wedding night," Johnson says as he walks up, holding hands with Chris.

"Yeah, yeah, yeah." I turn to face him. "Glad you could make it," I joke because I saw him sneak into the back during the ceremony.

"Gee, sorry. My asshole of a boss scheduled me to work today, so I was trying to keep Slate from being mauled out front." He rolls his eyes.

"Hey. It was cost effective. You were both coming to the same place anyway. No sense in paying another man when I can make you work for free." I smile and he shakes his head.

The week after Liv moved in, I decided to move the Guardian Protection office out of our apartment. When it was just me living there, it was convenient and really saved me on overhead. However, now that Sarah and Liv live there too, it was time to make that apartment a home. So Guardian Protection officially moved to the top floor of a building a few blocks away. Sarah has been instrumental in the success of the business. She's extremely good at the social side, and the clients love her. I kept my office in the security room, so she works from home most days after she drops Liv off at school.

"I want some cake," Liv says, pulling on my hand.

"You have to eat first, baby." I glance at Sarah, who is laughing with Chris. "*Si nos vamos ahora podrianos en secreto cojer un poquito de la guinda del pastel.*" (*If we go now, I bet we can sneak a little icing off the back.*) Her big, brown eyes grow wide and a smile lights her face. "But only if you tell me you love me first."

She begins laughing. "I love you, Daddy."

Yeah. That will never get old.

It's funny how life works sometimes. The day I met Sarah Erickson James, I was living an existence that couldn't even be considered a life. I was at absolute rock bottom. But I guess that's as good a place as any for your life to begin again.

Every day is a struggle. That will never change. I still have moments when I forget to breathe, but it's damn near impossible to focus on the darkness when your life is filled with lights as bright as Sarah and Liv James. Life is hard. That's a fact. But looking over my shoulder at my wife, while being dragged away by the hand of a little girl I love more than anything in the world, I can't help but feel like today might be the exception.

Easy.

Epilogue

12 years later...

Brett

"WHY DO I have to go?" I groan, rolling up the sleeves on the black button-down I just pulled on.

"Because I said so. Because Caleb is going. Because I'm really freaking happy and I want you and the kids to be there with me."

"Okay, okay, gorgeous. No need to get crazy and pull out dirty words like freaking." I laugh.

She levels me with a glare. "Come on, Brett. You told me you'd come with me. Slate and Erica will be there too. You know Madeline has a crush on Adam."

"Yet another reason why I should stay at home. Adam's a nice kid, but I don't want him anywhere near my daughter. Do you even know what thirteen-year-old boys think about?" I ask as she giggles from inside the closet.

We have been together for almost sixteen years now and that sound still silences the whole crazy world.

"He's thirteen, Brett. Worst case is he might try to hold her hand."

"She's eleven!" I yell, but it only makes her laugh louder.

"Hey, dad!" John calls, walking into our bedroom. "Wait! You're wearing jeans."

"Excellent observation, son," I say sarcastically, giving him a quirked eyebrow in response.

"Can I wear jeans to this thing? Mom gave me some khaki pants, but they make me look like a dork."

I try to stifle a laugh and fail miserably. Poor kid might be eight years old, but he's the baby. Jesse is having a hard time letting him grow up.

Jesse and I had a good bit of trouble getting pregnant. When we first got married, we decided to start trying for kids immediately. However, three years later, we were still chasing that dream. It should have been a time in our relationship that brought us closer together, but we both struggled with our desire to start a family in different ways. She did a lot of crying back in those days, and it damn near broke me when I felt so helpless.

Finally, we took a chance. We emptied the contents of our savings account and gave the miracle of In Vitro Fertilization a shot. It was hands down the best gamble I've ever taken. That one cycle of IVF gave us Madeline. Then, two years later, we thawed one of our frozen embryos and hit the jackpot again with John.

"No! You are wearing those pants. Don't even try it." Jesse says, walking out of the closet.

"Sorry, bud." I tousle his shaggy, brown hair, and he walks out with a groan.

"Now, can you hurry up? I want to stop and pick up some flowers on the way."

"So what am I getting out of this?" I ask with a smile.

"Um, I won't poison your food?" She offers me a sugary smile on her way to the mirror that makes me bark out a laugh.

"Well, I was thinking something a little more…um, stimulating." I walk up behind her and roll my hips into her ass.

"We don't have time for that, so stop." She rejects my advance, but with one glance in the mirror, I can see her cheeks flash to pink.

"Fine. Rain check. But I want you to do something for me before we go." I turn her in my arms and lift my eyebrows suggestively.

"Sorry to break it to you, big boy, but I just did my lipstick." She pats my chest.

"No, gorgeous. I want to hear you say it. Tell me what you want, and use something a little more descriptive than 'freaking.'"

She stares at me blankly, her cheeks growing pinker by the second. "Um…"

"Wrong answer." I scoop her off her feet, causing her to scream.

"Brett, stop!" She tries to sound stern, but she begins giggling.

"Say it, gorgeous." I drop her onto the bed and quickly cover her with my body.

"I love you," she says, leaning up to catch my mouth.

"And…" I prompt before kissing her again.

"And…I want you to fuck me tonight," she whispers, knowing exactly what I wanted to hear.

"There she is," I purr. "I'll be more than happy to oblige you when we get back."

"Ew!" Madeline cries when she walks into the room. "You guys are disgusting. Why can't you just be normal old people and not touch?"

Jesse's eyes go wide in embarrassment at having been caught in such a provocative position, but I just shake my head and stand up off the bed.

"I'm glad to hear you think that's disgusting. Now, let's talk about Adam Andrews?" I toss Jesse a wink and guide Madeline from the room.

Caleb

"EMMY, WHAT happened to the garage door?" I ask, walking into our bedroom.

"What's wrong with it?" she replies, fastening the necklace around her throat. Then she nervously drags her long, blond hair up into a ponytail.

"Um, it won't open and there is a huge-ass dent in the front of it."

"Oh, I'm not sure. I haven't noticed that." She turns away from me, but I can see her mouth, "Fuck," to herself in the mirror.

"Really. So you have no idea what happened?"

"Caleb, you need to get dressed. We're going to be late." She tosses me a smile that I know is only there to distract me.

"Collin!" I yell over my shoulder, and Emma's eyes go wide.

"Yes, sir," he replies from his room down the hall.

"You know anything about that dent in the garage door?"

"Um," is his only response as he walks into our room. His blue eyes flash to his mother, and I watch her give him the smallest shake of her head.

Collin has really filled out over the last year. It's hard to believe he's only fourteen. He looks just like I did at that age. If it weren't for Emma's white-blond hair, I would question if he got anything from her at all.

After Collin was conceived the old-fashioned *accidental* way, Emma and I were very careful for several years. We never really had time alone before starting a family, so keeping it to just the three of us was important to both of us. Right after Collin turned three, Emma sat me down and told me that she wanted another baby. I'd been thinking about it for a while, so that chat ended with us naked. Practice never hurt anyone.

The day Emma found out that we were expecting, she swore while hanging over the toilet that she would never get pregnant again. I laughed. She threw the plunger at me. It was pretty much business as usual in the Jones household. There was no way I was stopping with two kids, and she knew it. I made some lame excuse about the symmetry on my back tattoo, but the truth is that I loved Collin so damn much that I became greedy.

Eight months later, we both got our way. Lily Kate and Grant Walker Jones were born just two days shy of Collin's fourth birthday.

"Where are the twins?" I ask Collin. "Let's see if they know anything about the garage door."

"Shit," Emma mumbles, knowing Lily would never lie for her. She might have gotten her mother's attitude and looks, but she's a daddy's girl through and through.

"What's wrong, Emmy?" I toss her a knowing smirk.

"Okay. Collin, I need to talk to Dad for a minute. Tell everyone to be dressed and in the car in thirty minutes." She walks to the door, locking it behind him.

I stand in the middle of the room with my arms crossed as I watch her remove her panties from under her skirt. She reclines back on the bed and drops her legs wide.

"Come her, Caleb." She rubs a hand up her thigh, pausing on her wet pussy.

"Start talking, Emmy," I say but quickly make my way to the bed.

"Kiss me." She sits up to claim my mouth.

I'm more than willing to take whatever she is offering to bribe me with. I don't give a single fuck what happened to the garage door. I'm reasonably sure she hit it with the new SUV she begged me for. I tried to tell her that it was too big for our single-car garage, but the one thing I've learned over the years is that you can't tell Emma anything. You have to let her figure it out for herself. She won't ever admit that she was wrong. She will, however, apologize with her body. I chalk it up as a win.

"Take your pants off," she mumbles against my mouth.

"Now why would I do that, sweetheart?" I feign ignorance.

"Because you're about to fuck me and we only have a few minutes." Leaning forward, she pops open my button.

"Oh, Emmy, but then I would miss feeling you suck my cock with the sweet little mouth that keeps lying to me."

Her eyes perk at my comment before a slow smile creeps across her face. She stands up and pushes me to the bed, making quick work of pulling my pants down.

"Since we are running short on time, I think this would be an excellent opportunity to multitask." She climbs on top of me and spins to straddle my face. With one smooth movement, she takes my cock to the back of her throat and lowers her pussy to my mouth.

Yeah. We're going to be late.

Sarah

"MOM!" LIV calls from her bathroom. "Where's my straightening iron?"

I'm elbow-deep in cake icing as I look around to find somewhere to wipe my hands, but I come up empty. Why I didn't take Leo's advice and order a freaking cake is beyond me. But it's my baby girl's high school graduation party today and I wanted to make her something by hand. Leo hired a company to cater the party, but I quickly staked my claim on dessert. I had these grand plans of making this gorgeous cake. After I burnt the bottom layer, it quickly switched to gorgeous cupcakes. However, the ones sitting on the tray in front of me are seriously lacking in the gorgeous department.

"Ty, can you go tell your sister to stop yelling and to look under the sink?"

"It's under the sink!" he shouts from the couch.

"Well aren't you helpful," I reply sarcastically.

"No prob, Mom. I'm here to serve." He flashes me a killer grin that might as well be a Xerox copy of his father's.

"Right. Well, tell me what time it is at least."

"Four fifty."

"Shit!" I yell before turning to look at him. "You didn't hear that."

"He may not have, but I did," Leo says as he walks in carrying a cake box. "Go clean up, ángel. Everyone will be here soon." He slides the cake onto the messy counter and pulls me in for an all-too-brief kiss.

"Oh God. Have I told you how much I love you?" I breathe a sigh of relief that I won't have to serve the tragic cupcakes I made.

"No, but I'm fully expecting you to show me later." He winks and turns to Ty. "Aunt Erica and Uncle Slate should be here soon. They picked up some ice, so go outside and empty the big, white cooler and pull it around front for them."

"I'm on it." He jumps to his feet and heads out the door.

Two months after Leo and I were married, I got pregnant with Tyler. The panic attack that ensued after seeing those two pink lines was epic. I literally screamed when I read the test. Leo rushed in and then sat quietly on the corner of the tub while I spent the next hour pacing the room, rambling about how I couldn't be a mom. I have to give him credit because he managed to only laugh once.

Leo was ecstatic and more than willing to roll with a surprise pregnancy. I, as usual, needed a little time to adjust. Finally, he stood up, carried me to bed, turned off the lights, and held me until my pulse began to slow. Then he asked me to legally adopt Liv. And in that moment, being a mom didn't seem so scary. I loved that little girl, and he knew it. With one sentence, he put my nerves at ease and showed me that I already was a mom without even having to utter the words. By the next morning, I was completely on the baby train.

I was also on the nesting train even though I was only about ten minutes pregnant. I immediately started looking at houses online. Leo agreed, and four months later, we moved out of our downtown-Chicago apartment and into a four-thousand-square-foot house in the burbs.

"Dad, Johnson's here!" Ty calls from the front door. "Oh, and Jesse just pulled up. She brought her kids and husband too!" he announces excitedly.

Jesse has been a fixture in our lives for the last twelve years. Liv really took to her, and judging by the tears she shed as Liv was handed her diploma earlier this morning, I think Jesse is pretty attached to her as well. I might even be willing to say that we have become friends. I've seen Brett a few times over the years. We don't do barbeques together or anything, but it's not earth-shattering if we end up in the same room. We've even been known to have a conversation or two. It is what it is, and given our history, it's more than I ever expected us to have.

"What's up, man?" Brett shakes Leo's hand and tosses me a smile.

"Hey, Jess." Liv comes strolling into the room.

"How's it going, Miss High School Graduate?" Jesse laughs, giving her a hug.

"Soon-to-be college freshman," Liv quickly corrects her.

"Oh, don't remind me." I feign injury, grabbing my heart.

"Sorry we're late!" Emma announces, walking in the front door looking slightly disheveled.

"You're not late." Liv smiles, giving her a hug.

"I thought it started at four thirty? Sarah, you *specifically* told me four thirty." She gives me an appalled look.

"I may have lied." I shrug unapologetically.

"So I see it runs in the family." Caleb laughs, squeezing me on the arm as he walks over to the guys huddled around the cooler full of beer on the deck.

"You want me to get you something to drink?" Leo asks from behind me, brushing the hair off my neck.

"You know, sometimes, I think back to that time period right before we got together and I couldn't in my wildest dreams have imagined experiencing something as perfect as today. Did you ever imagine we would be here?" I ask, glancing around the room.

"Absolutely." He kisses the top of my head. "Thankfully, ángel, nothing's perfect, because oftentimes, the flaws are the most beautiful part."

I smile knowing he's never been more right.

In the end, no one was really wrecked or ruined. Our lives may have changed, but we're not broken and nothing was truly stolen but time. It's hard for me to reflect on the years of heartbreak and tragedy and feel anything positive about it. It was a journey, albeit a rough one, but we're all better people because of it. But as I look around the room today, it's easy to recognize that we all found the right course eventually.

Broken Course

THE END

Coming February 2015
Get to know Till Page.

Fighting Silence
(On The Ropes, Book One)

Acknowledgements

This book was definitely a group effort. It blew my mind how many people wanted to step up and help give Sarah Erickson a happily ever after. Some of you may not know this, but of all of my leading ladies, Sarah is my favorite. I cried (real tears) when I made her go crazy in Changing Course. It hurt. So thank you for allowing me to redeem her.

I'm going to try to keep it short this time, but please know there are many others who helped me behind the scenes to make this book a reality.

The Betas: Bianca (Mean B), Bianca, Tracey, Lakrysa, Natasha, Alexis, Ashley, Autumn, and Jessica. I'm not going to lie, ladies. Ya'll were not very mean this time. Thank you for reading…and fixing…. and reading some more. Then fixing some more. I love you each of you. Drinks on me!

The Proofreaders: MJ and Gina. Wow, ladies, what can I say? If it weren't for y'all, Leo would have infections. HAHA! Thank you. I know proofing is time consuming. You two rocked my world.

The Translators: Ciara and Wilma (my mother-in-law). I have no idea what you two translated for Leo to say, but here's to hoping it's actually what I wrote. HAHA! Thank you!

The Formatter: Stacey Blake. Thank you for not yelling at me when I message you every single day up until release day asking you to change things. This hasn't happened yet, but I'm sure it will! You are amazing.

The Editor: Mickey Reed. You are a rock star! Thank you for putting up with me and all of my seven billion questions.

The Bloggers: All of you. (Even the ones who have never read my books.) Thank you for tirelessly supporting authors. We would be nowhere without you.

About The Author

Born and raised in Savannah, Georgia, Aly Martinez is a stay-at-home mom to four crazy kids under the age of five, including a set of twins. Currently living in Chicago, she passes what little free time she has reading anything and everything she can get her hands on, preferably with a glass of wine at her side.

After some encouragement from her friends, Aly decided to add "Author" to her ever-growing list of job titles. So grab a glass of Chardonnay, or a bottle if you're hanging out with Aly, and join her aboard the crazy train she calls life.

Facebook: https://www.facebook.com/AuthorAlyMartinez
Twitter: https://twitter.com/AlyMartinezAuth
Goodreads: https://www.goodreads.com/AlyMartinez

Made in the USA
Las Vegas, NV
28 October 2024

10603137R00173